Cindy,
Enjoy!
Chuck McC

SHORT, SHORTER AND SHORTER STORIES

CHUCK McCANN

Short, Shorter and Shorter Stories

For information about Nightengale Press please
visit our website at www.nightengalepress.com.
Email: publisher@nightengalepress.biz
or send a letter to:
Nightengale Press
5250 Grand Avenue, Suite 14-110
Gurnee, IL 60031

Library of Congress Cataloging-in-Publication Data
McCann, Chuck,
Short, Shorter and Shorter Stories / Chuck McCann
ISBN: 1-933449-01-2
Fiction, short story
Copyright Registered: 2005
Published by Nightengale Press
A Nightengale Media LLC Company
www.nightengalemedia.com

September 2005
10 9 8 7 6 5 4 3 2 1
Printed at
Lightning Source, Inc
1246 Heil Quaker Boulevard,
La Vergne, TN 37086

SHORT, SHORTER AND SHORTER STORIES

CHUCK McCANN

Dedication

To Rita, my wife. She spent many an hour correcting my mistakes and they were not just mistakes in grammar. My gratitude for the guidance of my writing instructors: Pat De Prima, Diane Williams, Lisa Dieder, and Rita Eastburg, for their encouragement and ability to see something in my stories. Also to anyone with the title Teacher.

MYSTERIES

FACE TO FACE

Standing in the streetlamp's circle of pale light, Hugh Hawley relaxed his taut body muscles with a wide mouthed yawn, rocked on his heels and twisted his night stick tightly in his massive hands. A former ship's metalsmith and a dray driver, now Scotland Yard Officer Hawley, stood six foot seven and weighed eighteen stone. He had learned to read and write when the ship's captain watched him struggle to copy letters from bundles of cargo and rewarded his efforts with ciphering and writing lessons; albeit, not on a daily basis. Tonight he patrolled an area where the Ripper has been killing women.

London nights wore on everyone with the "Ripper" terrifying the starch out of very brave people. Many folks stayed behind locked doors, those that had to be out and about, walked swiftly, heads turning faster than the second hand of a clock. Sounds betrayed the listener and sparked one's imagination. A clatter of hooves could be the Ripper charging upon you, the squeak of a door, the Ripper reaching out for you and a scream sent a shaking body against the wall in dreadful anxiety.

A chilled London fog filled the streets, it created a floating circle of light around each streetlamp and soften the sounds of the night people. Business continued quietly, people gestured and spoke quietly, church bells rung quietly and fear settled in quietly. Time seemed to be waiting. The city, the people, the silent foggy night waited for the alarm that the Ripper had struck another woman, cruelly dispatching her and strewing her intestines about.

Hugh Hawley tensed, when he heard the shuffle of feet on the wet walk and... and the odd tapping between, not with the step. He recognized the approaching shuffle as the walk of an elderly person and the tapping of a crutch or cane. He relaxed, his breathing gained strength as he breathed again. He wasn't afraid, just alert, very alert.

The scream and sound of running steps came from behind Hawley, so close he couldn't prepare himself. The slight body thrust against him, one shoe stepped painfully upon his size fifteen brogan. Off balance, Hawley's head slammed into the wall. Dazed, he hollered to the advancing old man now defined under the street lamp, to stop his assailant. Hawley blew his whistle and with his nightstick beat a tattoo on the pavement. Shrill screams persisted from the doorway behind him, "The Ripper! It's the Ripper!"

Hawley watched as, under the circle of lamp light, the old man raise his cane to swing at the charging apparition. The fleet figure sidestepped, thrust its arms toward the stick and grabbed the cane from the old man. Now the cane became his weapon. Struck by a blow, the old man bounced off the lamp post and back against his adversary, both went down. Hawley struggled to rise but sore foot, wet pavement and his awkward position slowed him considerably. Screams, nightstick tattoos and whistles broke through the fog.

Two bodies wrestled for leverage, the old man bellowed for help, but none arrived. Hawley tottered, grasped chinks in the stone wall to stand and tried to make his feet obey his command, "Forward". He could see both men under the circle of light, their faces inches from each other; however, the fog prevented him from seeing any discernible facial features, even the color of the combatant's clothing was a neutral gray.

The cane rose and fell. The old man's cries stopped. The perpetrator scampered into the fog. The screams from many windows continued, some Bobbies arrived and a small group of curious people broke through the fog. The old man slouched on the dampness of a London street, his back sagged against the light post, his head hung down.

"What's happened here?", puffed the winded Sergeant.

"Was it the Ripper? True?"

"May have been, Sir. What little we know about him, could have been."

The Sergeant looked around at the small assembly, "Anyone here see him? Anyone hurt?"

A slight woman stepped out of the assembled group. In a mewing soft voice said the man had grabbed her in the doorway. She screamed, shoved him and knocked him down. He picked himself up and ran. She didn't see his face.

"Well Officer Hawley, can you add to this lady's story?"

"If you please Sergeant, I was knocked down at almost the moment the lady screamed. The blighter, ran into me and tumbled me over. My head banged hard on the wall. I became a bit befuddled and saw very little. But, we have a witness, a good witness that was this close to his face." Hawley placed his two hands before the Sergeant's face and spread them a foot apart. "This close."

Hawley reached down to help the old man to his feet. His hat still on, hid his face, his body shook from the night dampness or the shock of being hit. Hawley held him close.

"If you would sir, that is, if your feeling strong enough, tell us what the man you fought with looks like. I saw the two of you fighting, face to face, so you must have seen him."

"Can you describe him sir?" the Sergeant asked.

The old man's head turned and tipped up in the direction of the benefactor holding him so close. Without a word, Hawley turned to his Sergeant and shook his head negatively.

"What's this?" asked the Sergeant. "Can't speak?"

Standing in the circle of light previously occupied by Officer Hawley, the old man turned toward the Sergeant, his colorless white eyes blankly stared into the officer's face they could not see. He was blind.

BEETHOVEN AND BENJAMIN FRANKLIN

Doctor Nathan Tobias, placed the medical examiner's report on his desk, leaned back and allowed the music of Beethoven to flush his mind of today's problems. The report clearly showed lead poisoning as the child's killer. Accumulated in the small body over several years, abdominal pain, constipation and complaints of deafness should have warned the parents. The applause as the recorded piece ended brought him back into the reality of the world.

One of life's realities popped into his head, a long forgotten autopsy report, a medical school assignment. It had hinted at the possible causes of the death of Ludwig von Beethoven. The report showed hair samples of Beethoven had hundreds of times the normal presence of lead, than for most people of his time period. The assumption has been made that Beethoven's body absorbed quantities of lead in his life time. Pewter dishes, lead fumes, or water drawn from lead pipes, could have been contributing culprits, or even Benjamin Franklin's invention, the glass armonica.

Doctor Tobias again leaned back in his chair, swiveled it around and closed his eyes. "Suppose, just suppose, Beethoven heard about Mozart's composition for the glass armonic. Might he wish to compose a piece for the complex instrument also. If he did, would he invite friends and relatives to a private recital?"

Lulled by more music from the radio, Doctor Tobias imagined a room hushed into silence when two large doors are pushed open. A young uniformed man announces the potent planetary of the newly formed country of the United States, Doctor Benjamin Franklin. As enthusiastic soft applause fills the room the bespectacled man walks into the room. While their eyes were on him, his eyes searched the room for one man, Ludwig von Beethoven.

Franklin sat in the chair offered him in the center of a semi-circle facing a table covered with a large cloth covering a hidden object. His mind was piqued immediately, yet his head swiveled about, searching for the renown Beethoven. He came here tonight because he had been told Beethoven would be present and might even play one of his new compositions.

The soft murmurs of polite conversation stilled as several lighted candelabras were carried into the room and placed around the cloth covered object. Anticipation filled the room, the audience didn't notice the man that stepped quietly from the side of the room until he spoke.

"Ladies and gentlemen and my dear Doctor Franklin." said Beethoven as he stepped into the circle of light and extended his hand to Doctor Franklin. "I am so pleased you could come this evening."

"My pleasure." said the American statesman.

Beethoven indicated to two servants and the cloth was removed revealing the hidden curiosity. Benjamin Franklin smiled. A few spectators gasped in bewilderment others wrinkled their brows in wonder and others just sat. A machine of assorted bowls with rims painted in different colors sat in a shallow tray of water upon the table. In the soft glow of the circle of light everything sparkled.

Beethoven grinned. "This is the glass armonica. This," he pointed to Doctor Franklin, "is the inventor of this lovely instrument."

Franklin acknowledged the polite applause.

Beethoven stepped behind the instrument. "You should know that Mozart has composed several pieces for the glass armonica. I have heard it is wonderful music. Just wonderful. When

I heard that Doctor Franklin was returning to his homeland, I felt a strong desire to honor him with my composition, a heroic piece, for him and his brave country's fight for independence. I have created the music and will now play it on his invention." He poised his hands over the machine.

The sparkles of light danced as the composer touched the glass, producing crystal clear melodies. He repeatedly touched his fingers to the water filled tray or to his lips. A moist contact is needed to produce the sound from the lead crystal glass. The composer knew that to indicate the sound of each note, a different color is painted on the rim of the bowl. The attentive group leaned in, listening to this strange and wondrous instrument.

Franklin was very pleased as he listened, unfortunately some sounds never reaching his ears. He was having some difficulty hearing certain tones. He enjoyed every note he heard from his glass armonica, unforgettable, he would remember them and the man playing them. The audience begged the music master for more, but he wished some time with his special guest and declined further playing for the evening.

The two men settled in a studio of the main suite and discussed whatever came to mind. One topic was the metallic taste Beethoven mentioned after performing on the armonica. Franklin hadn't experienced such a taste. Neither man knew the metallic taste was the taste of lead. The taste might have been the precursor of Ludwig van Beethoven's complaints in later life of abdominal pain and gradual deafness. Both problems would be understood centuries later, when lead poisoning and its consequences were better known.

FIVE GRAVES

There were five of them, which was two more than what I'd been expecting. I work for the coroner's office. I'm the Coroner's Assistant, Sam Madison. We received a request that the family graves on the old Alsted farm be dug up and reintered in the church cemetery. My order specified the removal of Amond Alsted, his wife Clara and their daughter. They were former residents, legally buried on the family land. The new owners didn't wish to keep a cemetery on the property.

I lifted the cell phone from the pile of rubble on the front seat of the small van.

"Charlie." I said to my boss. 'Got a little problem at the Alsted place. Got five graves, not three."

"Huh?"

"Charlie, who the hell else is buried on the Alsted farm?"

"Damn it Sam. I don't know who else is buried there. I'll call Noel and see if she can give us some information."

"Noel is in Europe, on her honeymoon. Remember?"

"Forgot. Stay put, I'm coming out."

"Bring some hot coffee and some brandy. It's cold out here."

Both men walked around the 10 x 12 foot piece of the dry, weedy land. They couldn't be one hundred percent sure how many graves it contained. Three marked graves, the land flat on their surface. However, the small rises in two distinct spots might be graves. Graves that had settled in years ago. When in doubt, as they were, get another opinion.

Sheriff Kilabrew and Deputy Sloan stood with Sam and Charlie, each eyeballed the ground. Four knowledgeable and responsible men confused by what they saw, or didn't see.

"Sam, without disturbing too much around the site, dig up the extra two graves. Carefully!" he called, as Sam trod into the weeds with his shovel. "This might be a crime scene."

Sam pulled back, "OOPS. How careful you want me to be? I gotta get in there Sheriff." His hand wiped his brow, "You think there's more?"

"Yeah, yeah. Perhaps, just don't be a herd of buffalo. OK?"

"OK."

"Ain't no one gonna help me?" An exasperated voice pleaded for assistance.

"You start Sam, I'll get my shovel and give you a hand." Charlie bade the two lawmen goodbye, as he followed him toward the cars.

"Charlie, I'll get a court order from the Judge and send Sloan right back."

"I thought you would. Sloan, can you bring some sandwiches with you?"

The sheriff plopped into the squad car, and leaned out the window. "Oh, Charlie. Can we keep this quiet? If there is something out of line here, I'd like to examine facts without folks knowing about this." The transmission groaned into gear. "Old bastard just keeps going, but I hear a death rattle." Deputy Sloan coughed a laugh and waved toward the diggers as the car backed out onto the local road.

That night's news top story told of five graves and six bodies. The Alsteds and four others. In one a small child, in the other a woman and two infants. The coroner requested information from anyone knowing anything about the extra bodies. The newspaper from the Chicago carried the story. The TV news people came with their truck and left with nothing more than hearsay. They interviewed two neighbors, but no one elaborated on the graves.

The Coroner reported the small female, three or four years old, had no blunt trauma marks. She appeared to have died a natural death. The adult female, about thirty, seems to have died a natural death. The male infants, possibly still born, died within days of birth. Soil variations showed that the infants were later reburied in the same grave with the adult. He assumed she was the mother. Further tests would reveal if poisons or other factors contributed to their deaths. The Coroner also indicated the bodies were given a Christian burial, each box contained flower remnants and a cross. Some one cared for these people.

Sheriff Kilabrew investigated old death records, as the Coroner indicated the extra graves were actually older that the Alsted graves. This implied the graves were there while the farmer and his wife occupied and worked the land. They must have known about the graves. The sheriff needed help.

Intuition, dreams or a casual unrelated comment may unlock secrets history hid eons ago. The fossil records are examples of this. After two years, without identifying any of the grave's occupants, the files shuffled to the bottom of a heap and lay dormant. As time moved on Sheriff Kilabrew was voted out of office. Deputy Sloan fared no better, he opted to move to the city and sell insurance. The coroner, Charlie and Sam died. The buyers of the Alsted farm abandoned it and moved to Florida about six years ago. Dust collected on the forgotten stored files.

"Mr. Romeriez," said the insurance agent, "I need more factual information to settle your claim. Do you know how this policy was paid?"

Mr. Romeriez, shriveled as a tundra tree, leaned forward in the wooden chair. His hands wandered over the papers on the kitchen table. His "Chicago Water Tower" souvenir coffee cup stuck to the paper he withdrew from a tilted pile.

"This is the original paper." he said in English so fractured in dialect tones it was difficult to comprehend. "The old farmer gave them to me when I left him years ago."

Sloan looked at the creased, faded papers, the company logo barely distinguishable. The signatures had faded, but the office could photograph it and chemically make it legible. The amount was small, so he felt the old man would collect on the policy. With interest he said to himself. The damn thing could have been paid off years ago.

"Do you remember the farmer's name?" asked Sloan. Knowing this, should the signature prove difficult to read, might help the investigative staff. Hell, this case might produce some wonderful publicity he thought.

"Mr. and Mrs. Alsted, dead, gave me the paper. After my baby died and my little Rose. They said, 'Always have the insurance.' When my wife died I believed they were right. We gave each other some insurance papers. I locked mine away and forgot them. My friend downstairs saw them in my cabinet over there." His hand waved toward the closet behind him. "He called you."

Agent Sloan didn't understand half the words Romeriez said. A few stuck to the back of his memory. They could come forward if prodded. Which they were when the claims office called him to district office for clarification of the Romeriez claim. He saw the signature, A. Alsted, at the bottom of the policy. He had heard Mr. and Mrs. Halsted, died, when Romeriez talked to him. He thought the old man said the Halsteds were dead. He had said Alsted. Old memories and old times swept him back to the years of frustration and endless trails for the occupants of the two un-marked graves.

The old man settled back in the Lazy Boy and adjusted his glasses. The ex sheriff read then reread Sloan's letter. The ending, CASE CLOSED, at the bottom of the third page brought tears to his eyes. My, God. After all these years. Who is left to give a damn? Sloan's letter said he returned to Mr. Romeriez with a check for his claim and interest due. Then the letter related their conversation, word for word, as best he could remember. He started reading the letter again.

Hey Brew,

First I hope you're feeling better since you last wrote about your appendix surgery. Mabel Cole died of a busted one. Remember her? Well I got some real good news about an old case. The Alsted graves mystery is solved. I know who is in those extra graves. A fluke claim and a casual comment did it. I had to pay a claim one day.

"Mr. Romeriez, I have a check for you. May I come in?"

Tears shone in his eyes as he removed the taped glasses from the worn face. "Check? Come in. A check? You mean I get some money? Good."

Sloan noted the old man never asked the amount. "The company is paying you the full amount and some extra, because you waited so long to make a claim."

"That's nice for you to bring this to me." The frail voice cracked as the dry lips made an effort to speak. "Can I give you a drink?" He reached for the wine bottle on the shelf over the refrigerator. "I'm drinking, sore throat you know."

"Thank you, no. I wanted to bring you your money. It's quite a bit. Do you have a bank account? We can go there, in my car, if you want?"

The reply, still in a dialect that confused Sloan, indicted he and his friend would take care of the check. Sloan didn't relish the idea of a $4,300 check being left in the cluttered little flat, but, really he shouldn't be here either. He pulled out the old chair and settled at the table, his briefcase yielded the monetary treasure.

"This is the check Mr. Romeriez. I need your signature, here." He pointed to the bottom line with the company's blue lo-goed pen. "You can see it is for a large amount. Please be careful where you put it."

"In my cabinet." He walked immediately to the cabinet and placed the check inside. "Thank you much. You sure you don't want a drink? Huh?"

"I'm sure. Mr. Romeriez, can we talk? About the Alsteds, about the time you worked for them?"

"Yes. Sure. They were very wonderful people. Gave my family many things." His eyes clouded, voice softened and memories crawled back into view.

"Tell me about the days you worked for them. Please." Sloan leaned back in the chair he tilted to the wall and loosened his tie. Christ, he hated ties, but company policy demanded them.

"Oh my. I worked on their farm during the hard times. You know, the depression."

The word sounded French to Sloan. "Long time ago."

"Long time ago My wife, Freda, and I and our little daughter, Rose, asked for work at this farm house. Freda was so large, she expected, maybe two babies. So, the missus of the house took her man and talked to him. They let us stay in two rooms in a leather room."

"Leather room?"

"Yes. Where the harness and leather is kept. You know, for the horses."

Sloan rubbed his fingers through his thinning hair. "Leather room. OK."

"I worked the garden and cleaned the barn and coop. You know?"

Sloan nodded.

"Freda worked in the kitchen and the boiling pots for the canning. Rose stayed near by and both the ladies laughed when she did funny things. One day she went near the pots. Too near and she fell." Romeriez eyes flushed as the memory came to mind. Tears followed ancient cracks in his face. He hacked and spit into his handkerchief then rubbed his eyes. "Sorry. It is a bad memory. She fell against the fire and the pot. The water splashed her and she screamed as it cooked her skin. She died right there."

Sloan took the wine bottle and poured some in both glasses. He'd drink now.

"The farmers knew we had nothing to bury the child in. We wrapped her in a beautiful old blanket. The old lady put a cross on Rose and flowers. We dug a hole and cried and prayed over her."

"It was an accident. Do you remember reporting it? Did the Alsteds report it?"

"That I do not know. I didn't."

"I'm sorry. Please continue." He poured more wine from the nearly empty bottle.

Mr. Romeriez moved to the sink and withdrew another wine bottle from beneath it. He smiled as he raised it up and offered the bottle to his companion.

"Soon after the child died, Freda felt the baby coming. She had two, twin boys. We had two boys. She cried when she held them. One died that night. It was terrible. The next afternoon, as we began to bury another child, the second baby died. God took them before we knew them." More tears came with this bitter memory.

Mr. Sloan lowered his chair, shuffled his feet and just couldn't speak.

"Is OK my friend. I have lived for many years with these tears. I must continue. The agony of losing our children ate at Freda, she didn't sleep or eat. She could not enter the farmhouse. Slowly her mind left her. I worried, but even God turned from us. Freda died before the summer ended. We dug up the babies and placed them in her box. With my family gone, I told the couple I wished to leave. These nice people, that befriended us, were now expecting a child. I could not understand why God took mine and gave one to them. I was asked to stay. I could not. I took my things and left."

Sheriff Kilabrew read the hand printed postscript below, CASE CLOSED. That is the end of the simple story we never knew. Wouldn't the old gang like to have known that story?

Hope you're well and take care of yourself. Boyd Sloan.

A DEADLY SNACK

The smell of death smacked Mike's face as he pushed open the door. The stench of vomit, urine and excrement assaulted his nostrils. He couldn't check the gag reflex and cursed softly, forced to swallow the vile burning mess in his mouth. Not a good start.

The manager told Mike the maid had entered room 410 and keeled over. The manager saw her drop, rushed to and revived her, then called the police.

Detective Mike Lurie wiped his glasses with his necktie and surveyed the scene, then spoke softly. "Now what the hell happened here? What can you folks tell me? Hell, I can see you're dead. What else?"

The man, slumped on the sofa, 55ish, gray hair, wearing bifocals, weight 285 pounds, about six feet, didn't speak. Fully dressed, shoes off under the table, tie loose with his suit coat draped over the arm of the sofa he relaxed. His bluish face, one eye peered toward the closet door, saw nothing. "If I were a preacher I'd say you had a peaceful journey to heaven." commented Mike.

"And you my dear. Tell me anything, I'll listen."

He scrutinized the female about 50, dyed hair done up, weight 140, make up over done. Her glasses were askew, feet tangled under the chair, the right one in a walking cast. Her body was wedged between the table and the sofa. Pale green eyes searched the ceiling for the beyond.

On the table were remnants of a snack with coffee.

"Well there's no blood, everything seems in place. I'll rule out violence for now. Still has his wallet, her purse, even the rings on her fingers. Robbery's out."

Mike opened the wallet found the registered Mr. Nolan was really Dr. Nolan Everton. Why a false name? Mike's eyes scanned the little scene hoping to solve this riddle. He leaned over and smelled the mouth of the dead man. "Poison maybe? You're telling me very little people. I'll count on Doc for help."

Back at the precinct, Mike glimpsed at his notes. "That's everything I saw Nug" he said to a tall balding man standing near the soda machine, counting out change. "Let's see the video."

"Sure wish people would think of us first. Let's see this mess"

"Go on. You'd drop dead if they didn't die for you."

Nugent grinned. "You know taping the scene might let us solve cases from the office some day. I certainly wouldn't mind missing the smell at the scene."

The video offered no new information. Nugent thought the woman was familiar but couldn't place her. He had seen her somewhere. Perhaps known to the public?

Mike's cellular tickled his buttock. "Lurie here."

"Mike, Doc Laux. I have some very interesting facts on the two diners you sent me this morning. I'm not telling you, but they're interesting. Can you get your butt over here in the next half hour?"

"Nugent and I are out the door, quarter hour." He grabbed Nugent's arm as it reached for the soda dropping from the machine. "Let's go, Nug. Doc may have something."

"Meet Amy Gorman." said Doc, as the body tray slid from the cool wall. "Amy Katherine Gorman, author of several flower and herbal books. She's not giving autographs today."

"Could be why you thought you recognized the face, Nug." Mike grinned.

"How'd she die, Doc?" asked Nugent. "And do we know her as wife or a girlfriend?"

"Well Mike suggested broken neck and he was right, down

low, between the sixth and seventh vertebrate. It took a strong person to break it there. Mistress, I think."

"Could that old guy...", Nugent queried, "Was he strong enough, ya think?"

"Oh, I'd say so," said Doc, as he pulled the next drawer open to reveal the muscular Doctor Everton. "But there's more gentlemen." Doc picked up his clipboard and flipped pages. "The good doctor was poisoned. Matter of fact, with two poisons."

"Two poisons?" Nugent looked incredulously to Mike.

"Yeah, I thought so." mumbled Mike.

"There's another kicker. They both died within minutes of each other. Perplexing? But, I have a theory. Wanna hear it?"

"Speak your piece, Doc. We could use some help," said Mike.

"Yeah. let's hear it, Doc," interjected Nugent.

"I don't know why, but I see a suicide pact. The doctor killed her, then killed himself." Doc rubbed his day-old stubble and looked to Mike. "What do you think of that idea? And remember they died within minutes of each other."

"I can't go with you on that one Doc. No suicide note. My experience with the suicide thing is meager, to say the least; however, from police classes and old files, I'd say no to suicide." Mike turned to Nugent, as his cell phone beeped.

"Lurie. There's what? Same hotel? What the Hell. We're coming right over." He folded his phone and started to wipe his glasses with his tie.

"Damn. Another body at the hotel. Come on, Nug. Doc, if you got time, wanna see the scene?"

"Sure," said Doc, pushing body and tray back into morgue cooler.

As they drove to the hotel, Mike asked, "What were the two poisons Doc? Do they need to be ingested or injected? Any tell-tale smells or odors when they're used?"

"Hmmmm, left my notes in the lab, seems Aconium and

Vividyl. Likely ingested."

"Would this Dr. Everton use either of them?" asked Nugent. "In his work? I've never run into them before."

"What are they?" asked both detectives as one.

"Vividyl is an antidepressant, easily obtainable by Everton. Aconium is a plant derivative from ah," he paused, eyes rolling across the ceiling. "Monkshood, a flower. I'm sure Gorman would know that."

"Cripes Doc, it's winter. Where the hell would she get poisonous fresh flowers in Chicago during the winter?" Mike scoffed.

"Does it have to come from fresh flowers with, like, sap or something?" inquired Nugent.

"Not as I remember." Doc punched on the cell phone and winked at both men. "Marty? John. Need some answers. Aconium, from Monkshood, right? Right. If someone were to use it does it need to be fresh or can juice or powder be used? Either. Thanks Marty. Gorman? Oh, man. You are kidding me. No. I owe you one." Doc's smile lit the cold air as they departed the car.

"Fresh or dry. Hmmm. Did he say if one was deadlier than the other?" Mike asked.

"Fresh. All kill."

What's with the Gorman question Doc?" Mike queried.

"Ohhhhhh. Marty said if I had questions about these plants, I should ask Amy Gorman. She knows all about them."

"Yipes."

Nugent said, "I think we can get your plants Doc, at the Garfield Conservatory. They grow all kinds of plants all year. They might have it." Nug looked at Mike, "Well? Hell, I think they might."

As they walked into the hotel lobby, the harried manager directed them to a downstairs well. The body sprawled beneath the stairs. Mike knelt and peering into the bluish face with unseeing eyes.

"Shit. The same color, just like the other guy. Doc, I think we need to know what each victim ate and drank. You can do that for us, right? Maybe when and how much of both. OK?"

"Sure Mike, none of the autopsy materials have been removed from the morgue lab. We haven't closed yet." I can have staff..."

"Do you think you can do it, not staff. You know what we're looking for. Don't you?"

Doc's head bobbed in affirmation.

The next morning Mike's inter-office mail included Doc's filed report, with a note attached, "Very interesting, D.L."

Mike's tie made little circles on his glasses. "mmmm."

"Whatta we got?" asked Nug as he returned empty-handed from the soda machine.

"Patience. Let Doc tell us," Mike began to read aloud.

"Death caused by lethal dose of ...well damn. Vividyl and Aconium found in both males, none in the female. All died about the same time. Damn interesting."

"Sure is. Anything else?'

"Yep. The kid downstairs was their kid, Jamie Everton. The answer and the solution is here, in my hand. I think."

"Fine. Tell me."

"The doctor checked in alone having set up an 'important' meeting with Amy Gorman. He planed to kill her. That's why he used the phony name. She and the doctor breaking up and I think the kid's future was the problem, like the cost for college or something like that. They had some agreement before, now Everton wants out. She fixed cookies, knowing he couldn't resist them, but adds poisons. Why? Because she's fed up and knew their agreement would stand up in court if he was dead.

Her son probably drove her here since her foot was in a cast. When the two of them started bickering. The kid, without being seen, took some cookies and left the room. He went down-

stairs where he ate them. Back in room 410 the doctor, walked
about, got behind her and popped her neck. Before that, to Amy's
delight, he must have snarfed down the rest of the cookies, since
there were only crumbs on the table. Now, feeling woozy, he sits
down and... Bingo. Death tagged em."

"We'll need to test the crumbs."

"Could be. Sounds plausible enough to solve the case."

"It's solved, Nug. You type it up and I"ll get the soda."

"Machines broke again." Nugent shrugged. "I'll let you
treat later."

MORNING MURDER

Marie was dumbfounded when the sheriff's car, lights flashing out of kilter, siren chasing the quiet from the streets, screeched into the nextdoor driveway. Sheriff Doyle raced toward the house disappearing beneath the autumn canopy of rusty maple leaves. Across the street Marie saw Bonnie step out her front door holding the latest citizen of Holden Park, population 4,021, Several kids on bikes came barreling down the street, racing to the siren's call.

"What the Hell is going on?" she asked, heading for the side door. "Bill!"

Marie heard him holler from the backyard. "What's happening? What's up?" At that moment a yelp from Bill and the kitchen lights went out the dishwasher turned off as did the TV and timer, at 9:42 a.m. The squad car lights continued chasing one another from house to house, shadow to light to shadow again, a discotheque game of tag.

"Bill! Bill!"

"I'm OK. Damn electricity. Touched two wires. I'm OK." He walked into the kitchen clutching his forearm. "What the hell's going on? What're the cops doing here?"

"Don't know. I think something's wrong at Mitchell's place. Go see." The tone of caution belied her dread of something awful happening at her best friend's house.

"Sure. Yeah, sure." Bill touched her pregnant belly in passing, that little touch of reassurance couples share. Sally Bishop, the neighborhood gossip, approaching from the other side of the

Mitchell house, wore worry clearly on her face. Pivoting about to return back home when Bill waved her back. He mounted the stoop, pausing at the open door, knocking and hollering

"Mitch! Hey Mitch! Can I come in?" He began entering before an answer.

"Stay out! Don't come in." declared the firm voice of Sheriff Fred Doyle. A very business like order, thought the sheriff.

"It's me. Bill Mayhew. Can I help? What's going on?

"Just stay the hell out, Bill. And Marie too, if she's with you." Doyle's official reflection bounced from the mirror overhanging the antique hunting board. "Wait a few minutes, on the porch or at home." it said.

Marie came up, touching Bill's arm, giving him a weak smile. Mick Shay, part time Deputy, also the science teacher at Community High, Boy Scout patrol leader, nature interpreter for the county park system and contributor to the weekly newspaper, came around the side of the house. Already in a sweat, excusing himself, he pushed passed them.

"Sounds like the Sheriff wants you both off the porch. The ambulance is coming and we'll need some working room." he said. "No questions. We'll talk to you later."

Several hours elapsed as many rumors took hold. More official cars arrived, then a reporter for KMIT and their TV truck. The small neighborhood crowd grew when onlookers paused, then drifting away, armed with bits of rumors, they spread as gospel. When the ambulance left carrying something so did most of the officialdom. Sheriff Doyle saw Bill and Marie looking through the window, now beckoned them back to the house with his finger. Walking in was no different now than coming to any crowded party, except for the cold quiet. Both went to a red eyed Mitch, sitting next to the hunting board, giving him hugs and pats for unknown reasons.

"Bill. Marie. You better sit Marie." pointing to the chair

near Mitch. "I'm speaking as an officer of the law and want you both to know any information I share with you, is to remain in this room. Nothing about what I'm saying is repeated to anyone. OK?"

"OK." Bill answered, nodding a yes also.

Marie nodded yes and dabbed as tears of the unknown welled up, began trickling toward the tip of her nose.

"Bill, why don't you sit closer to Marie? Good. Might as well hit you both with it, can't sugar coat it. Mitch went to the store and returned to discover his wife, Carmen dead. Murdered."

Having them close together made checking their reaction easier for Doyle. Clues come from everywhere and anywhere at any time. Marie, clutching at Bill's shoulder, gasped, flopping back in a faint, her eyes disappeared up into her head.

"Christ. Get some water, Mick."

Shay left for the kitchen. Bill, staring heavenward, used his shirtcuff to wipe away unmanly tears. Mitch sat trance-like. All dutifully noted by the sheriff to be written as investigation notes later.

Deputy Shay held the glass out to the awakening Marie, then he leaned back against the door frame. He too watched the three people in the room, his pencil stub jotting cursory notes, Mitch holding his head, Bill rubbing his forearm and Marie unconsciously rubbing her belly and a future little Mayhew.

"Mick and I, maybe some District Attorney people, will be questioning most everybody in the neighborhood. We need answers." The Sheriff didn't feel comfortable with a murder investigation. In fourteen years the only dead bodies he saw came from the New Years Day accident on Toney Road. "We want the killer caught and out of the neighborhood. We have a few answers already and know something about this guy." Nodding, "A man did it. We've got KMIT helping us by asking anyone with any knowledge to call my office. Other then knowing she's been murdered, I can't give you any more information. I miss anything, Mick?'

"Nope."

"Actually I'd like you both to go back home and stay there. Don't talk about it to each other or anyone else. I'll come over in a few minutes. We can tell each other what we know and get to solving it. Any questions?"

At 3 p.m. KMIT let the world know Carmen Mitchell had been sexually assaulted and murdered in her bathroom between 9 and 10 that morning, the hour her husband was away from the house. Their informed source said, "She was strangled with a bathroom towel. The house hadn't been broken into. The police were baffled by the lack of clues." So much for limiting investigative information to the public and the killer.

The assistant D.A. had allowed Mitch, watched by Deputy Shay, to pack and leave with his sister. He would stay with her, on the other side of town, for a few days. He was visibly shaking and distraught. Questioning him for an hour or so had shed no discernible light on the killing. The other people the police had talked to were sent home after short statements and addresses were noted

"Mick, stay here, take more pictures if you feel they're needed and fill in any notes you need to complete. Call the wives, tell 'em we'll be late. You know." Sheriff Doyle adjusted the belt around his ample gut. "I'm going to talk to the Mayhews again."

The flashing lights of an approaching squad car, halted Doyle on the porch. "Oh Mick. Donalson just arrived. I'll get him to help you lock up and seal the place before you or Donaldson come over." Doyle headed toward his extra deputy's car. "Sorry to call you away from your mom's bedside.."

"S'OK. She's so out of it, she'll never know. Whatta ya want me to do? Gotta tell ya, I ain't never worked a murder. Can't believe Carmen got murdered." said Donaldson.

"You do nothing but secure the scene. No one goes in or out of that house."

Looking into the young man's eyes he said. "We'll catch the

killer. You'll be helping. Mick is going over everything upstairs. You stay here. When he comes down help him."

Starting his walk through upstairs, Mick Shay, scratched a few notes, turned off lights, closed windows and doors all through the house. He side stepped the area where the body was found and promised the outlined space, "We'll catch him."

Shay admired, with a touch of jealousy, the little plant potting area Carmen had on the side porch. Her cutting were just about ready to plant and it looked like she was preparing to plant them today, along with a few new plants. Jotting a note to ask Mitch about it, he moved along. The broken leaves on two Euphorbia had exuded some milky sap he noticed this too. The dim area was ready for Carmen to work, but everything seemed untouched, the spray bottle was full and plastic sheeting was still over some shelved plants. The porch's sun screen was still up also.

Leaving Donaldson on Mitchell's front porch, Deputy Shay walked a little quicker across the clean side area of the Mayhew's house. He heard the excited and condemning voice of Bill berating Sheriff Doyle.

"You're not thinking I did this, are you?"

"No Bill. No. Come on, calm down. These are questions asked of everyone when a murder is committed. Answers guide our investigation and finally lead to the perpetrator. No one is accusing anyone."

Marie and Mick nearly collide at the kitchen counter, as she carried a drink in each hand for herself and Bill. The Sheriff being on duty had refused.

"I'm here, Boss." declared Mick, more to break the ice than be acknowledged.

"Good. We've been talking, more or less, getting some answers to times and places. If you will talk to Bill, I'll ask Marie some questions." Doyle indicating the two of them would leave the room and talk elsewhere, Bill might feel more relaxed answering Shay's questions without Marie   Could make the investigation easier. He's such a hot head.

Bill sat, his sullen glare following the two from the room. Rubbing the raw welt on his arm he turned to Shay, "Hope your questions aren't as insulting."

"Insulting?"

"Yeah. Do I have the hots for Carmen he asks me, in front of Marie. Insulting."

"Cripes Bill. As good looking as Carmen is...was. A thought maybe. Huh?" The Sheriff turned a crimson hue and stammered. "Jeez Marie, I'm sorry."

"Well. Maybe. But hot. I got Marie. Pregnant Marie. Very pregnant Marie."

Mick watched Bill stroking his arm. His forehead wrinkling as he wondered if the rash was caused by anxiousness or worry? "God, that looks awful. What'd you do?"

"I was working on an electrical switch in the back. Juiced myself good." Mitch showed the Deputy his burns. "The Badge of Stupidity. Didn't turn off the power."

"You should get it taken care of. Looks bad." offered Mick.

"Maybe later. Too many things happening now."

Later, before the two officers started for the police station, they sat in one car and reviewed the information they had gathered. As they compared the answers, Mick's mind started clicking. Two and two make four but Mick didn't get four from the answers given and the evidence on hand.

The two men, Mitch and Bill, told near identical stories. About 8:50 this morning, as Mitch pulled out of the driveway, he had told Bill he was heading for the hardware store. Did Bill want anything? No. Carmen was in the house, just finishing her morning shower getting ready for some garden work. Bill had an outside electrical wire to repair. Mitch was gone about an hour, less he thought. He had showed a time dated store receipt from the store to both Doyle and Shay.

About 8:50, Marie was doing small household tasks up-stairs after completing some exercises to keep her weight down. She had seen her husband and Mitch talking and Bill heading for the back yard with a toolbox and stuff in his hands. She didn't see Bill again until he came into the house, after the squad car arrived. She was sure of her time because her exercises were timed and Bill had shorted the clock timer. Neither she nor Bill had been to the Mitchell house in two days. They had coffee Thursday evening, while Bill helped Mitch connect a circuit breaker. She had talk-ed with Carmen on Friday, over the waist high picket fence along the back half of their driveways, before Carmen went out to buy plants.

After talking to Mitch, Bill went to work on the electric switch and wire. He had no idea how long it took. The switch had given him some problems, as the wire needed to be pulled, cut and taped more than once. From his position on the ground in the back yard, he couldn't see either door at Mitchell's. He had seen nothing, heard nothing until the police siren alerted him. He had not been to the Mitchell's since the other night.

"Fred, ever know something and just couldn't push it to the front of your brain?" asked Mick. Plowing along without an answer, "Like a smudge on your glasses. You can see alright but it's not clear."

"Like what Mick?" asked Fred Doyle, brushing dandruff from his shirt front.

"Like Bill denying he wanted to jump Carmen. My God, every man I've ever been with, upon seeing her, said he wished to get her in bed or the back seat or under the stars. We even men-tioned it to each other. Yet Bill says otherwise."

"So?"

Mick looked into the Sheriff's quizzical face. "Sooo? So let me draw you a picture. Carmen is a gardening nut. She loves to try growing plants from cutting or other plant parts. She works in a small area out back. She is going to work in her garden this morning according to her husband. Her plants and the potting area are undisturbed. Except... Except some Euphorbia plants have leaves that are broken."

"Come to the point Mick. My ass is getting sore and my stomach is growling." Shifting, to ease his cramped position, the Sheriff asked, "Is there something we missed?"

"Not sure. Maybe." Deputy Shay continued rambling, "I just remembered, Euphobia produces a sticky milk when broken, behaves like Poison Ivy, causing blisters or a rash on some people. Mitch says Carmen was going to garden today. She hadn't been in her potting area today. The broken Euphorbia is dripping sap. The killer broke the leaves. Bill Mayhew is scratching at a rash on his arm, he says he got an electrical burn this morning. 'Could be its a rash? Or an allergy to Euphorbia maybe?"

"You think so? Bill Mayhew? They're friends, close friends. My God his wife would have been right next door." Whistling in astonishment at Shay's story, "That bastard. Tell me more. How?"

"Bill says he burned his arm, electrical burn, while working in the back yard. I came in to their house from there. The area is too clean for having worked there almost an hour. Some stuff, but no little scraps, waste trimmings. You know?"

"OK. Good observation. But how?" said Doyle, now intently interested.

"I'm only guessing. But here goes." Mick rolling his eyes, grunting and licking his lips begins unraveling a possible tale. "Bill resents the state of Marie's pregnancy. He envisions a body like Carmen's. Mitch says he'll be gone for an hour, at least. Marie is putzing around upstairs and can't see Bill. Knowing the Mitchell's so well, he could go through their house blindfolded. He beelines into the house, right to the bathroom where Carmen is about to get dressed. 'Clamps his hand on her mouth and when she resists he knocks her down and starts assaulting her. Then, knowing she recognizes him, he strangles her. Then runs from the house through Carmen's potting area, brushing against some plants."

Looking like Grand Canyon might, wide and dry, Doyle's mouth couldn't close. Tapping his forefinger to his lip, "Makes a good tale. Fairy tale Mick? Huh?"

"Could be? Shall I go on?"

"Please." The Deputy had the sheriff's complete attention.

"Now, we have a man, disheveled, sweating probably, return to work in his yard. He notices a rash forming on his arm. Mitch comes home and discovering Carmen, calls 911. Bill, hearing sirens and aware his wife might soon see him, looks for an out. What to do? Bill's fixed things before, he's a very handy man. Just fixed the light at Mitch's. He puts a wire on his arm, now reacting to the plant juice and grounds it. He has a reason for his disarray."

The question, "Any thing else, Mick?" catches in Doyle's dry throat.

"It's the Euphorbia. The answer, one way or the other, is the sap of the Euphorbia. Both Mayhews say they've not been to the Mitchell house since Thursday. Mitch and Marie say Carmen brought the plants home Friday. If Bill's rash is from the Euphorbia, then he's been in their house since Thursday. Makes him the killer. He brushed the plants in the semi-darkness of the potting area. Without realizing breaking the leaves or the sap was dangerous, he went to work on the electricity. In a few minutes the stuff is irritating him."

Again Doyle whistled. "Damn. Mick that's fantastic. Beyond belief. Go back into the Mitchell's, get your plant and let's confound Bill right now."

Marie was fretting that Bill's arm looked much worse and needed care, when the two officers called from the side door. The Sheriff asked if he could see Bill's burn. The four of them could see the burn and pustules. Nursing Bill's arm neither knew the Sheriff had Shay call Doc Sweeny, he lived four or five houses down. He was told the Sheriff wanted him at Mayhew's. Thinking it was the baby, the doctor came right away.

Twenty minutes later, after calling the doctor a quack with his diagnosis and telling both officers to go to Hell, a handcuffed, belligerent Bill Mayhew sat in the Sheriff's squad car. Bill's arrest stuned Marie and she went into labor. Doc Sweeny rode in the ambulance with her, since Bill couldn't. KMIT wouldn't know the murder suspect had been apprehended., until the other stations broadcast it.

"Got him Carmen." said Mick. "Got him."

NOTHING IS SOMETHING

"Geezas! Did cha see that?" Detective Mike Dickens howled, as he rubbed his head. He just hurled himself back from a display cage and smacked it into the florescent fixture hanging overhead. He rubbed the bump and checked his fingers for blood then stepped back for another look. Yep, there it was alright. The rolling coil was alive and slowly reducing its size.

"Does that happen every time?" he asked the grinning figure next to him. His bloody fingers indicated broken skin, another scar, but nothing severe.

"Yep. Every time, more or less. Let me explain." The man in the white coat handed Mike some paper towels to staunch the flow of blood, which trickled along his head toward his ear. Shawn Thomas, herpetologist at Brookfield Zoo, warmed to his task.

"The rat is prey. It must remain alert at all times to remain alive. If it ignores a warning, or even a hint of danger, its life is over. The snake is a predator, an opportunist, a skillful and deadly killer waiting patiently to survive. You just saw the completion of life's circle, well almost. After the prey's heart stops, the snake searches for the head and starts to swallow head first. It goes down, you might say, in one big gulp."

Shawn rummaged through a table drawer and held up a much used first aid kit. "Let's patch your head."

"For a scratch?"

"Around animals you cover every scratch. Sit." With his fingers, Shawn applied gentle pressure, "Fill me in Detective Dickens. Why the interest in snake feeding?"

"A thought. I read an article about a guy killing a python or some big snake. Family pet."

Big snakes don't make family pets." said Shawn, as the first aid kit tumbled about in the drawer hastily slammed shut.

"Oh?" One scarred eyebrow rose, curving furrows that time and worry had sculpted into Dicken's face. "They sell 'em in pet stores."

"Uh huh, so I hear." Shawn gave a bobble headed nod. "But, I said they don't make family pets."

Mike twirled on the stool, his voice blending in and out each time he faced Shawn. "Well this guy had one he called a family pet."

"You talking about the guy that found his son dead, squeezed by a Indian Python. Albertson, or Halberson? 'Went ballistic and hacked the snake to pieces?"

"Same guy. It doesn't seem right to me." Mike stopped the spin. "Ain't done that in years." His eyes glazed and he felt a grumble in his gut. "Won't be spinning any more either."

"Mike, I have lunch break. Feel like eating? We'll go over to the hospital and grab a bite. OK?"

"Hospital?"

"The animal hospital. Just outside." Shawn pointed toward the next building.

The entire lunch of burnt burgers with grease drowned fries and coffee, better if used to remove wood stains, sat in Mike's gut like a bucket of newly mixed concrete. A wiser Shawn feasted on fruit salad, the leftovers destined for bird food. Their casual exchanged conversation bonding the two tighter than Siamese twins.

The detective revealed why he feared snakes and refused to live in a house because the yard might have snakes. Billy Teason, third grade bully, threw him down before the other kids and dragged a dead snake over his face and chest. His screams brought a teacher to his rescue who later told him that screaming was unmanly behavior.

Shawn enjoyed a different attitude toward the reptiles, since the day a snake handler, in a school program, picked him to hold a boa. Afraid, but willing, it lead to a positive experience. Soon he looked for snakes, read about them and even convinced his folks to allow him to care for an injured snake one summer. Shawn promoted understanding and tolerance from the public for snakes.

Several days later Mike read that Mr. Albertson was released, the Coroner stating the baby's death was an unavoidable tragedy caused by Albertson's stupidity in allowing the snake to crawl about the house freely. The grief stricken father acknowledged his sin and accepted the chastisement from the judge, but Mike still felt something was wrong.

Tacit approval from the watch commander allowed Mike to look into the baby's death, on his own time. He reread the account, interviewed the reporter, discussed the case with two snake loving friends of Shawn's and went over the coroner's report. Nothing.

Mike revisited the death scene explaining to a weeping, hostile Mr. Albertson, that, yes the case was closed, but the law, bent by Dickens, required the father read the report and sign it for official approval. While Albertson read, Mike asked a few subtle questions. Frustrated by the man's attitude, Mike finally snapped.

"Didn't the baby scream when the snake bit him. Those teeth must have hurt?"

"Huh?"

"The bite?" Mike chopped off each word. "Didn't you hear the baby holler when he got bit?"

"I don't know. Don't remember hearing any screams. 'Kid musta been asleep."

Carmen Albertson opened the door and stepped back when she saw Detective Dickens. The package in her hand pulled swiftly behind her, her greeting, caught in her throat, came out in a garbled, boozy hiccup. A naughty child caught in the act by a parent thought Mike.

"Something happening here?" she slurred.

Mike looked at his watch. Eleven thirty-two in the morning and she's gassed.

"Honey, this is Detective Dickens. You remember him." He grinned in an effort to gain control of the situation. "He's come for...for me to sign the official police report."

"I didn't expect someone to be here. Surprised me." She walked through the room an unseen but alcoholic spirit moved with her as she deposited her package in another room. "You don't need me do you Detective?"

"No, Mam. All done and leaving. Bye" He walked out shutting the door gently.

Had he, out of sympathy, missed the woman's drinking problem? Mike decided to check the husband, see if there was a problem there. He was a gambler. He played the ponies, went to the Joliet casino once a month and played a little friendly poker, every Friday. He didn't drink but pumped iron regularly in a health spa next to the Three T's trucking docks, where he worked. He didn't cheat on his wife.

Today he was told to drop his interest in the Albertson case, the force needed more effort from him. Munching a dispenser sandwich, Mike looked at the coroner's file and pictures. He winced at the discolored bands across the small body, causing himself to bite into the lining of his mouth. "Yeow" He waved off the concerned faces about him.

In silent pain, like a hen on her brood, Mike smiled and grabbed the phone. A hunch.

"Connie, you gotta help me."

"With what Mike?" asked Connie Betts, part time computer operator in the morgue. "I'm as busy as caterpillar on a new plant."

"Could we talk? At your place?"

"You asking for a date or a free meal?" Connie knew Mike's favorite meal. "I can be fix something for dinner by six, six thirty. Then we can relax awhile."

"How about I see you in twenty minutes. There at the..." He just couldn't say morgue. "At your computer."

"OK. Sure. Twenty minutes." In a soft whisper Connie said, "Sex is out, huh?"

"For now. But, how about a rain check?"

Three days later Mike met Shawn and Connie at the Billy Goat. Shawn hadn't realized the girl he held the door for was meeting Mike too. After introductions, Mike smiled and childlike blurted out the reason for arranging this meeting.

"Because of the two of you, my friends, I got the Lieutenant to get me into the D.A.'s office this morning. I laid out everything I had on the Albertson baby's death. I explained all the things you told me Shawn. I showed him the enlarged pictures Connie did of the baby's body. He decide to reopen the case. By tonight that baby killer will be back in jail."

"Baby killer? What the hell are you talking about. I didn't give you any real help." The puzzled frown on Shawn's face matched Connie's screwed up face.

"Mike, I didn't see anything in those enlargements I did for you."

"I know Connie. That's the answer. Nothing."

Both, looked and spoke together. "Nothing?"

"Right." Mike leaned in conspiratorially. "I didn't find nothing and I should have. Remember the day that snake grabbed the rat? It grabbed it, twisted its body around the rat and squeezed it."

"I remember. I told you they all do that."

"Uh huh. That you did."

"You saw a snake kill a rat. I came to eat and you're throwing this at me." commented Connie.

"Sorry Connie." said Mike. "But there in lies the key to

the case. I explained to the D.A. that the bruises on the baby were made when Albertson hugged the baby to death. He is very powerful and could squeeze like a snake. The wife was out or bombed out. The kid was a bother to him and because the mother drank too much during her term mildly retarded which costs mucho moola. The clincher is the nothing. There were no teeth marks on the baby's body. No teeth marks. How did the snake grab the baby and squeeze it? Remember Shawn, it grabs and does that squeeze thing."

" I remember. Mike that's great. Storybook detective work"

"Congrads Mike." She winked, "Makes me love ya."

"Thanks guys. This meal 's on me."

THE BODY IN THE CAVE

Tim faced the narrow slit in the rocks thinking he could slip through it. If he became trapped, his friend Ken, having suggested the area for his geological explorations, would come looking for him. He left a marker at the opening and as he started slipping in, felt his heart beat quicken.

Tim Bemis positioned his head lamp to bounce light throughout the low roofed cave walls without creating shadows, as he continued to squeeze his body through the proverbial rock and a hard place opening. He stepped into a small vaulted rock room. He stood there feeling a wave of elation sweep over him. Had he discovered an undisturbed cave, new rock formations or treasured glyphs ancient dwellers painted on the walls? He took in the panorama with a slow rotation of his head. He would venture no further, no footsteps until he had some valid, measured photos of his find.

A large boulder just off the middle of the cave became the reference point for Tim's photos. One photo from the opening and nine paces placed him next to the rock. He bracketed his photos to each hour of the clock, then paced off each hour spot on the wall. If nothing more, Tim remained methodical with his geological research, each photo and measurement carefully recorded. Once he lost an opportunity to be published by his failure to record crystal sizes and growth in a Dakota cave. Never again.

All went well until he moved to the opposite side of the boulder. A chill shot through his body and the body refused to move or speak. The glow of Tim's headlamp circled a dirty boot and part of a trouser leg. He waited, as if the owner of the boot would speak. Not a word. Tim stepped away from the boulder and played his lamp up the still body toward the face. A dirty grey Stetson hid the face; however the hand was bones. He discovered a skeleton.

This was different. He supressed a strong desire to run and began to take photos, plenty of photos. If he didn't get recognition for a geological find, he might get recognition for chancing upon a mystery. He resisted the urge to touch or search the pockets for identification but opened the wooden box with the metal bindings near the man's hip. It was empty.

Once out of the cave, Tim headed straight for the State Police office. He had met Ken Stallwood in the field and both admired the other's approach to life. They also liked the Arizona Diamondbacks. Tim knew Ken would return the photos after they were developed and give him credit for finding the skeleton.

As Tim entered the busy office, he and Ken exchanged looks. Ken motioned him into his private office and followed him through the door. Funny how some people just know what the other is thinking. Privacy.

"What's up?"

"A body." Tim said soto voco, as if he might wake its ghost.

"Who and where?" Brevity seemed to suit Ken in this situation.

"Don't know who. It's in a small cavern I found this morning."

"Well, let's go see your body." Ken opened the drawer and removed his gun and gunbelt. "Eat yet? I'm hungry, mind if we stop on the way?"

"You won't be able to see the body. The cave opening is too tight" Tim patted Ken's paunch. "Too many lunches." Tim opened Ken's hand and dropped several canisters of film into it. "Get these developed and you can see the body."

"OK. We'll stop at the mall, get the one hour developing and have lunch. I'll make John a deputy before he developes the film. As a deputy he can't leak your body to the news people. OK?"

"Fine. You buy."

They took the photos back to Ken's office after lunch. "These are fine photos Tim." Ken said. He leaned forward across his desk. "However, we gotta get the body examined first then get it out. I think Bobby Burkett does forensic work in the medical examiners office, that would help us. Bobby's small, has a quick mind, strong stomach, excellent credentials and willing to work where others shy away."

"On your recommendation, get him in here. I'll pick you guys up at 8, sharp."

Ken smiling, waving good-bye and muttering, "We guys will be ready, 8 sharp."

The next morning at 8 sharp, Tim pushed his way into the office. The door hit something solid and bounced back into Tim's extended arm. A squeal of pain sounded from behind the door. Vapor trailed from the hot liquid as it splashed beyond the jamb.

"Watch where you're going. This coffee ain't for washing my face."

"Sorry. Sorry. Christ, are you hurt? Jeez, I'm sorry." Tim looked down into an angry face and small body sprawled on the floor, soaked and angry Bending over to help the young lady to her feet, Tim read the ID badge pinned to the stained denim blouse. BOBBIE BURKETT. Her look of indignatation and the heavy breathing pushing her small firm breasts up alerted Tim to possible trouble. Tim pulled his hands back, avoiding further embarrassment.

"Tim meet Bobbie." Ken's chortle filled the small office. Your faces are priceless. Bobbie, Tim thought you were a Robert and I didn't tell him any different. Looks like Bobbie wasn't ready to meet you, Tim."

The two shook hands and both apologized as they headed for the coffee pot. Settled into a chair, Bobbie focused on Tim perched on an ornate radiator cover. His demeanor and work attitude won her over and she knew she could work with him. But, she reasoned, she'd move carefully in close quarters.

Bobbie choose the backseat of the Hummer, her departmental vehicle because she wanted Tim to answer questions about the photos in more detail. Tim sat in the back too, as maneuvering in the front seat to view pictures might prove awkward. Somehow the body was tagged Slim, so it remained when they referred to it. Tim ventured a quick glance at Bobbie's hand, no ring.

Tim and Ken set a small gas generator away from the cave entrance to avoid fumes. Ken would be the "gofer" while she and Tim did the necessary examination and removal of the body. From the size of the opening Bobbie suggested that the bones be handed out one at a time, or in small bags. Tim labeled the bags or bones and took notes, Bobbie used a small recorder to tape her observations. All agreed several hours of continuous work might get the job finished in one day.

Dinner that night was very quiet, exhausted people have little to discuss. Tim did run his eyes over Bobbie's figure more then once. She did likewise and looked over Ken too. The medical report would be ready in a few days. Ken wanted to run down some old missing persons reports. Tim wanted to return to the cave, but it had been sealed.

"Possible crime scene." said Ken.

Three days later Bobbie called the State Police and reported to Ken that the case was officially closed. There were no indications of foul play. Ken conceded that he had found nothing in dated files going back to 1888. The body might have dated to 1870. Bobbie suggested the three of them meet, rehash their notes and speculate on Slim. Ken gently backed off and allowed the two might enjoy the evening without him.

Tim stood and waved as Bobbie entered Malcolm's, Fine

Food for Fine Friends. Her warm smile ignited Tim's hormone output. She approached the table with a bulging briefcase under her arm and sat across from Tim. The opened briefcase yielded Tim's photos.

"They belong to you. There is no case so the department allowed me to return them to the owner." Bobbie said.

"Thanks, they'll make an interesting wall display. Too bad they can't talk."

"Oh, Tim. They did talk and told a story filled with interest and fantasy." Bobbie fished a folder from the briefcase, now on the empty chair next to her. "I'll give you a step by step story and, maybe you can fill in a few gaps."

"Can we order first, I'm famished. My treat or Dutch?"

"Dutch." Bobbie smiled.

Tim picked up his coffee cup with both hands encircling it, put his elbows on the table and leaned forward to stare into Bobbie's face and said, "Read to me."

"Let's say Slim is almost 30 years old and may have been a bad boy. He had two different size bullets in him. I estimated he stood about five foot nine inches, weighed about a hundred fifty pounds, had brown hair and rotten teeth. He had just recovered from a poorly set broken right arm."

"Not bad for a made-up story." Tim interjected.

"That part isn't made-up. Sorry, Tim, bones do talk."

Tim leaned back and issued a low whistle, "Hey, I'm impressed."

"My job. From here on it's speculation. You took some wonderful shots. Ready?"

"Yeah."

"Remember Slim rested against the rock, probably seated himself. The old pistol, with one empty chamber in its holster. The pistol became obsolete during the Civil War. The shoes Slim wore were a new style that came out just after that war. So far everything clusters around the 1870's. With me Tim?"

"Hanging on every word."

Bobbie reached across the table to wipe Tim's chin and continued. "The box hasp had been broken from the box. The dent suggests it may have been shot off. Remember the pistol had one empty chamber. And, I'm pretty sure, outside the cave since we found no lock." Bobbie sighed. "Photo eight clearly shows the angle of the dent."

"Photo eight." Tim showed the picture to Bobbie. "Close-up and clear."

"Look at photos sixteen through twenty-two. Notice the horrible angle of the badly broken right leg. It was actually shattered. See how the pants are ripped just above the break? The discoloration is blood. I think Slim tried to shoot a lock off a box, probably stolen, and the bullet may have ricocheted and broke his leg."

"Shot himself." Tim suggested.

"Huh, huh." accompanied Bobbie' nodding head.

"Poor bastard. Guess he stole the box from a bank or stage coach, came here and tried to open it. After he shot himself, he still wanted the money..."

"There wasn't any money. You didn't find any before telling Ken, did you?"

"No money." Tim crossed his heart and raised his hand. "Cripes, he got zip."

"Looks that way, unless he had an accomplice that ran out on him."

"Could he have hidden it before he died?"

"That's doubtful, that broken leg negates his moving about."

"But he must have moved because you said he shot himself outside the cave."

Bobbie smiled. "Good point. I asked the doctor about the splintering break in the bone. He said the bone may have been fractured and after some movement, shattered."

It was Tim's turn to smile. "The shot outside the cave fractured the bone. then the poor slob creeps inside, ruins the leg and dies. Tough."

"Care to join me Monday morning to bury Slim in Potter's Field?" Bobbie asked.

"Sure."

The Fates weave and cut their threads in ways humans don't expect. Bobbie and Tim did not do the things people thought they might. In a few months they broke up. Ken married Bobbie. Shortly after the marriage they moved to the Canary Islands and purchased a home. Retiring at such an early age made for gossip at home. At about the same time a bank in the islands sold a treasure of old American, circa 1860's coins.

The story is Bobbie had discovered the coins in the debris next to "Slim's" leg on a previous incursion of the rock cave. Why she didn't announce her discovery is debatable, but one known fact is she had a fight with her boyfriend and was hiding from him when she found the room. Later they made up. To avoid taxes and litigation, they had Tim find the body, knowing he would go to Ken.

She had placed the coins in one of the small bone bags and Tim had passed it out to Ken. He didn't number it, so it was never recorded. Ken and Bobbie had the coins. They let Tim have the story.

Who was Slim? That never came out. A long time ago, out west, a thief met his Maker in a small rock room.

WASTED EFFORTS

Paul "The People's Plumber", signs plastered every side of the water-blue and white truck. Perhaps even under underneath, in case the truck should ever run down a pedestrian. The truck stood in the Brandon driveway nearly all morning. As it pulled out it narrowly missed Mrs. Bitterman as she exited her driveway. The squeal of brakes probably notified more neighbors of its presence in the area.

Katherine stood back in her doorway smiled and watched the truck pull away. Well they'd have pure water she thought. No more complaints about the fishy taste. She had never minded the taste but Herbert always mentioned it, even to company. Of course then they would notice the taste. It might have been missed, if he'd not mention the taste.

Eight years of marriage and only the first few weeks were free of his complaints. They frayed at her nerves, gave her headaches, kept her awake nights and upset her stomach. He would come home tonight, after the three nights at the luggage buyers meeting in Iowa, and complain about everything and everyone. He did it every time they had their company meeting. Every three months, off to Iowa. Why couldn't they meet in Chicago or some big town. She could go and enjoy doing girl things, shopping, a beauty shop appoinment, even visit a museum. She envisioned a billboard, COME TO IOWA, SEE THE CORN GROW.

Katherine wouldn't admit it, but she and Paul were, for the past three month, lovers. This time, she convinced Herbert a water purifying system had to be installed. He went along with the installation but almost ruined everything by calling the wrong plumbing company. She caught his error in the neck of time. The installation took half an hour, the rest of the time she and Paul had bopped each other in her very own king size bed. Better than the Pink Cloud and noisy next room neighbors banging their bed off the wall.

Back in the basement, to clean up the minor mess Paul must have left, Katherine picked up a brown clasped business envelope. Paul must have forgotten it. Perhaps it contained the warranty or parts list. But why was it so grimy? Katherine poured out the contents on the laundry table. Letters? Dozens of letters, from Iowa. Christ, these were love letters from Iowa sent to Herbert Brandon care of the Schlosser Luggage office. Her Herbert was shacking up at his company meetings with some dip named Zuzanne. He had a bitch in Iowa. And he complained she wasn't giving him enough, when he begged off most nights. "That son of a bitch. That dirty two-timing SOB."

The rest of the afternoon Katherine lulled on the patio, stared at the waves rolling flotsam onto the beach, as gulls argued over dead fish scraps. She measured the haves and have nots of her marriage to that two-timing twerp. She tried to picture Zuzanne, that husband stealing floosie, screwing Herbert. How could he do this to her? She wanted to call Paul, but indecision was one of Herbert's complaints about her and she remained true to that complaint.

Herbert arrived at the house at 6:30p.m., tossed his luggage and brief case in the alcove near the dining area, walked out onto the patio tugging at his tie, looked at Katherine and their lie together continued.

"Damn it's hot. The roads are jammed with trucks. Kissler, that stupid moron, kept the meeting going with some idiotic idea to display an open suitcase, with clothing in the display window. There's no room for an open suitcase."

"Anything special this trip?" came the soft, calm reply.

"Always something special. No bonus this year, but the life insurance value went up. Dead I'm worth two hundred thousand dollars. If I die in an accident."

"That'd be special for me."

"Are you wanting me dead?" came the subtle complaint. "You'd miss me."

Katherine gave him a small smile, as she rose from the chair now in the light of the late afternoon sun. "Would I? With two hundred grand, I could buy happiness." She couldn't believe she said it. Just like that, she had kicked out at him.

"Well, listen to this?" His voice drawled out the question. "I bust my butt working for the two of us. I ain't even dead yet and my wife is eager to spend my life insurance." Herbert slumped into her chair.

Katherine wanted to turn on him, challenge his fidelity, but didn't. For a moment she paused in the doorway. "I'll fix something for dinner. You want dinner, don't you?"

"If you haven't fix it yet, forget it." he whined. "Had a late lunch before starting back. Good thing too. The stuff on the plane looked lousy. Probably tasted lousy too. I didn't eat it."

"Have lunch with anyone special?" an almost sexy voice asked.

"Huh? Oh, no. Just two of the guys. You know them, Paul and Norton."

"Norton? Don't know Norton." She caught the look on her face on the pitcher just removed from the refrigerator. A sinister smile of remembrance of this morning. "I know Paul."

"Oh, speaking of Paul, the plumber guy is a Paul. Did he get here?"

"He worked here all morning. Nice looking guy, with a quiet voice, big icy blue eyes. A girl's dream prince."

"He's probably a fat ass. Why was he here all morning?" complained Herbert. "To push his bill up?"

Katherine smiled, covered her face and muttered, "He

might have pushed it up."

"Where's his bill? He gave you a quote, remember?" her husband whined.

"Two hundred eighty dollars he told me. He charged five dollars more."

"That's nice. He ripped us off for five bucks. Bastard." He came into the house and crossed over to the stairs. "I'm going to take a quick shower. Down in ten."

Katherine's nerves were stretching. Good God, this man complained for five bucks. He's spending hundreds on some gold digging tramp in Iowa and complains she spends an extra five. Cheapskate came the thought from behind a furrowed brow. She should bump him off, collect on that new accidental death clause and run off with Paul. Her mind toyed with the idea as she lifted the heavy broiler tray. Get rid of him, get peace and quiet with Paul.

Without a plan Katherine took the broiler tray up to their room, entered the steamy shower and bashed Herbert's head as he sang Old Susanna. She Zuannaed him.

Oh God. Now what should she do? Herbert didn't die from the blow. She'd toss him down the stairs. No, that wouldn't work. Bang his head on the floor. No. Obvious. Take him out in the boat and toss him in the ocean. Yeah. Wreck the boat and get rescued. Here was her accident.

Katherine worked feverishly to complete her little murder. She put the stopper down, filling the tub with water. Using her feet to hold him under she compressed his chest and released. The body shuddered as the lungs filled with water. She pushed down to fill the lungs completely. Getting clothing on his wet body took some time and she made sure, keys, wallet, coins and handkerchief were with him.

Hefting her late, now uncomplaining spouse, Katherine checked the yard. The sun set a few minutes ago, and most of the neighbors, like she and Herbert, shielded their yard for privacy.

Bent like the Hunchback of Notre Dame, she hustled her load to their boat and slid the body into the cabin area. In less than an hour Herbert had returned from Iowa and left for Hell. At least that's her place for him.

Pulling out she waved back to a neighbor's wave, eased the boat through the harbor that had filled with boats since they moved in, and headed for the shoals. She strapped the wheel to continue on a straight line and tugged the still warm body of Herbert into the small always stocked galley. She restrained from kicking him, no bruises for an autopsy. She uncorked a bottle of wine and returned to the deck. Check and double check, she opened the throttle and headed straight toward the dark area with breaking waves.

Katherine clung to the bobbing life preserver, she had forgotten how cold the salt water could be as the tides came in. The fiery wreck must have been seen, but she couldn't be sure. She reproached herself for acting without a plan. Then she saw lights and yells from a boat headed toward the wreck. She waved the emergency flashlight.

Somehow she had managed to cut and bruise her body. Good. That made the incident more an accident. She told the police she and Herbert went out for the evening to celebrate his return home. He had gone below, then asked a question about cooking oil. She left the wheel uncontrolled to help him. Her tears were real. It was a horrible thing to happen. Everything moved as if she planned it, the police, the hospital and the TV news all accepted Herbert Brandon's death as an accident. She slept soundly that night, with a little help from the pills the nurse gave her.

Two days later, Herbert's lawyer called on Katherine. The police called at the same time, to arrest her for the premeditate murder of her husband. Dumfounded and shocked Katherine leaned back in her bed. For three days she had gotten away with his murder. In her dreams she spent the life insurance money on trips and the good life. She and Paul traveled and lived, lived, lived.

What the Hell happened to change it?

Abraham Bemis asked Katherine, "Do you want me to represent you?"

"Certainly. Ask them why they think I killed Herbert?" She turned toward the policeman. "You think I'm some poor woman and you can yank me around? I'm not. Herbert left me plenty of money."

"Mam." The very polite young officer said. "Your husband's autopsy, showed he drowned."

"We know that." the lawyer said. "And Katherine, your husband left his money to a Zuzanne. A Zuzanne in Iowa. That's why I stopped to see you today."

Katherine's face flushed, her knees crumpled beneath her tipping her into a chair. Her voice sputtered vague meaningless sounds.

The officer looked at the scene, wrinkled his brow and firmly said, "Please advise your client not to speak. You know the Miranda thing."

"Katherine, I advise you to say nothing until we know why they suspect you."

The officer glanced over his shoulder and bent down. "I could let the D.A. tell you, but it's a no brainer. The guy drowned in the ocean, but his lungs were filled with pure fresh water."

THE BURNED LETTER

Another abandoned house, left by owners that couldn't afford the repairs or to pay the taxes. First discovered by teens wanting the freedom to booze, have sex, or do drugs, now the foul-smelling and decaying, derelict building served as a flop house by local winos and those irresponsibly homeless by choice. Tonight residents were Mike and the nameless old man. Both men had fallen through the system's paperwork, wandering out of a mental halfway house and lost on Chicago's streets.

Mike had found a dollar and shared his cheap alcoholic purchase with the old man. Together they prowled the empty house and decided a fireplace needed a fire for the night. Mike started the fire with old letters, tied with a faded ribbon and old newspaper clippings. The old man had gone off to urinate on the floor of what had been the family's bathroom.

"What are you reading, Mike?" the old man asked warming his hands in the fireplace.

"Just some old letters, come out of the box in the wall. Good enough to warm us up, but personal, nutty letters." Mike added a few more unread pages to the flames.

"What makes you think they're 'nutty' letters? You should open old envelopes, sometimes you might find some money." said the old man.

Mike rubbed the saliva from the corners of his mouth and tipped the bottle hidden in the brown paper bag. "Ahhh. One letter I tossed in was nutty. It was a late valentine to this guy's mother. Said he loves her and must leave town because he saw the guys killed in the garage."

"What?" The old man jumped up from his squat position. "What did the letter say?" Excitment sounded in his whiskey seasoned voice. "What did it say?"

"Let's see," Mike scratched the stubble on his chin and stared into the fire. "Dear Mom, I love you. Sorry I missed you Valentine's Day. I saw those guys get killed in the garage that morning. It's in all the newspapers."

"Oh my God! Oh my God!" The old man danced before the dying embers. "You didn't really burn the letter, did you?"

Mike frowned. "Sure I did. It was a nutty letter. Want to hear any more?"

The old man nodded and put his hands to his face and cried.

Mike continued his reminiscence of the letter. " I met Doctor Schimmer, our eye doctor, outside a garage on Clark Street. I told him my glasses hurt my ears. He said he was going into the garage for coffee and if I went in too, then latter he'd take me to his office and look at the glasses. When we got inside, he told the men there who I was. I had to pee so they pointed me to the toilet. Mom, I heard the machine-gun shooting. I was so scared I missed the toilet bowl. Part of the door frame was loose, I peeked and I saw two cops and a guy I seen in the newspapers holding machine guns."

"Oh God." the old man tossed his head, eyes rolled back so only the whites showed. "You burned that letter? You're sure you burned that letter? Positive?"

"Sure as I'm standing here. Something I shouldn't have done?" asked Mike in the voice of a child caught in a lie.

"Maybe. Did it say anything else?"

"Yeah. It said, the guy with the machine guy looked like 'Machine-gun
Jack...(over). Well I was cold and just threw the whole thing on the fire."

The old man's puffy red eyes stood out above the faint smile. His head shook back and forth as he stood before Mike and the ashes of a dying fire. "You're young, but ever hear of the St. Valentine's Day Massacre? When Al Capone's gang, some dressed like cops, killed a bunch of guys, with machine guns, in a garage on Chicago's Clark Street. 'Know the story?"

"Yeah and no. I think I know the story."

"Well Mike, that shooting has never been solved. Newspaper people, reporters, even the police might have paid us for that letter. I think you just burned the identity of the killers in the St. Valentine's Day Massacre. 'Coulda been heroes. Pass that bottle."

❧GROWING UP❧

BENJAMIN

In 1997 Benjamin began serving a life sentence as a habitual criminal. He never killed or hurt anyone. He just would not work at a job, instead he would pull a job with unthinkable results. More often than not, he got caught and sentenced. Many times he fell through the judicial system's loop holes, allowing him to stay on the streets for years.

Everything about Benjamin is continually shouting "Loser." If things began to happen favoring Benjamin you could bet change would soon follow. Looking for an explanation? Why bother? Except the fact, he's Benjamin.

Benjamin was a screwed-up, under educated teenager, floating about in a society passing him by or ignoring him. His opportunities are few, others take advantage of opportunities whenever possible, he fails to recognize them or twists them until useless. We can give Benjamin many excuses for his behavior. In truth he fails himself.

In 1930 a fifteen year old girl, frightened, confused and with little going for her, left her new born, Benjamin, in the hospital and never looked back. He couldn't be called cute, pretty or darling, but homely, plain or even a tad ugly would best describe the boy. Placed for adoption four days after birth, he became an unclaimed blessing and remained a ward of the state until fifteen. A few families brought him into their homes, never for more than a week or two. Once he stayed for an entire month, but soon came back to the institution. Rejected and unloved, he soon built a wall between most people and himself.

Charlotte, the home's assistant cook, doted on Benjamin. He allowed it. Charlotte, herself an orphan, understood the loneliness deep within the boy. When she died, Benjamin became belligerent, disruptive and began running away.

Incongruously, Benjamin had two loves, music and art. Classical music, not the soaring arias of operas, but the music. Tuning the radio to Herbie Mintz, he would drift into dreamland as the piano played Chopin, Herbert or Gershwin. Walking about the Art Institute, almost every free day, Benjamin stood for long minutes admiring paintings by Rembrandt, Monet or Rubens. After observing students copying paintings, he stole some supplies and tried. According to his own assessment, he couldn't paint.

At age 16 he was 5 foot 10, weighing 138 pounds. His deep set brown eyes, darting, always darting, peeked from a gaunt, acne-pocked face. Several inches of raised scar tissue adorned his right temple at the hairline. A broken hooked nose, he thought too large, angled in different directions. When he smiled, which wasn't often, the small mouth with razor thin lips revealed poor teeth. Benjamin cocks his head when listening, indicating a serious hearing problem. Poor depression care of teeth and hearing would keep him out of the armed services in the '50s. Slightly built and stoop-shouldered, his movements presenting a ape-like caricature. He kept his brown hair in a crew cut. His fingers were long, nimble and dirty most times. A gap between Benjamin's front teeth allowed him to spit saliva forcefully ten feet. He enjoyed maneuvering behind his tormentors, squirting spit somewhere on their lower backside.

Clothing presented no problem for Benjamin. He wore hand-me-downs, patches on patches or stolen thing which were often too large for him. Standing still Benjamin appeared to be in constant motion. A hat was a necessary part of his dress, fedoras preferred. Shoes were a problem, each foot was a different size, consequently he wore them 'til they literally fell off his feet.

Because Benjamin feared heights, dark or close spaces and

scary movies, he had nightmares. He fought off his nightmares, screaming himself awake. Often, during an expected scene in a movie, Benjamin closed his eyes. Walking across a bridge became an exercise in quickening the pace and looking straight ahead. If you're in a small narrow area, shut your eyes. Logical, isn't it?

Benjamin ministered to a rough, reddened, dripping nose by dragging his sleeve, already glistening with shiny mucus crystals, across his face. Actually Benjamin is allergic to dust and fungus spores, which made the warm months hellish and the cold months Hell. Once the Summer sneezing began, Benjamin sounded like a Fourth of July evening. He lost sleep and weight, which he couldn't afford to lose and became lethargic. The powerful sneezes damaged his middle ear. Someone once said his honking could decoy a flock of geese from the sky. He is also allergic to tomatoes and would find out in the1950's he was allergic to penicillin. He binged on candy and cheesecake when he could get them.

Afflicted with teen age anxieties, pimples, chronic hunger and misunderstood sex drives, Benjamin advanced toward adulthood. Already clumsy, he shied away from doing things that would test his abilities. Running. Running, he enjoyed running. Running everywhere just for the joy of running. He tried running and jumping, but fell over a garbage barrel and broke an arm. For the second time a nurse befriended him, reinforcing his fondness for the profession. On a home adoption visit a dog bit him. His teasing prompted the dog to bite. It was a white starched capped angel that held him on her lap while stitches closed the eyebrow. Frightened by dogs, Benjamin avoided them. Nurses were different, he couldn't assist them enough, often going out of his way to hold doors, carry packages or offer his seat on the streetcar.

In the Jackson Street Home, Freddie, a seventeen year old orphan with a personality problem, connected with Benjamin. Their relationship became closer than fuzz on a peach. Seldom apart they fed on each other's egos. Both were reckless with boyish daunts and dares, yet neither allowed anyone to transgress against the other. Freddie played games in the dark or in high places holding Benjamin's hand but couldn't abate his terrors. Freddie attacked an older, bigger boy for hitting Benjamin and received a beating himself. A month later the bully found his shoes filled with dog shit. Oddly, no one noticed Benjamin was developing a personality, coming out of his shell.

On Benjamin's sixteenth birthday, they ran away from the Home and found a small flat near the stadium. Petty shoplifting, once a game for Freddie and Benjamin, became their source of income. Pick up two small objects; pocket knife, candy, or doohickey, hold one up and examine it, while the other is hidden in the palm. Put the examined object back, pocket the second. If you were caught stealing or going into a restricted place, pretend you're supposed to be there doing whatever you're doing. Lie. You can run later, when your antagonists drop their guard.

Benjamin became a loser and loner after Freddie died. It happened when they were breaking through a restaurant skylight just before Christmas of 1945. Freddie was holding the steam heating pipes near the skylight, a small flashlight securely tucked into his mouth, when he slipped. He landing on his face fifteen feet below, the flashlight punctured his brain. Benjamin spent a few months under psychiatric care, but soon drifted back onto the streets. Some of the people he and Freddie associated with, fences, bookies and their ilk, had Benjamin run errands, or bought what he stole. They were never his friends and thought nothing of cheating him. Tiny came close to offering friendship by allowing Benjamin to flop in a room above the pool hall, with an outside entrance, but charged him rent.

On his own Benjamin knew little of the niceties of life, except what he saw in the movies. Without skills he tried to imitate what he saw on the screen, forgetting the person he was imitating was a loser. Benjamin lost too, often. That is why he is serving a habitual criminal's life sentence.

FORTUNE COOKIE

Pushing the last noodle onto his fork with his finger, Benjamin smiled at the waiter putting the dish with the fortune cookie on it before him. Beneath the cookie was his bill. Dry crumbs fell on the dish, tab and table as he opened the cookie and removed the fortune. For some obscure reason he put credence in fortune cookie messages. Twice his fortune had come true, sort of, at least he thought they did.

"Ask politely and you will gain many rewards" was printed on the slip of paper.

Leaning back, Benjamin allowed daydreams to float about in his head. What could many rewards be? Ask who? He beckoned the waiter for more tea. Playing the "What If" game, he wondered if asking for change he would get back more than he should. Or calling for three cards he would fill a royal flush. Or, if the Dwyer girl would agreed to lay him. Benjamin came back to reality when someone left and the cool night air came caressing his neck.

Looking over to the register he saw the tiny woman returning his look, as she continued counting the cash drawer. Focusing on her, he saw her slipping money into a cigar box and putting it under the counter. Another sip of tea while gazing about the restaurant confirmed that only the cook, waiter and cashier were in the place. It was just after 9:30 p.m. according to the wall clock and the place was empty. Few people would be coming for Chinese this late. It was mid-week and most people would be working tomorrow. Up early and that kind of stuff.

In the movies if you put your finger in your pocket and point it at people they think you have a gun. He would hold up the place. She'd never question him and hand over the box.

Pointing his pocketed hand, Benjamin asked politely, "Please give me the money from the cash register and get the cigar box from under the counter." Nervously she showed Benjamin the empty cash drawer, while handing him the cigar box. Several blocks away Benjamin opened the cigar box. Empty. Except for a fortune.

"Plan ahead for rainy days."

PAY ATTENTION

Hands digging deep into his pockets, head tucked down into his shoulders, Benjamin raced along the cold air biting his ears. Pushing blindly through the pool hall door, he bumped against the august bulk of "Tiny" Ponizzi. His ready snarl died below his Adam's Apple when he recognized the bulwark before him.

"Jeez. Tiny. Jez, I'm sorry I run into you."

"You should look where you are going. You could have hurt me."

Benjamin giggled at the thought of his 147 pounds hurting Tiny's 380. "Funny."

"You OK, Benjamin, not too cold?" Patting his back and looking him over, Tiny assumed he wouldn't answer. "Want to run an errant for me Benjamin? I need change and the bank is almost ready to close. Closes at noon today."

Rubbing the cold from his ears, Benjamin said, "Sure Tiny. Sure. The bank two blocks over. Right?"

"Right. Get ten rolls of quarters, four rolls of dimes. two of nickels and one of pennies. Go to Hugo and have him take it out of the pool hall account. Here's a withdrawal slip, all signed."

Benjamin ran through the bank door rubbing his ears and his mouth pumping vapor. The guard shot him a glance as he stepped into the teller's line. Eight minutes 'til noon. It would be cold going back he thought.

"You sure you want cash?" the teller asked the woman in front of him.

The word cash piqued Benjamin's curiosity and his cold

red ears listened as the cashier counted out eleven hundred dollars in twenties. He watched the envelope go into the large black pocketbook. He stepped out of line, contining to watch the frail old woman exit through the bank door. He didn't even notice the guard held the door for him too as he followed her out of the bank.

Benjamin's larcenous mind already assumed the eleven hundred dollars was his. He'd miss getting Tiny's rolls of coins, but he could get and pay for them at a currency exchange. He mentally moved in on the woman and pushed her to the ground, hard. The shock would keep her from hollering. He'd grab her pocketbook and run.

Cold as it was, Benjamin's thoughts warmed him as he walked on the opposite side of the street. following his prey, step for step. She paused in front of the 5 & 10 window, then went into the office supply store next door. Benjamin started to jay-walk across the street, but a street car clanged its way between him and his eleven hundred dollars.

The woman was still in the store. Looking through the "O" of Notary Public, printed in gold letters on the front window, he watched the woman take a small slip of paper from the person behind the desk and poke it into the black bag. She exited, walking passed Benjamin and struggling with her gloves. One glove fell from her hand and she stooped to retrieve it,

In the manner of a diving bird of prey, Benjamin streaked passed her, seizing the purse and moving toward the alley. The move sent her sprawling, spread eagle, on the cold pavement. Loss of breath stilled her screams

Two blocks away, in an alley behind the theater, Benjamin peeked back. Seeing no one in pursuit, he stepped into a doorway. Time to reap his harvest.

No envelope. No money. No treasure. A dollar, eight cents in a ratty coin purse.

Benjamin tore out the lining, nothing. He dug into each

zippered pocket, no money. A piece of paper. "Received of Mrs. Dugan, $11,000 down payment 12/6/47.

It was too late to get to the bank. Slouching down, reducing the cold wind, he began walking two blocks to the currency exchange. The man told him a bank withdrawal slip didn't work there. He headed for the pool hall and Tiny. His lie about the bank being closed already, maybe their clock is off, didn't satisfy Tiny. He didn't have the coins he needed. Tiny told Benjamin he was disappointed and he couldn't hang around the pool hall today. Benjamin left hungry, defeated and cold again. Another unlucky day.

THE FIND

The second floor window displayed, in gold letters, Objects D' Art, bought and sold, Abner Golden, Prop. Izzy stood at the window and watched Benjamin, only Benjamin looked like this character, kneeling and digging at something on the sidewalk. Izzy went back to his desk to attend to important business, the scratch sheet.

Across the street a sparkle in a crack in the sidewalk had caught Benjamin's attention. He knelt down, blocking the way for some pedestrians and dug out the sparkle, a faceted object. He didn't know if he had gem or a glass shard.

He crossed the street and mounted the smooth wooden steps. Walking into "Izzy the Fence's" office, he set the object on the cluttered desk.

"How much?"

Izzy gave a quick glance at Benjamin's sparkle, a passing roach might have gotten more attention. "Drop it in the wastebasket as you leave Benjamin." Izzy replied, his heavy eyelids returning to the racing form.

"Testing you Iz. Just testing."

Izzy returned to the window and stood, watching Benjamin crossing the street waving his arms about as he talked to himself. Stepping to the wastebasket to retrieve a half carat or so of yellow diamond.

Izzy returned to the business of picking a winner while talking to himself. "Benjamin, you putz."

THE PRIZE

Slouching in his seat as the movie theater darken, Benjamin would finally see Snow White. The bitter memory of missing the movie the first time around flooding his mind. The pain lingered in that memory. He remembered the day the prize slipped away, every detail, clearly. Back went his memory, back to the third grade, seeing himself years ago.

Benjamin's ears perked up. What was Miss Cohen saying? At times his hearing problem allowed information to skip passed him. A free ticket to a new Walt Disney Movie, Snow White, to anyone turning in a perfect spelling test paper tomorrow. They would get to attend Snow White in a downtown theater, free. Benjamin didn't know the story of Snow White, or care about it, but free tickets interested him.

Benjamin asked to stay and study after school, an advantage of being in an institution where you live and attend school in the same building. The courts had placed him here, to await a formal hearing, after being caught in a store after hours. He looked at the words and wrote each one. A careless mistake, he crumpled the paper and began again. Many attempts and still not perfect. He requested to return after supper and study some more. At last, after several hours, a perfect paper. Benjamin used chewing gum to hid the paper under the bottom of his desk.

The next day, as the test progressed, Benjamin pretended to write on his paper. He covered the paper as Miss Cohen walked the aisles calling out each word. He took last night's paper from under his desk and passed it forward. He had succeeded.

Miss Cohen called Benjamin to her desk the next day. He beamed as he stood next to her and saw his paper and the movie ticket. Today was a day he'd remember.

Miss Cohen beckoned Benjamin to lean down and in a low whisper asked, "Benjamin, did you cheat on this test?"

Horrified, he denied cheating. He called on God to prove his innocence.

"Benjamin, I wanted you to tell me the truth. The plain and simple truth. I know you cheated, but I don't know how. I mixed up the spelling words, your words are in alphabetical order."

NOT NOW

Before Benjamin dropped out of school he experienced a sexual problem. During math Benjamin was daydreaming. Looking at Peggy Berg solving problems at the blackboard got under his skin. And he was daydreaming, allowing nature to pursue her course was inducing an erection. If this had happened at home he would take things in hand and resolve it immediately. But sitting here in a math class, watching Peggy and permitting a temporary body growth to occur could present a problem.

"Benjamin, take John's place at the back of the room."

PROBLEM! Miss Cohen, calling on him? Oh no. No. No. No. Everyone'll see my hard-on. Benjamin's mind commanded. Down. Go down. He didn't stand, move or respond to the teacher's directions.

"Come on Benjamin, we haven't all day. Get to the blackboard. Do problem 8."

Problem 8. I got a problem here. But he moved and felt his tight skin slipping between the buttons of his undershorts. With less pressure maybe, just maybe, no one would notice the bulge in the front of his pants. He stood, turning toward the blackboard and problem #8.

Fliesher popped off with, "Hey Benjamin, your fly is open."

Benjamin's face flushed, red-hot. Reaching down to cover the gapping area, he felt every pair of eyes in the room center in on his fly. They'd know. They would see the tell-tale bulge. They'd all laugh, at his expense. Pulling his knees together, left thumb and forefinger seizing the material below the zipper while the other hand is grabbing and pulling up on the zipper tab.

Stars. Colorful, dancing stars jumping in his head and excruciating pain. Haste had moved the zipper up until the skin escaping between the buttons of his shorts stopped it. Caught in the closing teeth, the skin locked the zipper painfully in place. Words unheard in a classroom came spewing from Benjamin's mouth while dancing up and down, round and round, then, holding tight, beelining out of the door. The class wouldn't know about his erection but it would remember the zipper incident. Always.

LUCKY BEN

Benjamin sat on the Washington Park Express mulling over his good fortune. An hour ago, flat broke, looking for something to turn into cash, he strolled into the Palmer House shop area. A wallet, propped against the leg of a bright red cushioned chair, caught his attention. Benjamin retrieved it and headed for the men's room. He found in it thirty-eight dollars, a round trip ticket to the track and assorted pictures and notes. Dumping the wallet into a waste basket, without money or train ticket, Benjamin beelined for the Randolph Street Station.

Sitting in the smoking car, he perused the Green Sheet assessing his chances of winning by his usual, but unusual method. He always bet on the second horse listed on the line-up sheet to show. Departing the train, he slipped his hand around the money in his pocket, dreaming big, Benjamin walked to the entry gate.

Club House entry fee, a coke and hamburger, smokes and he still had over thirty-five bucks and change. Today was his lucky day, he just knew it. He would bet as he did with Tiny's bookie, holding his winnings in a different pocket. But regardless of how things went, he would hold off and bet ten bucks in the ninth race on Lucky Ben to win.

Benjamin's method paid on the first three races, lost in the fourth, but won for the next four races. He toasted each win with a coke. Nervous and excited, standing at the bet window, he changed his mind. He bet his winnings.

"Got yourself a winner?" asked the clerk, who had taken all of Benjamin's bets.

"You bet. And if you can, bet like me. A winner for sure."

Not many people stood at the pay-off window after the ninth race. Benjamin did. Lucky Ben paid $8.20 to win. Benjamin, grinning at the clerk, cashed for $620. Folding his hand over the money and shoving it deep into his pocket, he headed for the toilet . Too many winning toasts.

Standing at the urinal, one hand clutching his winnings, he felt a cold object pressing into his neck. A voice whispered, "Grab your pecker with both hands." As he complied, a hand dipped into his pocket and removed the folded bills.

Benjamin had a round trip ticket, he wouldn't walk home. Lucky Ben.

DOC WILL SEE YOU

"Number thirty-eight. Thirty-eight."

Approaching the desk quickly, Benjamin handed the woman cardboard number 38. His bladder was so full it hurt to move and pissing hurt so much he tried to hold it in. Right now his groin itched, but he couldn't embarrass himself by scratching there in front of everyone.

"Why are you here?" the receptionist asked.

Flushing red, Benjamin leaning toward her and whispered. "My pecker hurts."

"Is this an injury?"

"No injury. It just, sortta, itches and burns. I need the Doc to fix it."

She scribbled something, handed it to him, smiled and pointed down the hall.

Entering the door he was directed to, Benjamin grabbed his crotch through his pocket and began fidgeting with his penis. His obvious discomfort brought a smile to the dour face of the man standing next to the examination table. He opened the folder he took from Benjamin's other hand and glanced at it contents

"Having a problem in there?" he chirped.

"The problem in there itches. And when I pee it burns like hell. Can you help me Doc? Huh?"

"Got a sore or scab on your member? Been burning long? You're a little young, but have you been playing house with the girls?"

"There's a red pimple on the end of my dick. And I ain't

too young to lay a girl."

The doctor looked, "Clap. Young fella, you got the clap. Gonorrhea. Better tell your girlfriend to get in here and get some treatment for herself too. Might last...forever."

"I got the clap. From screwing some girl? Hell Doc, I don't know where to find her. This gal asked me if I wanted some? We done it in somebody's car. In the back seat. I run off after, so I didn't pay her."

"Well", he looked at Benjamin, "you didn't pay her and you don't pay here at the clinic. However, for a lifetime you're going to pay for your pleasure and pay and pay."

BAIL BOND

Benjamin was walking out of jail, a free man. The woman claiming he was stealing had failed to show in court and press charges. Besides, she only thought Benjamin was stealing, when he really was contemplating stealing. Waiting for a better opportunity you might say.

Now he had an errant to run. Largo, a friend of Tiny's, sitting in the lock-up, wanted out. So, as a favor, Benjamin was going to get a hundred bucks from Tiny for Largo's bail, plus a sawbuck for himself. Benjamin headed straight for the pool hall. This was doing a favor for both men, Benjamin might benefit from this errant in the future.

Tiny counted out ten tens and had Benjamin count it again. Crushing the money in his fist and shoving his fist deep into his pocket, Benjamin headed back to the lock-up. No screw ups this time, people would learn they could count on him. In the entrance hall, he felt hurried and sweaty, like he needed a cold drink. He fished a nickel from the money in his pocket and bought a coke. Guzzling the drink, but not finishing it, he stepped into the elevator with the rest of the small crowd. He held his coke close. He didn't like people jostling against him.

The official behind the desk, smiling as Benjamin came toward her, couldn't understand the sudden change in behavior Benjamin exhibited. He had stopped, screwed up his face and was bending his body around, thrashing his arms and moaning loudly. He began cursing and jumping about. A police officer started toward him, but Benjamin ran for the stairs.

His dream of people trusting him, counting on him were gone. From the time he bought his coke and exited the elevator, someone had picked his pocket. There were thieving opportunists everywhere.

A PARROT

Few opportunities for a quick buck escaped Benjamin's eye. A bright red and blue bird setting on a branch began squawking loud aggressive words, "Help." "Don't touch me." " Love you." and "Up yours." as Benjamin strolled passed the tiny novelty shop. The bird was being used as an inducement, a lure to get people to enter the shop.

Two woman walking out of the shop, turning to glare at Benjamin, when the bird got their attention with, "Cute ass." Benjamin turning several shades of Autumn red, began pointing to the avian culprit. Seeing no one around, Benjamin threw his jacket over the bird. Making like a football player, the bird buried deep in the crook of his arm, darted across the street and down the nearest alley, heading for home.

The shop owner gave the police plenty of useless information regarding the theft, because he didn't see the bird being snatched. He told a radio reporter he would pay a $1,000 dollars reward. The bird, an unusual hybrid macaw had an unusually large vocabulary and had just been signed for a part in a Frederick March, Florence Eldridge movie.

The person having the bird should feed it fruit and nuts and give it plenty of drinking water but no chemically treated water. Never, under any circumstances give it tap water. The owner repeated his offer of a $1,000 dollars reward, no questions asked. Just call the novelty store if you have any information.

Benjamin perched the bird on the foot of his bed and stared. The pinioned parrot walking back and forth, cussing in

Spanish and talking up a storm, sent Benjamin into giggling and dancing around his luckless avian captive. He repeated the bird's words. "Pay the girl." "One vote, one buck." "Craps." "Shut up and deal." "Bueno."

He knew he'd get some money this time. He sat on the bed reviewing his options. No one he knew had birds. He could sell it to a zoo, or a pet store. He could look in the want ads, someone might be looking for a talking bird. He reached over to turn on the radio, unconsciously stroking the bird's breast. A foolish thing to do.

Screaming in pain, flaying his arm, with the bird gripping his little finger, Benjamin began cursing and screaming. The vise-like beak was drawing blood, panicking him. He fell to the floor in pain. He began banging the bird on the floor. Even as the bird's spirit flew out of its limp body, Benjamin knelt there and cried, prying at the horny beak gripping his bloody finger Finally, when the bird no longer held his finger, when the pain and panic eased, he heard the radio announcer speaking.

"Blah, blah, blah For the return of this rare bird, the owner is offering one thousand dollars. No questions asked. Maybe the thief could collect this reward."

Wrapping the parrot in old newspaper, Benjamin went to an alley garbage can and tucked the bird into the bottom of it. He was feeling a different pain now. He was throwing away $1,000.

HANGING AROUND

Reading glasses perched on the receding hairline, arms folded across an amble belly, the elderly figure stood blocking Benjamin's entrance into Nussbaum's Clothing, Inc.".

An old country accent said, "Not today my little thief. You stay out today."

"Ah, Mr. Nussbaum. I don't steal from my friends." Benjamin's toothy smile tried to block that lie. "I just come from back in the alley and somebody put a hole in your wall."

"I know." said the man, now moving closer to Benjamin. For my new ventilator fan. To cool the heat from my shop. So go." a gentle shove promoting his departure.

Benjamin, skirting around the men unloading the truck and carrying large tubes into the store, stood aside, watching. He saw Mr. Nussbaum's head at the end of a tube a worker had on his shoulder. Putting his face to the tube, he hollered. "Bye, Mr. Nussbaum." The startled old man jumped, hands across his heart..

In the alley, after midnight, Benjamin could see the reflecting light shimmering dully from the metal framework around the metal tube in the wall. Moving a garbage barrel under the iron bars covering the opening, Benjamin pulled his body up and squirmed into the narrow opening. Crawling toward the dim light, he soon arrived at an opening above the table with the shirts on display and dropped down. The streetlight reflected enough light for Benjamin to look in the long mirrors and see himself dressed in a new suit, perhaps a dark blue, with a bright tie and a pinstriped shirt.

When he opened his shop the next morning, Mr. Nussbaum didn't understand the stool in the aisle or the shirts on the store floor. He understood the legs dangling from the new ventilator tube. He had caught a thief. A thief in a Nussbaum suit.

The fan installers, several neighborhood gossips, four policemen and a newspaper photographer stood around the shirt laden table under the dangling legs. They took turns hollering to the body attached to the legs, but got no answer. No one went out to the alley to look through the tube. The shirts were moved and an officer stepped onto the table, he grabbed the dangling legs. Pulling and twisting the body came loose and popped out, falling to the table.

The wide eyed, dirty, sweat covered face of Benjamin looked at the faces looking at him.

Arms akimbo, eyes on fire and breathing in short pants, Mr. Nussbaum said, "So, Mr. Thief. You don't steal from friends."

WINDY CITY

"Winds gusts, 35 to 40 miles an hour." the radio announced. "With temperatures below zero tonight. Right now it's officially 24 degrees." The little radio switched to music and Benjamin leaning back, clutching his sandwich between his teeth, heard "Claire de Lune." A quarter to 12 is a bit early for lunch, but he wanted to eat early.

Benjamin actually had a job, started two days ago at a small shop, 5th floor just off Lake and Clark Street. Realizing, at long last, a job would give him access to other offices and shops in a building there-by reducing the time wasted casing a place. Already he knew the glass shop on the third floor put out packages at their front door, for a trucking company to pick up and deliver. They made things that were small and expensive for homes or shop window displays. He also found the emergency doors, delivery doors and a roof door that lead to the fire escape and access to other roof tops.

Finishing lunch, Benjamin walked down the stairs, perusing each floor hallway. Dawdling as he went, looking into each office, he read each painted door, noted the occupant and hours. He thought to himself, "Jackpot". With care he could slip out of the cubicle lunch area, prowl the building and snap up things from carelessly unattended offices or shops, like the antique shop where two women employees left the door open while both of them were elsewhere.

The next day, the weather report seemed the same so Benjamin repeated his actions of yesterday. Outside the glass shop a box waited for pick up. Benjamin picked it up. In the stairwell, he decided to hide it on the roof. No one at work would see it or ask him questions, or know anything if asked by someone looking for the box. The box was heavy and the wind made the door impossible to open, so Benjamin leaned heavily against the door. It opened with the windy gust, he fell out and the door slammed shut quickly.

Benjamin's body had smashed against the door jamb. The package split open to release hundreds of brochures to the wind. Rolling onto the roof Benjamin felt his arm break and heard the lock snap shut as the door closed. Benjamin has a problem.

SHOE REPAIR

With his usual ineptness Benjamin bungled his latest attempt to exist in this world without the exertion normal people apply. Entering an unoccupied hotel room from the fire escape, he had gone into the hallway empty-handed and accidentally allowed the room door to shut behind him. He effectively locked himself in the hotel. The hotel Dick, Patterson, knew him and would try to collar him on the premises. So, rather than getting caught with any thing stolen, Benjamin opt to walk down the stairs, locate Patterson, then dash out of the building when the opportunity arose.

Benjamin saw Patterson talking at the newspaper counter. Easing into the lobby, he saw Patterson looking in the mirror and saw him smiling and turn. With a burst of speed an Olympic runner would die for, Benjamin ran for the lobby door. Slamming the door open, he stumbled on the metal door jamb and nearly ripped the sole off his shoe. Running toward State Street, his every other step give a loud clap, a slap to his foot.

Benjamin ducked into the alleyway behind the Fair Store. Leaning against the wall, he removed the shoelace from his shoe and tied the sole and shoe together. It quieted the slap walking. He didn't know if Paterson was following him. Well, I'm free, for now, Benjamin thought, stepping into Kresge's Five and Dime.

Marching through he swiped a tube of model airplane glue and marched right out again. He picked up a piece of cardboard from the alley behind the library and headed for Grant Park. Ensconced on the park bench, Benjamin began a simply repair of his shoe. Tearing the cardboard to fit inside the shoe, he spread a glob of glue to hold the sole and shoe together. Satisfied, he slipped the shoe on then sat watching the passing parade.

Benjamin snuck into the afternoon movie at the State and Lake. Then he slipped onto the I.C. suburban at Jackson Street to get home. He stopped at Carmin's little deli and stole a package of Twinkies. The shoe creating no further problems for Benjamin. Well, until bed time. Benjamin pulled one shoe off, but the other remained on his foot. It hurt, a lot, when he pulled at it. He called his landlady for help. She laughingly cut sock and shoe from his foot. The wet glue had seeped through bonding both to Benjamin's foot. He would face new problems tomorrow. He only had one pair of shoes.

THE JEWELRY SNATCH

December 26, 1947, dawned cold with freezing rain icing every street in Chicago. Benjamin found himself locked out of a hotel party he had crashed and wondering how he would get home from the Loop. His stomach, bloated from rich foods, grumbling like a volcano, the molten lava burning his throat when he belched and his eyes kept seeing twin everything. His thin, mismatched clothing suitable for the Chicago summers, not winters, wouldn't keep him warm or comfy if he had to walk home.

The wind blew off the lake. He avoided its bite by turning south on La Salle and found himself wishing for a men's room. His bladder had become the container for every dammed lake ever made. The post office toilets were ahead, but he couldn't wait. Pushing into the first office building, the directory posted a restroom on the ground floor. Benjamin can't fly, but his feet didn't touch too many floor tiles hustling down the hall.

Relieved, he began walking down the hall. Hanging golden arrows caught his eye, they indicated an antique jeweler and two diamond merchants had offices down the hall. Above the arrows a red emergency exit sign pointed down the same hallway. Benjamin walked casually, slowly passed their shops, studying each one through the plain glass doors, noting which were wired with a burglar alarm. A janitorial style tool box lay near the emergency door. A gentle push and the lock mechanism clicked open. Benjamin's thieving little mind was giving birth to a plan.

Attempting to enter the diamond dealer's office, he found the door locked. The clerk, hearing the door rattle, buzzed the lock open. Benjamin found himself about to enter a small cage. He held the door open, waving a sorry, "OOPS", to the clerk and retreated. He'd steal nothing from this place, nor from the near identical set-up in the antique shop. Bingo. The small shop, just a short way beyond the emergency exit, had no cage.

Proceeding outside, then estimating the location of the shop door, Benjamin paced off eighty-one steps to an alley. An emergency exit, opening onto a loading dock, slanted into the building with easy access to both ends of an alley. Benjamin peered into the loading area. The emergency door, he had tried, opened onto the dock, about 40 feet from the loading dock doors. Benjamin thought this situation held promise.

He reentered the building and went to a drinking fountain near the emergency door. A quick look down the hallway, no one. He retested the door with a gentle push. Click. Benjamin had visions of sugarplums, nearly wetting himself with anticipation. Wow. Back outside, gripping his thin coat close to his chest, he checked the distance by repacing the eighty-one steps. His larcenist intentions were keeping him warm.

"Hey! Stand on the curb." A policeman waving his arm and pointing toward Benjamin. "Pay attention huh. Let the truck in."

"Sorry. Daydreaming." said Benjamin, now watching the truck marked, Bibion's Antique Movers, back down the alley. Street traffic had stopped as the policeman waving his arms back and forth, guided the behemoth into the narrow opening. Cold, Benjamin walked back into the building, then stood watching the policeman walking off. He was finished with the truck. Benjamin felt the urgency of his bladder again and headed back into the restroom.

He slicked himself up before the mirror, then stepping into an empty hallway Benjamin started walking toward the last shop. Why wait, sometimes the spur of the moment worked quite well.

Holding the door of the jeweler's open, the man leaving said, "Welcome. Come in." Turning about and calling back into the shop, "Just coffee, no roll?"

"Right." Then addressed Benjamin. "May I help you sir?"

"I hope so. I need an engagement ring. Not big and not fancy. Plain"

"Not big and not fancy. Plain" repeated the clerk. "I know we can do that."

A black velvet tray of rings was set gleaming on the red cloth swatch covering the counter. Benjamin felt his eyes glazing over, his breathing quicken.

Benjamin glanced through the window into the hallway. Clear. Snatching rings with both hands he bolted for the door, not understanding a word the clerk screamed after him. Pell mell, his whole body hit the emergency door, releasing it. He flew out onto the dock .

Later, sitting in the squad car handcuffed and dazed, with a horrific, pounding headache, Benjamin heard, "He ran out that door and smacked into this antique armoire. A truck just delivered it to the loading dock. Knocked himself cold. The jewelry guy that got robbed called the cops."

PICNIC

Sunny, not too warm, with a breeze smelling of the lake stirring his olfactory senses, Benjamin had nothing to do and nothing to do it with. He was just wasting the day, walking, day dreaming, feeling funny, but couldn't understand why.

Stepping into the garlic laden atmosphere of a small Jewish deli, just off 71 Street and Jeffery, he looked about and did nothing. The man with the odd hat was watching him from behind a meat and cheese case. Smoked sausages lay in a window display next to the door. Turning, Benjamin departed immediately, so did several sausages. Curses following his rapid retreat, caught only his ears. Running through several gangways, he arrived on 75th Street with no one behind him.

Relaxing, wiping his arm across his brow. The muted murmuring of lake waves dragging the shoreline beckoning, he headed toward part of Chicago's treasures, the lake front.

Sitting on the concrete retaining wall, Benjamin watched the waves caress the shoreline. He watched the birds making a playground of the sky and marveled at a natural vastness he saw only parts of when downtown. Far to his left the Loop's towers outlined the horizon. Taking off his shoes and socks, burying his feet in the sand, he began strolling, yes strolling, toward the water's edge. Standing still, the chilly water buried his feet. At 17, he was feeling funny, a different kind of funny. His stomach started growling.

Benjamin picked up bits of wood and paper lying on the beach while walking toward a firepit. He soon had a small fire going. Gathering some more wood, he spread his jacket out on the sand and pulled the purloined sausages from his pocket. In minutes the smell of fat dripping into the fire nuzzled his nostrils, a build-up of saliva ran down his throat. His stomach began growling in anticipated approval.

Benjamin missed the approach of a small, dirty four legged stranger. Furtive movements brought it close to Benjamin's remaining sausages. A quick jump, a snapping mouth and the thief was darting passed the relaxing chef. Benjamin rose at once, chasing after the opportunistic sausage snatcher. His chase and curses were of no avail. Benjamin returned to his fire site. The wooden skewer had burned through, and the sausages had fallen into the flames, becoming charcoal ashes.

Benjamin's stomach growled in disappointment.

QUEST

Benjamin pulled the drape back and looked out at the traffic on the Outer Drive traveling passed the Drake Hotel. Pretty, I could live in a place like this. Enjoy a view and even give parties with girls and stuff. Turning away from the early evening scene and scanning the parlor with its paintings, fancy figures on the tables and trophies on the fireplace shelf, Benjamin felt truly envious. He wanted things like this.

Putting on airs was easy for Benjamin. Much of his world consisted of dreaming in the darkened movie theater, putting real life aside for a few hours. Now he found himself in a Michigan Avenue house that by chance he had overheard would be empty for the holiday weekend. He managed to wiggle his body through the coal chute door and could take his time stealing whatever appealed to him, if valuable and small enough to carry. He'd go out the front door with his loot and casually walk down Lake Shore Drive.

Benjamin took a large valise from a closet and laid it out on the parlor floor. He began rifling the bedrooms first dumping jewelry and things into a pillowcase. He took the silverware and a gold figurine from a special cabinet. Some items he found interesting, he'd keep those for himself. Finished, he took some wine from the pantry, popped the cork and settled down in the Morris chair. Ahhh. Just sit and enjoy life's good things. Turning the radio on, he tuned in Herbie Mintz for some light classical music. Revel's Bolero, not a piano piece, but nice. Closing his eyes, he let the music lift his spirit.

Opening his eyes, he saw an elderly man, a woman and a cop before him. His fogged mind wasn't figuring the tableau out, nor were they offering any help. The radio was off, all the drapes were open and the sun was shinning. Was he dreaming? Dead?

"Young fella," entoned the cop, "What are you doing in this house? These people, the Keelys, tell me you broke in. Are you a burglar, stealing their stuff?"

Poor Benjamin. He looked at the couple, the cop and the valise. His liquored mind, the relaxed mind, the dreamer's mind had fallen asleep. He had been caught in his own daydream, the dream of having everything he wanted.

ICE

April 8th and the kind of a day every Chicagoan loved. Benjamin walked into the pool hall just after noon and caught Tiny's hand wave before the door closed behind him. Without breaking stride, Benjamin went directly into Tiny's sacred chamber.

"Yeah Tiny, I saw you wave. Want something?"

"Need a favor Benjamin. Do a favor for me? Huh?" the big man asked.

"Sure Tiny. Any time you want a favor, you know."

"Sure. Just want to see if you was going to help me?" Tiny said.

"What? Where? How soon?"

"Good kid." Tiny pulled open a drawer of the small unkempt desk and pawed inside. "Get yourself some coffee Benjamin and for me too."

"Black, like always?'

"Like always." Tiny replied.

Benjamin stepped back into the pool hall, the clicking of balls on felt as audible as his heels on the ancient wooden floor. He walked straight to the coffee urn, grabbed two mugs, topped his with two sugars and cream and straight back to the office. Not even a nod to several players moving around the tables. He was in conference with Tiny today.

"OK, kid. Here's what I want you to do." Tiny took the steaming mug from Benjamin's shaking hand. "No need to be nervous kid, this is an errant."

"Just excited. You know, doing you a favor." Benjamin said.

"Yeah. I guess it's exciting. Anyway, you know Ralph's Pawnshop, State Street, just south of Van Burean?"

"Next to the stripper theater? I know it."

Benjamin took the I.C. suburban train to Van Burean, walked over to State Street and turned left. The pawn shop, almost even with Goldblatts Department Store, was next to the penny arcade, not the stripper theater. The woman behind the counter buzzed and a small man, neat as a movie matre de, came toward Benjamin.

"I'm Ralph. You asked for me?"

Benjamin had pictured a man like Tiny and flustered said, "Ralph sent me to pickup Tiny for him.'

"Tiny sent you?"

"Huh, huh. To pick-up a package."

"Stay here." The neat little man gave the woman a toss of his head and walked back to wherever he had come from.

"Relax kid. Sit in that chair there." she said and went back to adjusting watches in a display case. "I can watch you from here."

"OK. I can watch you too. We can both watch watches."

Benjamin couldn't hear everything the man said on the phone, but he wasn't happy. He heard the receiver click down and the door opened. Like Tiny did that morning, Benjamin got a come here hand wave. He stood and the woman bounced her head in the display case as she attempted to stand. The thud brought her a warning.

"Easy Toots, that display case is valuable." said Mr. Neat.

"Thanks a lot." she hollered back, hand vigorously massaging her scalp. "Damn."

The office was neat, desk clear, leather chair, file cabinets lined one wall, a safe, a small sink and a refrigerator were all crammed into the small room. Many unclaimed valuable objects, for now and maybe forever, hung from the ceiling and walls. There must have been a trophy for every sport crammed on the safe.

"Didn't know Tiny was sending a kid. So I checked you out. Bengy, huh?"

"Benjamin. Don't like Bengy."

"Tiny said you'd object to Bengy. OK, Benjamin. Doing a job for Tiny?"

"A favor." said Benjamin.

"A favor?" With his back to Benjamin, head cocked, the man slipped an icecube tray from the fridge. "I'm Ralph."

"Hi."

The tray slid on the polished desk top and stopped in front of Benjamin. A black cloth was dropped next to it. Benjamin looked at both, then to Ralph and into the tray.

"You're taking Tiny some ice. Diamonds. He didn't tell you?" said Ralph.

A sad faced clown looked at Ralph. "Uh, uh."

Flipped over, the tray spilled out a sparkling mound of shinny diamonds. They were all, nearly, the same size and color. Before Ralph could stop him, Benjamin poked his finger into the pile.

"Hey! Don't touch."

"Sorry, I didn't know not to touch. Really, I'm sorry, Mr. Ralph."

"Yeah, yeah. Ralph counted as his finger puhed, "...15, 16, 17. One's missing."

"I ain't got it." Benjamin said. He pushed back his chair and stood, holding out his hands.

"I know that. You couldn't steal something from under my eyes."

Ralph counted again, banged the tray and recounted, final number 18. Ralph swept the diamonds off the cloth into a thick red lined leather pouch.

"There's nearly half a million in stones in this bag." He

grabbed Benjamin's hand and smacked the bag into it. "See that Tiny gets it. He said on the phone nobody would think a dumb kid like you would run around with ice. Clever guy, Tiny."

Benjamin dropped the bag as though it had burned him. His voice failed him and his legs wouldn't hold his weight. "I can't carry them. No way." his sputtering voice finally said.

"You're doing Tiny a favor. Remember?"

"Cripes, Mr. Ralph. Half a million? A real big favor I'm doing. Someone could know I got this ice, these diamonds and kill me." said Benjamin.

"Yeap. Bye." Ralph was pushing Benjamin out the door. "Hurry on. Bye."

Benjamin's hand, wrapped around the bag , never left his pocket. He plopped into the corner seat of the first car on the train and sat so his cramped fist tried to dent the metal side of the car. He sweat and chewed away part of his inner cheek. Benjamin's mind urged the train forward, closing every door at every stop. The twenty one minute ride lasted for twenty one hours and a life time. Exiting the train, he ran down the station steps and continued running town 75th Street all the way to the pool hall.

Wide-eyed, dripping sweat and shaking he headed straight for Tiny's door. There wasn't a pair of eyes unaware of his entrance to the poolroom. Benjamin swore one or two started toward him. He squeezed juice from the door handle, bend the jamb as he forced the door open and broke the glass top on the desk as he banged the leather bag before the awe struck Tiny.

"You look like shit kid. What's wrong?" the big man asked. His hand immediately taking the bag out of Benjamin's hand. "You being chased or something? Huh?"

"Scared, I guess. Cripes Tiny, half a million. That's a big favor. Real big." Benjamin gasped each word. His control over his own body coming in short, deep breaths.

"Half a million? Half a million what?"

"Diamonds. Half million dollars in diamonds. I saw

them." Benjamin was still sucking air into his tortured lungs. "I saw Mr. Ralph put them in the bag. Diamonds."

Tiny poured the bag out. "Diamonds? No diamonds." A watch slipped out of the bag and Tiny wrapped it around his wrist. "My watch. Ralph fixed it for me, after it broke at a poker game. Diamonds. That son of a bitch. He fooled you Benjamin. He used to be a carney switch man." Tiny roared with laughter. "Go get some coffee. I'll call Ralph and tell him you didn't even sweat it. Teach him he can't fool my guys."

Benjamin went straight to the coffee urn. He saw no one and hoped no one saw him. At least he knew he hadn't wet his pants. Stupid trick.

EASTERN DIAMOND

Mopping along Clark Street, just south of Lincoln Park, Benjamin cursed the rain keeping careless shoppers indoors. It was after three and he hadn't eaten all day. He needed to steal something, anything, to get a few bucks and a meal. He had an aversion to work.

The mail truck slopped a curbside puddle toward Benjamin as it stopped in front of a jewelry shop. The driver entered the shop and Benjamin retaliated by throwing some of the muddy puddle onto the driver's seat. An opportunity blossomed before his eyes as the water cascaded over the seat and a shoebox sized package. Box and Benjamin departed.

Benjamin walked into Moocher's "private office", shaking the now soaked and tattered package, hoping for a clue to its contents. No sound from inside. An almost illegible label had "DAN" on one line and "Eastern Diamond" on the next. On the third line were the letters "re Ope" The address label was gone.

Moocher came in, the quintessential hoodlum of the 30's movies. He eyed Benjamin then the package.

"What cha got for me Benjamin? I could use a broad, but you ain't got one in such a little box?" He flashed a self approving smile. "Let's see. Dump it out. Here..." A fat hand cleared a space. "...on the desk."

Benjamin picked up a pair of desk shears, cut the string and flipped the box over. A pale cotton bag, nearly the size of the shoebox, tied with a string and tag rested on the desk.

"Well open the bag." said Moocher, without looking at the

tag.

As Benjamin cut, Moocher grabbed and poured the contents out, his greedy eyes envisioning the treasures of Sinbad.

A snake. A large brown and black checked snake coiled on Moocher's desk, its tail rattling against some loose papers. The snake and the rattling buzz caused Benjamin to empty his bowels on the spot.

Someone slammed the lid of the rolltop desk down, trapping the snake. Moocher picked up the tag that had fluttered to the floor. It was a copy of the original tag on the outside of the box.

DANGER

"Eastern Diamond Backed Rattlesnake"

CAGE BEFORE OPENING.

Moocher turned on Benjamin. "You stupid stinker. You coulda killed me. Some body throw "Shitty Pants outta here."

Benjamin's butt hurt from the kick he received and he was still very hungry.

LOCKSMITH

Benjamin stood at the counter watching the locksmith probing into a lock with a pick. While waiting to have his key duplicated he became fascinated by the man's ability to select a probe, poke about and open a lock. Day dreaming Benjamin imagined how easily he could break into a store or house with that skill.

"Seventy-five cents." the locksmith said to the man waiting beside Benjamin.

"Thank you." and the man left.

"OK, young man, what can I do for you?" the locksmith asked Benjamin.

Benjamin held out his key. "I need another key."

"Ummm. This is an old one. Might have a blank in the back?" The man's eyes scanned the blank key rack as he spoke. "Wanna leave the key or wait?'

"Wait. I'll wait while you check."

Wait. Benjamin waited about three seconds after the man stepped into the back area before he reached across the counter, to the cluttered desk and swiped three picks. He slide them under his hat, then stood and waited, an innocent customer. Once the keys were duplicated, Benjamin hastily left the store. Actually he grabbed the hat off his head, clutching the picks in it and ran out the store door and for a couple of blocks. Then he slowed to a walk and checked the picks.

Crouching down in the basement stairwell of his apartment building, Benjamin began teaching himself how to pick a lock. Twenty minutes and nothing but perspiration. The Yale remained unopened for ten more minutes. The locksmith made it look simple, easy. Subtle curses were slipping out between his clenched teeth, when he heard a distinct "tsssk". He had opened the lock. Hidden in the stairwell, out of sight, Benjamin locked the door and started picking again. It took less time to get it open the second time, less as he picked it several more times. Inside the basement he later picked a Sergeant lock. It took longer but he opened it. He stole nothing. Yet.

Benjamin took the streetcar to Western near Belmont and began walking through a neighborhood of apartment buildings. When he found a basement entrance out of view to nosey neighbors, he would pick at the lock for a few minutes. If he didn't get in quickly, he moved onto another building and another lock. He was chased away twice by nosey inquirers. The locks he opened were practice and he didn't take a thing all morning.

That afternoon Benjamin decided to try the front door of several buildings. The vestibule offered a haven from prying eyes. Opening a door he, reached over and rang the doorbell in the mail box of 2A. No answering buzz. Benjamin went up the four steps, put his head against the door and listened. Quiet. He quickly knelt down and began fiddling with his pick. He heard the tell-tail click. An unshaven, pot-bellied monster stood looking down on him. Benjamin bolted, leaving behind the pick he favored most stuck in the door. Panting and trembling he boarded a streetcar and headed back to the southeast side.

Benjamin had heard that the liquor store off Cottage Grove Avenue and 87th Street, kept Sunday's cash in a small locked area behind a mirror. After the 2:00 a.m. closing, the clerk put the register receipts and cash behind the mirror. He cased the place. Walking through, he saw the mirror through the doorway, and its proximity to the rear door. Around the back, in the alley, there were two rusted garbage barrels near the door, a barred window, a broken light above a door with two Yale locks. He even noticed the old burglar alarm and a disconnected wire. The alarm didn't work.

Three nights later, early morning to be exact, Benjamin moved one garbage barrel nearer the back door and slithered down behind its shadow. Feeling the pick sliding into the lock he started a gentle twisting. Within seconds the first lock clicked. What luck. The other lock proved more daunting. He switched back and forth with his two picks, wondering if he would... CLICK. He pushed the door open, slipped in and shut the door.

The clerk had forgotten to turn off the light in the storage area. Benjamin casually strolled to the mirror and took it down. "What the Hell. Not a Yale or Sergeant lock, an old Masters combination padlock grasping a hasp." He returned the picks to his pocket and pulled at the padlock.

He heard the toilet flush. The clerk was still there. Benjamin ran for the back door. He had closed and locked it. Trapped.

The following afternoon, after the bondsmen had Benjamin's signature and the police returned his personal belongings, sans the lock picks, Benjamin returned to the scene of the crime. Hoping perhaps things hadn't changed. No such luck. There were electricians working on the light and uniformed Brinks employees installing new locks and a new burglar alarm system in the building.

THE FINGER

Benjamin took the jacket off the back of the chair. It wasn't his. He walked quickly from the drug store, heading for a south bound State Street streetcar. It was chilly, so swiping the jacket pleased him. Examining the pockets, gave him nothing but a hole. Hell, he had the two quarters pilfered from the State and Lake newsstand. Why not take in movie? Angels With Dirty Faces was showing in a dinky theater on 63rd Street. Benjamin loved that Jimmy Cagney movie, that Rocky Sullivan, what a guy.

Sitting in the darkness, through a second showing, Benjamin mimed Cagney's character. He knew the lines and gestures as if he owned them. Benjamin heard and felt the not too gentle pangs of hunger. Fumbling in his pocket, he refound the hole in the jacket pocket. Continuing his search, he found nothing He had lost his last dime. Trying to see its reflection on the dimly lit floor produced nothing.

Outside, he found the weather had changed, tiny ice crystals stabbed at his skin. Hitching a ride on the back of a streetcar was out of the question, too slippery. Just off the corner was a small family grocery store. He thought of Cagney pointing the pack of gum he had in his coat pocket at the boys in their basement hideout. Once before he had tried robbing a small store with his finger in his pocket and was given an empty cigar box. He'd look in the box this time.

"Help you?' asked a soft voice at the counter.

Benjamin sized-up the situation in an instant. Just a tiny wisp of frail womanhood in the store. Putting his finger to his lips,

"Gimme the money box." Gesturing, with his other hand in his pocket and poking it menacingly at the woman.

"Paw! Paw!" She swung at Benjamin with a punchboard. Slapping at his bewildered face. "Paw! Thief!"

"Christ lady. Stop it. I'll shoot you!"

The pounding that old lady was giving was causing bodily harm. Pain, too. Why wasn't she begging, pleading for mercy? Looking down, Benjamin saw his forefinger protruding from the jacket pocket. The hole, that damn hole.

REMEMBERING

His head hurt, his body hurt even this eyeballs hurt. Benjamin was waking to his first hangover and feeling downright miserable. His misery increasing when his sodden brain refused to recognize his location and he was alone, no one to ask or help him. Looking out the window scrambled his eyes, the sun shinning in from a window next door, lit the room with searchlight brilliance.

The bathroom was empty except for a dingy gray nameless towel and washcloth. A hotel. He was in a hotel. Where? And how did he get there? Benjamin was fully dressed, albeit, like a discarded rag doll. Not a penny in his pocket, well there seldom was. His stomach gurgling, sent regurgitated slop to burn his throat coming up and going down. He adjusted his clothing before looking into the hallway. Empty. He stepped out of room 19, closing the door and heading for any exit.

The clock behind the empty check-in desk said 10:40. The sun was shinning, must be morning. The newspaper on the lobby table was the Milwaukee Journal. Sunday's Milwaukee Journal. Was it Sunday? How in the hell did he get to Milwaukee and how could he get back to Chicago? Benjamin had a problem which his mind didn't seem to want to solve.

There weren't many people walking about and public transportation didn't seem to be running. He headed toward a stoplight, he'd make a decision there. He began walking toward the sun, south and Chicago. Tired, confused and testy about his northern location, Benjamin attempted to review yesterday or the yesterday before. A brief glimmer flashed in his head. He had a cold, he couldn't talk. He stole some new cough syrup for his cold.

That was it. He couldn't talk his throat was so sore. This stuff would clear it up. It must have been bad, made him sick or something. It hadn't tasted too bad. He didn't remember drinking it all. Feeling sick, he had stowed away in a bus. Things were becoming clearer now.

He approached a stranger, held out his hand, but nothing came from his throat. The stuff hadn't worked. He still couldn't talk. It's a long walk, thumbing to Chicago.

GUMBALL

Benjamin walked through the Randolph Street Commuter Station, poking his finger into every telephone coin return slot. He had three nickels this morning. Upstairs, next to the library steps, he clicked a nickel on the newsstand, loud enough for the vendor to hear, smiling as he took a paper and a dime. Crossing the street, he headed into Pixley's where he sat with his coffee and doughnut skimming the newspaper. A visit to the men's room, allowed him to tuck a roll of toilet tissue under his arm. He returned to the train station and went about a coin collecting scheme.

Standing with the phone to his ear, talking to himself, he wadded the toilet paper and forced it up into the recesses of the coin return slot. There would be no refunds in the few phones he disabled this way, he'd collect later. He kicked the candy dispensing machine and heard a coin rattle into the tray. He extracted two bits, not a bad investment for a kick.

Benjamin smacked the glass globe holding colored gumballs in the "L" waiting room. His finger probed the little cup. Finding nothing, he looked about for someone he might complain to about the penny stealing machine. Seeing no one, he retrieved from his pocket a piece of a coat hanger. A very serviceable tool Benjamin had often used to persuade a coin machine to cough up its goodies. Seeing the coast was clear he slipped the hook onto his finger and poked it into the machine.

CLICK.

Trouble. Benjamin was in trouble. The elusive mechanism had shifted and the probing hook tripped the release, closing on

Benjamin's finger. The Monkey jar snare could not have caught him more securely. The little wire hook compounded the holding power of the trap, by bending the joint so he couldn't straighten his finger. He could twist the finger, possibly losing some skin, but he wasn't the least bit fond of the accompanying pain. He couldn't walk off with the machine since it was bolted to the floor.

It seemed like hours that the fireman and a gumball machine mechanic fumbled with Benjamin's finger. Amused passenger passing by laughed at his predicament. The moment Benjamin felt his finger coming out of the machine, he broke away and ran. He headed back to the Randolph Street train station. He ran right passed a telephone repairman coming up the steps carrying a hand full of wadded toilet paper. Later, after exiting the train, he stopped and picked up a small stick, to scrape a wad of gum from his shoe.

EASTER HAT

On a Spring Sunday in 1947, pleasant temperature, people moving about outside, kids dressed up, a smiling Benjamin exited the I.C. suburban train. He had successfully avoided the fare which he usually did. This Sunday brought him to the Loop. Perhaps some careless person would enrich his day. He'd make an effort and if unsuccessful, he would sneak into a movie.

Leaving the Randolph Street Station, he saw, in his opinion the funniest Easter hat ever created, much less worn. Lining up behind the woman, he traipsed behind her up the stairs. Many people turning for a look, actually gawking, at the hat perched on the dyed red hair. Benjamin saw a smirk or two. One man actually laughing, 'til the lady next to him gave him an elbow, damn near broke his rib. Benjamin continued smiling and following behind the hat.

The nearly twenty four inch wide white hat, had small pink balls attached to the brim, three or four long scarlet feathers along the side and an absolutely huge cluster of assorted flowers across the crown, each a different pastel shade. The front had a large brooch like pin, in the shape of a hand, holding the brim up. From the back of it trailed a yard of wide, multicolored ribbon, in shades of red. Benjamin was simply enjoying the faces moving toward him and passing him. They were as funny to look at, as the hat.

At the corner of Randolph and Wabash, the hat stopped for the traffic light. Benjamin stopped, other walkers stopped and crossing traffic nearly stopped. The only thing not stopped, a pigeon perched on the elevated train metal framework. It picked that moment to express its judgment of the hat. The glob descended with enough force to tilt the hat, splattering the luckless Benjamin. He saw what came flying toward him and started raising his hand in defense.

The hat appeared to turn the head under it, the face, seen by Benjamin for the first time, wreathed by the red hair, lit with fury, challenged him. Without warning, a hand reached out, smashing Benjamin's face, followed by another slap with the backhand.

"Don't you dare touch my hat!" she screamed, then turned and walked off.

Benjamin stood in shock. Reaching up, rubbing his throbbing cheek he watched the smiling faces walk passed the hat. It was so confusing. He turned back toward the train station and again boarded a train without paying. His pride was hurt, his cheek hurt and the conductor caught the stow away, booting him off at the first stop. It began to rain as Benjamin started walking home.

BON APPETIT

One of Chicago's new ambulances turned on its siren and pulled into traffic, taking the elder woman stricken while walking home. She had shopped for her meager weekend supplies and the heat had overcome her frail body. Someone had called the fire department and now she rode to the nearest hospital.

Benjamin announced, "I have a box. If you'll help me collect her groceries, I'll get them to her apartment." Actually he didn't even know the woman.

People quickly began to pick up the strewed items. Some told Benjamin they thought it was a nice thing he did for a neighbor. A few people placed coins in Benjamin's hand. "To replace the broken stuff."

"Thank you. You're very kind." He smiled and nodded his head.

Unbeknown to anyone, a cracked bottle of syrup found its way into the box. It slowly began to soak the cardboard container. Benjamin picked up the box and began his walk down the street. The glow on his face belied the truth. He had conned a group into a bold theft. All this stuff would soon be in his pantry.

Benjamin set the box on the stone banister, fished out his key and unlocked the door. As he wrapped his hands around his ill gotten treasure and lifted, the box collapsed in his arms. The goods spilled on to the concrete stoop. Benjamin yelped when some falling objects smashed his toes. Boxes broke open, glass shattered and dirtied Benjamin pants. Two boys grabbed a package of cookies and some canned goods and ran quickly down the nearby alley.

For his effort Benjamin found out that afternoon he had two broken toes, the pants were also cut, all glass containers had broken, the small boxes contained special diet preparations and the two cans he had managed to keep were mushrooms. Benjamin is allergic to mushrooms. Bon appetit Benjamin.

MASTER KEY

Wishing it were anyone but Benjamin, but there was no one else, Mrs. Paige pleaded with him to mind the baby for just an hour or two. It was an emergency. She pointed to the prepared bottle and diapers, in case, then flew down the steps to the hospital and her injuried husband. She didn't argue when Benjamin insisted on a dollar in advance.

The baby was sleeping in the buggy. Benjamin spotted the ring of keys on the hall table, and heard Opportunity knocking. Each key was labeled, office, supplies, storage. Keys opened doors and open doors had things behind them. He had blundered upon Pandora's box to open and loot. If he acted, now.

Bouncing the buggy down the steps, Benjamin headed for the hardware store. He spent the dollar and some of his own money, having each key duplicated. Getting the buggy back up the stairs wasn't easy. But once he did he sat back listened to the radio and dreamed. He even had a balony sandwich and some milk.

Stirring to wakefulness, the baby began whining as its mother entered the apartment. Giving the baby the keys from the table, she paid Benjamin another dollar and thanked him. Standing in the doorway, a sinister, clever ploy began dancing in his head.

"Mrs. Paige, those keys can get lost if the baby plays with them."

"Huh? Keys?"

"The keys from the table. Those keys the baby is chewing on."

Wanting Benjamin to leave, pursing her lips, she said. "Oh,

the baby plays with them all the time."

"Just the same. It's a bad thing if keys get lost. Right?"

"Not these keys. They're from where I work. We changed all the locks last month. Now the baby is teething on them."

The mother smiling and cooing at the little one slobbering on the keys didn't notice Benjamin wasn't smiling.

BARKING DOGS DON'T BITE

Luigi, a.k.a. Lug, detested Benjamin's presence. If Benjamin came into the room Lug flew off the handle and left or if Benjamin were already in the room Lug stayed out. Lug blamed Benjamin for the loss of his leg. OK, so both of them were once friends, close friends. So close they were breaking into a store through a sewer one night, and Benjamin let the cover drop on Lug's leg. Lug insisted that any fool could hold a manhole cover.

He never forgave Benjamin. On his death bed Lug swore that if he could come back, reincarnated, he'd come back as a dog and bite the bastard's leg off.

Benjamin learned about the threat, but pooh-poohed it as the kind of thing Lug would say, because he knew Benjamin didn't like dogs. Dogs often barked at Benjamin, often spooking him when he was prowling around looking for an open door or window. Any place that had a dog was safe from a burglary attempt from Benjamin. Besides when he snuck up on that dizzy, red-headed Irish kid, the kid's dog bit him. You know, once bitten... And, yeah. Ain't no such stuff as reincarnation, that's movie stuff.

Today, short cutting through Marshall Fields, Benjamin spotted a tall figure, in a natural full length mink coat, paying for cosmetics. He gave her the once over, twice.

Benjamin heard the clerk say, "Take care, Mrs. DePew. And I'll see that your order is sent at once. Two-three-one-four North Michigan Avenue, apartment 3."

"Not before 3 o'clock mind you. I'm going to the hairdresser's."

"Not before three. Yes mam."

Benjamin swiped a coin from the news stand and took the bus to the Lincoln Park area. He had no trouble finding the building or in slipping through a carelessly left open basement door. Smiling to himself, his furtive steps had him on the third floor in moments. Remembering caution, he knocked softly on the door of 3 A. No answer, so he knocked louder. Still no answer.

The hospital staff laughed as the policeman told of Benjamin's woes. He had been bitten by a Basenji, the barkless dog, when he broke in. Reincarnation? Hmmmmm.

VISITING CHURCH

A Chicago wind blew the cold dampness through Benjamin's meager jacket. Before the traffic light changed, the waiting pedestrians hunching their shoulders and bowing their heads began stepping off the freezing slush at the curb as one body, then fragmenting as they reached the opposite curb Benjamin shoved his body through the massive wooden doors of the Cathedral, attempting to blink icy tears, that were now creating mosaic colored panes, from his eyes.

Sitting on benches, the people listened to a preacher far in front of them. He spoke a language Benjamin didn't understand, bowing often as he spoke. It was warm, he understood that, and slid onto a bench to enjoy it. Chiming bells tinkled from the front and people began moving toward them, toward the preacher. Two ladies rose in front of Benjamin and moved into the aisle joining the group.

They left their purses on the bench. Unguarded purses caused his heart to flutter. A quick glance about him, he saw people moving toward the front and toward the back doors. No one was moving near the small doors along the side wall. A little red light went off above the door as a lady stepped into the church. He snatched the purses, shoving them beneath his jacket, while moving toward the small door. Stepping in, he shut the door behind him. In the dim light he saw there was no exit. People walking outside the door stopped. A weak sobbing reached his ears. A murmur, purses had been stolen. He'd wait, quietly, crouching back, allowing his racing heart to slow down.

The door opened, many strange faces were bobbing about, all staring at him. Among them stood a short, paunchy man in a long black dress, studying him. Next to him, a policeman rocking on his heels, a wide grin on his ruddy face.

"My son." said the man in the black dress. "You're in the confessional. Do you wish to make a confession?"

Benjamin's face wrinkled in confusion, his hands shook and, the purses dropped to the floor.

"Father, that is his confession." said the grinning officer

&FABLES & TALES&

FINDER, LOSER

Sitting behind a brush pile, a lone wolf, I was allowing my-self some time for introspection. My mind mulling over my con-tact with this herd of sheep and I was talking to myself.

This is getting ridiculous. Every time I get near this flock of sheep the damn dog detects me and runs me off. I guess I could take it better if her teeth weren't so sharp and she wasn't so damned mean. Being bigger helps too. Honey, you old bitch.

Here I sit, looking at some of the cutest lamb chops and this old wolf is dying of hunger. There she sits looking like a hill of dung. Ha. Ha. A joke. Well that's not going to feed me.

Let's see! If I just go... What's this? What's this? Right at my feet. A sheep skin. A full and complete sheep skin. Where the hell did this come from? I look around and there no one about. It's a ram's skin I thought. I know ram when I smell it. A big ram too.

I shook the skin out and spread it on the grass. Out loud I counted the legs. Four. The tail, one. The ears, two. Hell even the nose is attached. Who in God's name has gotten in here and copped a critter from my flock? Even skinned the sucker. I start-ed looking around little more slowly, a little more carefully, but I couldn't see a soul.

I'll just take this baby home and sleep on it tonight. And all the following nights too. No more cold cave floors for me. Com-fort and... and... and... What am I doing? Looky here. If I put this over my back and shoulders, I would look like a sheep. I could mingle in with the flock. I could go into the pen tonight, pick and choose whatever little ol' lambypie I want for din-din. O' boy! I've got it made now.

I draped the skin over my shoulders and wouldn't you know it here comes Honey now. Dizzy old bitch. Calm. Stay calm. She can't smell you, her sense of smell has been gone since she last had pups. I'll mix with the flock and lose her. My God! I'm doing it. She wants me in the flock. I'm in. Look at the smart ass bitch limping over to rub the old man's leg. While he's walking yet. For me there'll be a hot time in the old pen tonight.

You're in. Don't get excited now, just lay here in the corner, under the window and watch dinner walk about 'til it gets dark. Tonight I think I'll have lamb. Tender succulent, delicious lamb. I can taste it now. Who's coming? The shepherd? What's he hollering? Yeah. Yeah. He needs what? I can't hear him now that he's indoors. A bit of mutton for tonight. Why not, there's plenty. That's what I'll have tomorrow night.

The window above me is opening. Shit, he's groping me. No grabbing me. He'll drop me the moment he finds I'm a wolf. Drop me you jerk. Drop me! I'm a wolf damn it. A wolf. Too late. The shepherd, with the wool brushing his cheek, in one quick movement, pulled the "sheep's" head (my head) to the side and slits the "sheep's" throat (my throat).

The last thing my fading vision saw was the shepherd wrapping an arm around Honey's neck. The last words I heard were the shepherd saying, "Mutton tonight." I wonder if he'll know?

GODS' GIFT

Long ago, before time began, the gods of man discussed the feelings that man should live in harmony with the creatures the gods had put on Earth for his happiness. The gods wished to nurture man and gave him a share of their feelings, pride, happiness, strength, conceit, faith and self-importance. However with just these feelings man would be a god and this could not be.

The self-important gods met and bickered until all agreed, man would have the opposite feeling of each feeling he now knew. They almost over did their gift, for often man wished he never had these opposites. When man complained, the gods were furious and talk soon filled the heavens to destroy this undeserving and insignificant mortal, this toy. Fortunately they didn't or you wouldn't be reading this story.

When the gods gave man a mate, called woman, for she was drawn from the belly of man, they gave her feelings also. It was agreed, by the gods, that woman's feelings, while the same as man's, would often be more profound, sillier, unimportant or in some way different than man's. Poor man. Poor woman. What they each felt, they could not share, what they both felt was often shared and neither understood how this could be.

This gift the gods called, The Battle of the Sexes. The battle is not resolved yet, to the merriment of the gods.

Man's feeling run deep and somber, flamelessly burning his soul. He feels his strength, built on years of practice and natural abilities, can provide everything he and woman need to survive. He forgets his unquestioned gifts. Woman meanwhile, believes in his abilities, she does not question him, aloud, but prays he understands that she is there and will share and help when he beckons. Together they can achieve their goals. However; they are not alone, for wisdom, a godly attribute, often unknown to man or woman, gave other men and women the desire to help. This feeling, between choice and faith, allows hope to grow when shared.

The gods decreed long before the bones of time became dust, that each species give to the next a token of themselves. This would be an everlasting memory. The millennia have passed, and man continues giving the token, his offspring. We take pride in giving and seeing the gift accepted. The ability to accept warms all in the circle of family or friends. Unfathomed is the wisdom of the gods and we are wise not to question it.

MARY CONTRARY

Mary was quite contrary to everything anyone suggested to her. Except to the suggestions boys made to her. She didn't bother to take precautions when doing what girls are warned not do to with boys. In time, Mother Goose changed Mary's name to "The Little Old Lady That Lived in a Shoe."

FOOLISH

"Kittie Byrd, you listen to me. Keep that money where no one can see it or know you have it. You hear me child. Hidden."

Gramma Byrd worried about this child. Twenty years old and while a Byrd, behaving more like a caged bird in nearly everything she does. How Gramma Byrd dreaded sending this frivolous flake off to help her daughter-in-law, but she was needing help with her little ones since her sickness laid her low.

"Just don't you worry none. I"ll keep it here, pinned under my dress collar. It'll be safe and Sissy will be right pleased to get it too."

Turning and smooching Gramma on the hairy side of her cheek, Young Miss Byrd started up the aging steps of the Chicago bound bus.

"You all take care now, hear?" Gramma Byrd called out.

Stopping abruptly on the top step she came bouncing off the busty young woman boarding behind her.

"Sorry." said the newcomer, looking up into Kittie's wide eyes along with the entire apparition before her. Including a peek of green pinned beneath a blue collar. "You coming back down?"

"No, no. I just..." breaking off, waving to Gramma, then starting down the narrow bus aisle. The newcomer following her, looked about then sat next to Kittie, leaning back into the worn plush seats of yesteryear. Smashing a kiss against the gritty window pane, then mouthed, "I love you." to Gramma. Both were waving as the driver ground gears, commanding the road weary relic to move into the hot crowded street.

"We got three hours of travel time folks. There'll be food and a rest stop then. Sit back and let me take you folks along home with me." Chuckling at his humor, he placed himself and human cargo behind a Mayflower Moving van., adjusting to its speed.

"First trip?" asked the newcomer. "My names Rennie. What's yours?"

"My name is Kittie and this is my first trip myself. By myself." she corrected.

"Vacation? Going to school? Looking for work?" asked Rennie, pleasantly.

"None of those really. I"m to help Sissy, my auntie, in Chicago. She's sick and no one will keep her kids."

"Well you're nice to do that."

"That's the way a family should help. Do things and help with things and stuff. You know like clothes and things." said Kittie. She thought of money but didn't say it.

"Yeah. I know. Family helps family. It's the truth." said Rennie, looking toward Kittie. "You know it helps sometimes to bring more than just the clothes and things. Money is often needed but folks, even family, hate asking for it. You feel guilty like."

Kittie's hand came up, touching her collar and squeezed the small folds of green. "Yes, there is always the needed for money." The split seam of the coach seat held her head. "Money seems to mean too much to some folks."

"Not to me. I never have any, to speak of." responded Rennie. "Now if I need money, I usually gotta tell folks I'm poor 'cause my father left us and didn't help us none, or most of the time."

"True? Really?"

"Of course true. Hell, I got no money even to eat 'til Chicago. And that's nine, ten hours to go." Rennie's eyes fell on the little triangle of green peeking from beneath Kittie's collar. "Truth is I'll most likely sleep all the way there. Then I don't know

I'm hungry. I'll be sleeping next to a very nice, helpful person. You are nice."

"Oh God. You hungry now. I got..." said Kittie, standing and swaying to the rhythm of the bus, "I got some snacks right here in this bag. You help yourself. Here."

"Thanks. I really need this. You're wonderful. I said you were nice. Didn't I?"

"Go ahead and eat and when we stop I'll even buy your lunch." said Kittie, fingering her hidden treasure.

The two of them giggling and snacking began to share each others thoughts and dreams with the snacks. Rennie praising Kittie for helping Sissy and how she might be owning a shop for selling baby things or going to work at the hospital in the nursery. Or perhaps she would travel, doing things for poor people in distant lands. Both soon succumbing to the drone and swaying of the aged land rover and napped.

After their quick lunch, Kittie expressed a need for the powder room. Rennie said she would be waiting for her outside in the shade or be on the bus.

"All aboard folks." called their driver. "Chicago bound folks all aboard."

"Oh Lordy. I need to go and we ain't paid our check. Gosh Rennie, please tell him to wait. And here", unpinning her secret from under her collar, "I gotta go." Running toward an alcove marked "Dames" in block red letters, hollering, "Pay the bill."

Kittie, watching her bus pulling out for Chicago said, "No sir, I don't know her last name or where she comes from or really where she was going."

The police officer nodding, continued scribbling in his notebook.

"I met her on the bus and we talked. I shared my snacks with her and was going to buy her lunch. I did buy her lunch. Then I had to pee and asked her to pay the bill. I gave her", Kittie began crying again, "all the money." She rubbed her swollen red eyes for the umpteenth time, "Then I got on the bus. She wasn't there. The driver started off and I was screaming that Rennie was still back there. He stopped and let me off to look. The station master, that man there." her finger gesturing toward a balding fellow in a red jacket, "he told me a girl got a ride in a car going that way." Her gesturing finger sweeping an arc, now pointing homeward.

The officer nodded, "You gave her your money? All of your money?"

"Every dollar Gramma Byrd gave me."

"Maybe she should've pinned it someplace on you so no one could get it."

"She did."

WANT AD

Reg Foxx, called "Rusty," since nature had oxidized his mane, stood listening as clarion chimes were arousing Mr. Leontine, telling him, he had arrived.

The ad had read, "Bright, honest, willing to work, young man wanted. A future fortune can be made," A "future fortune," had piqued Rusty's curiosity. A fortune he wanted and the sooner the better.

"I'm interviewing applicants at my home today. May I make an appointment for you at 1:30? Please be punctual," said Rex Leontine, responding to Rusty's phone inquiry.

"It's a contemporary museum," Rusty remarked, crossing the rug with Mr. Leontine.

"Thank you. Please, sit in the red brocade chair. I like nice things and indulge myself with a few knickknacks now and then. If you're working for me you may be indulgent yourself." A Mona Lisa smile was hiding beneath the mustache and sparkling eyes.

Rusty's eyes continued to caress the office treasures. Win the lottery dreams careening the labyrinths in his head. "Maybe? Some day? What do I do for such wonders?" he asked Mr. Leontine, now reposing behind a large paper and mail cluttered desk.

Twenty minutes into the interview, of rosy prospects, glowing promises and plenty of Horatio Alger stories of past employees, Mr. Leontine dropped a bombshell.

"To start you off with all the materials and possible client list Rusty, I require a fee of $1,000 dollars. You'll make that back in a week or so. 'Ready for it?"

"Nope," said Rusty, with the confidence of a poker player holding four aces in five card stud. "You asked for a bright, honest young man. I'm bright enough to notice several unopened envelopes from your bank and utilities on your desk. Your phone is ringing, but unanswered. I've seen no employees. I'll invest in more than your pretty picture. I see future treasures here, for you, not for me. Thank you and Good Day."

COLD HEARTED

She stood patting his cheek while looking over his shoulder at me, flashing a smile which licked my soul, burning it with tongues of passion. I didn't even know passion. I felt the searing heat of a speared shis-ka-bob on the grill. Pain.

Without knowing, without realizing, the emotions of love and hate torched my heart, my mind, my being. I stood for a moment, her smile knocking me senseless. My being simmering, bubbling, volcano hot. Now cold, so cold my teeth chattering together in a Tommy gun staccato. Urges, which I didn't know either, tried wandering along unfamiliar parts of my body.

If I were asked to explain my thoughts, my actions, to save my soul I couldn't. Without compelled effort, my breath hissed through clenched teeth, muscles became rigid, fists of fingernails drew crescents of blood into my palms, tears began chasing each other down my cheeks. Alternately green and red explosions illuminating my wretched mind.

I had to separate her from him. I didn't know why. I just had to. Had to.

I couldn't see the eyes she now looked into, but I knew they were blind to what she was doing to me. I couldn't see if he smiled at her, exciting her, daring her to touch him more. I knew he didn't feel the warmth, the urges I felt.

The cold hearted son of a bitch. I'll kill him. So help me, I'll kill him.

I ran at him, attacking from behind. I jumped, grabbing him around the neck, ripping his hat from his head. Sliding around him and smashing at those black unseeing eyes. I knocked the smile from his face. Screaming, no longer smiling, she stood staring at him. He was no more, just the snow he had been made of.

THE TRUTH ABOUT GOLDILOCKS

Her golden locks froze to her face, the biting cold wind filled her eyes with tears and mucus froze on her upper lip. The lost child continued her desperate walk through the forest. Pushing through the drifting snow she unexpectedly stumbled into a tiny woodland cabin. The inhabitants were delighted to see her. They would have meat with their porridge today.

A FAVOR

Bradley Crane didn't like to be called Brad and didn't like to be called into Coulton Wolffe's office either. Many young execs had walked into his office and kept walking right out the back door. Coulton Wolffe was a hatchet man.

Knocking and entering the office with one motion, Bradley announced himself.

"Here I am Mr. Wolffe. How may I help you?"

"Yes. Here you are. Come in, come in. Sit here. I have a real problem and I thought you could help solve it with me. Not for the company. For me. Perhaps if you would assist me, we could solve it."

"Well Mr. Wolffe, that's why I'm here."

"Yes. I'll make it well worth your while. You know I can do that." said Wolffe.

"Certainly. What can I do for you?"

"You heard that office gossip about Ms. Shadley and me? It's true. I had her in here earlier and in my haste I..." Wolffe stood up, his fly was open with a piece of white shirttail with a red stain on it was sticking out. Blood?

"I zipped my pecker and shirt", Coulton said, " and.. and my pants together. I can't leave the office this way and I can't get out of here without help. Will you please help me? Please?"

Bradley almost laughed aloud, but choked it and a smile back down his throat. He felt a twinge of pity for the guy. There were rubber gloves in emergency kit in the private washroom of Coulton's office. Also plenty of gauze and a scalpel, ointment and handy wipes were there. Enough to work with Bradley thought, after checking everything.

With diligence and tender effort the shirt and pants were cut from the skin. The zipper was then removed from the pants and the bloody penis hung limp, but free, albeit, hanging as a sorry excuse for a male dominate symbol. The two conspirators left by the executive elevator into the garage, then out onto the streets in Coulton's light-blue Caddy. Neither man talked much during the hour drive to Coulton's Long Island home. Since his wife was in California, Coulton had let the house staff take a week off. No one was home. No one would know what happened.

A few months later, a new company position was announced. Bradley wanted that job. He approached Coulton Wolffe about it. When denied the job , he reminded Coulton of the delicate favor he had performed.

Coulton smiled and said, "Friend, who in the hell will believe a story like that? And, if they did, they might think you a ... You know. You wouldn't want that, would you? Also, Ms. Shadley has informed the front office that you have made advances toward her. You know it's against company policy to fraternize with staff. You're being released tomorrow so get your sorry ass out of my office. No one will ever believe your story."

As so many others before him, Bradley Crane found doing a favor may not have the expected reward.

IN YOUR OPINION

The audience was up and applauding, whistling and calling, Jack Corvus loved it. It was the same each year, the end of the local musical ending with him doing Cagney's "Yankee Doodle" dance down the White House stairway. True there were fewer steps, but he went up and down three times. The audience would take more; however, it was tiring.

That night, after the cast party at Reverend Cain's community meeting room, Jack popped a Gene Kelly dance routine into the VCR and lolled back, feeding his ego. He knew, just knew, he could dance as well as Kelly. He carried a tune with the ease of Little Red Riding Hood carrying her basket. Flatley, of River Dance, might learn from him too. He was persuading himself to chuck Kansas and go for it on Broadway. Hell, why think about it, pack up and high tail it out of nowhere. He'd give up a lot, his room, Mrs. K's meals, his job at Krogers, even "Yoda", his rusting, haul it all truck.

Two days later he was in New York walking along Broadway. He couldn't believe it. Corvus grinned at gawkers passing along, gawking himself. He found the neighborhood changing he'd been warned to stay on the main drag. Retracing his route, he asked a policeman where he might find shelter for a couple of days, 'til he showed Broadway his abilities.

Following the officer's directions and wondering why he had laughed as he gave them, Jack was soon in front of The Little Hideaway, transients welcome, pay in advance by the day or week. Not exactly what Jack had in mind, but for a few days, one week,

OK.

The next day, bright and early, the early bird gets the worm, grandpa used to say, Jack was rapping on the glass doors of the theater featuring River Dance. His knuckles hurt before somebody inside the building hollered. "What you want? Why are you fooling with this knocking. Go away."

"I want to show someone how well I dance and sing, an audition" Jack hollered back.

"That ain't how you do it. Ain't no body here 'til 2 this afternoon, come back then." Turning and shuffling off, he hollered, "Come back then."

Jack returned just before 2:00, the doors were still locked but someone was standing in the inner foyer. Tap, tap, tap, the coin beckoning the person inside; however, it didn't move him. He saw movement in the box office and proceeded there, where he again rapped with the coin.

"We're not open 'til 4 o'clock." came from the barred empty cubical.

"But I need to see someone, to talk to someone, to show someone my dancing."

A head looking over the shiny brass ticket slots said, "No one here does that. Go get an agent." and vanished ala a magician's bunny.

In the store's phone directory, under theatrical agents, Jack found a name on Broadway. Following the building numbers and their directories, he finally blundered into, on the eleventh floor of some place, a door with an aging golden scrawl, Bob Olor, Theatrical Agent. Knocking softly and opening the door he entered a small office.

"Yes. May I help you?" the dyed red-headed toothpick thin girl at the desk queried.

"The man at the theater said I needed an agent. So I came..."

"You got an appointment? Or a letter from someone?"

she sang. Finally looking up from the magazine in her lap.

"Do I need one, I'm right here now." Jack didn't wish to, but sounded exasperated.

"Oh. Mr. Olor never sees any one without an appointment. Never. Not ever."

"Do you know who might see me without an appointment?" he asked with controlled restrain.

"My gosh. I would never sent someone to another agent. I'd be betraying Mr. Olor."

Her look said, "Get lost fella."

The following afternoon Jack was back at the theater. He saw several people heading around the building and thinking they may help him, he hustled after them. The door was closing, his holler caused a balding head to peek out.

"You're not part of the group. Take off." The door closed.

Jack had no better luck the next three days. People weren't willing to help him. He ate but one meal a day, slept poorly, and had begun to look a little seedy. The rent was due this morning, but he didn't have another week's rent.

"Too bad." the landlord said. "The sign says, In advance. And no, you can't go up and get your stuff. You're overdue. Get out."

Now what? No money. No food. No place to live. No work. What's a guy to do? I had everything at home and pissed it away. There's nothing here. I've failed. He thought all these things to himself as he filled out a job application at a grocery store.

Like the pages of the Book of Life for so many people's lives, Jack Corvus' life, has no ending. His life book starts, goes along and never ends. Never ends.

THERE'S HOPE

The radio went off after announcing today's weather and no winners in last night's lottery. Foxy flipped over in her blue silken cocoon cursing her bad luck. Not a winner again just another day toiling for Mr. Feeney in his hot close quarters greenhouse. Barnyards were at least outside, his smelly garden of hot house blooms never allowed her a gasp of clean air.

Foxy slid past a waiting customer, dropping the correct change and breakfast check onto the candy and gum cluttered counter. "See you George. It's the correct amount. Bye." half turned she didn't see the bundled body pushing into the store. The glass door, her face imprinting onto it, the Thank you covering her cheek, stopping her desired exit.

Indignation left as she realized blind Mr. Sus was the entering body. Both began apologizing immediately. "No, no. Mr. Sus, it's me, Foxy. Sorry, I was hurrying and didn't see you coming in. Are you OK?" His response confirmed for Foxy that he wasn't suffering any damage to his aging person or belongings.

"Mr. Sus, why are you here? It's twelve below zero. You're going to catch your death for sure." Foxy scolded.

"Well the lottery is rolling over and I want a winning ticket. I need my walk for the day. I can handle this weather, have for 72 years." There was pride in the soft but assertive voice. "George, if no one's in line can I have a two dollar ticket, please."

Admonishing the neighborhood icon, Foxy said, "Well you could wait for better weather before you come out."

"At my age you wait for damn little. If you do, you miss

out on lots of things Foxy," said Mr. Sus. "Besides, I don't bother a soul doing things my way, do I now?" he said, poking the expected treasure ticket into his mitten while shuffling toward the door.

"Thanks George. Keep in mind Foxy, I'm ready to win, if the good Lord wants me to. Ready to leave if He's calling too."

Stepping into the outdoor icebox, crunching the salt shards under foot, pulling down into the fleece lining, he turned for home. After all he thought, there's always hope and the quiz show was on TV.

CHICKEN

The short Old Capricorn bridge had long ago ceased to carry traffic. Very narrow, it had become a one car crossing a real bottleneck, holding up traffic rather than moving it.

The town petitioned the county and a new bridge was built, the old one never came down. The temporary road connection remained too.

Once in awhile some pranksters would detour the unsuspecting onto it. They would sit on the rocks next to a billboard advertising, Grants Union Store, everything half price, waiting to see their poor victim's behavior, gave some jokesters a big laugh. Many nights, some stud's hormones would assist him in pulling the barrier aside then drive over for the seclusion and backseat romance the darkened overgrowth provided.

One early May evening Billy Kidder talked Cindy Ewell into such a liaison. It wasn't difficult since they had tangoed there before. The only foreseeable problem being Ron Roach. Ron usually took his dates there on Thursdays and today was Thursday.

Billy figured they might share the solitude; however, he didn't mention it to Ron, because he didn't see him that day.

Both cars arrived at the bridge at 9:45 that evening and both young men, neither having established his dominance postured and bluffed themselves into the impossible manhood dilemma, the challenge. A chicken run. The girls would stand at the bridge to signal the start. The drivers would race their cars down Hill Street passing the Main Street curve and straight to the bridge. Winner crosses, loser is aced out for a year.

The entire town attended the funeral, only double funeral ever held. Obstinate fools wouldn't give way. Their fiery explosion had lit the night sky. Now the twisted, burnt remains, are eternally welded to the iron of Capricorn bridge, blocking forever passion's portal for any and all would be lovers.

LAMB EATS WULF

"I've asked you here for only one reason and you know that." Desmond Wulf sat behind his desk pointing to a chair for his guest. "So why are you resisting me?"

"I want to know why you are doing this to me. Why are you trying to take my business away from me?" Now seated, Mr. Lambkin's face and voice expressed anger, his hands trying to squeeze the sap from the oaken arms of the chair. After all this was his life. Mr. Wulf was trying to steal his life.

"I want to buy your business. Nothing more than that. I have no desire to hurt you. Just sell me your business. I am offering a very good price."

"But I'd never thought of selling. I'm happy with what I have."

Desmond Wulf rolled his green eyes up into his head, stuck out his hands, ala Al Jolson and precisely enunciating, word by word, said to the little man in the big office chair. "I have a need for your company. Now do you understand why?"

Lambkin's slight frame shook as he looked across the large desk to Mr. Wulf, who had risen as he began speaking. "You have the largest electrical connector production company in the country. I'm small potatoes next to you, yet you're gobbling me up. I see no reason for this."

"Yes, small potatoes, but there are other small potatoes too. I need materials to finish my orders. I can't be waiting for small potatoes to drag them in." A sneer crossed Wulf's face and a bit of spittle shone in the corner of his mouth.

"I can meet your demands," said Lambkin. "Just give me time and an amount for an order in advance."

"That's the problem with you. You think I have advance time to meet my world wide obligations. I have no such luxury."

"With computer, e-mail or fax you don't have enough time?" asked the bewildered Lambkin.

"Right."

"How about a week's notice? One week? Guaranteed delivery." There was hope in the sound of his voice Lambkin thought. Wulf can't be that big of schmuck.

"Can't wait even a week. Too long."

"Isn't there any way to prevent this. This is everything I've worked for." Tears began to form in the baggy folds under Lambkin's eyes. A prayer seemed to form on his lips. "Everything, everything. You do know that there is a debt on the place don't you?"

"Yes and that will be paid by you, in the selling price." Wulf replied. "Remember part of that debt was co-authorized by me. Now sign these papers and go clear out your piddlely cracker box office." He pulled an envelope from the tray on the desk and poured the paper contents before Lambkin. "Sign now."

Lambkin scrawled his name across the bottom of the familiar forms before him. A teardrop punctuating the end of his signature. Slouching down, pressing back into the cushy office chair, a small sigh issued from his mouth. The bowed head was unable to even glare at the man that had just hustled him out of business, his business.

"Thank you and good bye Mr. Lambkin. As you now can see I get what I want. This time it took a little longer. But, you're out. Close the door after you."

Lambkin sat at his desk dialing a familiar number. "Pack your bags Lambykins. Wulf bought us out at our price. He'll never know you were the ordering company. He skinned us in the past, but we got him back. The headline will read, Lambkin Eats Wulf."

THERE'S A REASON

Lars had given serious thought to purchasing the black Labrador pup. The price, well beyond his meager means, would require most of his squirreled away money. He would fulfill a dream by buying a dog. Since boyhood he wanted a dog, like the one he saw in a commercial. The shinning black lab took his breath away. He would run to the television set the moment he heard the commercial music. As a kid he pestered his mom for a dog on birthdays and Christmas. Her words comforted him, a little, but always came out as, "Honey, we can't afford a dog." Or, "Our place is too small for a big dog.

Isaac Pleese sent him word that his prize bitch had whelped seven healthy pups. Five were promised and he thought he'd keep one. The last one, a runt, Lars could have for a reduced price. Isaac wanted Lars to have the pup. But a business man like Isaac needed money and couldn't afford word get out that he had given Lars the pup.

They sealed the deal on the phone. Lars stopped often at the house to hold and admire his dog. He named the little female Flow, an obvious name, for she urinated on everything, including him when he held her. Isaac offered to keep her for training and to instill a few good doggy habits. Lars would hear nothing of the kind. He would train her, his way and relish the pleasures and disappointments that training involved. He took her home the day Isaac said she was weaned.

Lars spent hours pouring over training books. He took Flow out and taught her to heel, fetch, come, sit. Well you know, the things a dog should know. No sleeping on the bed. It didn't last the first night. Bark to go out, that took months. Chewing objects, well that came after a few non-violent rebukes and the lose of a handmade pair of moccasins which became shredded garbage.

Flow came into the world in February and to Lars in May. He wanted to use her for the coming duck shooting season. An early Saturday morning in September Lars took the soft decoy, purchased for training Flow and placed it in her mouth. She spit it out at once, he replaced it and held her mouth softly shut. "Stay." The moment he released her the decoy fell to the floor. By noon she held, fetched and dropped the decoy into Lars' hand on command. Lars was very pleased with the dog's quickness to learn and obey his commands. All afternoon he guided the dog through the lessons.

Sunday morning he again went through Flow's lessons. Then he took her to the lake. Here she could go through the fetching under near actual conditions. He would have to teach her to hold unfrightened when he fired the shotgun over her head. That would come next week.

Lars heaved the decoy in a high arc and watched it settle in the water. Flow sat at his feet and watched, tongue out, eyes following the "flying duck".

"Fetch."

Flow bounded to the water's edge. There she stopped, turned and looked at Lars.

"Fetch, Flow. Fetch." Lars pointed toward the decoy.

Flow walked forward. Lars blinked in disbelief. He rubbed his face and eyes. His voice sputtered. He looked about for other people. He wanted someone to verify what he saw. Flow actually walking on the surface of the water. That's right. The dog walked on the water. When she reached the decoy, she picked it up, returned and sat before the bewildered Lars.

Lars threw the decoy into the water several times. Each

time Flow walked out on the water and retrieved the decoy. Astonished Lars flipped his cell phone open and called Isaac. Without telling Isaac why he must come to the lake, Lars got Isaac to say he'd be right there. Lars could hardly control his nerves, the excitement had him walking back and forth, the dog faithfully at his heels.

Isaac watched Flow's retrieve. Lars wanted to know why. And more.

"Easy." Isaac said. "Ain't seen it before. Never. But that damn dog don't know how to swim."

LUNCH ON THE HOUSE

My wife saw the place from a curve in the road. "If that's an eating place let's stop." she said.

"No problem. If, I can locate the entrance."

It appeared quaint from the outside. Yes, quaint. We were given a table with a beautiful view of a creek, bridge and small goldfish pond. A light salad and sandwich were ordered and taking the waiter's suggestion, homemade soup. The rising voices of a group of men in the bar area wafted into the dining area. Loud, but not violent. We could not help but listen to them. I turned to look and saw a heavier man poking his thick finger into a natty sweater of dull green worn by a thin, freckle faced redhead.

"I damn well can bet a few dollars." the heavier man insisted.

"I'll whip your ass in a cross-country race."

"Old man, you are full of crap." came back a quick, laughing reply.

"Don't laugh at me, pip-squeak" said the heavier fellow.

"I'm not laughing at you. I'm laughing at the situation you're getting into."

"Look I said I could do it and I can."

"Ah ha. I am in complete accord with you." freckles dancing on the wrinkles of the face. "We, the two of us, start, in the morning, racing to Milshire and back. From where? Outside, by the ... No, from the bottom of the stairs. There at the pond."

"Stop listening to them. Turn around and eat your lunch." my wife said, diverting my attention back to her and the meal.

"Can't help it, it's one of those times I can hear everything."

"I don't care. It's just a local argument." she hissed.

"Not really. Not an argument. You can hear it. It's a dumb bet. Look at the older guy. Overweight and old. Maybe sixty-five, seventy?"

"Makes no difference to you or to me. Come on, eat."

"Come on honey, what do you think? Who would win?"

"The kid. He looks fit enough" she retorted, biting into her sandwich.

The voices grew louder. They seemed to be changing the time of this great race.

"When?" "Right now?"

"Why now, of course." the older fellow responded.

"Right this minute?"

"Here and now." the old man said.

Several patrons of the bar area pressed in on the pair. There was a rife between them, each bettor offering to back their favorite with hard cash. I would guess that all the spectators lived near by and knew both challengers.

Someone voiced this opinion. "We need an unbiased judge. Someone, other than 'Old Vulpes' here. He's betting on Chelonia." Old Vulpes, I soon learned, was Fred, our waiter, the only waiter and perhaps the owner. He came toward our table.

"Excuse me. I can assure you this little race we're planning will be over long beforeyou finish your meal. And... And I will present you with no bill, if you would start our race and judge who crosses the finish line first."

I looked to the wife. My look, asking her opinion. Affirmative.

"OK with me" I said, looking to Fred, adding, "The soup is delicious."

"Thank you. You will do it then?" Fred asked.

"Yes."

"We gotta judge guys. Let's run us a race" Fred shouted. "Lettum run."

I started them off with a wave of my handkerchief. Every bettor cheering them.

Across the lawn they went. The old man seemed to be a failure from the first step. The young man had already crossed over the small hill and curve from where Rita had seen the inn. The bettors and I returned to the bar and dinning area, to finish lunch and wait for "The Great Race" to end.

"How far is it to Milshire?" I asked Fred.

"About eight kilometers, give or take." our host replied.

"With a couple a hills." added the lone female in the subdued gathering.

"Yeah!" said Fred satirically, "But Chelonia s' been doing those hills twice a day since before I was born." He gave half a generic laugh. "I was finishing the second half of my sandwich and caught a move outside near the goldfish pond. I didn't jump or holler. It was Chelonia."

He was returning. Already? I looked at my watch, 43 minutes. He was there and back in 43 minutes? My God. He must be in great shape. But why is he coming from the backside of the goldfish pond?

I now saw the young fella coming down the hill from the place I had seen him disappear. Chelonia was to beat him sure. By a minute or two. I was amazed.

"I'm back!" Chelonia hollered as he placed his foot on the bottom stone pond step.

He looked as I had seen a survivor look in some dramatic movie. Would he now be dropping dead, just as the Marathon warrior did? The rash one, Bunny, as his supports called him, came in gasping for air.

"You cheated! Damn it Chelonia, you cheated me. You cheated."

"No I didn't Bunny. No one would cheat you. You know

that."

"You never passed me. You didn't, you admit it now, or else."

"Or else? Bunny I didn't cheat you. I took a short cut. You went round the Benet farm, I went under the culvert at creek's end. You went round Mailer's hill over near Cooper's garage. Right? I crossed behind his barn and through the old gas station area.

"That's cheating. That is cheating." He puffed out each letter. "C H E A T I NG."

The apparent winner turned to me. "Did anyone tell you the course we had to run?"

"No," I admitted. "I expected you knew the course and would run accordingly."

Chelonia smiled and turned half back to the group, "See, no course set. Here is the Milshire Weekly Minute, which I didn't have before we left. You know Mr. Hunt only puts it out on Fridays, at noon. I grabbed it when I passed his place. It proves I was in Milshire today. At noon today."

I looked at the paper he held out to me. "He's got today's dated paper."

"Does he win?" asked Fred.

"Yeah. Does he win?" asked Bunny's supporters?

"Let me think about this for a moment," I replied.

Rita was coming down the steps. "Thank you for lunch. Wonderful. I'll tell friends about it." She stepped past me, winked and got into the car. She was going to drive. I too stepped into the car, saying as I did, "Chelonia wins. The old man out foxed you all."

PARKING SPACE

Double parked, Mike sat watching some poor son of a bitch screaming curses at a tow truck driver. Every time he came near the driver, he waved him away with a tire iron and he didn't need a weapon. This gorilla would destroy the illegal parker if he closed in. As the truck began pulling the car from under the no parking sign, the beleaguered driver ran after it then stopped and returned to copy information from the no parking sign.

Tooting his horn, Mike tried to get the writer out of the empty parking spot. Finally parked, he stepped from the Audi convertible, the writer came over, warning Mike and pointing to the sign.

"They just got my car."

"Yeah, I know. I watched him tow your car away. Parking's a bitch in this area."

"Don't you care if they tow your car?"

"Sure I care. That's my baby. But he just took you out. I got time to have a drink, pick up a broad and get out of here before he gets back."

Mike walked passed him laughing out loud. The man stared at Mike in disbelief and continued to stare at the parked car, the no parking sign and Mike's back walking down the street.. He stood simmering in anger and resentment, then flipped out his cell phone. In minutes he stepped up onto the curb grinning, as a tow truck backed in and attached a hook to the illegally parked car.

The tow truck driver rolled down the window as the man, cell phone in hand, walked toward the truck.

"You the guy that called our office?"

"I am."

"The reward for reporting illegal parking ain't much. But thanks. Thanks a lot."

He looked at the twenty. "Let's just say, 'Parking a bitch around here."

"For some it is." said the driver, pulling the Audi from under the no parking sign.

HEAR ABOUT SNOW WHITE

The seven miners stepped aside as one, allowing the young man to come forward and view the recently deceased Snow White. All seven men, their faces puffy from crying, watched the strange conduct of this new fellow. Well dressed and handsome, he respectfully bent over the casket and kissed Snow White. To the astonishment of everyone, she awoke

Several of the miners subdued the young man, while some of the others held Snow White down and drove a wooden stake through her heart. They'd have no living dead wandering about their area.

WANT A DRINK?

"Want a drink?" I asked in the softest voice possible.

Saying nothing, while keeping her eyes on me, her body language said yes. Angling around her I poured. She's being difficult. Again.

"Enough?" I asked.

She had emptied the container. This wasn't like her, turning her eyes up, waiting, giving no response.

"More?" I didn't wait for an answer, but began pouring, her willing servant.

As she turned her head to drink I began to nuzzle her neck, stroking her long hair. Expecting something for my efforts I continued sitting, stroking and waiting.

She dropped her head into my lap her tail drumming the kitchen floor and barked.

MOUSEY

The screams were pitiful in their urgency. My death is near they said. "Help! Help me! Please!" The pained screams filling the abandoned factory vaulting against the walls and bouncing through the glassless windows. Hearing them was one thing for the people on the streets but they wanted to know where they came from and who was screaming?

Officer Leo, the new beat cop, never asking where or who, he just ran toward the screams of despair. A quick run found him turning left, then continuing to the left, passed the factory, stopping and returning to the factory dock door. It was open a bit and shouldn't have been. An excruciating scream rent the air. Into the darkness and dirt of the building he went. His flashlight beam imitating the screams by bouncing off everything it touched. He stopped again to listen. Silence. Was he wrong in coming this way? More screams assured him he was in the right place. They came from directly below him.

A hole in the floor, which must have been the service elevator floor with a miriad of wires hanging into it, caught Leo's attention. The sounds were coming from there. The wires were moving. Careful he thought. Officer Leo approached the hole and knelt, allowing his flashlight to probe the darkness below.

A small boy about eight years old, lay entangled in oily multicolored wires. He was not moving, for all movement bound him tighter in the web into which he had fallen. A weak, sincere smile, haloed in the light, flashing up to Leo. By laying on the dirty floor and reaching down, Leo was able to pull the frightened dirty scamp up from this dragon's lair.

Unhurt, but really frightened, Mousy, Del Moskowicz was his family name, thanked officer Leo and wondered how he could escape any outside attention. Some of the curious people were beginning to gather outside the factory already.

"You OK?" asked Officer Leo.

"Oh, yeah. Look I can stand and walk. Maybe even run." He took off for the open dock area before Leo realized he was moving. Stopping, Mousy spun a 180 and hollered back. "Thanks. Maybe I can help you when you're in trouble. He 180ed again and was gone. Poof.

That evening Mousy hear shooting. The first shots had everyone in the street scattering and everyone in nearby flats ducking below the window ledge but dearly wishing and often trying to see the shooting outside their refuge. Who was getting killed now? Neighbors, sprawled on their apartment floor, prayed it wasn't their children while the godless thought of themselves. Was this the usual shooting from the flats, where a drunken live in boy friend or pissed off husband hit his wife or she banged his head with a pot?

Officer Leo was on the evening beat and just outside the apartment building when the shooting began. It was in Mousy's building. Hell it was Mousy's sister's boyfriend doing the shooting. Mousy ducked under the tumble of bed clothing and thrust his hand out to create a tunnel to view the other room. Sirens were wailing outside.

It was the boyfriend, The silly son of a bitch had his half-sister, Louise, in a neckhold and was facing him.. The loud knocking on the door, forced him around, turning his back to Mousy, "It's the police. Open up in there!" accompanied the pounding.

"Get away from the door cop. I"ll kill her."

Leo didn't know there was a hostage. Drawing back the beloved size14 clodhopper he sent the door into exploding shards. Seeing the hostage and ducking in time he was missed by the shot from the boyfriend. Mousy, quickly tossed the bedding off his small frame and screamed. The gunman turned, pointing the gun toward him. Leo began firing. That quick it was over. One shooter with a broken hand, three unhurt innocent people.

Looking at Mousy, Officer Leo asked, "Don't I know you? Have I seen you before?"

"Yeap." said Mousy. "I won't say where, but let's say you helped me out of a tough spot and I was able to help you out of a tough spot."

Both were smiling at the thought they were sharing.

SOUR GRAPES

A beautiful young blond, green eyed, 36-26-34 with a distinctive wiggle in her walk, sashayed along the sidewalk near the new office building construction. The construction workers were at lunch. She could see, as she had from the office where she and watched them for days, they were all hunks.

She didn't look at them but knew their eyes were glued to her bod. She put a bit more sway into her walk. She paused to adjust the neckline of her peek a boo blouse and stopped once more to look at the bottom of the three inch spikes, which pushed her to 5 foot 6. Continuing her walk, a little slower, she traversed the entire block. Not a whistle not a catcall. Nothing. She wanted to look back but didn't dare. Were they all dead?

Stepping into the doorway of the small sidewalk cafe, she glanced back. Those hunks were there. Some were still looking her way. Had she missed something? Was something wrong? She glanced in the window at her appliquéd reflection, just her. A very pretty woman. Not a thing out of place that she could see.

Leaving the cafe with a tiny white bag of soup de jour, to go. She retraced her steps of six or seven minutes ago. This time she looked and made sure those hunks were looking too. They were. The rhymic sway of the cobra to the fakir's flute with just enough feminine mystique to draw their collective breathes and get a few hearts a flutter she thought. Not a peep, a "Hey babe.", or a wolf whistle from the gallery or box seats.

She entered her office building thinking, I know they're not dead. So if they can't show some spirit, some manliness, to hell with them. They must all be priests or married. Or...or...or...not interested in women?

BUFFET

Rather a large crowd of people I thought, as I entered the room. I recognized a few sports figures and public office personalities; however, I didn't know them and just nodded in their direction when they looked toward me. My invitation was just a come on for a donation, that was a given, besides I wished to see what these gatherings were like.

The buffet was under the organization's symbol toward the back of the large hall. Many guests already had small plates of various fruits, little finger sandwiches and things I didn't recognize. I stepped into line and started along with the others.

"Would you care for the tongs?" asked the gentleman in front of me.

"Thank you." I said. Upon looking at the offering, I put the silver tongs down and passed it up. Along the line I moved. No, not that or that. This didn't appeal to me either. Many people seemed to be stopping ahead of me at one section of the table. Perhaps it was something special, maybe the items I hadn't recognized earlier.

Ahhh. No. Not caviar. One of my unfavorite foods, pass by. I looked down at the next table, almost bending under a most exotic and colorful display of pastries. Being diabetic, I would pass this table too.

I came to the end of the line to see the hostesses taking money from each guest. The donation. The only thing to do, grab the next item and donate for it. I looked at the meal I had just paid twenty dollars for. A package of saltines. Wow!

RESCUED

Trazee didn't hesitate for a moment. She dove into the swirling river water, ignoring the initial icy shock and with powerful strokes headed directly to the splashing flounderer. Grabbing hold she turned, but the struggling victim broke loose from her grip. The current pummeled them and they separated. Trazee, doggedly following, grabbed hold again. Her steady, strong paddling brought both to shore. She sat, waiting, with a pat on the head she released the duck.

FLIGHT

Tommy Hawke didn't understand how it happened, but one day he could converse with his dog, Duffer. He scolded the dog and the dog scolded back. Tommy was dumbfounded. It went further, he understood the bird at his feeder, the one near the porch swing, asking him to fill the feeder. "Thank you." in bird talk was high pitched, yet easy to comprehend. Tommy soon found he could talk intelligently to many animals. Amazing as this was he never considered telling another human of this ability. Never.

One fine Spring day he met an eagle, migrating north to Alaska. Something the eagle said revealed it to be a shaman, capable of ancient magic spells, such as becoming an eagle. Tommy, now a young man, had desired to fly since early childhood. He wanted to fly high above the earth, to swoop down and skim the edges of the trees and fields then soar upward punching through billowing clouds. He told the eagle, who, in an offhanded matter of fact manner indicated it wasn't that easy.

"Sometimes it's scary. You might not be so enthusiastic particularly on a windy day. Or when a flock of geese in formation doesn't get out of your flight path."

His negative comments were a gauntlet across Tommy's face. More than ever he wanted to fly. He cajoled, begged and whined for the opportunity, he even offered a rich reward for one flight.

"If I cannot be an eagle, would you carry me up and drop me? Let me soar, dive into the wind, glide over fields, just once.

Please?" he begged.

"You are not prepared, that is, made to fly. You have no wings, no knowledge of wind currents, or how to stop your flight when landing." said the eagle. "However, if you insist and will not blame me if..."

"I insist! I insist!"

The eagle took Tommy high above the clouds and released him. He didn't fly.

Tommy examined the feathers on his wings as his Guardian Angel came toward him. He's getting his first flying lesson today.

HOW IT STARTED

I lay there, under a bush, listening to the warning wondering all the time why warn them? They had everything. I mean everything.

But I heard Him say, "Do not eat of every tree in the garden." Asking myself, who else, "Why not eat of every tree? Was there something special about one tree?" I suspected Number One was hiding something from them. No, from me. What?

To find out I would eat from every tree in the garden.

Now I'm not a vegetarian and eating fruit is unappealing to say the least. But I tried, climbing tree after tree, eating fruit 'til my belly ached. Finally, in a tree He called an apple tree, I gagged. My stomach revolted. I hollered out, "Hey, Eve! Want a bite?"

PERFECT FOOL

Cyril Laurence, looked at the face in the mirror and saw the small wrinkles in the outer corners of his eyes. He pulled at them with his finger. He leaned closer to his reflection and searched for other signs of the human curse, growing old. The skin looked a tad loose. He didn't wish to grow old, alone, without children. He was a brilliant, handsome and wealthy man. He must find the perfect woman to give him beautiful children. They would inherit everything he had.

Mr. Laurence hired a marriage broker. Of course the best, Dolly Levi. His faith in Dolly Levi bore fruit in days. In the next county, just outside New York City, lived August Fromm, a farmer with three marriageable daughters. They were educated, said to be "rivals of Helen of Troy" and still waiting for their true love. Dolly visited the Fromm farm and talked to August and his daughters. Her glowing report fascinated Mr. Laurence.

With Mrs. Levi as chaperon, Rose Fromm accompanied Cyril Laurence to New York City for dinner, to talk and become acquainted. Upon their return on the 10:41 night train, Cyril had made a decision. Though late, he and Mr. Fomm walked the gravel path between the dairy barn and the spring house. They stopped for a draft of the cool milk at the spring house and talked about Miss Rose. Mr. Laurence allowed that Rose was absolutely gorgeous and intelligent, knew something about practically everything. She would make some man a excellent wife, but not him. He saw in her an imperfection, not much, just a little bit. Rose had an eye that wandered in its socket. He was afraid his child might inherit this imperfection.

Flora Fromm had no reservations about dating Mr. Laurence. Since she had visited an old friend at the hospital that day, she joined Mrs. Levi and Mr. Laurence at the Alhambra for dinner. Mr. Laurence was impressed by her manners, knowledge and social graces. With regards to beauty, she rivaled her sister Rose. They took the 10:41 back to the Fromm farm also. Once again the two men walked the small gravel path. As before, with deep regrets, Mr. Fromm was informed that Flora had an imperfection, not much, just a little bit. When she laughed, her mouth opened wide and he saw her crooked teeth. He feared it might be passed on to his children. Dahlia Fromm accepted Mr. Laurence's request for a chaperoned evening. It was the most perfect evening Cyril Laurence ever spent, alone or with someone. Dahlia Fromm made it perfect. Upon their return to the farm, Mr. Laurence blurted out his desire to her father. He wished to wed Dahlia and the sooner the better. He knelt before her and she accepted his proposal. Dalia insisted they wed at once, the sooner the better.

Mrs. Levi made the wedding arrangements. The wedding became the talk of the farming community and New York City. Mr. Laurence bragged about his perfect wife, of his hopes for the perfect offspring and the perfect life they would live. They would live in New York and winter in the Mediterranean. The child would attend private school and finish his, (he was sure he'd sire a boy) education at the Sorbonne.

That May, when Cyril Laurence gazed upon his first born, a girl, he gagged. He held the child at arms length and immediately passed it to the nurse. His child, bearer of his perfect features, born to the most beautiful mother God ever created, was ugly. At least he thought the child was ugly, for she looked like neither parent. Why didn't the child fit his expectations. He asked Mr. Fromm this question in the hospital anteroom. His response was simple. When they married, Dahlia was pregnant. Not much, just a little bit.

❧ONCE UPON A TIME☙

ANOTHER RUMOR

The hollering and shooting from the far off stagecoach, proceeded it like a long shadow cast by the rising sun. People turning, pointing and speculating as to what event could cause such a commotion. On the outer edge of town, folks near the road caught passing dust and fragments as the vehicle wheeled by.

"Robbers." "James." "Shot."

It made no sense. Townsfolk began hitching their teams, following after the crazy carriage bounding by, heading for the depot on Center Street. The driver urging the horses on, careening through the streets, sending onlookers scurrying to the boardwalk. Often raised fists and profanity followed the cloud disappearing down the street.

"Killed." "Stopped." "Boys."

The stage went on by the Wells Fargo station stopping instead at the doctor's house. Squire Logan left his suttler's store to join the gathering crowd. Mr. Pike, puffed short gasps as he ran from the station to join the group. The bank staff stood watching through the windows across the street. Widow Haines and several boarders hung their bodies out the upper windows to inquire what was happening. Two farm wagons and a mule pulled buggy arrived from the edge of town, just as the doctor opened his front door.

"Bleeding." "Fell." "Helped."

Amid the confusion, folks jabbered, or stood and watched Mitch, the driver, and two strangers, lift Clancy, the weak minded guard, down from the stage. Moaning to the movement of his blooded body, Clancy and the strangers quickly disappeared into the doctor's home. The gossiping throng sounded like locusts advancing on dry leaves. They were single minded and milled about uninformed and directionless, as a swarm might do.

"Road." "Brothers." "Money."

The Squire, knowing as little as the group, clambering to the seat of the stagecoach, turning round and round, waving his hands and shouting, he began, slowly, quieting the mass of humanity. This calmed things down. Squire looked at the bloody front of Mitch and made an assessment of the situation.

"Mitch, are you shot, too? Are you hurt?"

"Nope. Just that damn fool Clancy got shot."

Some noisy murmuring from below, impatient for news, brought Squire Logan's hand up. Quiet resumed.

"OK. Tell us, we all want to hear. Explain the ruckus. Who shot who? How'd Clancy get shot?"

Mitch bit into a chaw and coughed. The sun shone on him alone for the moment. He began racing through the events.

"Mitch. Mitch. Mitch, for God's sake slow down. We don't understand a word. Start talking again. Talk slow."

"OK Squire. OK. Slow. We got held-up by the James boys. Clancy got shot. The James brothers got killed." He was hollering and dancing on the top of the stagecoach. "Me and Clancy, we get the reward for getting the James brothers."

Hurrahs sounded from parts of the crowd, accompanied by a loud whistle.

"Dang it man, talk slow, stop this dancing and shaking this coach. You and Clancy shot the James boys. Fine. We'll get to that later. After you tell us what happened."

"Come on over to the saloon and tell us." boomed Froggy Dunne.

The widow Haines screaming and banging her cane on the boarding house porch roof hollered, "Some of us women don't enter your place Froggy. You stay put and keep talking from there,

Mitch. Or you might not get your supper tonight."

A few laughs and calls for Mitch to keep talking, killed Froggy's idea. Someone got a bucket of beer up to Mitch, to clear the dust out of his throat.

"From the start, you all know the bend afore the log bridge. We slowed down and two men in dusters came out on the road." Mitch, pointed toward Doc's office. "Like the dusters them two strangers went into Doc's office had on. One man grabbed the reins and the other pointed a brace of guns on us." The beer dribbling down his chin glistened.

Mitch changed his voice, "We're the James brothers. We don't want no trouble. Throw down the box and mail bag." His voice shifted to normal, "Our horses began slipping in the soft ground. The man holding the reins started sliding and hollering. The fella with the guns on us turned, looking toward the front where the horses was held. That's when stupid Clancy pulls the shotgun off his lap and shoots." The last of the sparkling suds glistened on Mitch's chin.

Murmuring from the folks in front accompanied Mitch's slow telling. The crowd had grown and people on the furthest edge couldn't hear, one shouting for Mitch to speak up.

"Need refreshment to speak that loud."

He heard an order for beer, adjusted his volume and began again.

"When the shooting starts, the stage lurches off the road. The man that slid gets drug under and run over by a wheel." Mitch became animated and thrashing about. "He's screaming. The gunman turns, knocks into the harness and loses both guns. He reaching down when the lead horse kicks out and brains him. I gets down from the box and see this guy's brains, just like the Rebel's brains when they left him on the rail fence during the war. 'Member that Squire?"

The crowd made no sound, silent as though they stood next to a fresh grave.

"Anyway, the wheel crushed the guy holding the horses. Crushes him dead. Bloody bubbles blowing out his mouth. Me and Clancy get the horses turned. We had to move the stage right over the dead man. I took the canvas off the storage boot in the back and wrapped his body. We lifted it into the coach. With the shovels, we dug the squashed fellow up from the muck, wrapping him in the horse blankets and lay him on his brother. Then that stupid Clancy picks up one of the brace of guns. Bang. Off it goes into his upper arm. Knocks him off his feet, on his ass. Out cold."

Loud guffaws and laughter rolled up from the crowd.

"Lord God. There is two bodies in here" said Pike, pulling the door open.

The closest folks pushed to see, this prevented many people from looking into the stagecoach. But the pressure tilted the coach and Squire Logan started teetered on the top. He hollers for folks to stop pushing and stand back. The two men on Doc's porch ran to the stage, pressing their bodies against the wobbling vehicle.

"Show some restrain people. You nearly knocked me off my perch here." Logan said, wiping his bandanna back and forth across a red sweaty face. "You'll see the bodies, the James boys bodies, as soon as Doc has 'em ready."

"Doc wants the bodies inside. Want more help?" asked the shorter stranger. "My brother Frank and I are already bloody."

Four men from the crowd, the Squire's choice, assisted the strangers empty the coach and carry the bodies into Doc's. Not one spent any time inside the office. The strangers paused on the porch listening to Mitch elaborating on his hold-up story.

Applause broke the silence as Mitch, downing the last drops of beer licked his lips. Bragging, Mitch's favorite pastime, stopped. The crowd wanted to hear more. Mitch turning the pail over and heard orders to bring more beer. He declined none.

Doc came out , motioning to Squire Logan, then retreating back inside the building. The two strangers stepped aside, the shorted fellow asking if they could help any further. Squire nodded an affirmative, beckoning the men to follow him. "Seems ashame to take folks away from Mitch's story, you two don't seem to mind missing it." The four men looked over the bodies, each in their private world, stood in silence.

"Squire," began Doc, "these two fellas are the James brothers. And they ain't the James Brothers."

The helpful strangers looking at each other, appeared bewildered and amused. The Squire rubbed his chin, glancing at each face in the room and grunted.

"It appears like somebody is fooling somebody. These strangers seem to think you're mixing things up. In your head or on those tables. They can't be brothers and not be brothers. Can they?"

"Would seem not. But look here." Doc pulled the bloody duster back and removed an envelope, that he had seen and replaced. "Read."

The unposted letter, muddy and pink with a bloody watermark addressed to Mrs. Amy Louise James, St. Louis. The letter shook in the Squire's hand, "Dearest Mother, mumble, mumble, mumble, our love, your sons Arnold and David James." Squire's features hid the laughter in his soul. Clancy and Mitch would get no reward. Mitch, he'd soon to be a bigger fool than Clancy. As if he knew, Clancy began to giggle in his sleep.

"Gentlemen, a favor." said Squire Logan. "Mitch is a pompous thorn stuck in this town's side. An embarrassment you might say. I would love to get the railroad people here, set up a big to do for Mitch. Clancy will go along, simple as he is. And before they hand over the reward, have Charlie print in his newspaper the letter and the truth. Could you not say anything to Mitch. Or anyone, please?"

"Here for bank business. Be riding right out. Won't mention it to anyone." said the shorter and obvious spokesman of the two. His brother Frank nodded.

Both men stepping off the porch, passing the thinning crowd, nodding to townfolk, walked toward the bank. The on-lookers in the bank window were gone. Unbuttoning their dusters during the short walk, both men, adjusted their gunbelts.

"For a while I thought we were dead Frank." said the younger man as they took two step at a time up to the bank.

"Me too." The usually quiet Frank, now in the lead, pushing open the stuck door with his shoulder. With a devilish smile, stepping back and with an elegant flourish, bowed, "After you brother Jesse. After you."

A PIONEER DAY

All through the night the constant rushing of wind snapped the corners of the canvas and rocked the wagon just inches above the Storey family. At 4 they were up, not that four a.m. ended the night, it only started another day. The eighteenth since the small wagon train of eight wagons, eleven families, left St. Louis, Missouri. The group took six weeks to stock supplies, prepare the wagons and get livestock together. They were planning to settle on open land near the eastern foothills of the Rockies.

Liz Storey, expecting her seventh child, bent to the task of bread making in the cast iron pan at the edge of the low fire. Rita, her eldest, now nine, helped the younger children with toilet and dressing. Aaron helped his father care for the livestock and harness the team, while the twins scouted nearby for burnable material for the fire. Liz turned and dipped water from the barrel for Naomi, taking a deep draught herself before dropping the ladle on the hook.

Dawn set the low grasses aflame and hid the stars in the sky. A great day.

Today the Storey wagon would be last in the train's rotation. Aaron listened to his father's reminder that Indians did make off with stray cattle, so keep his eyes open and the mind alert. Liz Storey set to walking for awhile, the hard wagon seat kept her unborn awake, at least that's what she said. Close to the wagons her children ran and played with many of the train's young ones. Mrs. Phillips and Mrs. Pratt walking along with her, talked the talk of mothers, wives and women, enjoying each other's company.

Sometime later, while Liz sat on the swaying wagon seat, a sudden shivering, a violent wrenching in her gut and she was projecting a copious stream of vomit onto the lush grasses. At the same time her eyes glazed and she was fighting to hold herself on the wagon seat. Miles Storey stopped the team, hollering to the wagon ahead of them to hold up. He came around to assist his wife out of the wagon. Prone on the ground, she heard someone ordering the children away, her twisting body discharged her stomach and bowels together. With a violent heaving and piteous wailing, she aborted her child.

Mrs. Pratt recognizing the problem, she had experienced it before, warned the group. "Cholera." Everyone, hearing her pronouncement, moved back. "Cholera. Liz Storey has cholera. Everyone, keep back and keep your children away."

The train stopped as shouts reached the lead wagon. Silas Edgars, elected leader, quickly riding back to the stricken group, just as quickly called for a meeting of the families. Afterward he spoke Mr. Storey. The train voted to wait, but no longer than tomorrow's dawn, then move on regardless of Liz or other family member's condition. One condition, their wagon stay apart from the other wagons. A brave act for people mowed down often by illnesses like cholera, influenza, even measles.

Liz Storey, healthy and happily alive at four in the morning owned her own piece of open land by one in the afternoon. The burial over, the Storey's wagon rejoined the train for another few hours on their westward trek.

The families gave the Storeys their condolences and many sharing their evening meal. Broken hearts and swollen, red eyes accepted such kindness but there were problems with the smaller children's behavior. Miles Storey would need some answers and some help, right now.

Sending Rita to fetch Mrs. Pratt and bring her three to play with his children, Miles went to the Phillip's wagon. He asked Ted Phillips to walk with him, to discuss an important issue between

men. The issue, plain and clear, Miles desperately needed someone to help care for his family, other than himself. His oldest, at
seven, was far too immature, breaking up the family wouldn't be
considered, for the moment. Mindy Phillips, now fourteen and
only twelve years younger than Miles, could join his family. Would
he and Mrs. Phillips consider it.

"You mean Miles, you want to marry Mindy?"

"I know she ain't grown into a full woman yet. But she is
a woman. I've seen her off caring for woman's needs."

"Yes. I know that she's a woman. But she's still a child."
the father replied.

"My God. Look at Ben Lowe and John Bellup. Both their
wives are as old as Mindy. John's wife is already with child."

"I know. Are they happy married?" asked Mindy's father.

"Ted, look, I don't know if anyone is happy if they're married. Well Liz and I were, most of the time. How about you and
the Missus, happy?"

Ted Phillips looked into Miles eyes, "I'd say so." Ted placed
his hand on Miles shoulder, "I'll talk to the wife. I'll even support
you. But even then we ask Mindy. Stay here, have another cup of
coffee and a biscuit too. Mindy made them."

August 11, 1882 Liz Bowman Storey died of the cholera
- just past noon on the grasslands of the United States northwest
territory. August 11, 1882. Millicent Sarah Phillips became Mrs.
Miles Storey just as the sun set. I witnessed. These were the words
written into the diary of Mrs. Irene Holt Phillips. This diary was
found in the belongings of Amy Storey deceased grand daughter
of Mindy Phillips Storey. Since Miss Amy Storey had no living kin
the diary was donated to the local historical society by the Christian Hospice. Miss Storey has resided at the hospice for the last
four months.

PRACTICE

Revenge. Luther wanted revenge. Crane had shot Luther's brother in the back.

The canyon echoed with slow deliberate shots. Luther practiced, hour after hour, every day, becoming quicker, more accurate.

Finally, Luther stood before Crane's house shouting his challenge.

Stepping from behind the barn, Crane shot Luther in the back.

THE DAY THE ICEMAN DIED

Otzi stared into the vile brown pile of his own excrement and saw the worms wriggle. They came from his body. Bewildered, he knew they were part of the weakness slowing his fortyish body down. Yes, the pain in his ankle and knee effected his body too. But the Shaman had marked and prayed over those areas. Usually these pain causing spirits entered a person's body at night and withdrew the day after sacrifice. Otzi wondered why the spirits had returned to bother him.

He plucked several hairs from his head and wet them with spit before dropping them into the small fire, today's sacrifice. From the mouth of the shallow cave, Otzi gazed at the snow covered mountainside and wished he had crossed yesterday. However, too many things had happened, each slowed him up and now he wondered if he'd get home at all. He noticed a new pain in his jaw as he bit into the charcoal flecked bread, nearly losing the bit of meat already in his mouth. The last of his food.

The braided grass cloak warmed his torso and the grass filled shoes his feet. He pulled the fur cap down on his thinning hair. He tucked his scabbard and ax into his belt in preparation for continuing his journey. The food in his mouth slid down as he reached for the quiver and a bow taller then his own body. Fresh blood flowed over the back of his hand, a reminder that his progress might still be followed. Otzi was a fugitive, running for his life. He limped into the morning air, homeward bound.

Four mornings ago Otzi had wandered into a group of flatland people gathering planted roots. They had welcomed him and

traded bread from their crops for copper nuggets from his northern mountain homeland. His first encounter with these strange
people, nearly naked and painted with odd marks, intrigued him.
He accepted the offer of a place near their fire. He ate their food
and watched them dance. He did not relax, survivors don't relax
fully, in a strange situation.

As the sun passed its zenith, Otzi prepared to leave. The
cautious movements of these people made him wary, his signal of
danger. He left with a hand wave and moved with haste along the
riverbed and into the hills

Just beyond their crop area he felt the arrow pierced his left
shoulder and heard the yowls of a pursuer. Like a mountain goat
Otzi ran up the rocky hillside, his leather clad feet moving easily
over the sharp stones. His unshod pursuers soon fell behind and
disappeared. Blood coursed down the small body leaving a clear
trail for any follower. On the run, he reached back and snapped
the shaft protruding from his shoulder. The stone point would
remain stuck in the bone for now. Otzi chastised himself for not
detecting his attackers sooner and for the trouble he had brought
on himself.

He stopped to gather lichens and moss which he pressed
against the bleeding wound. It hurt. Running was difficult, but
Otzi had moved through the lower tree line and onto an alpine
meadow. The wound would effect his hunting ability and early
spring plants were not growing above ground yet. There was
another problem. Arthritic pains began to rack his body as he
continued walking toward a pass in the mountains. Otzi hunkered
down and slept without a fire the first night. In the morning he
checked the mountainside and moved on as the sun's rays touched
the stone peak. His jaw hurt while chewing the hard bread of the
flatlanders, but it satisfied him for awhile.

His next food came when he found a dead furry animal
the cold mountain air had preserved The weary traveler cut small
chunks from the bones and ate them raw. He tucked a meaty bone

into the grass jacket and proceeded upward along a goat trail. He didn't progress very far that day, numb, cold and weak he couldn't. Diarrhea also slowed him down. He knitted his gray eyebrows in perplexity. Was he getting old?

The next day he found a small cave and holed up. Fortune smiled on him that day, a larger boulder held the material that when struck with flint sparked.. Otzi used an arrow head and grass from his shoe lining to build a small fire. Animal dung and nesting material found inside the cave kept the fire burning 'til dawn. His efforts to chip off some of the fire making material failed. Sleep and the fire's warmth lifted his spirit.

He stopped where the sun had melted small patches of snow and drank from rivulets of water to quench his thirst. He hoped home was just beyond this slope.

Suddenly the field of snow shifted. The entire slope began to move. In his weaken condition Otzi struggled to flee, struggled and failed. In the blink of an eye he disappeared. He never saw the sun again; however, the sun did shine upon him again.

It's believed, from the evidence found, that Otzi lay under the snow blanket from 4,309 BC 'til 1991. His body and possessions, created a scientific sensation. Dubbed The Iceman, Otzi, this wonderful relic from our past, is being carefully studied. The body of Otzi has already told us much about his life and may reveal mountains of information from his environment or his wellbeing. We must wait and learn from a single traveler traversing a isolated mountain trail, whose journey home was interrupted.

THE BLACK RIDGE PACK

Stretching his arms toward the silver knob in the cold heavens and twisting his hands, Martin listened, as if turning the moon would silence the wailing of the Black Ridge pack. Listening intently he assigned the howls to different individuals. Vocally Rufus, the alpha wolf, grated the starry sky, while an unknown voice rose, taunted him from the far left ridge near Indian Hill. Lumpy and Greeny could be heard yowling their calls after Rufus barked at the unknown intruder.

Since he arrived in the basin, Martin spent hours watching and listening to the pack, he called The Black Ridge Pack. The pack had brought down an elk across the river from his first night camp. He had not seen the actual kill, but heard the snarling and yelping as the wolves tore into the flesh. He watched through the telescopic sight of his rifle, entering, albeit, uninvited into the life of the pack. He wanted to know and understand them in fact, not in the distorted stories he had heard from frightened people. He stayed in the basin knowing he shouldn't and with time permitting followed and studied the pack.

He thought himself fortunate to follow them and observe their behavior. After months, he learned to recognize individual voices, footprints and position in the hierarchy of the pack. He began understanding the selection of prey and the difference between play and the deadly business of remaining alive. He saw the consequences of attempting to advance in the pack and the submissive attitude of the dominated. He felt sometimes that, because the pack didn't attack him, they had accepted him. Where did he fit?

Late in the afternoon, Martin heard something behind him while cutting a stake for a trap. In turning he fumbled the sharp knife, driving it deep into the calf just behind his knee. Two days from camp and a fresh snow covering an already thick blanket of snow, he knew trouble had settled into his life. He tied off the leg reducing the bleeding, but found moving nearly impossible. The rocky ledges near the beaver pond, while not deep, could provide some protection from the threatening elements. Wedging his blanket into a crevice he then weighed it down at the corners. Next he began pulling nearby branches and build his fire, before easing his body down to inspect his leg.

During the night he saw the embers of his fire glowing in the eyes of the wolf pack just beyond the water's edge. Approaching in silence, they remained silent, drifting about vigilantly in the veiled darkness. Martin studied the movements as he shoved a chunk of wood into the low flames and bit into some pemmican, the hard trail cake of dried meat and berries mixed with fat. The snow had stopped falling but had deepened since he made camp. Anything moving about would have difficulty, hunter or prey.

Martin reviewed his chances of surviving the situation. He had pemmican for several days, snow for water, matches and eight shots for the rifle. He had met some friendly Indians wandering the area in search of meat, but doubted they would be moving in this weather. If they did they might smell the smoke and stop by. He could cache his gear and head for lower land. Not the best survival chances. Attempting to move, he found his bloody leg frozen to the snow.

Rufus howled to the empty sky. The cacophony came across the beaver pond bouncing along the shallow rock ledges, into Martin's heart. His blood froze as stiff as his leg. His hand held tightly to the loaded rifle, his body tensing, waiting. Had he become the pack's prey?

The Black Ridge pack had nine members, counting the

three pups of last summer. The severity of the past few months limiting their kills, made them more desperate and less cautious. He could not count on killing one wolf per shot; however, if he shot Rufus the pack might back off. He needed to keep the fire up and if he could, remember how to pray. He might hold out 'til dawn. He eschewed hope. He thought of God, settled back and bracing his rifle in the compacted snow, composed a prayer.

The night air, so crisp and clean, carried the rifle's echo many miles. It also carried the howling of the pack. Days later an Indian hunter found an empty rifle sticking out of an undisturbed blanket of snow, Why it was there and what happened must wait for the Spring thaw.

FRIENDLY MURDER

A shout stopped the small boisterous group moving along the corridor. Everyone knew the friendly, smiling face approaching them. Their hands extended to congratulate the slight, balding figure coming into their midst.

At a friend's signal they seized his arms, making him helpless. After stabbing him all withdrew in haste. Julius Caesar's sightless eyes followed them.

THE BUNDLE

Billy McCory cinched the knot of the bundle tighter. This bundle, Murphy, wasn't going to slip from the blanket or the travois. Just past sun-up and sweat was already dripping from Billy's face. Summer-like weather, he couldn't remember it being so warm so soon in this part of the Black Hills. Flipping his coat over the saddle horn and mounting Murphy's old horse, with the sun warming his back, he headed for Territorial Seat, the bounty and some easy living.

Waiting all night for Murphy to move about Billy stiffened when Murphy stood, coffee and bread in his hands. Coughing, Billy shot him as he turned. You don't shoot a man in the back, but you don't let him draw either. Particularly with Murphy's reputation. Neither Murphy nor McCory were fast with a gun; however, both were sneaky.

Billy's old buffalo gun near tore Murphy in half. Laying in his own gore, just as so many of his victims had, Billy let him die while finishing the coffee Murphy had prepared. He toed the body onto Murphy's blanket and began his rope and spider routine, blood quickly, quietly oozing through the dead man's blanket.The sun cooked the earth and everything on it. Flies buzzing their kin, soon covering the bloody bundle. A sickening sweetness clung about the rider and his bundle. A poor start for a four or five day trip.

The first night Billy hung his bundle from a cottonwood. Jerky sizzling on a stick didn't mask the stench. By morning Murphy was an unbearable fly covered stink. Billy's rigging allowed the travois to drag behind him thirty feet or so. No breeze, hot sun and no way to hurry along, the dozing Billy continued moving. By nightfall Billy didn't want to eat. Murphy was weighted down in a creek that night, but he bubbled up to foul Billy's air. The flies ate Billy's meal.

As the moon slunk beyond the hills, a coyote slunk in to begin his dinner of "offal a la Murphy". The snarling and odors didn't keep Billy McCory awake, he just couldn't get to sleep. A shot put flight to the coyote. A piece of blanket and Murphy took flight too.

Noon, the fourth day, found Billy, the traveling stench and flies, poking along, when three Indians stepped from the rocks in front of Billy's horse. Raising no ruckus and Billy offering none, they indicated that Billy should dismount and give them his horse, gun and saddle bag. He did so, willingly. The Indians, smelling Murphy, decided there was nothing they wanted from the travois. Billy began walking one way, dragging Murphy, the Indians, two riding one walking, went another.

Next morning, Billy wading into the creek where Murphy's body was stashed, stopped dead in his tracks. "Oh God. Oh God. He's coming back to life. Oh God."

Billy saw the blanket twitching back and forth. A turtle poking its head up sent small fish darting about, all were feeding on the shrinking bundle that was once Murphy.

Billy McCory was a slow learner. But he learned sooner or later. Standing in the icy water, he started pulling the fetid rags from the body, wrapping the skull in the remaining pieces of blanket. The rest of Murphy he buried in a shallow ditch.

The townsfolk knew something horrible was coming before Murphy's stench or Billy McCory came down the dusty street. Gagging, people ran to their houses shutting their windows and doors. Plunking his sorry, stinking bundle on the boardwalk, Billy walked into the sheriff's office. The sheriff walked him back out, telling him to get out of town and take the stinking bundle with him.

    Billy never did collect the bounty for bringing in Murphy. Seems there wasn't enough of Murphy to prove it was Murphy. The townsfolk knew how sneaky these two could be. Why Murphy could be out there, somewhere, just waiting for Billy. They'd high-tail it to Mexico and spend the bounty.

THE KNIFE

Thomas Bernard "Skip" Towne, an American expatriate living in France, enjoyed the challenge archival photo interpretation presented. Cursed or blessed with a mind that forgets nothing, he could see in the faded, torn picture relationship without any connecting dots. Now his reputation for recalling old photographic evidence would be severally tested with the fragments of photos decades old. Contractors while knocking down the old newspaper building for a new shopping development, discovered an old, unused vault. Workers found boxes and boxes of photographs without any identification. Sensing a story, the publisher, managed to talk Skip into the task of making sense of the photos.

The name Skip came from a salesclerk in Chicago's Fair Store. While shopping with his mother, he took a hat from a mannequin and put it on. The clerk said, "My, my, my, my, my" in a sing-song style. "Doesn't he look just like Skippy?" Skippy was a popular comic strip character at the time. His mother agreed.

She started calling him Skippy, the family began calling him Skippy, as did the kids at school. He was able to cut it to Skip when his voice began changing. Now retired from the Chair of Antiquity Studies, he continues researching, cataloging and pasting together historic photographs for museums around the world.

Vault photos soon carpeted every available flat surface in the small house Skip rented, including under the chairs and table. They were not schematically placed. The photos, boxed years ago, began crumbling as they were moved, thus scattering their contents in total disarray. Dr. Towne planned to create order out of the chaos the newspaper people had created.

Walking from room to room, coffee cup in hand, Skip began sorting the pieces of his latest puzzle. If the photo had a single face, on the bed, a group shot, the bedroom floor, publicity, on the sofa in the spare room, scenes in the kitchen. By noon everything, more or less, arranged so he could find it and he was only on his third pot of coffee.

Many photos were in extremely poor shape and would be discarded. If he thought modern methods might salvage a picture, particularly one that intrigued him, he placed it next to the coffee pot. After three days of judicious sorting he called the publisher and invited him to the house for coffee.

The publisher, with two advisors, went over Dr. Towne's special photographs and heard his suggestions. They weren't the most pleased people in France that morning. Cave paintings and prehistoric artifacts were of particular interest to Skip. At Skip's urging they did agree to spend some funds on digital enhancement of many scraps of photographs they considered junk. Reluctant to trash the entire project, they agreed to fly Dr. Towne to America for some research and to spent more time researching Lascaux cave artifacts, as well as other European caves. He must then concentrate on something they wanted researched.

Returning to France, Dr. Towne contacted Jean-Marie Chauvet, discoverer of the Grotte Chauvet. Unfortunately, Chauvet's commitments forced him to decline Skip's request to work together. The two men perused the photo and identified a few locations. Rouffignac, Malt'a, in Siberia, Cougnac and some small sites were passed over at once. Lascaux, Altamira, Brassempouy, Abri Bourdois and Cap-Blanc were considered, but then dropped. It seemed possible that Louis Jullien or Edouard Piette may have taken some of the photos in Grimaldi, but neither were sure. At least Skip had a starting point, of sorts.

Dr. Towne expended his energies on several photos clipped together. Photos of an obsidian stone point embedded in a rib bone of a buried caveman. He recalled seeing catalogued photos of several obsidian knives, one missing its tip. He thought they were exhibited in Spain. Altamira possibly? But didn't remember if the photographs had identification on them. Contacting Altamira, he found the knives had disappeared when the exhibit burned. Two burial photos were in the files. The photos contained the bones of two male adults buried in a common grave. The Radius of one man scratched with strange lateral gouges.

In America, Skip found the computer scanning electron microscope identified the scratches as coming from the side of a stone blade, dragged along the forearm. It appears to be accidental. Photographs with microscopic enlargements matched the gouges to the obsidian blade. While the pictures were taken by different photographers at different times, he was able to match them.

Skip Towne hired his cousin's daughter to take notes and handle his less than acceptable filing system. Fortunately, she provided the patience and skills that made his job easier and fruitful. Within two years the following story emerged from the crumbled photos, albeit fictionalized. It was published with great fanfare, as unlocking a thousands of years old murder. The entire mystery being solved, the newspaper announced, by Dr. Skip Towne's critical examination of the old photos found in the vaults of the newspaper.

Caveman's Murder Solved

While photographs and records have been moved about and lost, Renown archival photograph expert, Dr. Skip Towne, believes the following story may have occurred. The story explains the stone tip in a caveman's rib and identifies scrapes from the same stone blade on the Radius of another caveman buried 33,000 years ago. Dr. Towne has named the victim and murderer, for clarity, with fictional names.

Muss crouched close to the fire his hands extended and warm, his rear extended back and chilled. He watched Culth twist and turn two stone in his hands. Slowly, chip by chip, one stone became longer and sharper, its ebony surface reflecting the fire's dancing flames.

Culth could achieve the workmanship that Muss could not. His thick fingers were unable to grip the tools necessary for the task. He had actually tried once, only once, with half hearted effort. When he needed tools he bargained for them or used inferior ones which often failed him and caused him physical and mental pain.

Culth spun the blade in his hand, its sharpness split his skin and drops of blood hissed when hitting the flames. The blade fell and Muss grabbed it. He drove it into Culth's chest causing a rhythmic gush of blood to ooze between his clutching fingers. Culth's eyes glazed over, his face contorting into a dying question. "Why?"

The stab caused Muss to cut himself as the rib bone's resistance pushed the sharpen stone along his wrist and lower arm. A slippery bloody blade sliced tendons and muscles, while howls of pain echoed through the huge French cave. The blade fell, fractured into several fragments, its beauty and usefulness lost.

Muss, in his greed and haste to have a sharp stone, killed his brother, lost the very thing he desired and caused his own death. Many years later this story was discovered in photographs in an unknown cave burial. The rib of the victim chipped by the blade, the Radius of the murderer scraped by the stone blade. Which cave the murder actually occurred is impossible to say.

ESCAPE FROM SALEM

Goodwife Bonafield, earlier in the day, felt the prickling sensation throughout her groin. The Master was notifying her with waves of pleasure, the kind that all members of her ilk recognized. But watching the swaying body of Rebecca Nurse, hung as a convicted witch, had thrilled her. So ignoring obvious warnings she returned home. Now they had trapped her. They were moving toward her house, down her lane and from the lane on the Commons. Torches burning, screeching awful oaths of damnation, the mob advanced on her.

In the past weeks panic had seized Salem. Three lying children had sworn under oath they were tormented by witches. First Tituba, the black one, had succumbed to their accusations. George Jacobs, Margret Scott were convicted and poor Giles Corey, was pressed to death. Goodwife Bonafield knew the children were lying, but speaking out could reveal a true witch. Herself. Many families purged their pets from the house, they were considered witch's familiars, their contacts with the devil. Poor innocent creatures.

Parents looked at children, children at adults and friend at friend suspiciously. All feared any sign or happening, even a bug found in the house could bring suspicion. It might be the Evil One or his minion.

Peering through the window at the torches advancing toward her, Goodwife Bonafield set aside her supper bowl and reached for the earthenware container hidden in the churn. Mindful that speed was needed, she began to cast a spell to save herself. She made a circle of forbidden herbs and crushed ingredients known only to witches. Then, wetting her finger, she drew a flying bird in the dust, uttering a short chant, she knelt inside the circle. Thimble, her cat and faithful familiar, crouched near the fireplace, eyes wide, back arched.

Dust clouds flew about the room as the door came crashing down. The burning fire sent a spark into the traces of a circle on the floor and a supper bowl fell from the table, upset by the mob pushing into the empty room. Empty, but for the cat settled on the warmth of the hearth, feathers protruding from its mouth.

❧MISCELLANEOUS❧

NO FUTURE

In a few minutes it would be too late. Burt could see from his upstairs window that Andy was crossing Depot Street and would be in their little computer lab in minutes. Andy would see the timing device on the computer was released and pre-set, he'd press the page up button, as they did before and Burt would return.

Burt stepped onto the platform, sliding the cover over himself and the control panel. The setting of April 29, 1906 was correct, the digital clock flipped, 7:10 a.m. Two minutes. Everything he wanted since purchasing the old book on the e-Bay auction had come to this moment. He released the timer.

In 2002, Burt Crowley, computer geek and dreamer almost missed the e-Bay auction deadline. He was tinkering with an old cathode board and just shocked himself by touching the exposed rim of the tube. He reset the rheostat and noticed the time. Spinning around in his chair, he saw the latest bid on the H. G. Well's notebook and upped his bid. He was confirmed the winner and the book would be sent from England as soon as Burt's payment was received. He made an electronic payment.

The day the package arrived Burt could barely control his fingers as they removed the wrapping. He held the first page at an angle to read the faded writing, his writing. It can be done. H. G. Wells. From that instant Burt put his life, time and funds into their dream, his and Wells', time travel. Having no family and a modest income from the old railroad station, his aunt had converted to living quarters and left him when she died, he was responsible only to himself. Some of the stored railroad equipment remained in an unused portion of the building Burt always intended to clean out, but somehow never found the time.. Burt swore his only friend, Andy, a research assistant at the university agricultural extension, to secrecy and together they began work on a dream

The second night of reading slowly and allowing himself the luxury of pretending to be the renown author, Burt noticed pages stuck together. With a gentle wiggle, probing finger separated them and found a faded newspaper clipping.

April 28, 1906. An unidentified young man was struck and killed this morning outside the railroad station by the 7:12 train. From his dress, he appears to be an out of towner. The young man had no wallet on his person or marks on his body that might help the police identify him. His face was badly burned by a broken steam pipe. The body has been taken to Toomey Mortuary. It may be identify there. Mr. P Quigley, the train's engineer said the man appeared out of nowhere and was struck down before his eyes. Mr. Quigley has worked for the railroad for twenty-one years without an accident. He is deeply distressed.

Burt was distressed also. He talked to Andy the following day. Both felt obligated to go back in time and save this young fellow's life. For some unknown reason, Burt's affection for the dead man took on a deep significance.

The faded writing on some of the pages made reading difficult There were marginal notes, scribbling, diagrams and some complete paragraphs of some earlier stories, The Time Machine, When the Sleeper Awakes and Man in the Moon. The book had a musty odor and might be missing pages, missing diagrams. He spent hours deciphering these notes, checking with Andy and feeding the incomplete notes into the computer. They realized the information was old and incomplete, but, like the Gordian Knot, solvable with time and effort.

Living in the older part of town, 10 Spur Street, the address given the old station when it had been moved onto the removed rail head, Burt pursued his own interests at his leisure. He managed to become a well known hacker, able to solve problems the computer companies whizkids couldn't. Computer companies supplied him with their latest equipment problems to solve and if he wanted he could ask them for the moon and get it. Everything he did was computer connected, or he wasn't interested. Until the two of them began to delve into Wells' notes and diagrams neither man thought their aspirations would be more than a dream. Burt's biggest thrill came the day he discovered, on the edge of the notebook, in invisible ink, "It can be done."

Eighteen months to the day he first opened the notebook and read those faint formulas and diagram, Burt saw on the screen a workable possibility for a time machine. Andy and he made some calculation changes and discussed, over and over, what they thought would span time. But, they had no vehicle, no transportation and no assurance that they could return. After Andy left for the night, Burt played with the digital camera and various light settings on the pages of the old notebook. Failing to develop anything new, he relaxed and fell asleep in the Lay Z Boy, notebook in hand.

So many magnificent ideas of what the future might hold. Wells saw some in his lifetime, but many other came years later. Like DaVinci, Wells perceived a new and unbelievable world in which man would fly, visit distant planets, slip through time and even create life. Burt Crowley dreamed these things too. Tonight his mind churned with ideas.

During the night the old notebook dropped from his hands, pages broke from the binding sliding across the floor. Burt gathered them up and placed them on the table with the digital photos. The morning sunlight bounced off the shiny paper, revealing the words, TIME REVERSE. He hadn't seen them last night. But what did they mean?

When Andy came in after work, he told Burt about the latest development with DNA. Everyone in the genetic research program at the University Agricultural Farm talked of nothing else all day. Seeds from Egypt were dated by the gen/tech department, showing dates with a margin of error at less than ten years. Last year's corn showed the changes for at least 150 years. If they had a means to retrieve plant parts from the past, they could pin-point the year they grew.

Great news. Now both men pondered TIME REVERSE. It plunged them into many fantastic possibilities, none seemed resolvable in the computer. Burt's fingers hurt from tapping the keyboard. He poked at nothing, just poked the keys to calm his frustration. TIMEREVERSETIMEREVERSTIMEREVERSE-TIME. In that simple exercise of futility the answer leaped from the glowing screen. REVERSE TIME.

Set the timer and date to go back in time, set the retrieve timer in reverse. Why not? Set the clock to advance the seconds and minutes counter clockwise. My god. The simplest of actions. Wells had seen this possibility. Had he tried it? Had his Time Machine worked? These questions crossed Burt's mind. But to prove it. He quoted the Bard, "That is the question."

"Suppose, just suppose, we break down the defrag chip and work it into the fax machine? Would that break the living molecules down?"

Burt took off his glasses and tapped them to his chin. "Haven't we tried that?"

"Don't think so." Andy replied. "Here." He sat and tapped in a code on the keyboard. Both read the screen. "We must have mentioned it, but didn't enter it."

"Well GIGO. Or we get something better. Go for it."

A bit of this and a bit of that added to previous entries and spread sheets were soon giving them alternatives to many possible options. Their spirits were up, hours passed without their awareness, before they realized it, this one step lead to many possibilities.

"This has to be the way." Burt blurted, looking at Andy.

"Let's do it.'

"Let's. What's first?"

"Can you get someone at gen/teach to test something we bring back?'

"Think so." said Andy. "Might be able to myself by the time we bring something back."

"Who or what should be sent back?"

"It can't be one of us. We have to remain here and control everything."

Burt frowned at this remark. "You can handle things here. I really wish to be the first."

"Not in the trial stages, Burt." Andy seemed horrified. "We need to send... to send a camera. We send a camera, with the timer set. It takes a photo and returns."

"Possibility. Yeah. A good suggestion. We send a digital and know the minute it goes into the computer."

It took time, weeks and weeks of time to construct their machine. Testing and resetting, changing and adapting crucial parts, the two men became slaves of the machine. So devoted to its functions they grew thinner, because they skipped meals. Their eyes were ringed in darkened shadows from lack of sleep and like automatons seldom found a need even to speak to each other. At the gen/tech station, Andy's co-workers, asked if he was ill, shortly after his promotion to testing DNA samples.

The day the digital camera was set on the platform for projection back in time, called for a little toast, a speech. They took some orange juice from the fridge and stood before the platform and an array of cannibalized computer boards and paraphernalia.

"Success."

"Success."

Burt downed his drink, waited 'til Andy took the cup from his mouth and pushed the Crtl button. No hum, no flash, no whirring noises. The camera was gone. The camera was back. In a trance, both men stared at the camera. Burt finally reached out and picked it up. Neither even looked at the clock on the wall, the timer settings or the exposure number on the camera. He stepped to the computer, inserted the camera, pushed the button and on the screen an out of focus picture appeared. Out of focus, yes, identifiable, not really. However, it was a picture of plants.

"We did it. Oh God, we did it." Andy tried to scream the words, but couldn't.

Burt continued to stare at the picture, mumbling softly. "Success." over and over.

"We have some things to do. Before we send the camera back, we have some adjustments to make. Let's do them quickly and send the camera back.'

"Right. You name it Burt, put it in the program, while I do as you direct."

"OK. "One," he typed in, set the camera in the opposite direction from the first time. Two, set the focus for less distance. Three, set it for greater color contrast."

"Done. Turned it, set the focus and the contrast."

"Let's do it." and again the camera disappeared and reappeared.

"Time?'

Burt looked at the screen, "six seconds."

Andy brought the camera to Burt, he placed it in the computer. A different picture. "Plants, actually weeds." Burt murmured. The leaves were a mixture of grasses and a hirsute notched leaf, like a sunflower. There appeared to be a building or a wall in the distant background, nothing positive.

They took more pictures and had a few more things in the pictures. But no way of telling exactly where the camera was sitting in the past. They knew it was on the ground. Tomorrow they would try different dates. This would clarify that they were going back in time. After all the pictures taken today were of the present season. They needed more results. They slept in the lab that night, if you could call their dream filled night sleep.

In the morning Burt set the machine for the snow storm last year, calculated the going and returning factors, while Andy placed the camera on the platform.

"Wait! I got an idea." Andy took a kitchen timer and placed it under the camera. It turned slowly. "We'll get a full circle of photos."

"Good idea."

Disappointment can't be hidden when great expectations fail. The photos came back dark and blank. All of them dark and blank.

"Something went wrong."

"Yeap. But what?"

"Look," said Andy, snapping shot after shot. "The camera is working."

Burt tapped the button enlarging the image. In the corner, with all the darkness, faint shadows stood out. Shapes. Crystal shapes.

"Andy, oh Lordy, look. The camera was under some snow. Look. It worked."

Delirious with excitement, Burt slid to the floor, hollering. "EUREKA! EUREKA.'

Andy joined him on the floor. Hugging and crying in their happiness. This emotional collapse draining their bodies of all the worries and frustration since the experimenting began. If someone had come upon them, speaking gibberish and sprawled out on the floor, a stay in a mental hospital would be suggested.

Sucking in his breath, Burt stood and extended his hand, pulling Andy up, so they could survey the lab.

"The lab is big enough. We need to increase the size of the defrag platform." Burt casually remarked. "We also need to sent living material. An experimental animal, or even a bug or bird."

"Hadn't considered doing that yet. Are we ready?"

For the first time there was a touch of urgency in Burt's voice. "I want to do it. Go back. I want to see what it's like."

"I understand. But, but..." Andy's response died in his throat.

"I know. I'm rushing. Foolish. We will wait." Burt turned back to the platform and running his finger over it, paused. "We have work to do."

By trial and error experiments increased their knowledge. The first mouse sent didn't return. After some thought they arrived at the conclusion that it had stepped off the platform. The second mouse was shipped off in a box and returned; however, nothing came back with it. Andy left the lab and returned with an old bird cage. He sat and silently removed the bottom, replacing it with a screen. He then, with a twinkle in his eye, put a mouse in it and adjusted it on the platform.

"What to you think? If we leave it for a few minutes, the mouse will grab some plant material. He comes back with proof."

"Ingenious my boy, ingenious." Getting up from in front of the computer, Burt sat Andy in the chair. "Sent the messenger."

Their messenger came back with several bits of chewed plant parts on the floor screen and was chewing on a seed pod. They quickly retrieved the pod. It proved to be a legume, beans, a very fresh bean pod. The plant fragments legume also. Andy took them to the gen/tech lab and came back with a smile worthy of Carroll's Cheshire cat. Positive results, DNA tests on the pod confirmed the little rodent had travel back in time. The messenger was sent back and forth that day, but returned with legume parts each time. Andy deferred a trip to gen/tech each time.

Many days with many tests on the materials the messenger dragged into the bird cage. Their results being more conclusive every time the data was programmed. A great deal of time was expended on rebuilding an enlarged platform. Not knowing what the actual defraging trip involved, Burt ordered a plastic cover to enclose him when he went. That day was close.

Saturday, Andy and Burt huddled around the platform equipment, checking the reverse mechanism of the calendar. Each month and day of the selected year dropping into place as expected. No hitches. The discussion drifted, as always, to the chosen date and time. It would take place one hour before the train was scheduled to arrive at the station. This would give Burt enough time to find the man and keep him away from the railroad tracks. They punched in the date and time. Everything was ready for tomorrow.

"Tomorrow."

"I'd stay tonight, but Mom's got something go..."

"I know Andy. It will be a busy day tomorrow. I'll get a good night's sleep. Then, as soon as you get here." Burt began singing a song, from the stage show "Annie," "Tomorrow. Tomorrowwwww" and stopped. "Never could sing."

Turning on the computer, Burt saw the blinking message telling him the clock had been changed during the night. He looked at his watch, an hour difference. They were now on daylight saving time. He didn't have an hour to find and save the stranger. He looked out the window and saw Andy crossing Depot Street. For once Burt's cool left him, only saving the stranger filled his thoughts. His actions were hurried, decisive, but hurried. He stepped onto the platform pulled the cover down and released the button.

The experience of molecular breaking apart and coming together again frightened Burt. The crowding of compressed sounds while traveling disturbed his equilibrium and jarred his position on the platform as it settled. Off balance Burt attempted to fling himself from in front of the steam engine moving toward him. He was back in time. But time back then didn't change on the last Sunday in April.

Engineer Quigley saw the young man on the tracks for an instant. He seemed to have come from nowhere. After being told the young man was dead and no one knew him, Quigley collapsed.

Later, when he talked to the police officer he said, "If I had seen him sooner, I might have blown the engine whistle, might have saved his life."

Trying to calm the distraught man, the policeman said, "If you had, you would have changed the future."

MEMORIES

Marie studied the tinted photo in the silver frame for a moment, then slipped it out and dropped it onto a growing pile of refuse. As she wrapped the frame in folds of newspaper, her daughter Callie, came into the nearly empty room.

"Need some help mom?" Her eyes sweep the vacant shelves and cupboards and stopped on the picture in the rubbish box. Retrieved from the pile, Callie turned the picture over, "No names, guess you don't know them, huh?"

"Oh, I did and I didn't. They're your great grandparents, my mother's folks."

"And you don't want their picture?"

"Like I said, I didn't know them,' Marie sighed, "and they didn't know me."

Callie looked her mother in the eye and detected a note of sadness in her voice.

"Were they alive, you know, when you were?"

"Very much so, for more than thirty years. We, your Aunt Sue and I, never knew them and they never knew us." Marie reached for more newspaper while she continued closing the house she had lived in as a child. "It was one of those things that happened and it shouldn't have."

"I've heard some of this haven't I? It's like a family ghost in the closet story?" Callie squealed with mock anticipation. "Can you tell me?" Please?"

"Sure. But we keep packing things, your dad will be back with the truck soon and we have to pack and unpack everything by tonight, so the truck can be returned without extra cost."

"OK. I'll pack this stuff," Callie pointed to the pile of knickknacks near the window, "and you tell me the story."

"Fine. Do you recall any of the things you've heard?"

"Not enough to make sense. Grandma's folks didn't talk to her or grandpa, or to you or Aunt Sue. That's about all I know. Seems strange, kinda like, spooky."

"To you? Yes. However; spooky isn't the word. I'd say selfish, or petty."

"It started the year Aunt Sue was born. Grandma and grandpa had told her folks they were married in the county clerk's office. Eloped, after dad's divorce. Grandma didn't like the idea of her daughter marrying a divorced Catholic. When Sue was born they brought her to grandma's folks to see. The visit was short.

By the time I was born they exchanged few phone calls or letters. My mom wrote each Christmas and sent pictures of Sue and me. She didn't even know if the cards were opened or the pictures seen. Each Christmas her dad sent a card and some money for us. That went on for years. I once wrote to them and asked if they would see us. I never got an answer."

Marie looked around the boxes. "Have you seen the tape? Oh, there." She pointed toward Callie's foot. Callie nudged it toward her with her shoeless foot.

"Anyway, about ten or twelve years later mom's brother contacted her. We went to see him. They remained in touch with each other for awhile and then, POOF, the contact was broken."

"Why?"

"I don't know. After we were married and you and your cousin were born, mom read in the newspaper that her dad had died. The family never contacted her. A few years later her mom died. After that she received a check for some small amount, to satisfy the estate claim. She donated it to the arthritis foundation. Then two old photo albums of her's arrived. That looked like the end of her knowing her family."

"Just like that. Here's your stuff. Goodbye?"

"It seemed so. Help me move these two boxes nearer to the front door." Both women shoved the boxes across the wooden floor with little kicks. "Your dad should be here."

"Well everyone got together again. I've met grandma's siblings."

"Right. We're sort of together, as a family. Your great grand parents missed out on a lot. So did Sue and I. Funny what unspoken misunderstandings can do. Here's your father."

As Callie and her dad carried boxes to the truck, Marie retrieved the picture of her grandparents from the trash bag. She gazed into the faces that had rejected her in childhood. I don't think I'll ever understand, but I can tell you now that I think you missed a great opportunity to enjoy the lives to two nice people. You even missed out on knowing your greatgrand children. I"m really sorry, for you. I had a good life.

For the second time the picture dropped onto the trash, the lights went out and Marie stepped onto the porch. She locked the door and walked to the truck.

SOUP

Bent over, kneeling on a scrap of old rag rug, deep in thought, Louise did not hear the garden gate scratching open, metal on metal, nor the constrained quiet steps approaching behind her. Her flowers were in need of thoughtful ministration. She scraped the drying soil, knowing the roots were unable to poke through the brick hard clay of thin glaciated ground. Visitors are not the usual thoughts when tending one's flowers.

"Louise. Louise, don't you hear when a body calls you?" said the intruder.

"Oh May." she said, turning with a start, her trowel held in a defensive position. "I wasn't expecting you. Why are you here so early? Nothing wrong? Na...."

"Pish. Nothing's wrong." The folded little figure pulled, with gnarled roots, at the faded plaid shawl she had draped over stooped shoulders. "Just bringing something special. And... looking for a chance to talk and set awhile."

"You're so sweet." she said, reaching up with her twig like hand for assistance. "How's an aching old bitty like me to reward your precious care?"

"Do I ask for rewards?"

The two of them, one arm wrapped around the other, now headed for the back porch of the small frame house. Gently they helped each other to squat on the bottom step. The sounds of nature in the little garden were blending in with the constant drone of voices and machines of the city. A quiet, private spot. May adjusted her dress to hide the patch coming loose, again. A quart size Mason jar was extracted from the brown paper bag. A slight twist and a warm, odorous fog rose from the small bottle.

"That something special? Is for me?"

Nodding an affirmative, May set a margarine tub between them and poured the hot liquid, then took two plastic spoons from her dress pocket.

"Have a care now, It's still pretty hot. You know Louise, this soup isn't possible without your garden."

They both spooned a mouthful from the bowl. Eyes a twinkle they blew the vapor from the spoon. The elixir stung their tongues, hot, with a certain unnamable tang.

"Well how is it that my garden made this soup possible? I only grow a few flowers, no vegetables." Louise said, rolling the still hot soup around her tongue. A drop of yellow liquid snuck out from each corner of May's mouth. It looked like a ventriloquist's dummy's mouth to Louise.

"Tell you when done." May mumbled, tilting her spoon to catch the drop. They both took several more gulps of the delicious hot broth. May licked her spoon and returned it to the depth of her pocket. Louise stretched her legs and her arms out, digging her spoon into the clouds, like a stray cat waking from a peaceful nap in the sun. The cap went back on the bottle, now casting a shadow on the pavement and into the bag. A small bird dropped onto the edge of the garden path, right at their feet.

"Sorry soup's all gone." said May.

"Let's see. You said that I made the soup possible. How?"

May raised her eyebrows and cleared her throat. Casting her eyes down then looking into her friend's questioning gaze and smiled.

"Since I moved in. Let's see. Two months now. You've been given me your newspaper and your magazines when you're done. So I thought, after I read the article about cooking with flowers, in one of your magazines, well I'd surprise you. And I did."

"What did you do? What flowers? You told me you don't know about flowers or gardening."

"I really don't think that's too important. Anyway, I came over to your garden last night, you know it was full moon last night, and I took some of the flowers from back there." her gnarled finger poked through the railing slats. "So you won't notice, I cut real low and a bit here and a bit there. Even took some leaves to thicken it and add some color." She gave a slight, indulgent smile. "It's OK? Isn't it?"

"May, which flowers?" Louise was clutching at her bosom, standing as she spoke. The hint of alarm in her voice May's old ears didn't hear. "Which Flowers? Where?"

On her feet now and turning slightly, May pointed toward the back fence. "The tall pinkish, bell shaped flowers. Those, hanging down."

Fear had begun contouring Louise's face. Instead, an angel's whisper turned all her wrinkles toward heaven. She patted May's arm, avoiding the purple maze of those damnable weak blood vessels beneath her dry skin.

"Oh. It's OK. I don't mind you taking a few flowers or leaves."

She stepped over to her little tool box, reached in and pulled out the plant shears. Cutting a few more of this flower and that, then walked back to the porch, handing the small nosegay to May she said, "Sweety, I suddenly feel very tired and wish to lie down. Do you mind if we visit later?"

"Oh, no. You rest. And thank you for the flowers. They're so pretty. Pretty flowers."

"Thank you for the soup."

May, clutching the flowers between her arthritic twigs, passed through the gate.

"Auf Wiederschen mein Engel, haben zucker traums," came drifting back.

Louise moved through the house, dragging her fingers

over the kitchen table and chair, crossing the living room to sit on the edge of the couch. Staring out the window she saw nothing, not even the warm sun gazing in, nor did she hear anything, the humming city turned silent. She didn't tell May that both of them would soon receive their reward. Very soon. She just couldn't tell this dear sweet woman that her loving gesture, her soup, the flower soup with leaves, had been made with Foxglove. Digitalis.

She lay back on the couch, eyes shut, resting her head on the old doily, the way her Ollie used to do. She could feel her heart speeding up, the way it did with the touch of Ollie's hand when he was asking for her special favors. She spoke softly, "Bless you, May. I could not have picked a nicer way to go."

THE UNIFORM ATTRACTION

Becky always loved a uniform. She saw to it that Harvey Junior wore kid's clothing with a uniform motif. Later she saw that he joined the scouts and the R.O.T.C. and finally the army. He died over there, in his uniform. Now she's taken up with some smart ass guy in a uniform. It was just too much for me, her husband, to take. I followed her to several motels, where she'd register, then call him. Then they'd get together for their sordid little affair. Today, before she could call, I shot her. Then I called 911.

"911. How can I help you?" a tired voice replied.

"Someone's been shot."

"Where? How long ago?"

"Unity Motel, on Logan, unit nine." I said, being very cool.

"An officer will be right there. Who is this? Are you OK?"

"You don't need my name and I'm OK." I hung up.

The blue and red turret lights splashed across several Unity Motel units. A couple came out of unit four, then retreated and closed the door. Units ten and seven pulled aside their curtains to stare. The policeman tugged his utility belt and pants up to nearly reaching his navel and stepped to the door of unit nine. He banged his knuckles below the number.

"Yes?"

"I'm Officer McQueen. Did you report a shooting?"

"I did." I said in a firm voice. "She's dead. Door's open. Come on in."

The officer pulled his gun and pushed open the door. "You, in the room. Step out so I can see you."

I shot at the uniformed figure. Blood immediately stained his blue uniform. Officer McQueen fired several shots at me. As I fell over his body and as we both breathed our last breath, face to face, I mumbled, "Wife stealer."

THE QUIET ONES

He jumped up in front of me, his chair bouncing back and banging loudly off the tile floor, his hands slapping the Formica table top. The florid, freckled face, nostrils flaring, green eyes afire, glared at me, daring any reaction to his behavior. He spun around tugging at the gray and red local high school jacket now locked under the fallen chair. His violent tug ripped it, so it flew over his shoulder to the floor. Never said a word. Never bothered with the chair. Never went after the jacket. All over in, maybe, five, six seconds, from start to finish. All done. Off he went taking big determined steps. Out of the eating area and into the mall, around a corner and out of my life. Holding my food tray and shaking, I looked to the girl sitting at the table he had vacated. She sat absolutely quiet, not speaking, anguish all over face. The tears were coming. This tiny figure neatly dressed, for a kid, hair pulled off her cherub's face, just sat.

She slumped down and watched the young fellow stomping away. The tears came, copious quiet tears. I stood there with my shaking tray and asked the small figure if I could help. I asked twice. When she looked at me and didn't answer, I guessed she just couldn't speak at that moment. I looked over to my wife, shrugged my shoulders and went to sit with her.

"Does she need help?" she asked, as I plopped down into my chair.

"Don't think so."

"She is OK?"

"Pride's hurt, but she's not."

As we ate and talked about the clothing the grandchildren needed for Easter, I caught sight of the young man. He was down a bit in the mall, I could see his reflection coming off a shop window. The girl could not see him. Back and forth he walked, head shaking, arms gesturing. He walked a slow methodical walk, as I have at times of stress. I knew the feeling. He had just made an ass of himself and was trying to justify it or considering how to make amends. Either would cause him to swallow his pride. If the girl was worth it he'd come back: however, he was angry.

I looked to the girl, as I had done quite a few times already. The busgirl had picked up the chair some time ago. She must have asked the girl if she needed or wanted help. She had shaken her head, "No." The busgirl was there again, hanging the retrieved jacket on the back of the chair. She must have again asked if there was anything she could do and again the girl gave a negative shake of her head.

I went for a diet Pepsi refill and cruised passed her table. Her tears had etched dark graffiti designs onto her pink shell. Her napkin was shredded. She had pushed the food around on her plate, but eaten nothing. Her cup was empty. She couldn't bring her face up as the tears continued falling into the growing pattern of darkening, wet abstractions on her sweater. Twenty or so minutes had past since the chair hit the floor and there she sat. The hurt on her face pained me, it must be killing her.

Returning with my drink, I saw she was still alone at the table. I tried to see if his reflection was still in the shop window, but it was nowhere to be seen. He was gone. The reflection was gone. Where had he offed to? Was he taking a toilet break?

Sitting there I thought what is it about a spat that makes people, me too, behave the way we do? Are we so narrow minded about some tiny thing that we can't accept another's viewpoint? Too often we hurt the one we love with foolish, spiteful, vindictive behavior. I'll say this much for the older critics they already know how nice it is to make-up. I've found out too, over the years.

"Finished?"

"Yes." my wife said, pushing her chair back. "Time to go."

Ah, more shopping, my favorite form of exercise. This I thought, I'm too much the coward to say it out loud.

She started to rise. "Whoa. Hold on. Sit for a second more." I took her arm and gently eased her back into her chair. Walking slowly, head down but angled so he could keep his eyes on the girl, the temper tantrum youth was returning. She is worthy. Now if he can say he's sorry, appeal to her for forgiveness, he might return to her good graces. Her face came up and the weakest of smiles arched the corner of her mouth. She knew he was coming. How did she know he was coming? How do some women sense these things? She hadn't turned around to see him approaching, nor had he called out, yet she knew.

The head went down again. Tiny wet shreds of napkin dabbed the tear swollen eyes. He stopped just short of the table. Looking down, he paused and waited for her head to rise, to look up at him once more. As her head came up his fingers gestured. He was deaf, or she was or both were.

I understand some sign language and think he signed, "I'm sorry. I wasn't thinking. I'm sorry."

"I'm sorry too. I love you." her fingers said.

"I love you too." was the quick fingered reply.

No wonder she never spoke to me. Had she understood we had asked if we could help? He reached for her hand, taking care to grab their coats as she got up. They walked, hand in hand out into the mall.

We got up too. Hand in hand we followed their quiet example into the mall.

GETTING RE-ELECTED

I knew it. I knew it. I knew it. Why in the hell didn't I pay attention to my gut feelings? Why? I was looking with hindsight now. Too late! Way too late! Yesterday a Congressman. Today a citizen. Damn!

I wanted to be someone so badly. I saw running for office as a chance to better myself. The party needed a candidate, one with no damning history, a clean record. I had worked for other candidates in the past. So I asked, they talked it over, then blessed and anointed me.

Let's see. As I remember we discussed a platform and getting it out to the voters (schmucks). We would need to cater to the environmentalists, pro and anti abortionists, industry, labor, the graying generation and the baby boomers. Christ, when will the demands to appease stop?

Don't forget the special interest groups. Or the foreign policy people. Or ethnic people. Or the people chipping into your campaign fund. Hell, I even put in a few thousand bucks I borrowed to help. Where does it stop?

Now the running around the state I really enjoyed. I liked meeting people. Talking to them, tasting a few ethnic foods, telling a few stories and jokes. God that was fun!

My opponent is a do-nothing guy in my book. If he challenged my promises, I'd rip into his. If he flubbed a vote getting opportunity, I'd grab it. Never get angry at him but bait him into making mistakes. A game. Just a game. Big boys play this game.

But it was my big mouth that got me elected. Campaign

promises they call them. Promise the stars and the moon. I did,
and the stupes believed me. They pushed me into office and into
D.C. That day I became Congressman Bill Meelator. Not Mr.
Meelator but Congressman Meelator.

Some of the Party's boys in Washington helped me settle in,
then started to ask for concessions here and there. Others wanted
my vote too, on this or that bill. Sure, no problem. A lobbyist
made request to consider this and maybe they could do that. But
no restrictions. I did ask the voters what they might like. As if I
cared. But few answered. I followed the party line on most issues,
voting outside of it on the abortion issue.

Four years later I thought, hell this is a snap. I'll run for
reelection. 'Made some excuses for not keeping my earlier election
promises. I explained to my constituents that as a first time Congressman it was difficult to move things along. But the pot was
boiling and they should put me there to watch it and move it along.
The newspapers back home said I was ineffectual. The voters said,
"Bull shit!". Well I ran again. Those I helped, kicked into the "kit-
ty." Some, wanting help from a putz, did too. I borrowed some
more money. I traveled and talked and "glad handed" all over the
state. Meanwhile the Party whipped up enthusiasm at little rallies,
making them seem bigger and more important. The Party wanted
me back where I could be controlled. Running around the State
was tougher but still worth it. Freebies are fattening but they produce votes.

However; promises don't fill bellies, or pay the rent, or get
put in the bank. My people, the citizens I blew off. Well they blew
me off. If we ever meet, I'd like you to say, "Hello Mr. Meelator,
citizen."

GOOD MORNING

People listening to Margetta and Olaf talking with their heavy English accent, always thought they were peculiar, the way rich people are crazy, eccentric. They spoke of people long dead as if they were alive and socializing with them last night. They had dinner with Maximilian and Carlota, or tea with Albert and Victoria. They didn't argue if you corrected them about dates or events. A smile between them, a private joke, and they never broke away from their rendition of whatever they were talking about.

One intriguing story Margetta told concerned the pregnancy of Carlota by a Belgian Colonel in her husband's army. Margetta spoke of it in hushed tones, fearing Maximilian might discover her indiscretion. Such behavior from a royal princess, if true, might endanger France's position in Mexico. It sounded like Margetta witnessed this happen.

They had their arguments and fought with each other as folks living together do. But the next evening everything was lovey-dovey, no grudges held. Margetta and Olaf didn't do much during the day, lazed around watching TV probably. Their evening ritual of sitting on the porch shortly after twilight was when they spoke to and visited with neighbors. They stayed out for a while, but only as long as the stars were in the sky.

The original investigation into their disappearance is 95% hearsay evidence of their last argument, The last time they were seen or heard, they were overheard by Rachel Coombs. Rachel lives next door and as she says, is the neighborhood snoop and gossip. Detective Mike Dickens was assigned the case and it is from his report we get the following story as Rachel Coombs told him.

"Damn it! Damn it! Damn it!" Olaf was furious. "Margetta, where in the Hell is my screwdriver?" Stepping to the basement stairs he yelled up. "Margetta!" No answer. His mood blackened, he started up the stairs, mumbling curses as he stepped into the empty kitchen. "Oh damn. Where in the hell is that woman?"

Olaf walked into the next room, empty, with the television on. The whir of the sewing machine came from around the corner. A person could watch television from there since it was an L shaped room. Olaf swung his angry frame, pushing a little potbelly before it, into the space Margetta needed to see the program, a P.B.S. special on the transval area.

"Ollie, you're blocking my view."

"And you're stopping me from my project. Where is my screwdriver?" he huffed. "Didn't I tell you? DON'T TOUCH MY TOOLS!" His words were forced through clenched teeth, a bit of spittle dropped from his lips as he bit off each word. "I've got to repair those chests and can't find the tools to get it done, because you take them and never return them."

Margetta's mouth popped open and remained open during his tirade. She looked with disgust at the man she had spent years with, wondering if he'd ever grow up.

"The sewing machine was loose. Remember?" She tapped the edge of her machine. "Remember? I told you yesterday. You brought the screwdriver up last night and tightened it."

"I don't remember."

"You did." She turned slightly and pointed to the hutch. "There it is. Where you left it." Her yellow teeth showed a slice in her face, a condescending smile.

Olaf reached for it. "You should've made me take it back down stairs right away. You know tools can get lost or misplaced." He couldn't look her in the face. Starting for the basement he mumbled. "You took tools before and didn't put them back."

"Not lately. And stop with the cursing and temper tantrums."

The basement echoed his stomping on the steps, not the quieter expletives. Tossing the screwdriver on the workbench, it bounced and fell to the floor. Olaf smacked his head on the lid of the chest as he bent to retrieve it.

"Son of a bitch!" Loud and clear the words ran through the dirt covered basement, up the stairs, through the kitchen, finally blocking out the voice on the TV. Margetta rolled her eyes. A few more times Olaf damned the chest, the lid, the screwdriver and everything else. It was just too much, he couldn't contain himself. The flood gates of rage opened and he began throwing things, damning things and getting out of control.

Margetta called from the top of the stairs. "What's going on?"

"Mind your own damn business. Leave me alone."

"You're going to hurt yourself. Stop it! Stop it right now!"

Olaf continued cussing, less loudly and still slamming things about. Margetta opened a kitchen drawer and took out an apron, tying it around her slender waist as she descend the basement stairs.

"Why are you coming down here? To bother me?"

"To put the sewing I finished in my chest." She was perplexed by the clutter on the floor but thought better than say a word. She picked up a tool, or a whatever, and set it on the workbench as she passed.

Olaf sweep it to the floor. "Leave my things alone."

She spun about and glared. "What is your problem? We go along for years and years, centuries, no big deal. Suddenly everything is wrong. And, if you please, my fault. Well piss on you mister. I'm not about to have you dump on me. You open your snaggled tooth mouth again and..."

"Did you come down here and move the boards I had next to the shelves?"

Like that, the subject was changed. He was going to change the subject and blame her for something else. She would be wrong again. The thought raced through Margetta's mind. She threw up her arms, kicked at the pile of dirt on the floor and hauled herself back up to the kitchen. Olaf followed.

"Come up to find your boards? Do you see any boards?" Tears welled up in her eyes, shinning but not spilling onto her cheeks. "You stop blaming me and shouting and cursing. I have feelings." Her head fell to her bosom, her tears dropped to the floor. Sobbing choked her words. "Leave me alone."

"I heard that. You want to be alone?" Olaf grabbed his coat. "You're alone." He started through the back door. "I'll get my own meal tonight, thank you. You? You can do as you damn well please." The slammed door shook the walls and rattle the dishes, his crunching steps on the gravel driveway faded.

Margetta Gufenson fumed as she turned toward the back of their dingy house. Year after year their arguments seldom changed. Always his bitching about the way she did this or she did that. My God, he knew she wasn't perfect when he choose her. When he storms out, he always leaves the other women and comes back to her. She didn't like that either. Well, she could understand some of it, but there were a few things she worried about. There were times she thought her simple minded Olaf would really leave her.

Margetta Gufenson, born into a financially comfortable Romanian banking family, schooled at Budapest's finest, the Trans/ Gothic School for Young Ladies, spoke four languages, interested in social reform issues for woman and, unfortunately, afraid to make her own decisions. Well, not all decisions, she had picked Olaf from the men that chased after her. Some times she regretted that choice, like now.

The argument began the same way, she didn't put things

back where they belonged. That is, where Olaf puts them. Last time it had been, what, the heating pad? Yeah, the heating pad. Cripes, winter didn't start 'til next month and already he was complaining about the cold. She was cold and hungry too. She would wait, perhaps he'd be back in a few minutes. However, the longer she waited, the angrier she became.

"Well, la-dee-da-da. I'll fix his wagon. I'm sick and tired of the inconsiderate S.O.B." Down the basement steps her tiny feet went, the twinkle in her eyes sent sparks through the semi-darkness. "What was it old Doc Swenson harped on about anger? Beat the hell out of it. Beat a rug. Make bread, knead and reknead. Just do something physical to burn off the anger." Her eyes scanned the mess all about her. The boards, his damn boards were right there, out in the open. A blind bat could have seen them.

Up through the heating ducts came Snow White's, Whistle While You Work. When the whistling stopped, Margetta's voice cooed, "Nails where are you?" She pounded a hammer on the boards and chests as she looked. Her glasses slid down her nose as her head bobbed and weaved like a boxer looking for an opening punch. "Where does that miserable inconsiderate keep the nails?" Bang, bang, bang the hammer tattooed. "Ahhhhh." Her eyes lit on a shelf of assorted cans. "In there?"

She poured the nails all over the bench top. She placed a board over Olaf's chest and drove nails through it. Board after board she nailed helter-skelter to each other and if the nail bent she pounded it flat. When she finished it was a work of art, A Miro. A Calder. A Picasso. Finished it was nothing, she pushed it off the back of the workbench into the shadows of cans, shelves and cupboards. Back upstarts Margetta headed out the door, along the crunching driveway she tossed the hammer into the garbage can. She was eating out.

In time the kitchen door opened, the lights were still on but the house was quiet. "I'm home." Olaf's call was unanswered. "Hey! Anybody here?" The tone was a bit friendlier. No answer.

Olaf walked through the house calling several times. No answer. The house was empty.

It didn't take long his anger began fomenting, breathing became heavier and he blew his cool again. Screaming curses accompanied his marionette contortion as he bolted down the stairs. "Oh I'll fix her. Bet on it." Grabbing the electric drill he changed the bit, then dumped a large jar of assorted woodscrews on the bench, not noticing the bench was cleared of his stuff. He saw only Margetta's chest filled with her things. ZZZZHH buzzed the drill and screw after screw sealed the damn box shut from every direction. He even screwed the chest to the workbench.

The faintest hint of morning pink touched the eastern horizon as Margetta walked into the kitchen. She knew she was late, getting her own meal had taken more time than it did years ago. Olaf heard her scuffling across the kitchen floor. He'd run up and bring her down to see his handiwork, but when he looked at it he realized his stupid tantrum was going to hurt the woman he truely loved. He ran toward the stairs as Margetta started down.

"Might as well stay down here, it'll be daylight soon." Margetta said, giving Olaf a smile.

"I know." His smile took a bit of effort. "I love you, really love you."

"Me too."

Olaf turned toward the workbench. "Hurry. I did something dumb. 'Gotta fix it fast."

Margette, almost calmly replied. "So did I. The worst thing possible."

The two of them held hands and surveyed their angry accomplishment. Words failed them as both felt the rays of sunlight slide across them. In and instant their bodies painlessly began to decay, drifting down over their chest which in turn began to turn to dust. Centuries of devotion to each other ending for two vampires that had a stupid quarrel.

Detective Mike Dickens paper clipped a small note to his

report. "I don't believe in this vampire stuff, but just the same, I'm glad someone torched their house the night we found the dirt and "caskets" in the basement. I won't have to chase after any of this. I did find out from a history prof, Carlota did have a baby by some soldier."

DON'T WANNA

February 16, 1940

"Pauly, your daddy and I have made arrangements for you to attend a summer camp this year."

Ten year old Pauly wrinkling his pouty face said, "I don't want to go to a summer camp."

Momma's smile became a frown, "And why not?"

"I don't want to. I don't want to." The spoiled, belligerent child hollered rapidly reinforcing his words by folding his arms and tensing his juvenile muscles. "Why are you sending me away?"

"No, no. Oh, Pauly, no." came Momma's reassuring voice. "Momma isn't sending you away. I love you. Summer camp is a place to have fun. Cousin Frankie went last year, remember?"

"He didn't like summer camp." Pauly shot back. "He told me some kids jumped him, beat him up and threw him into the lake. They made him do lottsa things he didn't want to do." Pauly's mind went racing through his small memory bank looking for another unpleasant thing to mention. His face screwed up, "And they make you eat dirty food, dropped in the fire."

"Pauly, that's not true. Aunt May told me Frankie is looking forward to going to summer camp again this year. He must like it." Momma's whining voice continued. Placing her hand on her bosom, taking a deep breath, smiling, "You'll like it. Honest. Please try, for me."

"No." Pauly's determine posture and peevish voice caused Momma to swallow her smile. Wrapping her arms around the monster she created and continued creating. "OK, no summer camp. OK?"

"OK." Pauly said. Momma should have seen the devilish smirk delivered behind her back. She might have, just might have, swatted Pauly's butt and sent him off to summer camp.

"Honey, I've changed my mind. I want Pauly to stay home this summer."

Christmas, 1957

"We honeymoon on a cruise," chirped Marie, snuggling into Pauly's shoulder. "A week sailing in the Caribbean, just the two of us."

"Nah. No cruise. I don't like the idea and I can't swim if the boat sinks." Pauly didn't look at Marie, but he felt her body tensing against his. "Nope to a honeymoon cruise."

"Please. For me?" in a voice dripping golden honey. Her hands caressing his soft body, trying to weddle a concession from him. "Cruises are a lotta fun."

"Not for me. No cruise." Pauly said , lifting Marie's head from his chest. Holding her face between his stubby fingered hands and looking into her moist brown eyes. "No."

Cold, clear ice crystals started forming between them at that moment. Chinks and cracks, developing in their relationship. Marie soon cut through love's blind bonds and facing reality, returned his ring. The wedding never happened, they drifted along for awhile then alone, in separate directions. Pauly had it his way, again

June 10, 1969

"You may kiss the bride." echoed in the judge's small, simple City Hall office. "Becky. Pauly. I wish you the best of everything in the years to come." the judge said, as they were ushered out the side door into a City Hall corridor. The wedding had been a spur of the moment thing suggested by the parsimonious Becky. Pauly agreed. Nothing fancy, no relatives or banquet, a plain simple ceremony. The ceremony lasted less than five minutes. Would the marriage last longer, than the fourteen weeks they had known each other?

Becky, plain and hardworking, saved and planned vacations and trips for the two of them. Mostly visits to her brother or sister or an overnight with acquaintances or an old school friend. She planned, but each year they stayed home. One year they nearly went to Colonial Williamsburg, their wedding anniversary fell that week-end. Pauly found an excuse to cancel the trip, the dog was sick. You can't leave a sick pooch, can you?

Pleading with Pauly to leave the dog with the vet and complete their anniversary plans didn't work. It became an open sore in their live. It festered and grew, becoming the issue of every domestic quarrel, every decision. Neither wishing to separate or encounter the cost of a divorce. They soon slept in different rooms. Pauly pushing himself, working longer hours, eating out and spending his time in the house with his dog and the only toy he ever whined for, a Lionel train set now safely ensconced in the basement.

Becky began a catering business, that grew quickly with her astute business acumen. She was soon traveling about, locally, with business luncheons and company dinners. Overnighters, for international company functions, had her traveling cheaply, a business expense. She and Pauly seldom saw each other and talked on the phone, only when necessary. One historic nine day period, not a word passed between them. They were husband and wife in name only.

September 11, 1989.

Becky's obituary occupied the business section of the newspaper. It mentioned in lieu of flowers a donation to the Cancer Foundation. The blurb mentioned a marriage. She had no living relatives. Pauly found out Becky had died when an attorney called. He was inquiring if Pauly would be making funeral arrangements? No, the attorney should make arrangements. He mentioned to Pauly that as sole heir he would inherit a small fortune. Pauly requested the money be placed in the bank. He then forgot about it.

February 5, 2002

Judge Shine read the State's claim to Pauly's estate. Pauly had died two years before, leaving no will, or known heirs. His attorney, acting for Pauly, had paid off his debtors. A claim had been filed by a supposed offspring, but discounted after an investigation. The judge ruled for the state. The following day the newspaper headlines were, "State Claims 2.7 Million Unclaimed Estate"

Pauly had the time and wherewithal for everything. He choose not to spend his money or enjoy life, in the end he had gone nowhere and had done nothing.

CELL PHONE

When it's raining, standing under the Marshall Field's clock at State and Randolph in Chicago's loop is as uncomfortable as standing in the rain nearly anywhere else. But Louis had told him to wait there and he would be picked up at one thirty. Just be on time and wait, so he waited, cold, wet and pissed at Louis.

Lester saw another driver, cell phone to his ear, nearly knock down a pedestrian with a cell phone to her ear. They exchanged words and fingers flew up and out. Lester thought they were both stupid. Almost every time the traffic light changed, among the waiting drivers or pedestrians, a cell phone conversation was conducted. Lester imagined himself having a cell phone, he could stand inside the store entrance and talk to Louis until he saw the car or Louis told him he was approaching. Beat catching pneumonia.

Louis arrived and they drove to the Rosemont Arena. He was surprising Lester, a dyed in the wool devoted fan of Elvis, to an Elvis impersonator show. Lester pleased by his brother's treat dug into his nearly empty pocket. He had enough to buy each of them a Special CD Concert Set of Elvis songs sung by the impersonator.

"I didn't know you had a CD player Lester." Louis commented as they entered the men's room.

"I don't have a CD player."

Louis looked in disbelief and remembered this was his brother. "You bought CD's and you don't have a CD player?"

"Well maybe some day I can get one." Lester stammered.

"Maybe some day you'll get a brain too."

The fellow at the sink spilled his souvenirs and bent over to scoop them up. Lester saw his cell phone setting on the edge of the sink. The passing hawk swooped off with the mouse. Lester had a cell phone. Louis didn't like Lester stealing things, so Lester said nothing. He'd surprise Louis later.

The rain had stopped and Lester asked to be dropped off at Marshall Field's. No sooner had Louis drove off when Lester called him on the cell phone.

"Hi Louis, it's me. Lester."

"Lester?"

"Un huh. The guy you just dropped off. Your brother."

"How did you... Why are you calling?"

"To say thanks for today." said Lester. "I'm going over to eat and thought I'd say thanks first."

With the phone to his ear, Lester stepped from the curb. He distinctly heard three horns and a woman's scream, as the Marshall Field clock spun around building outlines and the dark cloudy sky. He saw the dancing, multicolored fragments of the Loop's lights. He even saw the purloined cell phone flying off on an unknown migratory flight path. The brightest light he recognized as a police badge, inches from the end of his hooked nose.

"You hurt?" asked the badge.

Not sure why a badge or anyone was asking him if he was hurt, or if they were asking him, Lester didn't respond. His vision cleared a little, enough to see a hand giving the badge a shattered cell phone and hear, "This is his. Using it when he got hit." Things got fuzzy and dark.

As the haze cleared Lester focused on the bright object at the end of his nose, a stethoscope. He wondered why. Where was he? He found out where, when a pleasant, but reprimanding voice said. "You're in the Stronger Hospital. You are not hurt too bad. That was stupid walking into moving traffic talking on a cell phone, you coulda got killed. Now, what's your name?"

NEWSPAPER CLIPPING

From the Chicago Tribune News Service, November 3, 2000, to Beijing, China To Kyle Owen. Your services are terminated today. Charges by staff employee, Rose Dumont, have been filed against you in court today. Butler: foreign serv. Ed.

To Chgo. Trib foreign service Ed. Nov.4, 2000 from Beijing, China. "Butler, keep me on. The biggest story in history is breaking. Urge you to beat others with this release." Owen

Front page this. The Tinder Ltd. mining camp in Chuyen, on the southern edge of the Gobi Desert, claims they have found the smallest dinosaur on record. Will Chase, an American geologist, assisting the mining company said, "This [the find] will change the scientific history of the world."

Chase found the 2.8 mm long complete jawbone attached to the inside of a section of fossil eggshell, only bony section found, embedded in rock formed 180,000 years after the dinosaurs became extinct. According to Chase the advanced development indicated the creature would hatch soon. It's teeth are similar to raptors found world wide. It is Chase's opinion this small size and development indicates the dinosaur's maximum growth would be six to eight inches. He has dubbed the creature, Gladii paulosarus, meaning "small swords." Thad Tinder, CEO and owner of Tinder Industries, Ltd., will surely add it to his private collection. China is inviting eminent paleontologists of the world to Chuyen to confirm this latest discovery. Digging continues at the site for more tiny dinosaur bones. Keep me, Kyle

      Nov. 6, 2000. The Chicago Tribune and its TV station WGN apologizes for the China fossil hoax played on its readers by a disgruntled ex-employee. Further details will be published as the story unfolds in court.

THE CHRISTENING OF BONEHEAD McGEE

The news of Bonehead McGee's death brought smiles to the old timers' faces. They knew him and remembered how Bonehead got his nickname. Many, as they gathered about talking, questioned how he had die. They were disappointed that he died in bed and not by some foolishness, which was Bonehead's trademark.

Arriving in the small fishing town, after losing three fingers and his job in the lumber camp, McGee looked up his uncle and got a job on his boat. He lost his fingers when they were dragged across a saw he had just sharpened. This wouldn't interfere with working the lobster pots. Besides, his uncle really needed a cheaply paid hand aboard his boat. Baiting lobster pots is a smelly dirty job, many people looked down on it, but it is a very necessary job.

The first day, before going out to sea, rain began moving into the area. McGee was told by his uncle to batten down the hatch and chop bait for the pots. The man figuring a fool could do two chores without supervision, headed into his shanty for a drink or two. He figured wrong.

McGee didn't understand the basics concerning the closing of hatches. After struggling a bit, without success, he attempt to cover the hold with a piece of canvas. The wind would have none of this. Spotting a gap beneath the pier, he untied one end of the boat and shoved the boat with its open hatch out of the rain. There was no room for him, so he took the bucket of herring scraps onto the dock under a bit of shelter and began cutting bait.

A booming thunder clap wouldn't drown out his uncle's

shouted curses. McGee ran around the shanty, staring back at the dancing, arm swinging, cursing man. Dozens of people from sheds, bars and boats came out in the rain, shouting and roaring with laughter. First his uncle pointed at McGee, then below the pier and back to McGee.

"Get here, you bonehead ass. Get here and see what you have done."

Wishing to flee, but drawn by the hypnotic hand movements of his uncle, McGee slowly approached the dock edge. Drawn upward by the incoming tide his uncle's boat, had risen smashing its running lights and wheelhouse. Yet, McGee always remembered, the boat's hold had remained dry, since that part of the boat was under the pier.

The next morning, still alive and still employed by his uncle, the two men began to clear away the shattered boards and electrical wiring. His uncle threw the boards up on the dock and McGee, thinking the boards came close to hitting him danced about. Collecting wood, he dropped the pieces into a metal drum, now burning intensely. He collected metal and wire dropping them into a wooden box to sell as scrap.

"Enough." said his uncle mounting the dock and accosting the sweating McGee. "I'm taking the truck to the city. We need new lumber, paint, wire and lights. An' a new wheel." He looked at the boat. "And more. I want the deck cleaned off. Burn every scrap. Dump the ashes and take care doing it."

They nodded to each order. Never said a word.

Scanning the sunless sky, he added to the orders already given. "Looks like more rain coming. Get the hold covered. The hole where the wheelhouse was too. Mind you no nonsense. Hear?" He waited.

"Yes sir. I hear. Be gone long?" asked McGee.

"It's three hours one way. Be back before dark. We'll eat, then unload the truck. If it's light enough." Walking away, he looked over his shoulder. "Get to work!"

The rains started about twenty minutes later. The canvas McGee had stretched across the hole lifted with the breeze. Trying to grasp it, he bumped into the drum with the burning wood, upsetting it into the water and on part of the dock. Quickly he swept the embers off the dock, averting a calamity for sure. Now looking about, he couldn't find the tarp. The rains came pouring down, pooling in the bottom of the boat and he had lost the canvas.

McGee knew he could tie the boat safely under the dock now. There was nothing on the deck to get ripped off or broken. He maneuvered his uncle's boat between two pilings under the dock, tying it with knots no sailor ever saw. Both ends were snug to the pilings. He climbed back on the dock and proceeded to look for another drum.

McGee didn't hear the truck return. He had finished his work and fallen asleep just inside the shanty. He awoke to loud deafening curses. Everyone, even the souls in the little cemetery heard them. McGee couldn't understand the screaming stomping man, but approached him carefully. He knew the boat was safe and dry, under the dock. Maybe his uncle hadn't seen it.

"I put the boat under the dock when the rain started. It's safe. Even if the tide comes back, the top stuff is gone and the boat is safe. Honest. Look!" McGee yelled.

McGee started down the ladder, stopped and felt his heart trying to exit through his throat. His feet were wet. Secured to the pilings were two funny knots. Between the ropes was the boat, under a foot of tidal water. Securely tied the boat hadn't risen with the incoming tide, instead the water crept up and over the gunwales, into the hold and technically sank it.

Bonehead was christened then and there, while clinging to the ladder.

Bonehead stayed in town, even lived with his uncle. He never boarded another boat. Didn't even try to get work aboard a boat. He cut bait in the bait shop just off the pier. People, wandering in, read the article in the fading news clipping and looked at the two pictures of a battered boat hanging under the pier while McGee filled their bait buckets. Sometimes he'd answer their questions, but not always.

MILLIONAIRE

"Please welcome Mike Quiller, from Round Lake Beach, Illinois" The audience roared its approval. The hostess of the TV super show shook hands with the slight young man. "Welcome to Who Wants to be a Millionaire." She pointed toward a chair, "Please be seated."

Mike climbed into the chair, his greeting lost in the noise of the studio crowd.

"So, Mike, you're from Round Lake Beach, Illinois. Is that near Chicago?'

His fingers caressed the arm of the chair. "North of Chicago. Right. Not many people know that."

"Now we know that. And you seem to know quite a bit too."

"I know a lot of things." he said, his voice indicating no trace of discomfort or fear, as so many contestants did sitting in that chair. "I came to win a million dollars."

"Well. Hey. Let's get on with it. The audience is with you." The audience applauded and shouted their loud approval to the comment. "You know the rules? And you have three lifelines. 50/50, audience, and a phone call."

"Know the rules. Don't think I'll need the lifelines."

"Really?" Meredith looked quizzically at Mike. "Ready?"

The blue lights streamed out across the studio and down to the floor. Both looked at the question and possible answers on their monitors.

"What might be commonly worn in a women's hair? A)

safety pin, B) bobby pin, C) sculpin, D) bowling pin."

"That's a dumb question. B of course."

Meredith smiled. "Correct. You have one hundred dollars." She looked about the studio. "A sculpin?" Her voice sought an answer.

"That's a bottom living fresh water fish." Mike interjected. "Quite common."

"Oh. Thank you. Fish. But you said B) bobby pin. Right?'

"You have a hundred dollars. Let's go for two hundred. From which country did Columbus sail on his first voyage of discovery? A) Spain, B) Portugal, C) England, D) Italy"

"Columbus was born in Genoa, Italy and shipwrecked in Portugal. He sent his brother to Henry the seventh of England to get money. He sailed from Spain, August 3rd, 1492. A Spain, final answer."

A look of bewildered amusement accompanied Meredith's smile. "My, my. That's a lot of information about Christopher Columbus. Did you study his life for some reason, like a school book report?'

"I read a lot." A smug smile wrinkled his face. "It was an easy question."

"You're right for $200. On to three hundred."

Both looked to their monitors, as Meredith read aloud, Mike moaned disapproval.

"In the chemical equation, NaCl, what element is represented by Cl? A) Carbon, B) Chlorine, C) Calcium or D) Cadmium."

Mike slouched in his chair and uttered a cry of disgust. "These are so simple. Is there any chance of skipping to the big money questions? The million dollar one?"

"Mike you said you knew the rules. We build up to the million. No way we're skipping any questions."

"OK. Yeah. It's a stupid, silly question anyway. B Chlorine. Final."

"Come on Mike. Play the game. Everyone is on your side. Right audience?"

Applause, whistles and cheers echoed through the large room.

"See?"

"OK. Keep going."

"For five hundred." Meredith cleared her throat. "Which of the following common composite flowers is edible A) rose, B) dandelion, C) Iris, D) violet."

Mike's head dropped to his chest and moved back and forth. He muttered, "Another stupid question."

There was a audience moan and a disapproving glance from Meredith that Mike didn't see.

An audible sigh preceded Mike's answer. "Oh, well. B) dandelion. They're all edible. The dandelion is the only composite. B) final."

"Lots of information again. Probably all correct."

"Not probably. All correct."

"OK. All correct. B) is the correct answer. On to a thousand."

"Finally."

"Right after this break."

The studio came buzzing to life. Someone stepped up to adjust Meredith's make-up. The floor manger took her position, stop watch in hand. Some one else began speaking to Mike quietly. Mike's head bobbed affirmatively several times. The studio audience cluttered the air with murmuring. A signal was given and the studio monitors showed the program restarted.

"So Mike, your work is not listed. What do you do for a living? She considered asking, "Besides being a jerk?" but didn't.

"I don't work. No job. I do what I want. Read a lot and just do what I want to do," He rubbed his fingernails across his lapel and gave Meredith a knowing smile.

"That makes paying your bills rather difficult doesn't it?"

He grinned, "I live at home. With my mother."

"Oh. No money problems then. Lucky you."

"Well she works. She's a music teacher."

"You have it made, sort of, haven't you? Ready for the $1,000 question?"

"OK."

The music and blue lights filled the studio. The polite applause didn't ring true.

"The Rosetta Stone was discovered by which country? A) Italy, B) Egypt, C) France, D) Germany."

"For some people this could require a lot of thinking. The question doesn't ask where it was found. In Egypt."

The camera zoomed in on Meredith watching Mike with a perplexed look. Her finger slid along her chin 'til it stopped and danced on her lower lip. She focused on Mike's face.

"Greek is one of he languages on the Rosetta Stone. Italy had nothing to do with the Rosetta Stone. Never did. Napoleon's army was fighting in Egypt at the time. So the question of which country found the Rosetta Stone would need the correct answer, C France."

"You're amazing. That your final answer?"

"Final answer."

"I'll not make us wait. Correct, for one thousand dollars."

The audience applause wasn't as enthusiastic as usual and died quickly.

"For $2,000." She read from the monitor.

The music sounded, the lights twinkled across the floor. There was polite applause from the audience. Oddly, both Meredith and Mike were seen licking their lips and adjusting their bodies in their chair. The pale blue studio lights glistened in their eyes.

"What Olympic figure skater became a movie star in the 1930's. A) Dick Button, B) Bill Tilton, C) Sonja Henie or D) Herman Brix?"

"One of my mother's favorite movie stars. I've never seen her movies. I don't think I have. Anyway, C) final answer."

"You never saw Sonja Henie skate? Wow. She was good. And you're right. Let's go for four thousand."

"Of course I'm right. I don't expect to give wrong answers." He grimaced and looked toward someone standing near the camera. "Oops."

"Something wrong Mike?"

"No. No, nothing is wrong."

"Shall we continue for $4,000?"

"Certainly." Mike returned his attention to Meredith.

"Which of following breed of dog is bred for lion hunting? A) Istrian Hound, B) Pharaoh Hound, C) Rhodesian Ridgeback or D) Wachtelhund."

Mike shook his head and stared upward. "It's not your fault Meredith, I know that. But some of these questions are dumb, really dumb."

"Oh, come on Mike. This isn't an easy question."

"Sure it is. A dog bred for Lion hunting. Lions live in Africa. Rhodesia is in Africa. Ergo, C Rhodesian Ridgeback is the correct final answer."

"Couldn't one of the others be lion hunters?"

"Nope. Wachtel is German for, let me see, for quail. Makes it a bird dog. Pharaoh Hound is a trick to catch the unwary. In ancient Egypt they were used to chase down small game. And isn't the Istrian Hound a European dog?"

A few boos came from the audience.

"You can stop that. Mike I don't know if the Istrian is European. Is C) your final answer?'

"Of course. Final"

Meredith pressed her hand to her head set. "We have a technical problem. We'll take a commercial break and be right back. I hope."

Meredith and Mike were quickly surrounded by several

people. The audience let loose with a few derisive catcalls and loud whistles. The gathered group soon broke up. Meredith said something and offered an outstretched hand. Mike shook it.

The camera refocused on Meredith. "Shall we continue Mike?"

"Continue."

"For $8,000 and you still have all of your lifelines."

Mike had no trouble answering that the author of Ben Hur, Lew Wallace, had been governor of Indiana. And for $16,000 that the Periodic Table of Elements was developed by Maleeveian. The answers were given matter of factually and Meredith winced as she saw the direction Mike was headed. The audience had turned on him, shouting out their disapproval.

"On your way to $32,000. A correct answer here and you can't leave here with less than $32,000. Ready?"

"Let's"

"Let's hear it for Mike." A few people clapped. An embarrassment to all.

"On the TV children's show, Arthur, what kind of animal is Arthur? A) aardvark, B) rabbit, C) cat, D) mouse." She looked at Mike, not a trace of knowing on her face.

No one heard the groan, but the pained look on his face told a story. Mike didn't have an answer. Many smiles lit the darkened area surrounding the center stage. Everyone heard one spectator, in a sotto voca tone, "Gottcha." A few giggled.

"Mike."

Barely loud enough for Meredith to hear Mike said, "I got a little problem. I don't watch TV much. Especially children's shows. Except I watch this show." He shrugged. "I want to poll the audience."

"Really Mike? Poll the audience?"

The audience reacted with shouts and whistles. Meredith waited politely, a benign smile played about the corners of her mouth.

"Come on guys, show some support. Mike needs your help. Punch in your votes." Quickly the results flashed on the screen. "Ouch. Mike not too much help here. The audience gives 52% to A, 20% for B, 18% for C and D gets 20% too."

"I know it's best to go with the audience. They're usually honest. A) final answer."

"Oh Mike, they're all honest. They really want you to win. Thank them for helping you get the right answer." She waved her hands in a grand circle.

Enthusiasm filled the domed room with assorted signs of approval.

A mumbled thanks and weak wave acknowledged Mike's acceptance of their help.

"On to sixty-four thousand dollars." Mike got the correct answer that the tallest plant in the world is a form of kelp. For the $125 thousand question, Mike opted for 50/50 then eliminated one on the basis of the word's root structure, correctly guessed the answer. It didn't shake him up. A few applauded his gutsy chance.

"Half million on this question. In 1953, which State had to ratify it's constitution, thereby becoming, legally, the 48th state. A) Indiana, B) Arizona, C) South Dakota, D) Ohio."

"This would appear to be a difficult question. It's not. If you read books about strange things happening or unusual facts, which I do, it's easy. The guy that wrote it was trying to be tricky. For half a million the correct answer is Ohio. D) my final answer."

"Mike, I am amazed at your behavior and by your intelligence. I usually say who's correct. But you are correct. Ohio, for half a million."

"I knew I was. I told you, I came to get a million dollars."

Commercials filled the studio screens and people talked in hushed expectations. Some wanted Mike to win, others to lose. Some stage hands were making side bets and the stage manager wished the clock would move faster and get Mike out of his hair. Meredith didn't show her feelings either way. Mike sat, relaxed and confident, a slight smirk on his face.

"4, 3, 2, 1"

Meredith sat back in her chair. "Nervous Mike?"

"Nope."

"I am. This is it folks. A million dollar question. And Mike, you still have a lifeline." With a gracious smile, she leaned forward and offered a high five. "For luck."

"For luck? OK. I'm ready."

"At the start of George Gershwin's, Rhapsody in Blue, what musical instrument plays a solo? A) piano, B) trumpet, C) clarinet, D) tympani"

Mike clenched his fist, "Damn." He bit on his lip. "A music question. My least loved subject matter."

"But Mike, you said your mother was a music teacher."

"Yeah, I did. But when I was little, she tried to teach me and I resisted. We fought about it. I hate this stuff. I really hate it."

"You have a lifeline left. Want to call someone? Your mom?"

"Un huh. I'll use my lifeline. I'll call my mother. She isn't going to like this." He rubbed his chin. "Call her. Her name is Louise."

"OK. Our friends at A T and T, we're calling Mike's mother, Louise."

The phone rang, Mike frowned, Meredith waited blank faced and the audience sat quietly. It rang again.

"Hello."

"Louise?"

"Yes."

"This is Meredith. I'm here with Mike and he needs your help."

"My help? Well, OK."

"Louise, Mike is going for one million dollars."

Gasp. "A million. Really? A million dollars?"

"That's right. Will you help him?"

"Yes. A million dollar is a lot of money."

"It is. Here's Mike. Mike you have thirty seconds. Starting now."

Mike stopped fidgeting with his finger nails. "Mother, here's the question. 'At the start of George Gershwin's, Rhapsody in Blue...'"

"Oh. A music question."

"Mother, just listen to the question. 'At the start of George Gershwin's, Rhapsody in Blue, what musical instrument plays a solo? A) piano, B) trumpet, C) clarinet D) tympani."

A silent pause.

"Mother, what's the answer?'

"Oh. That's it? That's the whole question?"

"Fifteen seconds mother. Fourteen."

"Well Michael. If you had listened when..."

"Mother." The panicy voice loudly interrupted. "Seven seconds."

"... you would have known that the answer...", his mother continued. Pause. "... a."

Three rapid beeps and a buzz, the connection was broken. Mike was cut from his lifeline. He pushed his hand hard on his forehead, his eyes rolled upward. Meredith looked quizzically at a face wreathed in perplexed anger. Not a sound. Not a single sound. Somewhere someone snapped their fingers.

"Mike. Mike. You OK? You don't have to answer. You can quit with what you have. A half millioin dollars."

"I know. But she said A. Just before the click, she said A. Didn't she say A?" There was a plea for some acknowledgment. "I'm sure she said A.'

"Yes."

"I came for a million." He hesitated. "I'm going to say

A."

"Final answer?" spoken softly by the hostess.

"Final answer?"

A long, unexpected pause. The monitor blinked and blinked again.

"Meredith, am I right?" Mike's face asked in silence.

The monitor flashed C) clarinet.

"She said A) piano. I know that's what she said A."

"Sorry Mike. She may have been saying a clarinet, not A) piano. Sorry."

Meredith handed Mike a check for $32, 000 and gave him a hug, he didn't return.

Music and lights. The hushed studio came back to life.

"Our next guest is..."

MODEL

The class focused on the model as she stepped onto the platform, dropped her robe and struck a nude pose.

"Thirty seconds." the instructor announced.

To the model he said, "I expected your mother."

"She wasn't feeling well. So I took her place, Daddy."

WHO ARE YOU?

I never liked manufacture's names on clothing, especially on tee shirts. Message shirts? Depends. Is the message blatant advertising with name and logo? 'No like. Just a logo? OK. A non-commercial message? An offensive message or logo, "The Bird", or American flag abuse. This is not for me.

Today's T-shirt read, S _ _ _. Not punctuated or high-lighted. Just white letters in a black square on a white T-shirt. The shirt was probably a XXX large, covering a hulk of humanity. As we passed, I checked the back of his shirt. Nada.

How do you convey to this walking brick wall, that his taste in clothing wouldn't make the worst dressed list if the wearer were the only candidate? Any comment, verbal or eye contact, might start trouble. Perhaps not. Sued? Well we are a nation of suers and he does have freedom of speech. Of course I don't have the same freedom. Ask any lawyer.

Can I explain this use of a socially unacceptable word to my granddaughter, as it walks toward us? I can't punish her for reading the word. Nor can I ignore what it says. It is a proper word and has a proper use. But here? Sorry, not in my book.

What does S _ _ _ say to the viewer? Is this his opinion of me? Of mankind? His political views? His life? Himself? What makes his inference important enough to broadcast it so boldly? Why should I, or any one else, accept or consider his view of life? It wasn't ask for.

Reflect on this, we conclude this is an opinion of himself. I can acknowledge that. Who would know better. Why is self esteem so low? Were there mitigating factors in his life to create such self abuse? I don't know or care. Is he the S _ _ _ of his proclamation? Wear the T-shirt and you become what you say you are.

TRAFFIC COURT

"Malcolm Burns."   called the deep voiced bailiff. "Burns."

"Here." a tired voice called out and rose from the bench before the judge.

The judge cocked his forefinger for the man to approach the desk. "Is the officer here?" the judge asked.

"Yes, sir." Officer Ostrowski, stepped to the desk and flipped his ticketbook open.

"Mr. Burns, do you know why you are here?"

"I was given a ticket by this officer, but I didn't..."

"Please, Mr. Burns. I'll ask the officer to read the charges. Then, I'll get your story."

Mr. Burns' head bowed. "OK, sir."

"Your Honor, I clocked Mr. Burns going 64 miles an hour in a 40 mile an hour zone. I pulled him over and gave him a citation for speeding and reckless driving since it was raining and he was endangering other drivers."

"Your Honor. Sir. I wa..."

"Mr. Burns, I asked you to wait. Please."

The Judge turned to the officer. "Any further charges Officer Ostrowski?"

"Yes sir. Mr. Burns could not show me proof that he had auto insurance."

"Have you auto insurance, Mr. Burns?"

Mr. Burns held a slip of paper out to the Judge. "Here sir. I got insurance."

"So I see. I'll accept this as proof of insurance. Now Mr. Burns, you can tell me your story."

His voice cracked as a large tongue protruded to licked dry lips.

"Easy Mr. Burns. There's no need to be nervous, take your time."

"Yes sir, Judge. When the policeman stopped me, I asked him why? He said I was speeding. Going too fast in the rain." The man twisted his hands together and wet his lips again. "It ain't raining I told him."

"Was it raining Officer Ostrowski?"

"Your Honor, when I started after Mr. Burns, it was raining. When I pulled him over and approached his car the rain had stopped. He mentioned the rain had stopped."

"See Judge. It wasn't raining."

The judge gave Mr. Burns a withering stare and put his finger to his pursed lips. "Now, Mr. Burns, were you driving in the rain when Officer Ostrowski pulled you over?"

"I don't remember driving in the rain."

"Officer, can you substantiate your claim that this man was driving in the rain?"

Your honor, here is my citation book, showing raindrop stains from a previous ticket. The location, the date and time show when and where I issued it. Sixteen minutes later I issued Mr. Burns a ticket about a half mile from that location. He was driving in the rain your honor."

In a stern voice the judge said, "Mr. Burns, it appears you are attempting to skirt the circumstances here. I find you guilty as charged. You're fined $95 dollars for the ticket and an additional $35 dollars for reckless driving. The charge of driving without insurance, which could have cost you a mandatory $500 dollar fine, is dismissed. Pay the bailiff. Bailiff, next case."

"Romero. August Romero."

Officer Ostrowski turned to the judge, "One of mine. May

I remain here sir?"

A head nod kept the officer in place.

"Mr. Romero, do you know why you are here?"

"I got a ticket from this policeman. He pointed to police-man Ostrowski. But, I shouldn't have. No, sir."

"Yes or no will do. Please wait, I'll tell you when to present your story."

"OK."

"I'll ask officer Ostr... Ostrowski to read me the charges. After that you may give me your version of the events. OK?"

Romero nodded, cleared his throat and eyed the Officer.

"Your Honor, I clocked Mr. Romero doing 73 miles an hour on the Skyway. When I gave pursuit he continued speeding 'til just short of the Indiana stateline. I told him he was speeding and in trouble for not pulling over when I put on my lights, and I had to chase him."

"Sound correct to you, Mr. Romero?" asked the night court judge. "Does it?"

"Your honor, sir. I'm telling the truth when I tell you what happened. This officer is picking on me. Being I'm Hispanic, he picks on me." Romero glanced at the policeman, "He picks me out and pulls me over for a ticket."

"That's against the law to pick on certain people. Isn't that correct Officer Ostrowski?"

The officer nodded in the affirmative. "Yeap."

"So, Mr. Romero, why do you say this. Truthfully, remem-ber you said you'd tell the truth."

Romero warmed to his story, started to speak quickly. The judge waved his hand to slow the man down. He swallowed and started again.

"When this guy, policeman, started to tell me I was speed-ing, I didn't know what to say. He tells me I'm going way too fast and asks for my license. He looks at my license, I got a hole in it along time ago. "Been stopped before he sez. I go, yes, once."

Romero paused, "I can see in his eyes he don't like me."

"Mr. Romero, just tell me how the officer picked on you."

"He sees my name and my color. He hears my accent. You're getting a speeding ticket. Jeez, I said. Why me? Why didn't you go after the red car?"

"The red car. Officer was there a red car? Did I miss something?"

"He'll have to tell us. He mentioned a red car when I stared writing him up."

"What about a red car?" asked the judge.

"Your Honor, there was a red car right beside me when the police car lights came on, right beside me. I asked the officer why he didn't pull him over. He was speeding I told him."

The judge passed his hand along his chin. "A red car, right beside you, was speeding?'

The officer smiled.

"Yes sir. I told him that car was speeding. He knows it too."

"Mr. Romero, I'm going over your statement, one item at a time. Say yes if I am correct. OK?"

"Say yes. OK."

"You were driving on the Skyway next to a red car?"

"Yes."

"The red car stayed right beside you?"

"Yes."

The red car was speeding?'

"Yes."

"You were not speeding?"

"Yes."

"My, my Mr. Romero, side by side but you're not speeding? Guilty! You're fined $95 dollars for speeding and be aware that I would like to fine the red car too. Perhaps I should ask you to pay his speeding fine? Pay the bailiff."

JULY 5TH

Young Malone was up and out of the house early, walking along the curb. He hoped to find unexploded fireworks from the night before. Wondering if the cherry bomb he had just picked up was a dud, he lit it.

"Three Finger" Malone remembers July 5th every day.

HE IS COMING

Tired from a long day and awaiting her relief, the receptionist peered toward the screams echoing through the hospital vestibule, along with the frigid night air. The screams chilled her. The fatigued afternoon team at Hospital Beth El Lam had already begun the transition of duties to the oncoming night team on this Christmas Eve.

"My wife! My wife! The baby is coming!" Joseph Carpenter, soon to be father, arms churning the cold air, legs pumping and eyes on high beam ran toward receptionist's station. "Help my wife!"

The tired receptionist pushed the ER alarm for Joseph's wife as she passed through the reception area counter. She heard part of the ER team starting down the narrow hall. The team sailing by the screaming man assisting his wife pushing them away from the rolling gurney to reach their destination, the ambulance, siren wailing and emergency lights dancing, backing into the emergency slot. Choreographed actions had all participants moving back along the corridor in moments. Mrs. Carpenter, who had slipped to the floor groveling in labor's agony, grabbed at a passing paramedic's leg, but couldn't hold it.

The tired receptionist, pad and pen poised, stood in front of Joseph. "May I have your insurance card please?"

Mary Carpenter let out a heart wrenching yelp.

"Please help my wife. Our baby is coming. Look."

"We will. May I have your insurance card, please, Mr..." she paused.

"Carpenter. Joseph Carpenter. I have no insurance card." He felt the receptionist with her hand full of papers pushing him back into the wall.

A second ambulance screeching to a stop outside, the paramedics crunching the doors into the entryway wall, storming through the crowded hallway.

"Out of the way! Move it!" hollered the giant pulling the gurney. "We got a pregnant flatliner." A bloody figure, the drunken husband-driver, came staggering along behind them, unassisted.

Mary Carpenter cowered down, screaming in fright and pain. Her child struggled in the birth canal. "Help me! Please help me." came her piteous cries.

The orderly chaos of the hospital's emergency teams ran smoothly except in the eyes and opinions of Mr. and Mrs. Carpenter. Bewildered and confused they were being ignored for the moment. Babies had been born before without hospital help.

As Mr. Carpenter knelt beside his crying wife, Doctors Milt and Roscoe Sheperd, twin brothers, were entering the hospital for their monthly tour of volunteer duty, assisting the ER doctors. A humanitarian program they had dreamed up to bolster the hospital's local image. Milt grabbed a gurney while Roscoe helped Joseph Carpenter lift his writhing wife onto it. Bolting for an auxiliary room, they tried to make sense out of pandemonium.

"You can't take her in. They have no insurance." hollered the receptionist. "Stop!"

"It's a breech. We'll need to cut." yelled Dr. Milton Sheperd

"You the husband?" Roscoe Sheperd asked Joseph. "How long ago did she start labor?" He bumped the receptionist, waving her papers. "Get out of the way. Damn it!"

"They must go somewhere else. They have no insurance. Who's going to pay?"

Joe looked at his watch. "Over half hour, a little longer maybe." he croaked.

"Damn. Milt we may have a problem. Mr., please wait over there." Roscoe said, pointing toward a bench. "We'll take care of things and get back to you real soon. Go sit over there. Please." Pushing Joe gently with his elbow toward the drunken man, now cursing a policeman, the doctor turned toward the E.R.

Dr. Lamb stuck his head into the room. "Need help?"

"Yeah Teddy. Got us a problem delivery. Give a hand, knock her out."

In the adjoining ER room the frantic pace eased up, a little. They had lost the flatline woman and were working in desperation to save the infant. The tiny body responding to their administrations, struggling to survive, but ever so slowly losing ground with every machine assisted breath. Tubes criss-crossed the diminutive human frame, still wet with embryonic fluid. A pump wheezed and pushed wisps of oxygen into the tiny lungs.

Mr. Carpenter swore vows to his God, vows he could never keep, just to keep his wife and baby alive. Head bent low, sobbing, a puddle grew around his shoes. The one vow he could keep, came easily and without thought. The baby would be named Christopher, Christopher Carpenter, for God's son. These prayers begging for life, came from a man who had never learned to pray. Factually, he seldom prayed or even attended church. He would start.

The drunk continuing his boorish, obnoxious behavior, couldn't even determine that he had caused the deaths of his wife and child. He loudly cursed everything.

Milt Sheperd, swearing under his breath, saw the child had ceased moving and he had not finished the surgical cut. He knew and looked tellingly at his brother, the birth process about to end before the life had began. Dr. Lamb shook his head, tossing the surgical gloves toward the container and stepped into the next cubical. The blurred lights cleared when he wiped the tears from his eyes. "Need help?"

"What's going on over there?" asked the surgeon, rolling his head at the other room.

"Milt is losing an infant. Too long in labor. The heart stopped."

"Teddy, I just lost this one and the mother. The car accident pretty much crushed the baby's brain stem. Hell, any chance we can save Milt's new born using support and good parts from this one. A shitty choice."

Doctor Lamb turned to the two doctors. "Will donor parts save your baby?'

"You're kidding. Teddy, don't josh us."

"Honest. The woman is dead. The father is...", Teddy spun around, pointing to the loud drunkard, "over there."

"Get his permission. Who's with the mother? Oh, Milt is. I'll get the donor."

Dr. Lamb called to Milt Sheperd and crooked his finger, beckoning him to follow. As the two men approached the drunk, Dr. Lamb volunteering to handle the situation and get the father's permission while Milt talked to the dying baby's father.

Milt Sheperd's presence brought Joe Carpenter to his feet. Their eyes met and without a word between them, Joe knew, he swayed and settled back onto the bench. He rocked back, muttered curses to no one and found tears in some bottomless well.

With gentleness, uncommon in men, Dr. Lamb attempted to console the drunken man. However, inhuman as it may seem, he began at once to solicit the dead child's parts. He softly stressed the need for quick action, the hopes of giving life back to a dying infant.

Dr. Lamb's words drummed into his ears, penetrating the besotted mind as slowly as the rising sun. Their impact exploding into the fireworks of a 4th of July night. Cut up his child? CUT UP HIS CHILD?. He didn't believe the request, he could not be hearing this.

"NO!" He screamed the answer louder than Mary Carpenter screamed in labor.

Both doctors fell back as the enraged man began cursing their souls, their parent's souls and their children's souls. His vitriol snarling curses were daggers to their hopes. Both emergency teams stopping their work and stared at the men in the anteroom.

The stars twinkled in the cold sky above Hospital Beth El Lam. One seemed to illuminate the hospital dome.

"I will never know my son. Oh, God! Why are you doing this. Mary! Mary!" Joe Carpenter rushed into the room and threw himself across her unconscious prostrate body. Dr. Roscoe Sheperd stood half way between the two cubicles, the covered body of the donor baby in his arms. Looking at the two doctors, shaking his head in disbelief and retreated, returning the bundle to the gurney.

The emergency team in the ER looked at the support machines as the electronic ribbon blipped a long continuous flat glow. They looked at the drunk, that took two lifes, now denying life to another child. They looked and wondered about life itself.

Dr. Sheperd mused aloud. "Suppose this had been the Christ child?"

DONUT SPECIAL

Lester stomped his freezing feet and exhaled his warm breath into his cupped hands. Monday morning, April 7, 2003 and Chicago was experiencing bone chilling weather, with snow snarling the city and its traffic. Lester waited near the bus stop for any commuter to trash his morning newspaper. His nose dripped icy mucus, the cold wind cut tears from his eyes and tucked his head lower into his hunched shoulders.

Finally, a bus crept to a crunching halt and a newspaper found its way into the ice encrusted garbage container. Lester retrieved his prize and headed for the newspaper machine outside a nearby restaurant.

"Buy mine" he said, to the man digging for coins in his pocket.

Newspaper and coins changed numbed hands. Lester rubbed his ears and hurried toward the doughnut shop just off Clark Street.

Inside he ordered the "Special" from the half awake kid behind the counter and contemplated which of the filled doughnuts he wanted.

"The large coffee and doughnut special ended at nine o'clock. It's 9:40."

Lester's eyes darted to the clock. "Aw, come on. I only got fifty cents."

The kid pointed to the sign. "No can do." he said and went about another task.

Lester walked out, pressed his hands against his ears,

"Dumb, cheap little shit." he muttered to himself. He headed back toward the newspaper machine. If he bought one paper with his fifty cents he could grab a few extra and sell those too. Damn, he'd get himself a regular breakfast. The thought of it made his mouth water and hastened his pace.

Two coins rattled into the metal box and the hinges screeched open. Nothing. The box was empty. Lester hadn't checked before depositing his coins. The weather probably delayed delivery just as it had tied up the city's traffic. Again he had nothing. Stomping his freezing feet and breathing into his cupped hands, Lester waited at the bus stop.

CONTRITE

Ramee wasn't sure what was happening. He'd been driving home after an exhausting day at work. He felt good about the progress he made with the blueprints and the revamping of the dam construction the chief engineer had assigned to him. Winter darkness seemed to be coming in earlier this evening as he drove through the small community of Contrite, pop. 78. Perhaps the weatherman had gotten a prediction right, the possibility of an accumulation of snow in the evening hours. He turned on his headlights.

Why were all these people so eager to have him join them. They were pushing and shoving to the point of hurting one another. And the cheering, why the cheering? Or was it yelling? Well, now what? They're picking me up, carrying me. Where? This is getting rough and I don't like it. I don't like it at all.

"Hey! Hey!" screamed Ramee. "You're going to hurt me. What's happening?"

A fist struck him in the mouth.

"Hey, stop that. That hurt."

"Shut up you son of a bitch!" hollered the man swinging a branch at his body.

The cheers weren't cheers. They were jeers and taunts. They weren't clear but explicit. "Kill the bastard!" "Hang him!" "Drunken fool, drove right up on the road edge and killed that child."

Killed a child? Drove off the road? I didn't drive off the road. It was getting dark as the storm must have been coming.

The weatherman said snow possible. Why are you hollering at me? You're hurting me. Don't hurt me. Somebody call the police, find someone to tell me what's happening.

"Here's the rope!" the burly man said, swinging a length of cord over a large oak branch.

A cheer went up as the rope swung over the branch and dropped down into waiting outstretched hands. One pair of large, reddened, rough hands quickly forming a loop, tossed the loop toward Ramee. Ramee shied from it, but the restraining mob held him fast.

"Why? What did I do?" squirming, thrashing, Ramee finally saw his danger. Saw at last an angry mob bent on killing him. A lynch mob driven by a lust for revenge upon a drunken driver that had invaded their community, their homes and killed one of their's. "I'm not drunk. I..."

The man with the branch swung again, jerking Ramee's head back and ending his protestation. The blow broke his jaw, he could no longer speak, no longer protest. As a matter of fact, the blow broke his neck, but the mob didn't know. They hung Ramee anyway. The father of the dead child stepped forward and punched the swinging limp body. Another man stepped forward and did the same, a woman spit in Ramee's florid face. The sputum mingled with drool from Ramee's mouth and the smell of alcohol offended the noses of those people standing close by.

A State Police car coaxed its way into the mob, siren blasts and turrets lights attempting to divide the crowd still yelling at the dangling bloody stranger. Cat-calls fell on the two officers shoving their way through the mingling slightly subdued mob.

"My God! What the hell have you people done?" office Tobias screamed. "Get back. All of you back."

The father pointed to the child's body lying on the ground. "Drunken son of a bitch killed my girl. Ran her down."

Several yells of encouragement arose from the throng.

"No more yelling." said the police officer. "Let me hear

what happened."

Again the father spoke, in a firm, loud voice. "That bastard. That drunken bastard ran over my little girl."

"Here Monty. Look at this." The office showed Officer Monty Tobias a wrist band on Ramee's dangling arm. "DIABETIC."

"Oh God. The man may have lapsed into a diabetic coma and needed help. Just his luck the first people on the scene smelled his breath and announced he was drunk. Mob instinct took over. They never gave him a chance."

"Bull shit. You can smell the alcohol all over him. In his car, you could smell he was drinking.."

"I'm sorry your little girl was killed. But, diabetics frequently smell of alcohol because of their diabetes. Diabetics don't drink." said Officer Tobias.

"I didn't know that," the child's father said.

The mob silently and surprisingly quickly began to dissolve. Snow began to fall.

FREE LUNCH

Lamont was usually unlucky. Lamont's letter to Santa was lost in the mail, as for the Easter Bunny, if he came, he would have left Lamont regular bunny pellets.

Lamont thought he found a good con for a free lunch at one of the local fast food chains. It was simple and fool proof.

"Are you the manager?" Lamont asked the man at Henny's Burger House.

"Yes. May I help you?"

In a demanding, but weak voice Lamont stuck out his chin, "Listen here fella. When I drove through yesterday I didn't get one whole family meal. I didn't know it 'til I got home. I want my money back, or my family meal."

"You say you got the order yesterday? Why didn't you come right back? We would have fixed it at once." the manager asked in a quiet voice.

"I was too far away by then to come back, all the way home before I noticed." Lamont's voice rose a bit.

"You got your order here at Henny's? Yesterday?" the quiet voice asked.

"I bought it. I want what I paid for or my money back." his voice a bit louder.

"Do you remember who gave you your order?" the same quiet voice asked.

The quiet voice bothered Lamont. He tried lowering his voice. It squeaked out. "I know I paid for a meal I didn't get. Here at Henny's, on 5th Avenue. I want it."

In short quiet phrases, "OK. You were shorted a meal, yesterday, which was Sunday, at the Henny's, on 5th Avenue. Right?"

"That's right. I paid for a meal I didn't get yesterday, Sunday, at Henny's on 5th.

"I don't know who sold a meal, but we were closed yesterday, Easter Sunday.

People who knew Lamont knew his luck hadn't changed.

END

Mike glanced down from the cockpit, riveting his eyes to the sandy shoreline. Nudging the dosing copilot, he pointed down tilting the large plane slightly, enabling Cook to see what he saw.

"Whatta make of it?"

Cook rubbing the sleep from his eyes, "Am I awake? Is the land breaking of into the sea?" Lifting his body out of his seat and leaning over Mike, he stared down. "Christ Mike. What's going on?'

"Don't know.'"

The intercom buzzed. "You guys fooling around up there?" came the head steward's voice. "Or have a problem."

"Don't know. Anything happening with your passengers?"

"No. A few are looking out the portside window in the first class section. One just hollered."

"Get ready for some questions and ..." The fasten seat belts signal went on. "I'm telling them to buckle up. Don't let them up or crowd one side of the cabin."

"OK."

People were looking out and seeing a nightmare or a creepy space movie. The sea was falling into itself. Huge whirlpools churning the open sea, white swirls dancing up from each vortex. Of course they heard no sound from below.

Cook had the nearest airport on the radio. He was trying to explain what he saw but couldn't understand himself. The radioman was asking him to get off the air because a local station was trying to warn... The radio went dead.

"Ladies and gentlemen. We were in contact with a local radio station, but they've broken off. If you have a cell phone, please do not try to call anyone. Please let us keep trying to contact someone. Please, for all our safety. Thank you."

A few prayers and curses filled the cabin. Calm would be difficult to keep in this group. The tension held everyone one's attention.

"The Captain again. Thank you for your patience. We still don't know what is happening. As you can see the land is disappearing into the sea. Like a big earthquake in a movie. I know we're safe up here. However, if you have a cell phone go ahead and call home. Maybe someone will have news of what is going on. If you get news tell a stewardess and we'll announce it to everyone."

The buzz of voices, demanding, frightened and unbelieving contributed to the air-conditioning hum and the constant hum of the plane's engines. Short sentences, oaths, finally yelling disrupted throughout the entire plane. Panic was setting in.

A shrill, ear piercing whistle punctured the growing sounds of disorder. The little flight attendant, smiled and began.

"The Captain told you, we are safe up here. He is talking to you now. Please listen."

"Who in the hell can whistle like that? Thank you.," The Captain's voice instilled a little confidence in the passengers, several applauded or giggled. They sat back and listened.

"What we are seeing below is local." Audible gasps came from a couple of listeners. "The few explanations we have been given by some of you from talking on your cell phones is inconclusive. Rumors mostly." Electronic crackling filled the cabin. "Whew. Hold on. An official report from Atlanta Georgia. I am putting it on the intercom."

"...unsubstantiated at the moment. I have spoken to their connection and am getting pictures from NASA at the moment and beg you to stand by while the Director there examines and explains the space shuttle footage. We will resume shortly."

Moans and groans of disappointment came from everywhere..

"OK. OK." said the Captain. "That's not what we wanted,
I am going to hold the plane steady for five minutes. Those of you
that have camcorders, video cameras or any picture taking devices
get them ready. I will then circle to our left, that side of the plane
takes pictures. When I complete the circle I will do the same for
the other side of the plane. Get the best shots or footage you can.
When we land TV stations and publishers will want them."

Twenty minutes later, after some grumbling the Captain
ordered snacks served and free drinks for those who wanted them.
One per. As the flight crew handed out the snacks the piped in
music was interrupted.

".. from Atlanta we are getting a report from Toronto, a
professor of astro-geology something or other. I'm have trouble
hearing him because of static so pay attention.'

The Toronto spokesman said, "Looking at the photos
from the space capsule and having talked with a colleague in Tel
, crackle, crackle sss the depletion of oil from, crackle sss created
vast cavern below, crackle, zzz isss causing zz ississ This means the
orbital zzzz iss earth changed and our planet crackle crackle zszs
further into space crackzz." Silence.

"Didn't tell us much. People, I don't know where home
is for you, but that's where we're going." Mike's assuring voice
calmed the passengers down a bit. "Settle back, I'll leave the music
on."

The cockpit crew noticed the sun seemed to be positioned
at an angle different from the bizarre instrument readings and the
color a bit pale as the plane banked to the left.

ESCAPE PLAN

Matlon planned for every contingence conceivable, every emergency imaginable and kept it all to himself. Every escape failed because the escapee had neglected to considered some small possibility or shared a confidence. After every attempt the prisoner, or part of him returned within the perimeters of the Highland Prison and displayed, proving escape impossible. Yet, all the condemned of Carrillon, as did Matlon now, considered it, some tried.

Matlon was not a political or simple criminal prisoner, he was a callous killer and never denied that fact. Executions of killers, or any criminals, had been banned when Ryan successfully campaigned against the death penalty. Now life sentences, lasting a century or more, thanks to longevity medicines and chromosome splicing, were common. All life sentences were served on Carrillon, third planet of the Bayard Galaxy. He'd been imprisoned since 2254, 42 earth years. Planning to escape for 42 earth years too.

Matlon developed two characteristics in formulating his escape plan. Listening. Listening to every thing, filter it for truths and remember it. Read. Read everything, and along with pictures remember what you read. Checking out library materials, he used the Sleepreader, passing information into his sleeping mind. He practiced a fasting routine that was as effective as hibernation without sleep. His daily workout in the prison gym didn't build a physical physique on his diminutive frame, it built stamina and endurance.

Matlon slipped through the electronic wall in that instant gap when the electricity switched from off to on. At that moment all electronic eyes were focus inward before random movements began their limited night range, scanning six feet above the ground with heat and pressure sensors. He jumped to the electron beam tower and froze, forcing his body temperature below 95 degrees and shrinking the diminutive body into the cramped shadows. He waited, silent, alert, observing everything.

Matlon stirred as the day began, the sensors shut down and surveillance eyes returned to skirted the interior prison grounds. By now the robotics guards were filing reports of a missing prisoner, feeding the electronic papers through the bureaucracy of prison life. He scampered down, blew a kiss to the prison and pushed into the jungle he knew from his books. Listen, learn and remember, if he had and did then freedom.

Matlon zigged and zagged along the trailless jungle floor, very little grew on the lower ground and he moved quickly toward the second sun. According to an old paper book, a river, flowing toward the escarpment plains, would bring him to a city. There, by stealth and determination, along with his survival skills, he could board a ship, any ship and get off this pest hole of a planet. After that he'd plan a return to Earth and living.

Matlon cursed his carelessness, stepping into that shimmering stagnant pool of water, could have cost him his life. Here lived the filaria, round worms, causing blindness for eons in Africa. They pierced the foot or leg of the unwary, devouring prey from the inside in less than an hour or two of sun time. He slowed his pace, allowing memory to warn him of potential dangers and concentrated on locating the river. His memory warned him to avoid walking under the red trunk Scarred Tree, as the tropical Manchineel dripped burning acid, so did the Scarred Tree.

Matlon proceeded in one direction for 38 Earth days, each day the possibility of finding the river woke him and drove him. Subsisting on scant insect proteins and vitamin rich shoots of invasive champagne grapes, the plant that shocked investors into poverty by growing rapidly but never fruiting. A financial guarantee of riches and luxury so positive that even he had invested a few hundred dollars. He enjoyed drowning the agent that talked him into such a foolish investment. That killing put him in the Highland prison, for natural life.

Matlon stood and stretched after his morning toilet, then slivers of reflected light danced into his pupils, narrowed them with their intense brightness. For just a moment, he felt fear. He had no remembered information to guide him, for none had been available. The old paper book had imparted no information, except that a river and a city existed. The Sleepreader never mentioned which river. Mentioned in a book, a river and a city, nothing more. This was Matlon's goal, his Nirvana, the city on the river with a port leading to Earth.

Matlon dug into the soft wood with the rock's edge, a primitive dugout to float to the city. Without entering the dangers of an unknown body of water, he crafted a well balanced, shallow surface boat. He could travel by day and veer into the edge of the jungle each night before darkness enveloped any dangers. The distance to the city was an unknown. He calculated an Earth month, allowing for the slow drifting water. He choose broad leaf bamboo leaves for dew to settle on, his source of water and scooped termite's eggs into a leaf pouch for daily rations.

Matlon eased "The Rescue", as he called his dugout, into the water 46 days after his escape. He paddled to mid-stream, felt the gentle flow and headed toward the city. Daily he followed a survivor's ritual. Look, with fervor, for any signs of human life, eat, drink and watch for additional sources of food. Shove off, stay alert and look for the city. Daily searching, searching and day after day, nothing. Nothing but hope. Despair scratched at his mind.

Matlon saw the water parting around an object as he drifted past. A man made shape. Man-made. A man-made shape. The tortured brain nearly lost the significance of what his mind voiced repeatedly. Man -made. The city had to be near. Where? He strained his body upward and ran his gaze along the 360 degrees of horizon. Where? Where was the city? Valhalla? Where?

Matlon circled the shape, choose a shoreline target and paddled to land. The jungle didn't exist at the shoreline. Instead a rust-red plantless soil of flaked material crunched, unyielding beneath his deteriorating boots. Scuffing this strange dirt with one boot he found he couldn't release flake from flake. Magnetic attraction. Metal soil? Piece by horrible piece Matlon's brain composed a mental picture of a city built and abandoned, in ruins before he was born. No city equals no port, which equals no ship, equaling no trip to Earth. Matlon had been sentenced to life in a prison. His escape from one small prison into a larger prison, didn't change the sentence. Natural life in prison.

OUR HONEYMOON SWEET

"I now pronounce you man and wife." The words murmured earlier in the afternoon still rang in their ears. And now it was just minutes before midnight the exhausted couple was slipping up from the reception downstairs and into their honeymoon suite. The reception was winding down and most of the guests are gone. They were on their honeymoon. A complimentary bottle of vintage 2003 champagne sat on the table, next to a beautiful bouquet of flowers. The couple laughed and read the card leaning against the bottle, "Welcome Mr. and Mrs. Bell, enjoy yourselves with our compliments. The Management."

"Want to open it?"

"Do you?"

"Look," said the bride, still wearing the heavy white brocade and pearl wedding dress, "I want out of this outfit. I'm hot and sweaty." She turned her back on the groom. Sweetly begging, "Be a sweetheart and unhook me. Please?"

"Sure." fumbling fingers responding "I didn't expect you wanted to get undressed so soon."

"Oh David, it's the heavy wedding dress that's making me hot, not you."

His fingers stopped moving, eyes widened and voice constrained, "Thanks a lot."

She stepped from the dress now embracing her ankles. "Whew. Much better."

Standing so close to a woman in her underwear, David's mind gave David's body a sexual shove. Reaching around her waist and hugging her, his lips nibble at the nape of her curly but sweaty wet hair.

"Wanna?" he asked, in a voice soft and sexy. His body had started mating behavior.

"Can we wait, just a few minutes. 'Til I at least rinse off?"

"You smell OK."

"David, we're going to be married for a long time, what's the rush?" Liz tilted her head, "Besides there are things to do before we..." her voice trailing off. "You know."

"I only know I'm getting the hots and ready to play man and wife."

Liz gave him that exasperated look that all women seem to know instinctively. "Cripes, I'm not saying no. Give me a moment's rest."

David shrugged, "Mind if I undress here? In front of you? With the lights on?"

"I did." Liz turned her face from David.

"Well la de da da." he minced. "So, I will, too." A moment later he was slipping his excited body between the cool sheets of the honeymoon bed. He patted the coverlet, "Want this on?"

"Come out of there, David." Liz said. "You're not ready for sex."

"Huh?" fell out of David's open mouth. "Whatta ya mean?"

"You didn't put on any protection."

David, face sagging, questioned, "Protection? Honey I'm your husband, we're married. We don't need any protection." His eyes narrowed to thin lines. "Like you mean a rubber? On our honeymoon you want a rubber between us."

"Oh David, not for disease protection. The doctor gave both of us a clean ticket. I mean.. So we don't... You know, we said no kids right away."

"No rubber. Not on the first night. Come on, for god's sake." smacking the pillow with the palm of his hand. "That ain't right."

"Please, David?" Her eyes shinning with tears. "I had my period two weeks ago. According to most evidence, I'm ripe. My eggs are just waiting to get fertilized. Right now." Leaning down, she touched the hand smacking the pillow. "For me?"

"OK. OK. But now we got a real problem." Pulling the covers back, revealing a potentially potent piece of masculine equipment. "I haven't a condom with me."

Startled Liz didn't touch or wavier or step back. "Wow. That's more than I'd been expecting." She remained standing beside the bed staring, wearing a timid smile

"I'll make you a very satisfied wife. Let's forget it for tonight." He pulled at her, hoping she'd fall into their honeymoon bed.

She pulled back. "Nope, I bought a package of them at the drugstore today."

Again his open mouth let "Huh?" fall out of it. "YOU ARE KIDDING."

Walking over to the table with the little white bag, part of her wedding trousseau, Liz began poking her hand into it. Her lacy white slip swishing and flipping while walking was turning him on. Her hand came out of the handbag with a small Walgreen's bag and from it a package of condoms. "See, I did."

"I'll be damned. You actually went in and bought condoms. The pharmacy guy give you a big know-it-all smile that said, 'I know what you're going to be doing?' Did he? Huh?" Getting out of bed and moving toward his new wife, David extended his hand, "Let me see?"

Dropping the packet into the outstretched hand, Liz stepped aside.

"I ain't never used these before."

"David!" The loudness and tone of Liz's voice freezing the grin on his face. "Don't you ever say things like that to me. Never again. Never." Her face clouding over with disappointment.

"Ouch. Sorry." This would have to pass as an apology. "What I mean is I have never used a rubber before. Sorry. So tell me, how did you get them?"

Liz let her mouth curl into a slight smile. "I went in and asked the pharmacist for them. I told him I was getting married and wanted them. I also told him I didn't know your size. He laughed. David, did you know a condom doesn't come in sizes."

"I know." a silly smile pulling his eyes down. "I know."

"Any way, he sold them to me. Then he said, 'You're a smart young lady.'"

"Yeah. You are. You picked me."

"Will you put it on? Then, we can have sex. Newly wed, honeymoon, wild sex."

"There better be instructions in here." said a sheepish David. "I ain't kidding, I've never worn a sheath..., condom."

"Nope. No instructions in the box. Not on the wrapper or inside?"

David looked incredulously at Liz. "No directions. Oh great, just great. I agree and I don't know what I'm doing." His fist knocked on his forehead. "Damn."

"Honey, let me tell you what the pharmacist told me. OK? It'll be all right. Honest."

"OK. Tell me what he said." David gave Liz a small smile. "Sex 101."

"Well, I did ask the pharmacist if anyone could use them? He laughed and said to me, 'Not everyone, but nearly every guy can.' Then he smiled and continued telling me, 'They just roll on... Lady, you sure you want me telling you all this?'"

David sat on the edge of the bed hardly believing what he was hearing.

"David, I felt real red and couldn't speak, so I nodded my head. Finally, I blurted out, I do, in case, well in case. Like.. Tell me."

"So he starts talking, 'Any way, they roll on, all the way down to be effective. That's important, all the way down.' With a shy grin he continued, 'If your husband has trouble slipping it on, they roll some times, tell him to wet his... his... member.'"

David, embarrassed by Liz's reddening face, hung his head and shook it. He couldn't say a word. If he could, his inner voice cautioned quiet.

"Wet? How do you mean wet his member?" I said.

"The guy is, is like, drowning, gagging and sputtering. I think he was embarrassed. And he sezs, 'Wet. Like spit on it.' He's getting red in the face."

"So would I." David whispered hoarsely. "So would I."

"Yuck. Oh, yuck. I said and sorta made a wretching motion."

"Now he's looking at me like... like I'm a nut case. Well, he can use some body oil or some lubricant, like suntan oil. A drop."

Taking the small roll of latex and turning it in his hand, David lay back on the bed. "Here goes nothing." It fell onto the sheet. "Oops."

"Come on David, don't clown around."

"Who's clowning around. This is awkward. You want to do it?"

Blanching, Liz tilted back. "Maybe, some day."

"This darn thing ain't unrolling." David said, as he held his erection and attempted to roll the rubber downward. Slouching back, eyes looking into Liz's face. "I need help. Honest."

An amused voice, stifling a giggle, squeaked, "How?"

"Pull the rolled edge over the tip of my.... member."

"I'll touch you."

"We're married, it's OK. You know?"

"David, I can't. I can't."

"You wanted me to use this." Holding the roll before her face and wiggling it.

"OK. OK." Liz stretched the roll of latex over the hard

surface and it slipped from her grasp.

"Yeoowww!"

"David, I'm sorry. I'm sorry. Did I hurt it? You?"

"Damn right you did. Gimme that thing. Hold my MEM-BER."

The demand caused Liz to forget her sqimmish attitude and she grabbing a bit harder than needed.

"Come on Liz, don't kill it before we to use it together."

Clasping her hands and maneuvering them, "Like this, I hope." The two of them, as a team, succeeded. They were on their honeymoon, happily consummating their marriage. However, there were more difficulties to come before they slept that night. The loss of David's erection caused the condom to roll up into the pubic hair. There was no loosening it. The two newly weds, with giggles and very somber care, used Liz's cuticle scissors, cut rubber and strands of curly hair until the condom was removed. They must have succeeded in using condoms with less trouble, since their first born came nine months after their fifth anniversary.

WAKE-UP

Dark. Rudy knew it should be dark. He had gone to bed about 11:30. Now he was straining his eyes and could see nothing. Nothing. He had gone to sleep was he still asleep? If so, it was wake up time. Wake up.

Damn he was awake. It was dark and he couldn't see a thing. He was lying down. There was an odor of dust in the air. A hint of panic touched him, I'll need to look into it.

Rudy's thoughts went back to yesterday. He had checked into the hotel about 6:20 p.m. February 13, 2001. His meeting was scheduled for 9 the next morning. Hopefully the engineering job was his and would last awhile. He wanted a life, not the job jumping existence he was living now. A month in Japan, two in Columbia, and six with that motley crew of Hasting's in Oman wasn't living. Then there were the girls, the flesh peddlers he hated and needed. Maybe, one day a sweetheart, a family, maybe?

Wake up!

Let's see, I checked in, walked around the block of the hotel, had broiled fish for supper in the hotel restaurant. Damn. Was the fish spoiled? Poisoned? Rudy's hand went to his eyes and pulled the bags beneath them. His eyes were open. It was dark.

He cautiously reached out, trying to calm his rising fears by ascertaining his location. He was on a rug, there was one in his room. His hand touched nothing above him, nothing in front of him. There was a wooden something across his legs just above the knee. Something jagged with smooth material covering one side of it. Paper? Paper on wood? What? He reached behind him, nothing. But he couldn't raise himself up. His leg wouldn't let him turn over and aside from the rug, floor, he couldn't support his body. He had to lie where he was.

He pulled the pinned leg toward him. No movement. He tried to lift the thing holding it, nothing. He tried to call out. No sound. And still the dark. Rudy had always had a fear of the dark and tight places too. Dark, close space were his nightmare. A dull pain started in his knee. In reaching to squeeze it his head bumped against something. Just over his head. It wasn't there before.

Flat, smooth, very smooth. Glass? Glass? A window? The mirror, the mirror on the dresser. How did it get on top of him? What the hell is happening?

Rudy tried to put both hands on the mirror, shove it off, move it out of the way. Maybe then he could see something, a clue to where he lie. His other hand didn't move. He tried the fingers, but didn't think they moved. This had to be a dream. It had to be.

Wake up! Wake up, screamed his confused mind. Close your eyes and let's start over again. Think. Think.

You went to bed. No television, no newspaper, no radio. You could have picked a better hotel. Yeah, like you could afford one. You fell asleep. You started dreaming. You were in Oman, Hastings was shaking you, hollering the insurgents were tossing gasoline bombs into the rigs and you had to get away. You put your feet on the floor and. And? And then what? What?

Did you just doze off? It's still so damn dark. What's that? The mirror? It's moved, it's closer to my head. Can't be. What's happening?

Wake up. For God's sake, wake up.

God it's silent. Being dark is bad enough, but it's silent too. I didn't notice the silence before, couldn't hear a thing. My leg is cramping and I can't reach it. If this ain't a dream someone help me. I'm going nuts. Where the hell can I be?

Recreate everything you can, repeat your every move. You

went to sleep, Hastings shook you awake. No not Hastings. The bed was shaking. Yeah the bed, the whole room was shaking. You woke up and started to get out of bed. The front wall started to fall out. No wall, you could see across the plaza. Then the other wall fell toward you. Remember? Remember?

Christ! An earthquake. You've been in an earthquake. You're buried but alive. They'll be digging you out soon. Just think about waiting. Sleep. If you sleep you can't panic. Relax, shut your eyes and wait. God, it's good to a least know what's happening. You could really scare yourself in the dark. In the silence.

Rudy had no idea of time in his darkened quarters. He awoke and felt the mirror. It was brushing his cheek. He tried to turn his face, his head, anything. His arm no longer moved out, the mirror was pressing on it now. Panic struck. He had no room to breath yet his lungs poured forth a screech painful to his ears. One long, loud animal screech. The weight of the mirror the wall behind it and the building on top of the wall robbed Rudy of room to breath one more scream, one more. The lungs struggling to expand, didn't.

Wake up, Rudy, wake up. It's a whole new world.

AN AMERICAN PRODIGAL

"Come on Mom." The young woman pleaded with the back of the small woman washing dishes in the sink. "Mom. Mom, turn around and look at me. Come on, listen to me."

"No. You listen to me. We've been round and round on this money business too often already. I said no a thousand times and I still say no." She turned from the sink to face her tormentor. Tear filled eyes blurred the image she spoke to, in a voice filled with constrained bites. "I will not give you money, today or tomorrow. Especially money that would take you away from me."

"Mom, it is for college. It will get me through college. I can work on my studies without spending time working a job. It will allow me to finish faster, get better grades, have a chance at a better job." Her hands reddened as she twisted and untwisted the unused dish towel. Her voice picked up speed as words cascaded from her mouth and her body fidgeted as a child in urgent need of the toilet.

"You'll still be away from me, from home. The college you picked is hundreds of miles away. Now if you went here, close to home, just think of the money and time you'd save."

"But this college is the best for me. Not our dumb community college. I will get a better, no, the best education in medical studies at the university." She seemed to sense a little of her mother's resistance fall away. "The sooner I finish, the sooner I can pay you back. Look mom it's not like I just want your money, which you know I'll inherit some day anyway. It's better for me to study while I'm young, alert and willing to devote time to books and serious things. Please Mom, give me the money for tuition and room and board now. It'll come back sooner, a thousand fold."

"Let me think. Give me to time to think some more. Just go do what you want tonight, go out with your friend, that Billup girl." Weary steps took her from the room. "I'll sleep on it. But don't count on my mind changing."

"OK. OK. Think about it." A hint of exhilaration crossed Clara's lips. "OK."

Coffee fumes filled the kitchen and waffed into Clara's bedroom, beckoning her to breafsat. Her mother poured batter onto the sizzling pan of bacon grease and Clara reached into the cabinet for maple syrup Her mind recalled the good things that happened on the mornings she ate her favorite breakfast, bacon and pancakes swimming through a lake of maple syrup.

"Need help?" she queried. "I got the syrup."

"Pour your coffee and get butter from the fridge."

"Can do." Clara couldn't container herself. "Did you decide mom? About the money for college?" In her heart Clara knew she had and the answer was yes.

Clara's mother slid pancakes unto their plates and sat, her eyes searching into the eyes of her daughter. She folded her hands before her, then touched finger tip to finger tip.

I called your sister, just after midnight last night. "Told her what I was thinking and informed her I would advance you your inheritance for college."

Clara squealed, clapped her hands and rocked back and forth in her chair. She didn't utter a word. Tears were caught by her smile. If mom had seen that smile, she might have changed her mind at once.

The next few weeks kept Clara busy and a dutiful daughter helped about the house. For once she bit her tongue and said nothing when things didn't go her way. She even went out of her way to be nice to her sister, watched the kids and helped with some cleaning. What a change.

When Clara flew to Massachusetts, she barely managed to get quarters some distance from the medical campus. She dumped her suitcase on the bed, then went to the window when she heard laughter and shouting outside. Girls were gathered around several boys in a convertible. Everyone looked well dressed, the latest of styles as seen on TV. She ducked back when one of the boys glanced toward her window. The following day as she signed up for classes, she made mental notes of what the girls were wearing. That afternoon she went shopping.

The male students gathered around her in every class and after every class. Their attention delighted her. Their attention diverted her. Their attention caused her to pay no attention to her studies. She was soon in academic trouble. Then, to give herself the hours she needed to study, she doused herself with caffeine and uppers. The boys began to drift away from her, as she changed from a bright witty girl to a zombie.

She called home each week to assure her mother everything continued to progress as they had hoped. Lies of course, but she couldn't go home. She sought out her instructors and their advice, but failed to heed their suggestions. Her spirits spiraled downward, along with her bank account. In desperation she sold a small share of her uppers. Then the roof fell in, she sold herself. She needed her pills and a roof over her head. But the landlord tossed her out for unpaid rent. Her cheaper lodgings took her away from the campus completely.

Clara drifted through the city, in and out of jail and rehab programs. Yet, somehow, continued to bluff her mother into believing she was doing well at school. No she would not come home during the summer break. By staying and studying she would graduate sooner and get a good job. Then she would come home and they could invite their family and friends to a grand party. See what hard work could do.

Clara lay near death in the hospital detox ward, a former classmate, serving as a candystripper, saw her. She went to Clara's former landlord and obtained her home address. In the spirit of friendship, she wrote and told of Clara's predicament. Her mom, concerned over Clara's missed phone call last week, immediately flew to her. In the hospital Clara didn't recognize her mother. She hallucinated, tore at her body, cursed the caretakers and swore even at her God. Mom was horrified and begged her God to forgive Clara and help them through this horrible ordeal.

In time, as costs mounted at the hospital and Mom's bank account shrunk, Clara improved and was discharged. She returned home with her mother. Ashamed and weak, Clara remained in the house, secluded from the world she once knew.

Week after week Clara received the care only a mother is willing to give. She began to return to her old self, only to fall into old habits. One afternoon her mother returned from work to find her small cache of money missing, the medicine cabinet trashed and Clara gone. It broke Clara's mother heart. She didn't look for her, she didn't even phone Clara's sister. There were no tears, no recriminations, nothing. Several days later the police called. Clara needed help. It was denied.

SOMETHING TO THINK ABOUT

Holding the door open Benjamin read, HOLMES, on the bowling bags. A smile and a nod passed between them as they entered the building. The idea of being close to professional athletes enthralled Benjamin. The idea of talking with one blew his mind. He tagged along after Holmes. Maybe he might speak to him.

When Holmes started placing his equipment out, Benjamin sat right behind him. Again Holmes smiled and nodded. Benjamin did the same. As Holmes dug for something in his bag, Benjamin leaning forward to look too.

"Bowl kid?" asked Holmes.

"Some. Not very good." came the reply.

"Come to watch and get pointers then?"

Benjamin gave his usual weak smile. "What is a good point? For someone starting?"

Tying his shoes, Holmes spoke to the floor. "Concentration kid. Concentration."

"How about throwing the ball? Or aiming? That kind of stuff?"

"Gotta concentrate on that stuff don't you?" Holmes said. Standing on the approach, he paused, then threw the ball toward the pins. "I'll need a different ball here."

Glancing about Benjamin saw bowlers practicing, photographers poising them on the alleys, equipment being prepared and never once thought about ripping someone off. The excitement had his stomach churning and his eyes wide. He followed behind Holmes for a practice round. Saw him pick up a 5 /10 split, go high and leave a 9, and not convert for a spare. When the games started, nothing escaped his eager eyes, he saw some great bowling. He even thought he was beginning to understand concentration and some other aspects of bowling.

After he swiped lunch, Benjamin checked the morning standing sheets. Next to him stood Lamps LaMantia, the gambler. With gestures and mouth to ear whispering, Benjamin concluded Lamp was betting on Holmes. Holmes? Lamps was betting on Holmes, just for one game. Maybe Benjamin could sit close and get into the betting pool.

Holmes would be bowling on alleys 15 and 16. Walking side by side with Lamps entourage, Benjamin sat behind Holmes and could also hear Lamps' frequent whispering. He smiled to himself after hearing Lamps mention the little hesitation Holmes took on his second step. He too had noticed the little movement. Such a small thing, but it showed he was learning.

Iron Stoker, the disbarred wrestler, bent over Lamps' ear and both nodded. Bets were being made on the game and in each frame. Sitting directly opposite Benjamin, Flanagan gave him the high sign with pretzeled fingers, a language understood by buyers and sellers on the floor of the stock exchange and gamblers wishing to remain unnoticed. Benjamin bet five dollars on Holmes to win the game, at three to five. Sitting back relaxing, Benjamin continued listening to Lamps' whispers.

"I wonder why that Holmes guy uses that falter-like step?" Lamps said to one of the bodyguards.

Hell, if he wants to know, I can find out Benjamin thought. I'd do him a favor and he might remember I did?

Benjamin leaned close to Holmes sitting between shots.

"Huh? Why do I step? What step?" A scowling Holmes stepped up to bowl, looked down at his feet and shifted them. He left a 7/10 split. Spinning about, glaring at Benjamin, he grimaced. Hanging his head he stepped up fot his next shot, his breathing audible to Benjamin, Holmes' body shuddered.

Realizing he had interfered with Holmes' concentration, Benjamin left the area and the bowling alley before Lamps could find out what had happened. Holmes lost his concentration, Lamps lost his bet and did find out what Benjamin had done. Benjamin lost his five bucks and decided to hide out for a while to prevent losing some part of himself.

ASSUME NOTHING

Awkward in death, the body lay on the floor in the Ki Kwa Dojo mat storage room. In this seldom used room the body might have gone unnoticed until putrefaction had begun. Discovered and reported by students playing tag, brought the police at once.

"Hamilton Paulie, a registered child sex offender. Lives a couple of blocks over."

Sullivan noted the remarks in his notebook, along with a body and room description. Any information might help his investigation. He noted the body showed no signs of a fight, scratches, blood nor was the room in disorder. His pants were unzipped, stained and one shoe was off. The head, bent back and torqued to the side, might indicate a broken neck. He guessed the man to be 6 foot, 240 pounds, maybe 40 years old. The coroner would fill-in many blanks after checking the body.

Kim Sue Yaskawa, mistaking the men for patrons brought them towels, smiling and bowing as she did for each student. Speaking little English, the tiny 4 foot 9, 91 pound, 71 year old illegal Korean immigrant was frequently mistaken for a child. Had she suspected the two men were police, they'd never have met. Kim Sue spent many hours cleaning and helping about the dojo.

The police began questioning students, Mr. Haramoto, the owner, instructors, service people and shopkeepers next-door. Paulie's landlord and the employees where he worked and the restaurant he frequented were questioned. Hard work began putting the puzzle together. Paulie appeared to have hidden in the dojo after hours yesterday, since he hadn't eaten in the local restaurant last night. He hadn't been home either. Or someone dumped him in a handy spot, a room next to an alley. The broken lock and door had been unused for a while. Things would come together in time.

Kim Sue moved about slowly that day. Old age? She smiled inwardly as Mr. Haramoto explained how evil a man Mr. Paulie had been. Oriental wisdom masking her face, she nodded agreement and went about her daily regimentation. After locking up the dojo, the two faced each other across the mat. Her bruised ribs hurt as Mr. Haramoto went over her shoulder and slammed onto the practice mat.

PREDICTED

"When you're nineteen you're immortal you can't die and nothing can kill you. Everything is there for the taking, the dames, the booze, the drugs, which he didn't need, and the means to get it, Money." Robert Norman Salton, a.k.a. "Salty", a kid growing up on the south side of Chicago, knew what he was talking about. He had all these things because he took them and never looked back or said he was sorry.

At thirteen he got his first lay from his older sister. He caught her screwing her boyfriend on the enclosed back porch of the bungalow and threatened to snitch to his boozy father. She'd get a beating and she didn't want that. Their mother jumped off the Calumet River Bridge one night, taking the scars of too many beatings from the booser with her. After that, Salty used his sister often and even sold her to his friends.

Salty was a sneak and a petty thief who thrived on not getting caught. He started that when he was eight. He'd put a quarter on the cap of his old man's beer bottle, open and sip, then recap, so the old lush didn't notice. The old man's beer would go flat some times and he'd swear that Salty was responsible. But he couldn't figure out how the kid was doing it. After a beating, Salty took some beer then pissed in the bottle. His father was so drunk he didn't even notice.

By the time Salty was sixteen he had a couple of older girls working the street for him. He won them from a drug addicted pimp in a crooked card game. When the pimp came after Salty, his lunge carried him through the window and onto the fire escape.

Salty maneuvered him through the iron framework for a three story drop. The girls didn't give a damn who they worked for as long as their habit was fed. When Uncle Paul, the pimp's brother tried to recoup the stable, they jumped him and dumped him in a trash container.

It might seem to the reader that an adult would step in and shove Salty out. They might have if Salty's close friend wasn't the biggest, blackest and strongest kid in the neighborhood. Onyx, didn't answer to any other name. Salty told several foolish local toughs to stop goading Onyx one day. Instead they went after Salty. Onyx didn't like that and stepped in with punishing consequences. His I.Q. didn't measure higher than a rooster's, his devotion came close to Greyfriar's Bobby. He never left Salty's side, unless Salty ordered him to or he was doing an errant for Salty.

Working his girls on the street wasn't difficult and he made a point of not roughing them up. However, getting the drugs for their habit did give him trouble in the beginning. The seller wanted more than Salty was willing to pay. They struck a deal that both could live with. Salty would provide girls for his affairs, he would provide the drugs. Unfortunately some people get greedy and demanding, as the drug dealer did. He told Salty that his source man, flippantly mentioning his name, Lyons, wanted more cash. Oh he was the Man, the Big Man, everyone on the street knew Lyons.

Salty, remember he's immortal, went to the source. He started to complain and the Man stopped him.

"Ain't no hike in prices. That son of a bitch is jerking you around."

"Well, damn. Why would he want to screw-up the nice thing we got going?"

"Money. That asshole wants more money." said the Man.

"Don't we all?' Salty looked the Man in the eye after that comment. His mind switched to money. He thought the Man would take more for himself, but wouldn't make his buyer knuckle under to get it. "You'd take more if you could, wouldn't you?"

"Don't need to hit up the price right now."

"I'm thinking this guy's between us, trying to take my money and give you a bad rep. That ain't right."

The Man nodded in agreement. "Ain't right."

"I'm not going to ask what his mark up is. I'm asking you if I can buy direct from you. I pick-up the stuff and pay on the line."

"You looking to deal with me?" the Man smiled. "Dangerous talk. Suppose he hears about it? What then? Do I lose you, 'cause he's going to kill you."

"Will you deal with me? And if, no after I take him out, do I get his customers."

"Whoa my man. Whoa. Do I get the idea you're going to take this guy down. He's a brother. You're a Honkey." Lyons reminded Salty.

"Not just a Honkey, a buyer willing to fatten your wallet, and work harder doing it." Salty stood up and considered what he had just implied. "Deal?"

"You're serious ain't you?'

Before Salty answered loud shouting and screaming came from downstairs. It sounded very much like a knock down, rock-em-sockem free for all Lyons jumped from his plush chair, "What in Hell is...", he rushed for the door. Salty followed.

Both men stared at a young girl, about 17, 110 pounds, dressed in a future rummage sale dress. She stood just over 5 feet tall with firm, small breasts, straw colored hair and screaming mad. She was throwing chairs and tipping tables toward a slightly built jockey size man and a overweight, busty woman. She was screaming at the two as they circled about trying to catch her in their arms, without any luck. She turned and ran blindly up the steps toward the two onlookers.

Lyons wrapped his arms around her as she topped the steps. "Easy Miss. What in the Hell is going on?" She struggled in his arms. "Easy." Lyons tightened his hold. "You two, don't come up. Stand there and tell me what is going on."

The girl screamed into her captor's ear. "They're kidnapping me! Help!"

Lyons winced as the scream shattered his eardrum. "Don't do that." He held on to the struggling body but shoved it against the wall. "That hurts."

Salty watched and devined now was a good time to step in, perhaps get some brownie points. "Can this Honkey help? She seems frightened. I'll take her into your office while you talk to those two. OK?"

Somewhat confused by the rapid changing of events, Lyons pushed the girl toward Salty. "Sure. Good idea. I'll talk to them and be with you in a minute or two."

It was nearly ten minutes later when Lyons pushed the door open and saw the two Honkeys sitting on his couch, talking like they were on a date, or husband and wife. She had calmed down but jumped and cried out when he entered he room. He carried an old tan Samsonite suitcase, belted with cord strap.

"Sorry. Didn't mean to scare you. Brought up your suitcase. It's yours?"

"Uh huh."

Salty stood. "So, can I know what the commotion was about?" He turned toward the girl. "By the way, this here is Gina Moreland, from Sioux City, Iowa and she's come to Chicago to find a job."

"Well, you know a lot. Louise, the woman downstairs, met her at the bus depot. She mentioned getting a room next-door and a job here. Good tips. When Gina, right Gina? When Gina saw the place she thought she was being kidnapped for a harem or some such thing." He looked right at Gina. "Did you think that? Honest?"

"Well, I sort of, I was thinking of something different from the way that lady was telling me."

"She wouldn't hurt a fly." said Lyons. "Look here, my

partner and I are just finishing some work. He's free now. Right Salty?"

"Yeah. Free." His mind heard partner. He was in. "Something you'd like me to do?"

Lyons pulled a roll of bills from his pocket. "Why don't you two go eat, go somewhere. Have some fun. OK, Miss Gina?"

"I'm sorry. I just got scared and..." She looked at both men. "You hear stories and don't want to believe them and this happens."

"Want to have something to eat? How long was that bus ride? You look famished." Salty rattled off his questions.

"I slept most of the way. I am hungry."

Lyons clapped his hand on Salty's shoulder. Take care of her for me. I'm trusting you."

"Like she was my sister." He took the girl by the arm and helped her from the couch. "Want to leave your bag here? That OK?"

Lyons nodded in the affirmative.

The two of them had a really delightful dinner. They spent a lot of time talking about Gina's background, the differences of living in a big city and a small town. Gina wanted to know about work and if Salty could get her a job, since he was Mr. Lyons partner. He convinced her he could get her a job. He mentally put her in his stable if Lyons would sell her to him. He drank a bit more than he usually did. Gina held her liquor well. It was common in her family to have alcohol with the evening meal.

After the meal they walked. The sounds of music and dancing neon lights bouncing off the buildings they walked by, clamored for Gina's attention. She wanted to see their source. Salty, remembered Lyons order, 'Take care of her.' So they headed toward the school grounds and the auxiliary carnival. They strolled, tried games, rode the carousal and the Caterpillar and filled their sweet tooth with cotton candy,

"Tell your future." called out the gypsy. "It's all in fun.

Tell your future." She beckoned them into her little canvas tent decorated with painted stars and moons. "It's nice to know what tomorrow will bring. Maybe."

Rubbing her hands over a lighted crystal ball resting on a zodiac encrusted tripod, the gypsy began some drivel and chanting. Gina giggled and Salty feigned attention. Gina would soon be with the people she loved and enjoy a new job. Cripes thought Salty, she's doing my job for me. Helping keep Gina here with a job. The loved ones was bullshit.

"Now for you young man." He turned to leave but Gina constrained him with a tug, a smile and a silent plea. Salty sat down and waited.

"This isn't what I thought I saw for you. It's strange. The fortune teller stood up. "I'm getting goose-bumps for what I'm feeling and... and... and... I think we should quit."

"Oh no," said Gina, "please."

"Yeah. Go ahead, it's all in fun. Remember? Besides, I paid for it." Salty said.

"The message, the feeling is icy cold. Says you will be killed..."

Salty heard her say, '...killed by a lion.'

The inside of his head flashed warnings, bells, whistles, alarms, horns all kinds of warnings. This goofy gypsy had strange feeling that he was going to get killed by a lion. It would be not a lion but Lyons. He wasn't going back to Lyon's place tonight. He took Gina to his place.

"That damn fortune teller. She scared the shit out of me." He slurred his words

"Awe Salty, it was just in fun."

"Look Gina, I know when to be scared.

"Really? You're scared?"

Salty looked scared and his voice cracked when he spoke. "Of Lyons, yes."

"Got something to drink?"

"I got something better. Real hard stuff."

Salty broke his own rules, he broke out his stash of cocaine, the girl's stuff. He laid some on the glass top of an end table. He stroked into thin lines and rolled up a dollar bill. This was the very best on the street, not even cut. When Gina protested, he forced her face into some of the pile, she snuffled, gagged and passed out. Salty considered screwing her after he snorted a bit of coke.

The police answered Onyx's call in the morning. He had gone to Indianapolis for Salty, that was why they were not together yesterday. He came into the house and found both bodies on the floor. He dialed 911 and waited. The paramedics took the girl to the hospital. She appeared to have inhaled a small amount of coke but would live. Salty was already stiff and blue, from a massive dose of uncut cocaine.

"One LINE of this stuff can kill you. Just like that." the paramedic said to the detective standing over Salty's hardening body. "One line."

DO'EN ME JOB

Being late for the start of the night's festivities, I was a pint or two behind the other drinkers and the most sober of all that was in Kiley's the night Frogger died. It has fallen on me to tell the story, a most sorry event, in me own words. So here I am telling it.

Frogger is dead. Killed by ignorance and nothing more. It was an accident sure as getting pregnant the first time you did it. All his promises died with him. There he was, standing on the curbside having words with ruddy faced Pat Humphries, as to who's to lead the dance at the coming St. Patrick's Day todo. They wasn't fighting, or hollering just talking a bit too loud, just a mite of bluster, caused by a brew or two.

Oxley, just over from the Ol' Sod, is the new bouncer at Kiley's Saloon and family dining. He sees them posturing outside the new window, Kiley had put in just last week, after O'Brien had thumped his own brother through it. To protect the new glass, with Kiley's painted on it, in gold and green, Oxley hustles outside and pushes between Frogger and Pat. Pushes right in between them. No one pushes those two. They took offense right then.

Now Oxley is bigger than his name and when they challenge him, he grabs both their collars and holds their faces up to his dark eyes. Well Pat hangs limp like, figuring to best this ox when he turns to Frogger. But Frogger, he's a kicking and flaying, a unionsuit hanging out to dry on a fire escape in a high wind. Now his foot buries itself in Oxley's privates and the roar of a dying dragon spews out his mouth. He tosses Frogger off and wouldn't you know it, through Kiley's new window.

Now a little toss like this wouldn't kill Frogger, but his body, in his new suit too, fell into the support of Kiley's hogshead of home brewed beer. The beam broke and fell onto poor Frogger. It was awful. Crushed almost where he sat each night. The beer leaked out and run all over him too. It was a terrible, terrible tragedy.

Kiley selected me to tell his missus, a whisp of Ireland she was. It broke my heart just thinking on what I would say to her. She'd want to come to Kiley's, but I was to dissuade her. "Get Mrs. Lanahan or Mrs. Burns to go in with you." ordered Kiley. "It'll help keep his missus' spirits up."

Me and Mrs. Burns went, she rapping on the gray door with her arthritic knuckles.

"Margaret. Margaret it's me Sally Burns. Open the door. I got news about Frogger."

Well soon as the door opens Mrs. Burns blabs out the horrible news and the poor thing drops to her knees, praying in the old tongue, the Irish. She sprawled backward a wailing like a Banshee, awful screeches of torment and thumping her feeble breast.

"How could this happen? How?" She mumbled of plans she and Frogger was making, for a family and new things and such. "You said Kiley's new man killed my man. He's big. How big? My Frogger is a big man. Was he bigger than Frogger?"

"Oh, yes. Bigger than Frogger. Yes um." I replied.

"Bigger 'n the fighter which won last month at Jerry's place?"

"Sure he is bigger than that guy, easy." came a dry raspy response.

"Bigger then..."

"Maggie, please. It don't matter how big he is. He didn't mean to hurt Frogger. It were ignorance on Oxley's part. He was protecting Kiley's window, his whole establishment. He didn't know Frogger and Pat was buddies and always talked to each other loud. I'm sure he'll tell you this his self. I'll be helping you move things 'cause they'll be bringing him home soon."

Frogger had a beautiful wake and all. Everyone praised him and told the young widow how sorry they was and how sorry Oxley was.

Oxley came himself, blubbering he was, as he told the poor thing his regrets. It was a brave thing he did to show his self 'cause he was jest do'en his job. I've told the story and done do'en me job I am.

LITTLE JOKE

"You can go to Hell! You, the company, the deal, every-thing can go to Hell!"

"But Adam, this isn't the end of it. It's still your baby, with a change or two."

"You heard me. Take the whole damn deal, shove it up your ass and go to Hell."

Adam Asell threw the folder at his boss's head, spun about, slammed the office door shattering the glass and stormed toward the open elevator. Inside he saw the perplexed stare on the manager's face rushing toward him. He casually flipped him the bird and mouthed, "Go to Hell." as the elevator doors closed.

In the downstairs garage Adam fumbled with his keys and cursed the Almighty. He floored the gas pedal, the car rocketed into the street and accelerated passed the speed limit in seconds. The street lights became connected dots and the buildings a complicated jigsaw puzzle. He slipped beyond one hundred miles per hour as the car ducked under the post office then lost control as it emerged onto the iron bridge. During this episode he continued to curse the heavens telling everyone and every possible thing to go to Hell.

Adam sat on the curb and watched the emergency crews cut his Mercedes apart. The body the firemen removed was zipped shut in a body bag. He wondered who had died. He watched as the tangled car parts produced bright red and orange sparks when metal scraped metal as the tow truck hoisted the wreck onto the flat bed. When the policeman waved the east bound traffic along,

Adam realized he occupied the body bag. He was dead.

"Adam? Adam Asell?" A quiet feminine voice spoke from behind him.

"Yes. I'm Adam Asell." He turned as he spoke and wondered who knew him?

"I'm Ryetta. I'm to guide you from here." The sweet voice came from a beautiful figure encased in a gown that shimmered with a glow Adam had never seen before. In her gorgeous gown she floated and moved gracefully away from him. Her finger crooked and her raised arm gave a familiar beckoning gesture.

"Come with me, please."

"Yeah. Sure. Where to?" Adam asked as he stood, but unable to maintain his balance fell forward. "What the hell?'

"No, no. Never say that word." Her face wrinkled into a net at the corners of the mouth and the corners of the palest eyes. "Never."

She eased Adam into an upright position. It seemed to work, but he stood still afraid to move. A tug at his sleeve started his movement beside her. If he walked upon a floor he didn't know it or see it. No problem, but different than walking as he did before.

"I'm not ready for this. Am I really dead? Really?"

"Oh yes. Really, really dead. I'm to bring you to the bookkeeper's station."

"What the hell is.. Sorry" A smirk crossed his lips. "What's the bookkeeper's station?"

"He will tell you your eternal destination. You know. Heaven or .. You know."

"There really is a heaven and.. the other place." Adam shook his head in a disbelieving motion. "I never really believed in that stuff. You know. Burning fires, God, angels. Are you an angel?"

"No."

The swirling clouds dissipated and a line of people similar

to Adam stood waiting. Waiting for what? Adam couldn't tell. He craned his neck, but the line disappeared into the distant horizon. He turned to Ryetta, but found she had left him. He stood, moved, stood, moved with the others. No one spoke. A rather unfriendly group he thought. Now images, vignettes of things that he experienced on earth, began to possess his mind. Some worried him. He'd not been free of fault, sin if you please and he had occasionally been down right rotten. Maybe he didn't believe in Heaven or God, but he asked Him to send many people and objects to Hell. Often.

"Adam Asell." The bookkeeper called in a voice Adam thought flat.

Adam stepped toward the podium and stood beside an older gentleman. "Here." said two voices.

"Huh? What's this?" Replied the bookkeeper. "Two of you. Not possible."

The bookkeeper glowered his disapproval, poked the feathered quill into a mass of tangled hair and rang a golden bell, that shed eons of dust as it clattered through the vaulted area. The two men watched as darkness settled onto the scene. They saw a flurry of commotion in all reaches of the visible area. Something happened, Oh yes, something happened.

Ryetta appeared beside Adam, an ugly crone next to the other Adam.

"Well." Said the sternest voice Adam had ever heard. "Explain. Ryetta?"

"I can't."

"Neither can I." Said the crone, her face contorted into an feeble grimace.

Oh my, oh my. Adam said to himself. It's just like the movie with Warren Beatty, where he dies too soon and they burn his body. Then the angel gets him another one, a dead millionaire's. If that's going to happen again, let it happen to me.

The three heavenly figures gestured and murmured out of

Adam's hearing. They often looked toward him. His mind raced along a plethora of possibilities for another chance. All favorable to him since he now knew there was a Heaven and God and... Well he'd live a better life next time around.

The bookkeeper reached out toward the two men, beckoned them forward with a motion. "There seems to be a small problem, which we can settle in time. You," he pointed toward the elder Adam, "may go in now. You," he turned toward the other Adam, "are not listed for entrance to Heaven on today's roster. We can not look into future roster pages before their time. So, as you often hollered to Heaven and God for people to go to Hell, you're to go there."

"Shouldn't say that word up here." Adam spouted petulantly.

"Never-the-less. You go to Hell."

Without realizing movement, time or changes, Adam found himself in Hell. "Hey, Hey! No fair! I shouldn't go to Hell for your mistake. Get me out of here! Now!"

Adam railed like this often, for many years. The imps and the Devil himself enjoyed his suffering. Fear and pain etched his face, he knew he'd been there for a while. But more than any other soul in Hell, he felt that one day he'd get out and they wouldn't. Always this thought filled his tortured soul. Hope is not for those in Hell.

One day, Ryetta stood next to Adam.

"Adam Asell, we have not forgotten you. The bookkeeper found your name today."

"Now? You've come to get me. I get out now."

"No. Remember, you told quite a few people to go to Hell. The bookkeeper says, 'You probably know and met many of the people you requested God send here.' That being the case and since you're already here you might just as well stay."

The echo, "Go to Hell!," replaced hope in Adam's soul.

NIGHT DUTY

"Matusek, see you for a minute, in my office?" Captain Flynn, Chicago cop for 18 years, made this request with a wave of his arm as usual, his ham sized fist held a wad of papers and some fluttered with his movement like released doves of peace.

Violet "Vi" Matusek, veteran of sixteen years on the beat, smiled as a petite shadow stepped from behind the Captain. She followed him as he reented his office, her head bobbling like a dash board doll.

Yeah. Sure she would have rookie Officer, Clementine Theresa Gomez, as her partner. Yes, she knew her years on the force would benefit the new officer. No, she didn't mind and no, she had no questions. Yes, her present partner began maternity leave today and she noticed the blank space on the assignment sheet.

The two officers took unit 402 on to Marquette Boulevard and swung east. The silence was broken when the radio crackled and through the static droned a voice with a domestic disturbance call. When the rookie failed to respond, Vi reached over and grabbed the mike. She responded to the call, snapped on the gum-ball and new team stepped off, on the wrong foot.

Vi breathed a deep sigh, pulled to the curb, and faced her new partner. "Let's get back to basics. Radio calls are not answered by the driver. You sit in that seat, you answer the radio."

Clementine's head nodded.

"Hell, girl, you afraid or something?" A pause, followed with icy calm. "Answer me."

The rookie, looked into her companion's face, determination forced her chin out. "I have some trouble with English words, when I'm nervous. I'm new today, OK? I admit I'm just a little nervous."

"Me, too."

Officer Gomez gave a weak but sincere smile. "Nervous about me?"

"You bet. All that stuff at the academy about partners and closeness is true. We gotta know each other, think and move as one, a team. No one does it alone."

"I guess I heard some talk about you, but didn't question it." said Gomez.

"Christ! Ain't that Baker shooting ever gonna die? I shot Baker when his team didn't tell us they were covering a drug bust. They went behind the building and shot at shadows. Honest, shadows. I shot back and he's on permanent desk duty because it ruined his leg."

"Ohhh, well...." Gomez shrugged and smiled back.

"Let's roll on this call and talk later."

Vi hit the siren button, snapped on the lights and the two officers headed for the domestic violence

"You go girl." Giggles floated on the siren's screech.

As the day dragged on, little else happened and the two women started to know each other and settled in for the duration.

As weeks turned into months, misunderstandings fouled up some routine work. Some paperwork came back for clarification and rewriting. Violet handled most calls with black people, Clementine made the Hispanic language cases simpler. Both did their best with the rest of the world. It worked. Well almost.

One muggy Chicago summer evening, as the last tint of pink in the sky faded into purple. The following true story brightened the somber squad room in all district stations, had officers calling off duty officers and everyone laughed about Violet and

Clementine's little incident of misunderstanding for days. Somehow, the newspapers never picked up the story. Or if they did, they couldn't bring themselves to tell the public.

It all began as Vi and Clementine polished off a Big Mac supper in their squad car, parked at the corner of Chicago Avenue and State. The car windows open, but the a/c on and pointed down, cooling their tired feet. Matusek, for the umpteenth time, explained the proper preparation of tripe for easy meals. Clementine for the umpteenth time said she would rather eat her pork with hot, very hot, salsa. Pedestrian traffic oozed along in that, "It's to damn hot to move motion".

A skinny fella, bare footed, tank top, his belt unbuckled clutched his pants with one hand rushed toward the squad car. There may have been blood on his hands, but it was difficult to tell because his hands clutched his crotch. His face twisted in a gastly grimmace of pain. It wasn't his pants he held as he approched the squad but his crotch.

"Espanol? Hable Espanol?"

Clementine's head popped out of the curbside window. "Yo hablo. Ben para ca. Que tu quieres?"

"Estoy mouriendo."

"Que? Digame!"

Vi munched her last bite and watched the world moving about her. She let Clementine rattle on in Spanish, sure the problem would be resolved. The man's excited yammer rose in pitch and she turned toward the man, as Clementine shouted.

"Alto! Alto en sequida."

"Jesus Christ!" Violet's eyes bulged, her exclamation blasted throughout the squad car's interior. "Hey! You damn pervert!"

Clementine watched stunned as the man pulled his manhood out of his pants. Amazed, she drew back in her seat, threw her hands to her face, all the while shouting in Spanish.

"Alto! Siere el pantalon. Alto! Alto!"

The man continued to fumble with his pants.

"Por favor! Pongas su connaho ensu pantalones."

Violet had seen too much. She grabbed her nightstick from between the two seats and swung at the pathetic, dangling mass that protruded from the man's pants. She wanted to knock it off. Well, she'd bust it up a little anyway. A scream told her she hit the target.

Clementine grabbed at the flying club. "No! No! Don't hit him, Violet. He's hurt." She hollered at the man now howling with new vigor. "Siere su pantalons."

"Let go a me, Clementine. I'll fix this damn pervert. Flash a cop will you?" Violet tried to swing another blow but Clementine gripped the nightstick like a boa grips it's prey. The nightstick still landed on the screamer's member. Louder howls and pedestrians gawked at the dancing man near the squad car.

"Violet! Violet, the guy's girlfriend stabbed him in the penis. He needs help. He's trying to show me where she stabbed him." Clementine's head turned, her grip on the night stick firm. "Callate! Siere su pantalons. Eres untonto."

Fate showed its hand. The nightstick slid passed the man's body and stuck through the window. The struggle between the two women, caused one to hit the window button. It rose and held the nightstick and the man's genitals, norrowly preventing instant castration. The man feared this and in pain screamed louder. What with the scream, the victim beating the car with his fist and the struggle taking place in the car, a sizable crowd began to gather to enjoy the free show .

Clementine turned to Violet. "Shit, we're going to be in deep trouble if we don't help this jerk. Get him in the back and drive to Stroger. Now!" Clementine's order came out crisp and rung with authority.

Violet exited their car and came around to man-handled the hysterical man into the back of the squadcar.

The sotto voco conversation in the squad car would have

given a sit-com writer a season's storyline. The man swore bilingual oaths and continued to whimper loudly from the back seat. Clementine, hollered at the man in Spanish and tried to calm Violet in English. Violet swore at the man for exposing himself, cussed Clementine for dirtying the squad car and insisted the man should have gone to Stroger Hospital in an ambulance.

Before they arrived at the E.R. door, Clementine leaned over and whispered into Violet's ear. She reminded her they were responsible for hurting the victim and they could be sued. Violet shut up but muttered under her breath all the way to the hospital. They took the man into the E.R. where the entertainment continued.

Two Chicago officers and a County Sheriff already waited in the E.R. processing family shooting and a drug overdose. They started snickering as Violet began her explanation of the man's injuries to the giggling paper shuffler at the desk. One officer opened his collar mike, which allowed his desk sergeant to overhear Violet's answers to the desk clerk questions. District personnel heard it on the intercom and contacted other districts. The Sheriff had an asthma attack when he couldn't stop laughing. Violet went to the toilet, to cool off and calm down. Clementine and the hospital interpreter interrogated the victim.

As I said earlier, I wonder why it didn't make the news or the newspapers.

By the way. Domingo, the victim, had been stabbed, mostly sliced, in the groin. Several days later, our lady officers saw Domingo and a woman, hand in hand on State Street.

WAR STORIES

A LONG SHOT

"Awe, God. Take him down Noah. Take him down. God."

A wiggling mass of maggots, smothered the faded blue uniform wedged in the tree fork, many tumbling to the damp earth. The stench hung in the still air. Fleeing the battle at Five Forks the two brothers had forded the James River. Tired and hungry they blundered upon this loathsome sight. They gagged, but had nothing in their stomachs to heave. Noah, avoiding the squirming, pulsating mass, picked up the telescoped rifle and three loose cartridges.

"God bless you fella."

"Amen."

Turning south, both began walking. April 8, 1865, another weary day of war.

"I know he's a Yankee, Noah. But a man. We at least could take him down and pray over him."

"We just prayed" came the grumbling voice.

"No Noah, a heart felt prayer. Cover him, so no more creatures hurt him. He's the image of God. We heard momma say many times afore the fighting, man is the image of God."

Groaning his exasperation, "We are fighting a war. He's a dead man. An enemy."

Matty's voice aching with a choke men have before they cry, "Please Noah. So we never dream him haunting us for a grave or a prayer."

"Christ, Matty. OK. Hide our stuff in that thicket. This

here telescoped rifle too. We bury him fast and get.'"

Gulping for breath, when they could, they poked the body from the tree fork with a thick branch. Prodding the oozing body into a slight depression, both knelt, dragging leaves and forest materials over the unfortunate solider. Each in reverie thought this man could have been either of them a few days ago.

April 1st, "April Fool's Day", the joke was on the Rebels. The Yankees attacked at Five Forks. The battle had started and finished in hours. In the fighting the Yankees cost them dearly. Lost supplies, horses, artillery, scant and precious food stuff and men. So many killed, so many more captured.

An hour into the fighting, it seemed to last forever, logs reinforcing the entrenchment began buckling. Both brothers were buried. Struggling like earthworms, they escaped their mud grave. In shock for hours these indistinguishable clods lay against the tortured earth. Hours later they emerged into a different world.

They saw drunken Yankee victors huddling, laughing over campfires, somber confederate prisoners huddling, sulking around campfires. Long lines of men and wagons were moving on Five Forks Road. Neither brother, wishing to join the bedraggled unhappy remnants of beaten men so they lay in the chilly mud, waiting.

Noticing a gap in the moving army filing along the road, Noah began moving, Matty following, Slipping between Mackenzie' soldiers and Ayer's men, unchallenged, they were soon wandering along the banks of the James River. They wanted to be somewhere. Anywhere but here.

Blundering into bogs and deep woods, lost for days they managed to stay out of human sight. Once a burned barn covered them at night. They feasted on rotting seed goobers in the morning. Mostly they were sleeping out, cold, hungry, angry and very scared. And now this. Burying a Yankee sharpshooter.

In their desire to be "good" men they let down their guard. A major mistake in time of war. Unseen and unheard two clean blue uniforms creep close to them. One, swinging his rifle club like, flattened the shorter soldier into the partially covered heap of putrefaction. While the other, wrapping his arms around the smaller man, prevented him from helping his companion. The rifle came down again and again, gore flying from the weapon. Stunned, the young man struggled against an iron embrace, screaming, begging, watched his fallen brother being killed.

"Lousy thieven bastards. What cha doing? Stealing from a corpse?"

His heavy boots furiously stomping the fallen body, cursing it, damning it,

"We was try'n.." wheezed Noah.

A large head with bushy eyebrows, bend nose and thick lips, now sent a huge hand and heavy ring into his face, driving the words back into the gasping throat. Then a kick, drove his testicles up into an empty stomach. From his knees Noah witnessed the brutalizer ripping Matty's pockets open, steal his pocket watch then standing over him urinate on the body. Turning again to kick Noah's head, the soldier sent him sliding down the dew covered bank, the rushing cold water biting into the fresh cuts on his face, dragged him under. He felt, without understanding, the budding branches of submerged bushes grabbing him, hiding him from view.

"You hear me you Rebel bastard? You tell them one Yankee beat the shit out of two Rebel sons of bitches. You tell 'em. Hear?"

Neither gray uniform answered his taunt. Neither could. Two figures in clean blue uniforms stepping off north, didn't see one gray uniformed figure struggling out of the water, heading south. Soft bird calls began filling the soundless woodland, a frog beckoning another frog and a single violet unfolding within a shaft of sunlight.

****

Light had just separated sky from land as a lone figure,

crawling then running bent over, headed for the approximate spot of yesterday's murder. For murder it was, not a death in war. Murder. Brushing debris from the body, Noah, grasping the stiff form rose with it dangling across his shoulder. Heading, in a half crouch for the thicket, he retrieved the weapons hidden yesterday, adjusted the burden on his shoulder and continued south.

Faint moving outlines of waiting men in the morning mist revealed his lines. Leaning with his burden against a shot ripped oak, he gave a throaty bullfrog grunt. Separating from the mist and moving through the split rail fence, several gray uniforms, hastily eased the stiff body from his back down to the dew moisten ground.

"Easy guys. He's my brother."

Returning to their positions the nine soldiers, shivering in the morning dampness sat staring. Nine strangers united in a cause, united over a hole in the ground, united to the dead by prayer. God made them dreamers and builders, a difference in opinion made them killers. Hunching over a vile brew of acorn and chicory coffee, they were attempting to induce their trembling muscles to calm. Noah recounted yesterday's events. It sent shivers through their souls.

His story was mesmerizing, but the telescoped rifle more so. Six of the nine men were sent off, scrounging for firewood, the three remaining sat marveling at the weapon. Awed by rumors of it's reputed killing power. It's killing power at great distances. Fascinating.

"Never saw a Henry before." said the smallest fellow.

"I did. O'Malley, he's gone now, picked up a Henry at Cold Harbor. Sold it for twenty-five dollars."

"I hear it can kill man so far off you can't hardly see him."

"More'n a mile off."

"Never." said the smallest.

The red head, with a broken tooth smile, asked, "Gonna

use it Noah?"

"Hope to. Maybe."

"Think it'll really kill a fella a mile off?" the red head said, throwing his cold, bitter coffee away.

"Don't know. I don't think shooting so far you could tell if you kill someone."

"Lemme see here." The red head, hefting the rifle, lay it across the rail fence, peering through the telescope. "It sure make everything closer."

"Let me see too." two voices spoke as one.

Passing the gun from hand to admiring hand, all praising it more than once.

Their comments blessing the rifle with super power, while their hearts filled with envy and covetness. Back in the owner's hands, he began sighting along the Yankee lines.

The April sun melted the mist away. Stepping forward, steadying his hands by placing the rifle on the top fence rail, Noah slowly traced the distant horizon. Turning, grinning, looking at the men behind him, then winked. He began loading the chamber, sliding in one cartridge found with the dead Yankee. Leaning forward, he again, slowly, very slowly, began retracing the horizon.

The small group of men stared in the direction the rifle was pointed. One shielded his eyes with his hand, another squinting into the glare, shook his head in bewilderment.

"You gonna shoot somebody Noah?" asked the redhead.

"Can you see the roan? Near that flap of canvas?" Noah asked, not looking back.

"You got the telescope thing, we can't see that far. See a flap of canvas off to the side of a clump of trees. No roan. Why?"

"Well the man that killed Matty is standing between the roan and the flap. I'm hoping he'll be with the devil just as soon as I shoot this rifle."

With a wry smile the brute in blue, gazing up from a chiming pocket watch, saw a flash in the low area to the south. A wisp of light gray smoke rose from the flash, a whirling eddy drifting toward the tree tops. He felt something hit him and could see men looking down at him. Why down? Something was squeezing his chest, silencing the chimes, darkening the morning sky.

Noah never knew if you could kill a man a mile away. He just had to try.

The brute would never tell Noah you could shoot and kill a man a mile away.

BUCK FEVER

"Congratulations Myloss." A firm hand squeezed his companion's shoulder.

Myloss reached up and seized the hand. "Thanks Ari. I'm honored."

"Nervous?"

"A bit. It is my first assignment." Myloss grinned. "Were you? The first time?"

"Yes. I can tell you. Even had a touch of Buck Fever. Shook something awful."

The two men hugged in comradeship, picked up their weapons and headed toward the dilapidated door. They needed each other, the support and assurance of men that might die in the next instant. Their cause and beliefs kept them alive, their friendship the reason to live.

"Ari, what's Buck Fever?" Myloss smiled, a maiden asking a man a question.

His friend saw the simplistic need in the question, not the ignorance. "Buck Fever" is an old hunting term. The first time a man sees a buck his urge to shoot it becomes so great he becomes nervous, shaky and he misses his shot."

"Yeah. It's what I sort of figured.' A grin returned to his young, unlined face.

Ari took hold of Myloss arm. "It's very common. When you line your laser on your target, if you start to shake, take a deep breath, hold it and count to three. Count to three, important. Then ever so slowly breath out and touch off your shot as you exhale."

Looking deep into Ari's eyes, Myloss whispered, "I can do that. Breath, hold, count to three and shoot. I'll remember. If I shake."

They laughed and went their separate ways. They each had an assignment and each had his own preparations and thoughts. They even had time for a prayer.

That evening a quiet voice monotonously droned from the television. No one seemed to pay attention. Ari set his rifle against the chair and threw his weight into its recessed cushion. His ears perked up as the reporter read the report.

"An attempt to assassinate the Premier failed today, when security noticed a laser beam's circle of light dancing nervously off his office wall. The attempting assassin was killed. An officer commented that assassin's nervousness was due to "Buck fever".

IN TIME OF WAR

"Never volunteer."

Dolph heard it first during basic training. When the sergeant asked for volunteers, his hand was rising, but Heller caught the movement and quickly tugged Dolph's arm down. Christian volunteered that day.

Whispering, Heller said, "Let's talk later."

"You can bet we will. I'm thinking the sergeant should be told of this."

Heller's eyes showed his displeasure at the remark. "After we talk. OK?"

"OK."

Sitting on his bed, Dolph began assessing Heller. A large man, thick in the trunk and shoulders, a slim waist and feet too large for the body. His unshaved beard remained a perpetual shadow on his face, broken often by a smile. The military haircut made his head, look like a billiard ball, smooth and black. His quiet manner and speech distorting the picture Dolph was getting.

"I wanted to show the sergeant I could be counted on." said a peeved Dolph.

"Never volunteer. Never. You can get killed. I just met you, don't really know you, yet. Don't screw it up." Heller's big smile slashed his shadowed mouth. "OK?"

"What do you mean killed? We can't get killed, not yet anyway."

"My friend. Can we be friends?"

"Sure."

"In the army you can get killed in many ways." a smiling Heller said. "Believe me."

Dolph, looking into his new friend's face. "You been in before?"

"Nope. I listen and learn fast. I want in and out of this war real quick. I don't want to be a hero, just alive when its over."

The call to mess stopped their discussion, hunger interrupting further talk.

Four months later, sweaty and louse bitten, the two men hunkered down in a dry trench somewhere along the skirmish line. The ensuing weeks brought them together as soldiering has done for ages, literally reading each other's thoughts. This latest battle testing their camaraderie to the limits. Both men trying to be near the other, which in the army isn't easy, even when you're in the same hole.

"Heller, get back to the officer's quarters." said a filthy orderly. "Post haste."

"Up yours." answered Heller, kicking the yellow dirt at the messenger.

"Hey! I deliver messages. I ain't gonna be delivering your answer. Move it." the retreating face said, sliding back from the grassy lip of the trench.

"Get going. I'll stay here." said Dolph.

"Bye-bye."

Twenty minutes later the orderly inform Dolph that Heller had volunteered for a mission behind enemy lines. Dolph knew that was a lie. Never volunteer, bounced around in his head. That night he stayed in the trench, true to his word to wait there for Heller. A pale pink crease in the eastern sky informed him how long Heller had been away. He also noted a furtive dark hump wriggling in the crease.

Sliding down, placing his helmet near his feet, cocking his weapon he waited. The dawn became pinker. Dolph wondered where the hell Heller could be. What should he do? Waiting, by himself, was agonizing. Poking his head above the edge of the ground, allowing only half eye above it, he scanned the growing pink crease for further movement. Nothing. Hunkering down, waiting, and wondering if anyone else saw the movement.

"Dolph. Dolph." Someone calling across the dry field. "Dolph. It's me. Heller."

"Heller?"

"Yeah."

Clutched his rifle, Dolph's mind fogged by the unexpected event. "Heller? What the hell you doing over there."

"Taking a shit. I got sent here. Didn't that messenger tell you what's happening?"

Dolph didn't think it right to talk to a voice coming from the enemy's lines. He didn't remember exactly what he'd been told. Except Heller volunteering to go behind enemy lines.

"You tell me." Dolph requested

"Tell you what. The Brass sent me over here to see what's going on."

"You volunteered?" asking a whining voice.

"Sorta." The voice responded. "An officer remembered my remarks about how I listen and learn. He asked if I could listen and learn for him? When I said yes, he thanked me for volunteering. I started to protest, but, you know. They made me a deal I couldn't refuse."

Dolph smiled at the answer. "Saw the Godfather, huh?"

"With you. And the two girls we met and took to the beach."

"Christ. It's really you."

"It is and Houston, I got a problem. I'm in an enemy uniform. I need to standup and run to you. I got no way of telling the other guys on the line. If I start running they may start shooting, or these guys over here may think I'm ducking out and pop me. I got a problem Houston."

A non-com, gasping for air scurried into the trench with

Dolph. Neither knew the other, but their uniforms were the same. Looking at each other, smiling that just met you smile, they were both listening as Heller gave his instructions.

"I'll wait 'til 0 six fifteen, then run like hell for your spot. Stick your rifle up so I can zero in on it. Try to get our guys not to shoot."

Zipping along the perimeter lines telling everyone not to shoot the running figure at 0 six fifteen, Dolph convinced them it was our guy in their uniform. Don't shoot him.

Returning to the hole in the ground, waiting in silence, their rifles pointed toward the enemy lines, Dolph and the non-com sat, waiting. O six fifteen, Dolph's rifle poked the blushing red sky, his eyes scouring the horizon.

"Here he comes."

The man next to Dolph fired at the running figure, sending it tumbling down. Dolph saw the flash of fire, then the weapon turning, pointing at him. The sudden pain and darkness never let him understand. Speed meant life, the non-com, crouching low, ran quickly from the dying Dolph, passing the kicking figure of Heller.

Dressed in an enemy non-com uniform, the young man saluted his commanding officer, both men wearing knowing smiles.

"So, did your suggestion to infiltrate their headquarters get us any information?" asked the officer.

"Sir, in this uniform I was able to overhear plans to move against our lines at the town church when the sunrises. I knew the time was close so I took a chance and headed for here. One of their spies, in our uniform, tried to return. I shot him and the one trying to help him. Then while they were confused I ran like a deer and made it back. Sir, may I request never to volunteer again. I might have been shot."

SETH

Echoing off very rock face in the small gorge, the shot alerted the unwary and weary alike. Missing his quarry, exasperated the hunter with limited ammunition, now forcing him to wait for another opportunity. Waiting in the woodland can be pleasant or dangerous when marauders and guerrillas or regular army are moving about. April something, 1864 and the Missouri war area had killings daily, with or without battles.

Seth Colfax, three inches shorter than the old Kentucky long rifle he was using, was thirteen years old, skinny as a fence rail and sole male member of the family. Seth sat pushing the ramrod back and forth, waiting. Right now the family's hunger would allow shooting any source of food, as long as it would feed everyone. Not properly dressed, the morning chill made him pull his shivering body down into his over sized coat.

Holding an arm high, stopping the three men behind him, the leader, stabbing his finger forward, directing their eyes to the stump where Seth sat. With hand signals, they encircled and captured Seth.

"Why you here youngster?" asked the finger pointing guerrilla leader.

The frightened boy didn't hold back. "Hunting food. For the family."

"What you shoot?" asked the man holding Seth and his gun.

"Missed a squirrel. Got nothing yet."

The leader sternly asked, "Your name fellow and point the

direction you shot."

He pointed up the rock face, "Seth. Seth Colfax, we live on the river road."

"Ain't no trees up there." said a old man holding a bloody arm and pointed below. Turning toward the leader, Seth's eyes ask questions his mouth couldn't.

"Appears you're lying boy. Ain't likely you're hunting way up here if you live on the river road?"

An answer never came.

Miranda Colfax went looking for the boy a bit after noon. Familiar with his hunting habits, she headed for the small gorge. She buried him there, that afternoon.

REMEMBERED

Miranda Colfax had no time to mourn a son or others of her family killed in this Civil War. Actually a most uncivil war American fighting American. She would hold the family together and wait for the war to end and family members to return. No other thought or persuasion would change her determine mind.

The day after burying Seth, she began turning the rich river bottom soil. Bending over the shovel, breaking the earth for planting seed, she nearly missed the approaching men. The doves, stealing feed from the chickens, flew up as they came from the direction of the little gorge. Squinting at the tattered scarecrows, carrying their rifles slung carelessly over their shoulders, she realized they were not military. Bolting into the house before they could stop her, she immediately barred the door and both windows.

Sitting on the chopping stump hollering, "We need some food old woman. Don't make us break in or hurt you." the leader made himself known.

The small fellow broke into the chicken area, grabbing both chickens, then marching toward the house while wringing their necks. "Wanna cook these for us?"

"Damn Thomas, you're making us unwelcome doing things like that."

Shrugging, he sat next to the old man and both began plucking the birds. Their three guns and an old Kentucky rifle were leaning on the fence rail. Their spokesman walking back and forth, cussing his men and the old woman, made it clear they would break in if she didn't open the door. Burn her out even. They, said he, were fighting men of the southern cause and it was her duty to assist them getting to their unit.

"I'm an old lady, alone. Can't trust no one any more. Stand out near the fence, so I can see you all. I'll put out the kettle with something to eat. Eat. Then go away."

Quick and proper, like children hearing the school bell, they moved to the fence. Even shouting thanks and sorry for killing the chickens. Seeing the covered kettle placed outside the door, the ran pell mell hoping to catch the woman. They ran into eternity as the gunpowder filled kettle exploded in their lying, thieving, killing faces.

"They were liars and killers, Seth. Liars and killers, they's answering to God now."

TAKE SHELTER

"Get the hell out of here!"

The four man patrol didn't question the sergeant's order. Returning to their own lines after executing a family of suspected collaborators, they blundered into an enemy patrol. So close to their own lines and this happens. Sergeant Perez recognized the protecting walls as his old church. He remembered practicing Latin and stealing tastes of sacristy wine and a secret. He moved into enemy fire rather than stay against its walls.

In the exchange of fire, Nolan took a bullet in the lower leg, another bullet through his radio. Bad luck, each patrol trapping the other behind their own lines. Sergeant Perez would not leave a man behind, not if he could help it. Firing so close to their own troops would certainly draw friendly and deadly fire on themselves?

"We got a problem. Perez announced. "Stay here and wait means stay here and die. The sun would be up in about half an hour."

"So Sarg" said Private Pritchard. "What's the plan?"

"I'm thinking. I'm thinking. The only thing is..." looking at Nolan, "is leaving Nolan behind."

Nolan winced. The idea of being left sickened him, knowing mercy from the enemy didn't exist. Well they had showed none to them either. Since when did mercy become a factor in fighting a war, a Civil war? Flopping his head back and staring into the pale starry heaven, Nolan wondered. Did God see his predicament?

Crawling beside his wounded comrade, Perez asked, "Nolan, can you sit up?"

"Sure. Why?"

"Listen to me. We're leaving you here, for now. We're going off left and fire on those guys. I want them to think there's safety between the two walls."

"What? Between the walls?"

"Between the walls. Safe between the walls. Dug in and safe."

"OK. I guess you got a reason."

"You can see those walls?" asked the Sergeant, eyes close to Nolan's frightened face. "Now, can you throw a grenade from here to those walls?"

Looking over at the spot indicated, Nolan gave an affirmative nod.

"Hit the corner of the walls. Throw two, even three" The Sergeant laid several grenades into Nolan's lap. "They must hit right in the corner. We're going to raise a ruckus on their left flank, trying to get them to take cover between the walls."

"OK. Right in the corner." Staring at the Sergeant crawling back into the darkness, Nolan whispered repeatedly, "Right in the corner."

Sarg and his men poured in rapid fire and tossed a few grenades, sure enough, the drab shadows, of save my ass soldiers, were darting for the walls and safety. Nolan pitched three grenades as quick and accurately as he could. Watching the dust and smoke billow up and the walls fall, he thought something swallowed the ruins. Behind him Sarg called out then flopped beside him. "Nice toss. We got them all, I hope. We'll wait 'til the dust settles and check it out."

The weary men listened as Sarg explained that he had been an altar boy in the church years ago. They would sneak in and go down to a cistern under the church to drink wine and screw willing girls. The entrance had been under the corner of the sacristy, right where Nolan dropped his eggs.

Later they examined the hole. The faintest light of dawn revealing the extreme depth of the cistern, actually a grotto. There were fallen statues along the wall and crypts. Turning to leave for their own lines, friendly fire began pouring in on them. The ground gave way beneath their feet, filling the void with tons of earth.

Only their God knew these circumstances, for the Lieutenant's daily casualty report listed the entire patrol as MIA.

SHOOT THE DEAD

Even as they ran away from the shooting, they feared for their lives. Royale and Shane were soldiers, Union soldiers, sworn in two days ago. Right now wishing they had not listened to their girlfriends and stayed home. They didn't want to be soldiers now.

Shots kicked dust spurts in front of them. They had run back into the fighting. Both dove for the stone wall, burrowing beneath the remains of a building. How they wanted to come up in China. Shots, shouts and screams squeezed into their tiny shelter, madness tried creeping into their minds. An artillery shell exploded, dusting their backs with the loose dirt. A swallowed heart beat hurts as it thumps in a nearly breathless body.

Silence.

Their movements were no faster than growing grass, as they pushed from their hole. The smell of battle, powder, blood, urine and shit assailing their nostrils. They lay flat twisting their heads the height of plow turned earth, to determine which way the fighting had moved. Then they'd move in the opposite direction, post haste. Both stuck closer to the earth than shadows, their eyes scouring the horizon in all directions.

A Confederate casualty hung limp on a split rail fence, his banner flapping slowly to a soft breeze. Two other bodies, as though picnicking, leaned against a broken hogshead. The bodies, the smoking disturbed farmland and silent fields presented a panoramic painting of war.

"Let's git."

"Before we move, we better shoot them dead soldiers.

'Could be fooling us."

"Shoot dead bodies? Not me." The youngster stepped toward the road. His companion reached for him and the soldiers, thought picnicking, shot them dead.

"Our ruse is work'n." said one Rebel soldier. "More Yankees coming." He closed his eyes and feigned death.

"God, Sargeant. Looks like everybody here has killed everybody else."

"Looks like; however, don't trust what you think you see. Shoot those two near the wheel, I'll shoot the one hanging on the fence."

SHARPSHOOTER

The pinkish morning mist, swirling to movement, stilled the sounds within it. The movement slow and deliberate, moving up and down, pausing, couldn't be identified by Ted from his side of the creek. Hiding behind an oak log, holding his rifle steady while pointing it into the mist. He waited. The sergeant had drilled his boys, "Don't shoot until you're sure you can kill your target." Ted could wait.

The gray uniform, a shade darker than the mist, floated into view. A Rebel sweeping a stick across the ground was picking up exposed acorns or mushrooms. Moving like a wounded man or an old man stopping and stooping often. Foraging the woods the same as Ted had been doing, but unaware he'd been found. Checking his weapon, Ted inserted a dry cartridge, gauged his distance and fired.

The exploding shot, smothered by the fog, was hardly heard, as it thudded into the gray uniform. A scream, freezing his blood, forced its way into Ted's head. The mist boiling up showed the area where the thrashing body and screamed oaths of damnation and beseeching God for forgiveness came from. Ted screamed too. Then calm.

"I'm shot and bleeding. You a damn Yankee or a blind one of us?'

"Ain't no Reb. And I'll shoot again soon as I can see you."

"You just stay there." the scratchy voice said. "I'm dying real quick."

"Why you foraging so far from camp?" questioned Ted, his voice quavering.

"Gotta eat."

Hidden against the log, peering hard into the fog, wishing someone would come after hearing his shot, Ted spoke accusingly. "Didn't have to die to eat what? Acorns?"

"Didn't want to die hungry, or a soldier either, but I am. Just wanted to farm my land and raise my family. Then comes..." coughing, the voice broke, "... along comes a war, changing the world."

"You got a farm? Family? Where? You have those things? Are you an old man or a dreamer?" The wavering voice seemed genuine in its concern.

The rattling of the dying man's canteen, stiffened the hair on Ted's neck.

"A thirst is starting to burn me up. I'm a fifty-three year old dreamer and I got plenty. Or had, 'til you Yanks stole it all." The canteen's rattling created a pause. "Got a hundred sixty acres south of Menard, Illinois."

Listening, but still searching the mist, Ted said. "That's near where I grew up. Only a little bit up, Edwardsville."

"Ain't that somethin'," said the dying man. "We moved from there when the wife passed on. In '57. Married the widow Shoemacker and bought land below Cairo."

Ted spoke in a musing tone. "'Don't 'member no widow by that name."

"Oh. She never lived there." Coughing interrupted him again. "She and her husband were heading for St. Louis and he died of the cholera. She stayed on then."

"You got kids too? Huh?" Ted had shifted so he sat against the log, rifle across his lap, waiting for an answer. His target was becoming intriguing. The screaming cut into the fog and Ted again. He wanted to get up and run from here. "What's wrong?"

"Pain. Please God, take me."

Tears crept out of Ted's eyes, dropping onto his weapon. His mind telling his body to calm down, while his shoulders bounced off the log.

"I'm sorry I shot you. I'll pray you die soon."

"I will. But thank you for your prayers to help me."

Leaning back, Ted began humming "Going Home", but stopped. "Old man, I left Edwardsville in '55. Run away, and took to the river."

"My son, Teddy, died that year. Drowned."

"My name is Ted. But you had more family? Right?"

Moaning in pain, "My youngest son is back in camp. Private Ronald Pipps."

"Oh, God. Pa! Pa! It's me Teddy. Theodore. I didn't drowned. Pa!"

Ted threw his rifle aside and vaulting the log, began running through the rising fog. A Rebel sharpshooter, having heard Ted's shot, had sat waiting for movement. He fired.

SOUVENIR

"Murrary! Murray! The war's over! It's over!" Howard screamed and danced and jumped and hollered, happy as a kid that got the unattainable gift for Christmas. Traveling through the trenches and across the battlefield, the rumor grew in the heart of every soldier, except in Murray's. Even the time and date were known by every weary man, Eleven a.m., November Eleventh, 1918. Howard hugging himself, kept repeating "It's over, over, over."

Murray sat in disbelief, his face a mask, mouth agape, with doll-like eyes wide open. His mind yelling one word, "NO!" He didn't want the war over. Not tomorrow anyway. Next week would be OK. Yeah, next week. After he killed a Hun. After that no one back home could say he didn't come back a hero, a real killer.

"Murray? You OK? Huh?" asked the exuberant Howard, finally settling back into the trench. "You OK?'

"You sure Howard? The war is really over? Really, really over." the flat monotone ask Howard

"Right from the motorcycle messenger that heard the headquarters guys talking."

"Geez. We just got here to fight. How many days ago? Three? No, we got off the boat, ship, then marched for three days. We been here a week. Only seven days and I...you..us...we.., never fired a shot and it's over." The soft mud splattering both of them when his weapon slapped into the ground. A violent reaction from a braggart.

"Damn, Murray, look what you done." Howard whined.

The mud freckling his face, his uniform had been muddy since their arrival. He handed the rifle back

"I told you I was going to kill a Hun. I told Ruthy, my girl, I was going to kill a Hun. I promised myself, I was going to kill a Hun. I was even going to get a medal, even a souvenir, like a helmet or pistol maybe. And now I can't cause the war's over." Murray's helmet went skittering across the wet mud, the spray freckling the dull gray sky, then he threw the rifle down again.

"Well ain't you something else?" sounding like an old school marm on the radio, Howard mocked his buddy. Turning away in disgust, then turning back again, he fired another stinging rebuke. "You know, you can buy a medal or a souvenir."

"Ain't the same. Hey, what time did you say the war's over?"

"I said tomorrow. Tomorrow at eleven in the morning."

"Then maybe I can still kill a Hun. I've got all morning. I'll kill one yet."

"You're a real jerk. I'm just realizing what a jerk you are." Howard walked off, no longer happy, he pushed his way through the men pressed against the earthen walls. With ever step he muttered, "Jerk."

Murray had not been a good soldier. Not in training, where he sloughed off training duties and skill and often been reprimand for dirty clothing and equipment. Also for being reckless and careless on the firing range. Now he was preparing to kill another human being as the time to stop killing approached.

Groping his way along the silent, wet reinforced walls of the trench Murrray kept moving toward an outpost close to the enemy trenches. Murray reckoned a foolish or rash act from some dumb soldier exposing his body and he could tell the world he shot a Hun during the war. He just had to keep that promise. A promise is a promise and to thy ownself be true. Something like that he thought, pushing his rifle out over the edge of the trench into the darkness.

Just after eleven, a single shot came from the forward outpost. Not a shot so much, as a very small explosion. The sergeant went forward to investigate, then wrote,

"The last soldier to die in the trenches, died when he fired his weapon celebrating the end of the war. His weapon must have been choked with mud and exploded in his face, killing him."

STAY OR RUN, BUT DIE

Peter was no coward, nor was he a hero. He had joined the military to protect his country. It was one of those things he just had to do. Training went well, with his body becoming stronger and he was making new friends. His orders came and he packed his gear, said good-bye to his family and left his home for somewhere. He was a soldier, protecting his country.

The explosions of the first bursting shells over his head were terrifying. Louder, closer than in training, they broke through his soldierly facade of bravery. Throwing his gun into the air, Peter broke from the ranks of buddies in the slight slope facing the enemy. He ran. He ran screaming, scared and fast from the field. Someone grabbed at him, ripping the sleeve from his jacket. Pulling away he ran harder. Never had he run so fast.

Then silence.

Peter returned to consciousness with pain. His throat was a column of fire, his eyes saw blurs of color and his arms were swollen and bent where they should be straight. The compression of the near-by explosion had knocked him out and blown him into a hedgerow. He listened for battle sounds, but heard only the sound of trickling water. Just below him a ribbon of water flowed, passing within inches of him. Reaching out was impossible, both arms were useless. He inched his body forward, but the trickle eluded him.

The earth shook, enough to know something was moving. Suddenly running, pounding feet were jumping over him and on him. Those that missed him muddied the water. He tried to stop a vaulting uniform, grabbing the flying leg. It crushed his face and continued running. He screamed, no one stopped. Then it was quiet again.

He heard the scuffling of feet moving toward him. His countrymen would save him. The enemy would imprison him. Struggling to his feet, he stood before the mass of movement. He heard shots then he was tumbling over, his mouth came to rest in the cool trickle. He didn't drink, nor would others, as the sky-colored stream turned red.

THE COWARDLY SAMARITAN

The screams of bursting artillery shells didn't drowned out the screams of Private Terry Katz. Digging doggy style, elbows flapping, he dug into the sandy muck without getting his terrified body into the ground fast enough. He knew he would die here. His rifle, atop the hole Terry strived to excavate, slid down onto his reddish head, stopping his frantic digging and gaining unwanted attention.

The source of pain went unnoticed, the actual pain couldn't kill him. The blood and thought of dying broke the shield of immortality protecting the young solider. In an instant, Private Terry Katz, in Union blue, underfire at Mobile, stood up, turned and ran faster than he had ever run before, from the battlefield, a coward.

Screaming incoherently, arms churning the air, Private Katz ran. He ran passed comrades, passed an officer on horseback trying to stop other cowards, passing those cowards too. He ran 'til bursting shells were soundless lights, until his oxygen starved lungs no longer fed his fatigued muscles, now they were moving by memory alone, turning to mush. He collapsed beneath a bower of wild grape vines. Sleep, the simplest of cures, spread its mantle over the torn wounded body.

Shots. Shaking the cloak of Morpheus from his mind, he tried to count the shots, determining if others went uncounted before he woke. His muddled mind failing to work, allowed his body to stay down, remain hidden in the blood colored stillness of early dawn.

Facing the sounds Terry's eyes combed the countryside,

finally resting upon the scene about a hundred or so yards from his ringside seat. Two men in Confederate uniforms were shooting at figures running from a burning barn. Burning and screaming they ran everywhere and died everywhere. Two elderly men were running toward him, fear ruling their contorted puppet movements.

Terry sank down as they fell before him. Down he willed his body, deeper. Both uniformed men ran up, snickering and firing their pistols at the fallen bodies. Uniformed men yes, soldiers no. Guerrillas. Fear immobilized Terry's body, but not his bladder.

"Let's get back to the bitch." said one uniform.

"I'm hungry." said the other, standing over the bleeding bodies. "Let's find..."

"OK, Daniel. You scrounge up some edibles, I'll find the woman."

"Always women, Charles?"

Words and footfalls were hushed as the distance grew between them and Private Katz. Then slowly, ever so slowly, he raised his head. Curiosity calling his body toward the bodies, causing him to unfold and crawl out of hiding. He had watched them fall and saw them executed but he didn't see them die. Two dead Darkes their eyes shot out, lay gawking at the morning sky without seeing it. Squatting next to the bodies, Terry stared toward the house for other victims or killers, he wasn't sure.

If curiosity killed the cat, then Katz would die soon, because he wanted to know what was happening in the buildings. No sounds reached his ears, save the crackling of the flames skeletonizing the barn. Above the building a hawk pumped the air to gain gliding height to observe his domain, as the breathing fire pushed gray puffs upward, tinting purple morning's reddish horizon.

Terry's stealthy approach, low and slow, kept the well wall between him and the house doorway. No one moving in or around the house could escape his view. It frightened him. He thought of running away, of forgetting everything that happened here, but couldn't. He had to know what happened.

"Getting water." said the voice stepping through the door. "I'll fill your canteen."

An unseen voice declared, "I'll get a fire going in here. No hurry."

Terry Katz, cussed himself silently, cowering lower than the dirt beneath his boots, he watched the approaching shadow tread the dust. The shadow pulled the wench pin and began cranking the bucket up from the well. The shadow filled several canteens, then the shadow turned its back on Terry to drink from the bucket. The shadow went down hard as Terry swung the heavy wench pin through the shadow and into solid flesh. A mouth full of water mixing with blood created the muddy puddle he stepped into as he disarmed the corpse and headed for the house.

Scurrying, as a mouse avoiding the circling hawk, Private Katz, self-created coward, scampered toward the open door. The smell of coal oil fled the enclosed room, along with the slurred words of a drunk soon to be arsonist. Looking in, Terry had the man's back to him. Lofty thoughts of chivalry and the fields of King Arthur's England filled his head; however, pure cold logic ruled the day. Terry shot the guerrilla in the back. One shot and he screamed. A second shot and he faltered, turning, he sank to one knee, clawing at his holster. Pulling the trigger of an empty gun is useless.

Retreating, Terry ran, again. This time however, he had a goal, the well. The man at the well had ammunition. Terry wanted it, needed it and got it. Running completely around the house, Terry forced his head up to peer through the chinking. The guerrilla sat, facing the door, head slumped, gun held on his lap, waiting. Was he dead or alive? Terry, never a bad shot, at a sitting target, fired his pistol at the back of the head, a shower of blood and tissue sprayed the door frame. Walking around the building, he cautiously poked his head around the gore speckled door, then fired one more time into the body.

A coward? Maybe. A coward and alive? Yes.

They were after a woman. Where could she be? He noticed a rug hanging in the corner, next to an open shelf, an empty holster on the floor and a torn dress crumbled next to it.

"Lady? Mam? Lady? You in here? Mam?" His soft voiced queries receiving no answer. Pistol reloaded and pointing it before him, he walked toward the rug. "Lady, if you're in there, I mean you no harm. I killed them, the guys that shot your people. I hope they didn't hurt you. Lady, can I help you?" Yanking the rug aside, revealed the crumbled half clad body of a bloody, violently abused woman stretched out across the earthen floor.

Kneeling down, gripping her shoulders and twisting her around, he feared the worse. Was she hurt, alive or dead? Tearing loose from his grip, she rolled onto her back firing a hidden gun. Through despair and fear she sought to live, brave at all costs. The once cowardly soldier, now the good Samaritan, died.

A MISUNDERSTANDING

Obergefreite Sigmunt Hollenzub, a sadistic monster, beat and killed on a whim. He bragged often of the inhuman treatment he was inflicting upon the hapless, filthy scum living in the Ghetto. Claiming he hated to supervise the Jews, especially in the Ghetto but proclaiming his being there helped rid the world of Jews.

Herman Adolph Schmid, a calculated coward, used his ability to understand Yiddish and Hebrew, to expose Jews. Someone else was exterminating the Ghetto Jews he betrayed, his mind claimed to be innocence of that cruelty.

These two men met each other once. A chance meeting on a Ghetto street.

Schmid grew up with a Jewish nanny caring for his daily needs. Herman heard Yiddish every day, often more than German. His father, a prominent engineer and his mother independently wealthy, gave him life, little else. Rumor said Prince Rupert settled a large amount in his mother's bank account to avoid litigation and family embarrassment, for a young man's indiscretion.

Hollenzub grew up a farmer's son, frequently destroying the family's farm animals with gristly tortured methods. The loss cost money they didn't have to lose. When his father found him killing piglets, he beat the youth unconscious. His mother saved his life when she dragged him into a closet and locked the door. From that day on, Sigmunt stole neighbor's animals, or took newborn animals, before they were counted. He didn't stop.

Herman, brilliant in school, learning with little effort and retaining nearly everything he learned. He found, even before he went to school, that if he lied he avoided trouble with authorities and his parents. His parents, gullible and ignorant, always accepting Herman's side of the story, except once.

He had turned fourteen two weeks earlier when his mother caught him in his own bed, screwing the new Jewish servant. Herman came into the kitchen as the woman, perhaps thirty, stood polishing the family silver. Being in a horny mood, he ordered her to his bedroom. If she failed to go, he would tell his parents she had stolen money. In fact he had stolen some money. The frightened woman knew a Jew faced a beating and jail, submitted to Herman's demand. He told his mother he had paid the woman, but she believed the woman had seduced him and maybe her husband. She fired her.

Sigmunt exercised his German birthright each time he hit a Jew. Jews were forbidden to strike back. Sometimes his small group would attack a Jewish boy, or smaller man wearing the cursed yellow star. However, as Sigmunt grew up, he often hit or beat bigger targets. To celebrate his seventeenth birthday, Sigmunt beat seventeen Jews, one of his victims died in the gutter. No one came looking for Sigmunt.

Herman Adolph Schmid, young and filled with patriotic desire, joined the army two days after his graduation. Twenty years old, he volunteered for combat and soon ran, screaming, from the Russians' return fire. Wounded, a bullet puncturing his lung, he returned to Germany and family, a hero. In the hospital he overheard murmured Yiddish conversations echoing through the circulation ducts. He waved a superior officer to join him and they listened, Herman translating as the plotters spoke. His comprehension of the Yiddish conversation allowed them to inform the Gestapo of a planned bombing

The Warsaw Ghetto, Hell if you please, found the Jews struggling to live, more difficult each day. Jewish people didn't need German soldiers stalking the streets to show their superiority. They definitely didn't need Sigmunt Hollenzub. The soldiers never walked alone on the Ghetto streets, since some of them and their weapons disappeared. Groups of twos and threes, often more, shoved their way along the sidewalks, breaking windows and overturning buggies and handcarts as they traversed the area. Once in a while a rape or a murder occured and laughter exited the ghetto with the soldiers. Sigmunt laughed very loud, his hatred of all Jews, even their language, grew daily. But most of all he hated a Jew to speak to him in his language, German.

Promoted to a position worthy of his talents, Lieutenant Herman Schmid began a new job for the Gestapo, a listener, an informer of Jewish plans. He succeeded beyond the dreams of high officials in the Gestapo, even Heydrick and Goring connived to meet him and talk to him. Heydrick brought him to Berlin and introduced him to the Fuerher. Herman's heart swelled as a medal, for the hospital incident, slid around his neck, delivered by the Fueher himself. Later in a Gestapo office, Herman helped plan an incursion into the Warsaw Ghetto. He would enter as a Jew, join in their street gossip and funnel information out whenever possible. He would use his code name, "der Sperlingspapgei", the lovebird, to escape the Ghetto or in an emergency to contact the Gestapo.

Jacob, of the Jewish underground, mistook Herman for the underground's contact from outside the Ghetto. The words flew from Jacob's mouth. He named two contacts outside the Ghetto wall, two more inside the wall, with hiding places and the time for the bombing this afternoon. When Herman muttered the old password, Jacob realized his mistake. Herman had vital information and must get out of the Ghetto, at once. He must abort his mission, his Jewish identity and warn his fellow countrymen of their impending danger.

As his group of rowdies rounded the corner, Sigmunt saw two filthy Jews and headed toward them.

Herman saw Sigmunt as his savior, his means of escape and started toward him.

Rage filled Sigmunt's biased brain as Herman hurried toward him, shouting flawless German.

"Ich bin der Sperlingspapgie. Ich muss sofort von hier heraus!" Herman shouted.

"Ah, Herr Schismeister, you wish to fly out of here. OK. How's this little lovebird?"

Herman viewed the Ghetto streets differently as Sigmunt spun his body high over his head, on his out stretched arms, above the cobbled paved street. The little lovebird flew from his grasp. The name "Lovebird" never penetrated Hollenzub's bigoted mind. Herman lay dead at the wall, the monster stood over him wondering why der Sperlingspapgei didn't fly.

FIRING SQUAD

"You three men, finish your coffee, get your rifles and follow me."

The three men and the October sun rose together. The men complained, the sun did not. Exhausted soldiers in dirty blue uniforms, following a sergeant, didn't attract much attention from similarly dressed and exhausted men.

"Halt." said an officer standing outside a guarded shed.

"These are the men you ordered, Sir."

"Thank you, Sergeant. Have you men been told the duty you'll be performing?"

"No Sir, Colonel. Just told to follow the sergeant here with our weapons."

"Under Martial Law we execute spies by firing squad. Can you do that?"

A young red-headed soldier spoke up, his voice quavering, "Well, Sir..."

"Son, these guerrillas were caught, just before sunset last night, cutting the telegraph lines. This would jeopardize the entire army stationed in northern Missouri."

The soldier looked at the other two men nodding yes. "We can, Sir." he replied.

"Guard open the door." It groaned in protest "You three, come out."

Out came three straight backed civilians clothed in rags, Southern sympathizers, two boys and a girl, none older than fifteen. They stood against the shed, the rising sun in their eyes.

Their dirty faces stared, mute, in defiance at their captors.

The Colonel read from a document already showing signs of overuse. He added, "Rebels have no rights in time of war. By your rebellious behavior, you forfeit even a simple trial, as guaranteed by our Constitution." He stepped aside "Ready. Aim."

The shots turned a few heads and divided a flock of birds overhead.

"Good work men. Dismissed."

Saluting, the red-head asked, "Colonel, Sir. Permission to form a burial detail."

"Soldier, go have some coffee and relax."

"Sir, please. One of them was my brother."

KID STUFF

MOTHER'S DAY BREAKFAST

Joel and Jamie had planned this breakfast for nearly two weeks. They had seen a picture and recipe in one of the old magazines in grandma's basement and secretly cut it out. Grandma wouldn't care, but she might mention it to Mom and spoil their special secret. Some times she would accidentally forget and tell family secrets.

"You get the big bowl, and be quiet."

"I'll be quiet, Jamie. You read what we need."

They moved about the kitchen, getting this and doing that.

"Here's the bowl and a spoon too."

"Got the milk and eggs? We need vee-nell-ahh too."

"How much milk Jamie? How many eggs?"

"Two cups of milk."

"Not enough."

"Have we got three eggs, Joel?"

"Nope. Only two."

"Well , if there's not enough we'll do like Mom does. Use something else."

"I measured the milk, Jamie. There's just a cup. Almost."

"Add some cold water to make two cups, then pour it in the bowl."

"OK!"

"Two eggs will have to do. They're extra - large anyhows."

"Sure that should work. Break 'em and put 'em in the

bowl."

"Now we need cooking oil."

"There ain't no cooking oil. Mom put it on her list yester-day."

"OK Joel, use something else then."

"What?"

"Let's see. Two Tbls. I wonder what T b l s means?"

"T B L S? Means tablets."

"No! It means something else. I know! It means spoons."

"OK! Spoons! Big or little spoons?"

"Tablespoons."

"OK! Big or little?"

"I guess big. Use the big wooden one. And we can use margarine for oil."

"Yeah!"

"Pour out the pancake mix. Use 2 cups and half a cup."

"Two cups and a half cup Jamie? Right? OOPS! I spilled some on the floor."

"Sweep it later. Put in the bowl. I'll mix it. Put butter in the pan and light the gas."

"How much?"

"Just some. Like half a stick. Put the dish and silverware on the tray."

"I did already. We forgot coffee."

"I don't know about coffee. Pour some O. J."

"OK with me. We need syrup too, right?"

"Sure Silly. You wouldn't eat pancakes without syrup would you?"

"There's only a little bit. A real little bit."

"Use something different then."

"Like what? Oh! Oh! I know! I'll get that cherry cough syrup that Mom likes."

"I don't know."

"It'll be all right. Trust me on this one."

"If you say so. Pour it on. Let's go."

"They smell good, huh? Jamie, you carry it. I'll get the doors."

As they pushed open the bedroom door, both sang out, "Happy Mother's Day! Surprise!"

"Have we got a surprise for you." said Joel.

'Wait 'til you taste it." said Jamie.

"Go ahead Mom. Taste it." both said.

ERNIE THE EAGLE

Ernie hatched soon after his sister, in a twig nest high on a canyon wall. Ernie was a fuzzy ball of white with a black bill, black eyes and born hungry. But he was the sloppiest eater his parents ever fed. He seemed to miss their offering, dropped it or just hooked the bit of meat on his beak and dragged it into his mouth.

Ernie would watch the sky as he waited for his parents to bring him food. One day he rushed to the nest edge as mom brought him food, he happened to look down, became frightened and tumbled back into the nest. He was afraid of heights.

As he grew up his parents wondered why he never rushed to the edge of the nest to be fed. Some days Ernie would look down through the twigs in the nest and become frightened all over again. Ernie looked up most of the time.

As Ernie grew his parents left his food nearer the edge of the nest. He would stretch out his neck and drag his food back to the middle of the nest. His sister would tease him and pull it back to the edge.

Ernie and his sister soon found growing feathers made their wings itch. They would flap their wings to stop the itching. His sister would stand at the edge of the nest and flap while the wind lifted her a little off the nest. When Ernie flapped he stayed in the middle and clutched the nest. When the wind lifted him a little he could see the bottom of the canyon. He would stop flapping and huddle down in the nest. He was afraid.

Ernie's sister soon flew from the nest. His parents brought

little for him to eat. He was getting very hungry. His wings still itched and he flapped them furiously. It lifted him and a strong gust of wind carried him out of the nest and into the open sky. Looking down frightened him. He shut his eyes. He shut his eyes very tight.

He immediately found shutting your eyes and flying was a bad idea. He smacked into a wall and fell down to a rock ledge. He looked about, the ledge was narrow and went nowhere. He looked down. Down was a long way down. He was afraid.

A Ranger saw Ernie flapping his wings on the ground under the ledge. Ernie had fallen off during the night and strained his wing. He took the fledgling to the nature center for care and treatment. They noticed Ernie's odd and messy eating habit. A veterinarian came to see the young eagle and determined he was nearsighted. Glasses were prescribed and contact lens were fitted over Ernie's eyes.

He was returned a few days later to where the ranger found him and placed on the ledge. He stayed on the ledge all night, hungry and afraid . The next morning he looked around but slipped off of the ledge when he moved. As he fell he spread his wings and found he stopped falling. Looking down made him shut his eyes, again. He just couldn't look down without being afraid. But he didn't want to fly into a wall again. He would fly with one eye open. Things looked different, but he wasn't sure. He shut them.

He glided in circles all morning, but he was getting very, very hungry. Where would he find food? He opened one eye and looked down. Below was a lake, a field some trees and a rocky canyon floor and his mother. He shut his eyes. The lake looked the softest, he would try to go there. Down he went, opening just one eye every once in awhile, or blinking to check his progress.

He turned toward the small beach. However, not knowing how to land, Ernie came down and rolled head over heels several times. He didn't hurt anything more than his pride.

Ernie's mother came and left a large piece of fish on the

edge of the water. Wonderful food for a hungry eagle. She watched him gulp it down and look for more. The beach had many fish on it and Ernie had no trouble finding or eating more. After eating his fill Ernie climbed up onto a small branch.

It wasn't very high and looking down didn't frighten him. His wings didn't itch but he flapped them anyway. The wind lifted him up, he shut his eyes and he flew out over the water. Soon he opened one eye then both eyes and he soared up higher and higher. His fear of being high above the canyon floor and lakes was gone. Ernie Eagle, was flying, no longer afraid.

LATE

"Brian, listen to me. You were late for school yesterday and the day before and the day before that too. Promise me you wouldn't be late today. Please?"

Brain gave his mother that, "Why are you picking on me?" look. "I promise."

Linda looked at her second grader, growing so fast and walking the two and a half blocks to school by himself. She was proud of him, very proud. "You're leaving five minutes earlier today, to make sure you're not late." She kissed her finger and pressed it to his forehead, spun him around and out the door with a gentle shove. It was too nice a day for boys to be in school having their heads stuffed with learning words and numbers.

Brian hustled down the empty school hall, but the door to his room was already closed. His room faced the school office and Mrs. Makey, the Principal, waved for him to come into her office. He felt his heart race and his stomach hurt.

"You're late young man." The Principal's voice, while soft, with her stare, turned Brian to quivering jello.

"Yes Mam."

"The first week of school and I know you've been late before. How come?"

"I don't know." Brian's eyes held back a floodgate, letting one tear escape.

"Didn't your mother send you off earlier today?"

He rubbed his sleeve at his eyes. "Uh, huh. Yes, Mam, I started earlier today."

"Well?" Eternity paused, "Why are you late?"

The tears gushed from frightened eyes. "I don't know. I walked right here."

Mrs. Makey took the tardy youngster to his classroom and returned to her office.

The next morning, a day as nice as yesterday, found Brian starting for school a little earlier than yesterday. He didn't notice the lady talking to the neighbor across the street, but she noticed him. She broke off the conversation and watched the boy proceed along the sidewalk. She followed him, staying on her side of the street.

Brian stopped a block away from home and shaded his eyes to look up into a tree. Mrs. Makey saw a squirrel bounding along a branch and jump to another tree. Brian followed the squirrel too. After it ran over the roof of the last house, Brain looked up and down the street before he crossed. Two squabbling birds caught his attention, he watched them attack each other. One fled and the other gave arial pursuit. Mrs. Makey saw this stop too.

Brian disappeared behind some bushes. She craned to see him, when his head bobbed up, then back down. She saw him crouched down, intently watching something on the sidewalk. No, not on the sidewalk, in the little row of flowers bordering the house. The boy moved slowly in an arc, before the butterfly took wing. They watched it fly off.

A half block later Brian disappeared. Mrs. Makey crossed the street and peered through the windshield of a parked car at a crouched figure drawing a twig along several stones next to tree in the parkway. He opened his lunchbox, pulled out a sandwich and broke off some crust. Mrs. Makey understood what he was doing. He fed the small hill of ants part of his lunch. He took several bites too, then continued to school.

Electric sound waves rolled from the building cupola. The tardy bell sound slid out through the nice day, warning everyone, a school day had started. Brian and Mrs. Makey were almost half a block from school. They would be late.

Finally in school she picked up the phone and made a call. "Mrs. Makey here. I followed Brian to school today, as suggested yesterday. I had forgotten how interesting a world we live in. He didn't miss a thing that happened on his way to school. He saw squirrels, ants and things I may have missed. He'll need someone to walk with him, to keep him moving, but still start him a little earlier. He takes a young boy's walk to school. He sees and stops for everything. He'll be OK."

The next day he left earlier again. "Don't be late." But in her mother's mind she knew the world called out to Brian with every step.

THE LAST EGG

Katherine turned three today. Earlier this morning Grandma asked her to help plant some flower bulbs.

"These will be flowers when you are four. You are planting the last one. Now we need to water them. Will you please turn on the water?"

Katherine ran for the hose. Suddenly a dark form rushed up in front of her. She fell back on the grass, hollering for grandma.

Grandma had seen the dark form fly out of the plants under Katherine's bedroom window. She rushed to Katherine and held her shaking body.

"A duck flew out of the plants under your window. I wonder what a duck could be doing under your window?"

"I don't know. " sobbed Katherine.

"Let's look." said Grandma, pulling back the plants. "Oh. Look Katherine, a nest. With eggs in it."

"...nine, ten and I don't know any more numbers Grandma."

"Eleven, twelve. You counted very well. There are a dozen eggs. A dozen is another word for twelve. You will learn more numbers in school." Grandma wiped her hands on her yard apron. "Right now, we will move the hose to a different faucet.

Grandma began disconnecting the hose. Katherine hurried into the house to tell Grandpa of their discovery.

"I think you would like to see mother on her nest?" he said.

"Yes."

"Well we shouldn't bother her on the nest. But, I think I can fix it so you can watch her and not frighten her off the nest."

Grandpa went into the garage and soon brought some tools, screws and an old shaving mirror to Katherine's bedroom. He opened the window and peeking out saw the duck on her nest.

"Katherine, I am going to work here. You must sit and be quiet."

Katherine sat and watched Grandpa putting the mirror on the windowsill and screw in the screws.

"Finished." said Grandpa.

Katherine gave him a funny smile. "The mirror is upside down Grandpa."

It was. The mirror was upside down and tilted. Grandpa sat Katherine on the floor so she could look into the mirror. She saw the mother duck on the nest.

Each morning Katherine would look into the nest then before her nap, after her nap and before she went to sleep at night. Some times mother duck left the nest. Katherine would count all twelve eggs. Always there were just twelve eggs.

"When are the baby ducks coming?" she asked Grandma.

"I don't know." said Grandma.

"I don't know either," said Grandpa.

The morning of the tenth day, Katherine looked in the nest and there was only one egg.

"Grandma! Grandpa! Come see. There is only one egg in the nest." Katherine had a puzzled frown on her face. "Where are the babies?"

"They must have hatched during the night," suggested Grandma. "Their mother may have taken them to the pond for a swim. Shall we go look?"

At the pond there were several mother ducks with babies swimming around. Katherine did not know which duck had a nest under her window. Neither did Grandma know. Katherine knew one must be her mother duck.

"There is one egg left Grandma. Will she come back for it?"

"We will wait and see. She should come back soon." Grandma said.

Katherine looked in the nest at nap time. One egg. She looked after her nap. One egg. She looked before going to sleep that night. One egg.

In the morning Katherine looked again. The nest was empty. No eggs.

"Can we look for a duck with a dozen ducklings at the pond?" asked Katherine.

REALLY DUMB

THE GETAWAY

"I don't understand. I just don't understand how it could go wrong."

Luther would have wrapped his arms around his brother Mike and consoled him, except he couldn't. They were both sitting in the back of a squad car, their hands cuffed behind them. Their big plans, their big score, had just gone bust.

Later, after Jules, the master planner, had threatened to kill him for the hundredth time since their arrest, Mike went over everything again. He started from the very beginning. He would figure out what went wrong with the perfect hold-up.

He was a replacement driver for Sonny, 'cause Sonny got busted for DUI. His brother, Luther, got him the job. Now they sat at the table listening to Jules going over everything for the umpteenth time. He wanted each of them to recite his part one more time. To make sure nothing, nothing could go wrong.

"I'll walk passed the car, nodding to Mike and enter the bank at 9:30."

"At 9:30." mumbled Mike.

"At 9:30, go directly to the end cashier's window. Stop, take out my wallet and look through it."

"I can see you through the window." Mike piped in.

"Right. When I nod, Luther comes across the street, nods to you and comes in the bank." Jules stood up and started moving around the table. "When I slip my wallet back in my pocket, Luther and I draw our guns."

"Yeah."

Luther gave Mike a shove, "Just listen." and put a finger on his lips.

Mike, grinning, put his finger on his lips too.

Jules had stopped pacing and stared at the two brothers. "OK? Luther jumps the counter, I cover the guards and any customers. Then it's out the door, into the car and away."

"Mike, it's important that the car is running and the locks on the doors are open."

"And Mike," said Jules, "It's important you swipe a good car and switch plates."

"Just like you told me, Jules. I know. And I should fill the gas tank too. Right?"

"Right, Mike. Right."

"It's important all these things go right Mike. Real important." reminded Luther,

"You forgot, Luther. I should be on time."

The next morning both Jules and Luther saw Mike sitting in the car, motor running. As Jules went passed the car, he checked the door locks. Open. He nodded and entered the bank. Luther nodded, smiled and entered the bank. A few minutes later, both men tumbled into the car.

"Go! Go!"

"Move it, Mike." said Luther.

The car moved forward. Half way into the traffic lane the motor died. Mike turned the key, but nothing happened. The bank guards were around the car in a moment.

"I don't understand what went wrong, Luther. I did everything like you guys said." Mike rolled his eyes and sniffled. "I got us a good car. I got some plates off a car at a motel. I bought gas. Luther, I got here early, 5 o'clock almost. I unlocked the doors and I kept the motor running ever since. Nothing should have gone wrong. Nothing."

Luther started to cry. "Nothing."

CIGARETTES

One cashier, three in front of me, no one in a rush, I stepped into line and waited. The person in front of me twirled a carton of cigarettes between two dirty hands, the frayed Bulls' jacket cuffs ate away the dirt at his wrists. The jacket collar seemed to be swallowing his head and the baseball cap perched atop the head went back and forth just like the tennis matches.

The first customer moved on and the next presented some money to the clerk. The man in front of me dropped the carton and looked up at me as he retrieved it. A small face with a scruffy beard with his uncombed hair peering from under the hat's bill, hiding part of one eye gazed up toward me. A weak smile showed stained, irregular teeth with several gaps. Erect, he continued to wait and twirl the carton of cigarettes.

His turn. His voice came from deep in a canyon. "I bought this carton of cigarettes here last week. And my friends have finally convinced me that smoking is bad for my health. So I'm quitting smoking. I wondered if you'll buy them back. It's not open or nothing. OK?"

"Nope. We don't buy back things."

The shoulders drooped and the head went a notch or two into the collar of the jacket. He turned toward me, the drooping eyes, asking my indulgence. I remained neutral.

"You don't have no sign you wouldn't take things back. Come on, huh?"

The cashier, a swarthy individual, perhaps of Eastern European ancestry, tapped the front side of the register, with a ringed finger attached to a ham sized hand. "Right here. No refunds." The accent, thick, flat and positive, told me I made a good guess. Eastern European. No return here. He waved the small man off with the other cigarette holding hand. "Good bye. Have a nice day."

I started to move to the register.

"You can just give me the price back. No tax. OK?"

The cashier threw his head in the direction of the door, disgust and anger on the face. This message hurried him on his way. Out of the cashier's sight a finger flicked up.

"Do you have a copy of the Chicago Tribune?"

"No, sorry. White Hen," his head turned and with a thumb gestured off to the right, "might have it. Sorry."

In the White Hen the Trib sat alone on the paper rack and my small friend stood in line at the register. He looked over the small offering of assorted donuts and put his carton of cigarettes on the counter.

I heard the same story of buying cigarettes and quitting and could he get his money back. I even got the same asking for indulgence smile, without recognition. He got the same answer, no refunds. As he left the store the cashier got the same finger flick as before.

With my Trib under my sweaty armpit I headed for the car, passing my little friend standing behind his car. He was talking to a policeman. The trunk of his car revealed a box of cartons of cigarettes. The dirty hand closing the trunk held a cigarette and the face blew a cloud of smoke into the warm air. Where to next I wondered.

ACCIDENT INSURANCE

"Baby. Baby. Baby. Listen to me. It'll be OK. Just do like I say and it'll be OK. It's the one way we can make some easy money fast."

Wendy, wincing at the thought of shooting her true love, was crying and pleading. "I'm afraid. If I screw up you could die. Really. If you die, I'll die. I'll kill myself."

"Won't happen. Listen for Christ's sake. Listen. I'll be reading the newspaper. You shoot right through the paper. Even the cops will see the bullet hole and know it was an accident. Besides, it's a small caliber, a 22. It doesn't kill nothing but small stuff, like rabbits."

Wendy's shoulders were sagging and not from the weight of the little gun. "But if I miss, you could die."

"Christ. How can you miss?" He held up the newspaper. "You'll be shooting just ten, twelve inches away. Look," he wiggled the paper in front of him. "Come on Baby. The policy pays for an accident. An accident."

"You sure you'll be alright? Sure? Positive?"

He stood and kissed her forehead. "Positive. Aim to the right. That's important. Aim right. And call 911 right away/"

He sat down and held the paper up as if reading. He felt her moving closer and peeked over the edge of the paper. His mind began screaming. "My right! Not your right! Mine!"

"Hello Nathan, What happened?" said the man walking into the room.

"Well Sargent, a got a call from 911 about a shooting.

When we got here, the landlord let us in and we found this." His hand swept the small room. "The guy slumped in the chair. Shot once, right through the heart. And the woman, just like that, sitting in his lap and holding the gun in her lap. Shot in the heart too. Both dead. No note. Looks like a homicide and suicide Sarge."

"Not an accident, that's for sure." said the Sargent. "Not an accident."

JOB OPENING

Lester's shaking body, covered with feverish sweat, wet the bedding. The droning TV news report shook him too. Did he hear the reporter correctly? Melvin Piper died last night in a botched burglary attempt. Lester tried to focus on the report as the commercial started. Might his fever have effected his hearing?

Saturday evening Melvin and he were planning on breaking into an apartment above a bakery. The Sunday receipts from the downstairs bakery would be kept in the baker's apartment. Lester knew the baker and his wife were attending the political rally for their cousin on Monday, a holiday. He and Melvin would break in and steal the money from Sunday's sales. Sunday was usually a good sales day in the bakery.

Melvin stopped at Lester's place at 7 o'clock on Monday. The job would have to wait, Lester was too sick to move. Earlier, Lester had dressed and started down the hallway when his stomach revolted, it's contents spewed all over the upper landing of the staircase. He went back to bed. He nixed Melvin's suggestion to pull the job with someone else. Melvin said he'd go home.

The reporter said. "The baker returned to their apartment to find a body wedged in the window above the kitchen sink. Mr. Anselmo, the baker, thought burglars might come after yesterday's receipts. Heeding his wife's warnings, he dropped them in the night depository of the new bank down the street, while going to a political rally, "

Melvin's mug shot flashed on the screen and the commentator continued talking. "This man has been in trouble before. But last night's break-in ended his life and his career. The officer answering the Anselmo's call, found Melvin Piper's body stuck in the window. Pushing his body far into the apartment and losing his balance, the burglar, unable to get leverage and right himself, died of a cerebral hemorrhage."

"Damn fool. Melvin Piper, you're a damn fool. Now I got nobody to help me on this job or other jobs either." Lester said, returning to his sick bed. The news droned on.

CHARGE IT!

It was a dream. Mary's worst dream was turning into an unbelievable dream, like winning the lottery.

Working in England, Mary missed her family. When the opportunity arose she flew her mother from the States for a month long holiday. She and Mom, after shopping and lunch at Herrod's, decided on a movie. They locked their packages and, foolishly, their purses, in the boot. Hours later they returned to find the boot ransacked.

The next day she received a phone call. "Ms. Mejer, this is Constable Clark, of the New Scotland Yard. I'm letting you know your case has been assigned to me. The thief that stole your purse has been caught."

"You're kidding? Caught? I've just spent hours canceling all my credit cards."

"It's the right thing mam. Anyhow, he was caught using your credit card."

"Oh my God!" Mary cried. "I don't have to pay? Do I? Did he spend much?"

"You will hardly believe this Ms. Mejer, but using your card made you some money and got him caught."

"No? Made me money? Honest?" Mary's voice rose half an octave. "How?"

"Well Miss, here's what the track police told me. Teddy, that's the thief, went to the racetrack after stealing your purse and made a bet with your credit card."

She interrupted, "Using my credit card? For how much?"

"Just listen Miss. He bet a hundred quid on the trifecta. The trifecta, a race what pays on the first, second and third horse winning in one race. It paid eleven hundred, sixty-two quid."

"He didn't get it, did he?"

"No." said Constable Clark. "But he tried. That's where he screwed up. He was raising trouble at the pay out window. He wanted his money. The cashier buzzed the security police and they arrested him. Seems you get the money. You won. When you use your credit card for betting in England, winnings go directly into your account."

"Really? Wow!."

COOL OFF

Thinking things through to their logical conclusion had always been bothersome for Lester. Sometimes down right painful, particularly to people waiting for Lester to end whatever he had to finish. It has been said, that if Lester had to think to breath, he'd choke to death while breathing.

There's a story about his thinking that tickles the locals. On a warm summer day in Chicago, when Lester was between jail terms, he realized he hadn't eaten for a day or so. Stepping into a small beanery off North Clark Street, he took the dishwasher wanted sign off the front window. He knew the word wanted, since he had seen it so often on his rap sheet. He handed it to the guy at the register.

"Does the job come with meals?" he asked and ran his sleeve under his nose.

"Ever wash dishes in a dishwasher?"

"Lots a times. Do I get a meal too?"

"Coffee and a roll for breakfast. Soup and sandwich for lunch. Work late and you get the day's special. Pays three bucks an hour, payday every Friday. Want it?"

"Huh huh. Could I have a coffee while I start? Huh?"

"Come on back, I'll get you coffee. What's your name? And you fill out job papers. You're legal ain't you?" The man, Ham, looked Lester over. "Don't want trouble with the INS."

"Born here in Chicago. Went to school here in Chicago. No papers needed."

Lester, once he got the hang of the machine, after a few

tries and a threat to be fired, enjoyed the constant pace of his job. He managed to wangle a donut with his second cup of coffee and two soups with lunch. A visit to the John and he pilched a two quarter tip off the back table. The work was easy and with the air conditioning running, a pleasant place to spend the day. He jumped when Ham turned the exhaust fan on, the sound and suction were unexpected.

Lester looked into the twirling blades of the fan often from his position under it. He could see right into the sky, even watch the clouds pass by.

"That hole go out on the roof?" he asked the short order cook.

"No comprede, senor." He didn't wish to be bothered by Lester.

All afternoon he crooked his head upward. He studied the frame held by six Phillips screws. He guessed the opening would allow a small man, like himself, to fit through it. If a fella could get in, he could walk out the front door. Passing Ham's small office, when the guy delivered the fruit for the week, Lester didn't see a safe. Ham must keep the money coming in after the banks closed, in his desk. Lester dreamed.

For three days Lester washed dishes, ate his meals, and dreamed of doing dirt to his boss. Oh Ham was nice enough, but Lester didn't really like washing dishes. Dawdling over his Friday special, clam soup, and fried breaded perch, Lester saw himself with bundles of cash, walking out the front door. He looked back and saw the frame of the exhaust hanging down above the dish washing machine. It needed a grease job.

Late that night Lester removed a screen from the roof top exhaust fan. He slipped easily into the chute, his feet didn't touch the fan, but he decided to drop down anyway. A few inches and he stood on the fan support housing. No problem.

Ham swore at the short order cook, threw some pans about and cussed the be Jesus out of the absent Lester. Where the hell was Lester? Dirty dishes were piling up.

"Hey! Jose, turn that fan on. It's getting too damn hot in here."

Loud screams came from the exhaust system. Ham could see shoes in the tube. He called the police. A shaken dirty Lester stood before the dish washing machine, blubbering his fears and the terror of his night on the fan. He couldn't bend over to loosen the screws, which were on the other side of the frame anyway. The lip of the exhaust system, on the roof, was out of reach. Lester trapped himself. When he heard Ham order the fan turned on he panicked and screamed.

Lester knew with his experience as a dish washer, he'd get a job in jail.

HOLDING THE BAG

His parents, teachers, the warden, parole officer and gang members thought Lester thirty-five and a half inches short of a yard. His rate of comprehension didn't move faster than exfoliation on a tombstone. Now fifty-seven years old and out on parole only three weeks he prepared for a robbery guaranteeing him funds. He'd retire from cold Chicago winters and spend his days in Florida.

The idea came to him as he watched some damn fool trap himself in a robbery by allowing the surveillance camera to catch him robbing the store. He could see the answer as the fool moved about the store. The police had caught him the next day. Lester figured out a foolproof method immediately.

The following day he went to the local electronics store and looked for the security camera. It was above the cash register, arcing slowly from the front door, down the aisle to the office cubicle. Lester walked through the store, checked the location of expensive items, the entry from the supply room and left the premises. He chuckled to himself, turned back into the store and checked it out again.

That night he broke in the back door of the store already wearing a bag over his head and slowly proceeded through the supply room. He covered the security camera, then walked into the store and fell over a pallet of paper. When he stood up he bounced off a rack of pens, pencils and small desk supplies.. He couldn't see very well. He could fix that.

He picked up a pair of small office scissors from the tumbled display rack. He stepped behind the shelves of merchandise, away from the covered surveillance camera, and removed the bag from his head. He cut two larger eye holes and put the bag over his head again. He now saw what he wanted, collecting it at the back door and easily putting it into the stolen car.

In the morning, watching the news Lester saw himself cutting holes into the bag. He never thought to look for a second security camera. The police were knocking on his front door as he was turning the set off. Florida and retirement would wait.

HOROSCOPE

Beaumont "Bo" Bindovasky, was unlucky most of his life. He slipped out of the doctor's hands at birth. His mother choose his name from a movie advertisement, then left the hospital never to return. The cops move him along every time they see him. In the last year, he found a fiver and split his pants picking it up, then lost the fiver at the track to a pickpocket. He pulled time for trying to hold-up a grocery store with a broken cap pistol. His daily horoscope, which he read daily and tried to follow but seemed to misinterpret, would change for the better. He believed.

Horoscope for today. "Make friends. They will benefit you. Make plans."

Bo thought about this as he danced with the girl from the plastic factory. He found a ticket to the dance and just bumped into her. They danced and talked and danced and he listened. Yes, he listened. She just got a promotion, from checking workers' hours to filling their pay envelopes. She explained everything she did to Bo. When he wasn't clear about something he asked her to repeat it. Soon he knew what time the money arrived at the factory, where it was stored, what doors led to places, oh so much. His mind was a whirl.

Horoscope for today. "Follow your dreams. Nothing comes easy."

Today, right now, he started following his dream. It was just after midnight, he was gulping down a cup of coffee after the movie and had nothing going. There seemed to be fewer people about and others seemed to be hurrying a bit. Now, he could get to the plastic factory and sneak in. Once in he would hide near the dock where the money comes in, jump out and surprise the Brinks guy and be gone before anyone knew what happened. Round and round his mind played out the scene, each time it became easier.

Bo remembered nearly everything the girl said, she sure knew the place, every door and turn was right. Everything seemed as bright as a new quarter. Getting through the back fence and onto the dock had been easy. Where to hide and wait wasn't. Bo selected an empty dumpster just off the dock. Climbing in he lowered the lid, checking his view before shutting it.

It felt nice and comfy cozy out of the chill of the night. He felt at ease with the warmth and quiet and the pleasant odor. He pressed the light on his watch, 2:13 a.m. Time for a short nap.

Monday morning the dock foreman called the janitor out of his cubby hole office.

"Why's the chemical safety box shut tight?"

"Hell, I don't know."

"Was it open or shut over the weekend? It was suppose to air out." Shuffling papers on his desk, the foreman extracted a blank form and handed it to the janitor. "We can't do it now the fume build-up can be dangerous if it's been closed for a while."

"Like I said, I don't know if it was open or closed. I was off for the long weekend too. Remember? Thanksgiving week end? The plant was shut."

Bo's horoscope for today. "You can't fix some mistakes. Be careful."

INITIATION FEE

Lyons was a street wise thug. He didn't give a damn for anyone. Even his mother feared his violence. She had suffered because of it. The people he dealt with and those that associated with him never gave him cause to explode.

The newest hanger-on of the unholy cadre, Will Dass, cocky gang banger on parole and a little short on the IQ scale, sat watching the poker game. Lyons knew his type, willing to do anything to rub shoulders with the underworld figures he admired. Figuring the kid might still have outside contacts, Lyons called him to his table.

"Rest your feet awhile, sit and let's talk." Lyons said, pointing to an empty chair.

"Sure." Smiling and pulling the chair back, Will continued. "You talking or me?"

Nodding his head and looking around the table at his minions, Lyons said "I think the both of us will be talking. OK?"

"OK"

"It's my understanding you got contacts on the other side of Monroe Street."

Will nodding affirmatively, didn't speak.

"You saying yes?"

"Oh, oh. Yes. I'm saying yes." Will was grinning. "I thought I should wait..."

"Yeah, usually a guy waits 'til I tell him to speak. Today, you should talk. OK?"

"OK."

"OK. You know Carmen? Or Thrush? Or Bingo? Or his brother, Louis?"

"Know 'em all. Everyone of them."

"How well?" asked Lyons. "Can you deal some stuff with them?"

"Deal? Me?" Rubbing his hands together and winking with a facial grimace, he said, "Maybe?"

Lyons, with a soft laugh, stood and walking around the table, lay his jeweled hand on Will's shoulder. "Thinking of joining us Will? Make some money for yourself?"

The weight of the world resting on his shoulder, sent a thousand tingles coursing through Will. "Uh huh. I am."

"Good. Very good. I want you ..." He whispered the entire deal into Will's ear.

Will would contact one of the drug dealers getting him to a certain garage for a deal. A small deal but an opportunity to see how Will would do. Will made a phone call convincing one of the dealers that he had some money and wished to buy high grade stuff. A meeting was arranged for the following evening at Dubert's Forwarding shipping docks.

"That's great." said Lyons, "You be there kid. We have a future together."

The following evening Will Dass welcomed Louis, the dealer, on the loading dock, for outgoing freight only. Louis was offering Will three decks of quality drugs, when Lyons, stepping from the shadows, executed Louis. Driving away, Lyons set the three packs on his lap, for Will to see.

"Now I get a third of this, off the top, since I am the boss." said Lyons. "And I get another deck, since we are partners and partners split 50/50. The third one I'll keep too. If you don't like it kid, think twice, then picture yourself as Louis back at the dock."

Will did just that, pictured Louis sprawled on the dock dead. He blew town.

"Hey, I ain't seen that Will kid around for a couple a days.

Anyone seen him?" asked Lyons as he dealt the cards.

Picking up their cards as they were being dealt, each man said, "No."

"Funny. I thought he liked us." Lyons chuckled at his comment. "Gimme two cards."

JAWS OF LIFE

The engine's sirens went off while the crew was pulling it out onto the driveway. It was practice but everything and everyone had to function as it should for every emergency. Lay out all the equipment, check it, clean and polish it, then put it away.

Syd stood with a group on onlookers. Staying in a crowd usually gave him an opportunity to walk off with something. He'd wait around, for opportunity's knock.

Fire Chief Omar Balissi, decided to show the crowd some of his men and equipment in action. The power of the "jaws of life" were shown first and set aside. Syd immediately moved to the outer edge of the onlookers. In a moment he was pulling the blanket, the devise lay on, around the corner of the building. In two moments he was moving down the side driveway away from approving applause of the crowd.

Stillman, the hot goods man, gave Syd fifty-five dollars for the tool, knowing the Coomer brothers would pay plenty for such a handy tool. Break-ins of factories and stores would be much easier using its power.

Syd, with his easy money, proceeded to the card game in back of the scrap yard office. It took all of twelve minutes for Syd to lose the fifty-five and owe Iron Nick twenty more. He hung around, hoping someone might feel a bit of pity for him, which they never did.

"Syd, want to make a couple of bucks?" asked a faceless man at the table.

Syd recognized the voice. "Sure Mr. Stillman. Whatta need

me to do.?"

"I'm hungry. You guys want to have some pizza, cheese and sausage, from Carlo's?"

Several OK's and one request for mushrooms.

"Here's twenty-five bucks. Go to Carlo's and get two large pizzas, one with mushroom, one with sausage. You hurry and I'll let ya keep the change, Might add a buck."

"Thanks Iron Nick. Two large pizzas, one mushrooms, one sausage. I'm off."

"OK. Go, and get your ass right back here. I'm hungry. Ya hear me? Get!"

Starting out the door with his pizza, Sid asked the guy coming in, to hold the door open for him. In front of him was this guy's car, engine running. Syd could see him ordering and pointing to the menu while giving his order. He slid behind the wheel and sped off for the scrap yard

"Dumb Schmuck." he said, talking to himself. Iron Nick would tip him for being so fast and probably give him a hundred or two for the car.

A light rain began falling, the speeding car didn't hold the road well. Syd began to skid out of control as he crossed Washington, hit a parked truck and slid into the traffic signal post. Crunch! Conscious, but in pain, Syd yelled for help. When a small fire broke out, keeping spectators at a distance, Syd began screaming in panic. The smell of the pizza reminded him he was doing something for a hungry Iron Nick and he screamed louder.

In the distance the sirens wailing song grew louder. Chief Omar Balissi and his men doused the small fire at once. Syd hollering all the while. The Chief assessed the scene and his men made every effort to pry open the crushed doors. They couldn't budge them, the torque of the heated sharp metal held Syd tight. They foamed down the area, waiting for another engine crew to arrive. Since late this afternoon, their 'jaws of life " tool was missing and it was needed to free Syd.

Forty minutes later, Syd was released from the wreck. Before the ambulance took him away he was arrested for auto theft. Iron Nick would go hungry, and want his money back. Syd moaned in disbelief at his bad luck.

BREAK-IN

"You know, these guys were begging to get robbed. Building a bakery in such a quiet, empty area."

Spike leered as he backed the stolen car to the back door. "Sure was."

"How much you think they locked up tonight?" Lester asked.

"Not important, a good guess is plenty but first we gotta get the safe"

The two men went behind the building heading for the supply room door. Spike dropped to one knee, poked a probe into the lock and picked the lock. The hallway light was on, so they sauntered down the hall to the office. A squat safe nested in the corner, but the two thieves found out quickly a small safe can be very heavy.

"Christ. We can't carry this. Besides, we couldn't lift it into the car."

"OK Lester, whatta want to do, forget it and leave?" Spike asked sarcastically.

"No way. There's gotta be another way." Lester's eyes grew bigger and he sang out, "Looky here. An answer to our prayers."

Spike did a 180 and looked through the office interior window. Back on the loading dock was a forklift. Spike could visualize the forklift picking the safe up and moving it out to the car. But in reality, after lifting the safe, Spike pushed down on the throttle too hard. He sent the forklift through the wall and off the dock onto its side. In an instant everything went dark.

"Must have cut the electricity."

Lester agreed. "Yeah, mustta. But other lights are still on, just not here. Guess we gotta cut the safe open here in the yard and quick."

Spike looked at Lester. "You bring the torch with you?"

"I sure did. It's in the trunk of the car." Lester's smirk told Spike he wasn't as dumb as some people though he was.

"Tanks too?"

"Everything we need." said Lester. "Tanks, cutter, hell I brought a lighter and even matches."

Spike thought he might have broken some things but didn't have time to check that out.

"Keep outta my way." scowled the harried Spike, as he pulled stuff from the car. "Light that son of a bitch up and let's get outta here. OK?"

"You do the cutting. I'll light up." Lester thrust the nozzle at Spike who released the safety on the nozzle. When Lester struck a match, the entire yard became a bright ball of blue flame and rolling thunder.

Neither of the men seemed to comprehend what happened next. The police at the hospital were generous with their explanations. The newspapers and the TV newspeople were generous with their quips about the careless burglars. They called the episode, "Bungling Burglars Botch Bakery Burglary".

Spike's intuition had been correct. When he knocked down the wall, he cut the electrical power, putting the lights out and he had also cut the natural gas line. When Lester struck the match to light the torch, gas had already filled the yard. It blew up. The explosion knocked out both crooks and destroyed a new business. The noise alerted the police. The police found both men in the yard, clothing singed and a few burns on their bodies. Somehow Lester acknowledged to a newspaperman that he'd like his old job back when he returned to prison, working in the prison bakery.

ONE DEPRESSION EVENING

The stiff, cold wind blew the firehouse door open and threw the man and the bundle in his arms toward several relaxed and quiet men seated at a long table. The man nearest the heavy door, jumped up and forced it closed. Every pair of eyes in the large room impaled the snow covered diorama, voices choked into silence.

"Gentlemen." said the white frosted figure. "If you can't feed me, can you at least feed my little girl?" The rasped plea, became a prayer. "Or allow us to rest in your warmth 'til we can search some where else for help?"

For a moment no one moved, then all motion could be measured as a blur. A chair clattered, then another, men moved, arms outstretched, to help the figure that tottered near the door. Two men supported his arms as another lifted the child from the near frozen embrace. The ensemble moved, cloud like toward the warmth of the small kitchen behind the long table.

"Get some coffee," two voices called.

"Get the soup, two bowls and two spoons," called another.

A red-faced giant, gently cradled a skinny, wide eyed child, perhaps tw years old, in his tattooed arms. They stared into each others faces, bewildered and amused. A smile curled the child's mouth, as a heavy ringed finger scratched her chin.

"Thank you. I got nothing right now for us." The slurp, slurp of the spoon pushing hot soup into a hungry maw, interrupted his words. "Just come in the city and don't have an inkling where to go or who to see."

"Eat man. Eat now, talk later." said the giant. The child grabbed for the soup as he blew it cool. "Wait there little one. Just you let Charlie cool it off."

The firemen sat around the table, barely mumbling, they patiently waited for the coming story. One went for his blanket and wrapped it around the two as they warmed themselves inside and out. Someone placed his cardboard stuffed shoes near the radiator. Finally, as so many families did that December, the man related his desperate struggle to live without work, money, food or shelter and care for the child.

Adolph Stinson, farmer and farrier lost his shop then his farm. His wife ran off, sick and disillusioned, with a former boyfriend. Stinson traveled close to home for awhile, then in desperation broadened his search for work. Small jobs, here and there kept them going for a time. Then nothing. He knew there were places in the city that would care for them, or at least his daughter. So he came to the city.

"Robinson, can we put them upstairs for the night?"

"Sorry Red, that can't be done. You read that order yourself. 'Read it here."

"That order was to keep bums out. Those guys were stealing everything. I'm asking for a man and a kid. Right guys?" The red head bobbed on the hugh frame.

A chorus of approval filled the room. They decided the two strangers would be their overnight guests. Beds were set off in the corner and a small blanket hung on rope became a privacy barrier. The man wept and knelt in prayer with the child.

Twenty minutes later an alarm emptied the fire station. The men endured an agonizing hour of freezing weather subduing a house fire. At quarter to midnight they returned to warm coffee, warm clothes and empty, pockets, drawers and cubby holes. The down and out Adolph Stinson had used a child and a story to prey on the good Samaritans.

Charlie spoke up after listening to their swearing complaints. "We did what we thought was right, took care of a kid and a guy down on his luck. I'd do it again too."

Freezing air came screaming in as the door to the fire station opened. Epaulets of snow and a dunce cap melting snow and tiny icicles framed a small man standing at the door.

"Can you guys spare a little warmth?"

THE PACKAGE

Joey didn't know if the heat or the smell of spoiling garbage was bothering him the most today. New York City's heat didn't bothered everyone, but this heat wave, now six days in the 90's, had the whole town bothered. The garbage strike had people thinking Hell would be a breath of fresh air. Right now Joey felt queasy, like his stomach wanted to be outside of him. Tank top, shorts and floppies on his body, nothing else and these were wet as the sweat looked for new paths to roll down his face.

The subway draft tried sucking the heat away and many residents plopped down on the available benches before exiting, getting some small amount of relief. Joey didn't have that luxury, to sit and relax, life didn't treat him with such kindness. Joey was a thief, opportunities were opportunities, regardless of weather, hot, cold, rain or snow. At the moment opportunities awaited and he went after them.

Joey hit cars for his daily bread. Walking the streets looking into every parked vehicle, appraised the value of objects left on the seats or floor, he'd try to claim them. Right now, with the garbage piled high and getting higher and wider every day, he and the garbage were in the street. Car owners had difficulty finding a parking space, while Joey had trouble looking into cars from the street side. He much preferred working from the curb, most drivers didn't lock that door, the other door they usually locked.

Joey's routine was simple and fast. Look into the car, see something he wanted, pull on the door, if it opened, grab the object and move on. Quickly, faster if pursuit ensued. Once around a corner or in a doorway, he'd drop his booty into a shopping bag and continue looking for more a block or so away. With a margin of success, five or six treasures wound up in the bag and he would head for Flag's place.

Flag, he once declared winners at the motorway, now spend his time evaluating various objects that different customers had for sale. Flag didn't ask for documentation of belongings or even request if the customer had a price in mind. He didn't haggle, take it or leave and don't return again. Most of Flag's sellers were cheated, they knew it, but where else could they find such easy accommodations for their newly acquired goods.

Joey first three items were open door jobs, a camera, a pair of binoculars and an old P.C. Oh, and a breakfast meal with one bite out of the egg and muffin. The jerk had milk instead of coffee, but there was change in the bag. His last attempt nearly broke his elbow.

On the seat of a Lexus convertible lay a package that made him drool like a new father in the maternity viewing room. A lovely bow tied box of flowery paper with a note tucked under the ribbon. It read "to my on... and ..ly". Joey liked the mushy stuff, poor sap would have a rough time explaining to someone why he didn't have a gift. Joey brought his bent elbow down on the canvas, ripping the roof. In his haste, he misjudged the position of the roof strut and yelped in pain when the elbow took the brunt of his blow.

Two men, standing a few doors away, turned and saw Joey reaching through the roof. They began running and yelling at him. He had the package and reached down for his shopping bag, but while turning he slid on a plastic pile of garbage. Scrambling like a goose trying to take off on a frozen lake, Joey managed to out run the beer bellies running after him. Twice he slid on the slop stuck to his floppies, but winded and sweating profusely, he out ran them and bolted down an alley then started walking a bit slower.

Flag didn't get a change to evaluate the pretty package,

Joey didn't remove it from the bag. He took the $185 bucks, Flag offered and headed for the subway. On the train he sat, cooling and dreaming about the contents of the mystery box. He kept stroking it, like a puppy getting a belly rub. He imagined some thing lady-like, something for the gal upstairs. He'd give it to her and perhaps get his way with her. Maybe? Should he open it first or just play Mr. Big and drop it in her lap.

Entering his dump of a room and a half, he opted to open it. Popping a beer and pulling out a kitchen knife, he slit the ribbon. The carefully prepared package poured out its contents, all over Joey's table and floor. The S.O.B. had wrapped his garbage and left it out for some one to steal. Bet the S.O.B. left the curbside door open too.

SURVIVAL LESSON

Matt Laurie loved Millicent Baumann from the day they met 'til the day he decided to kill her. Once he reached that decision, his plans moved, without a flaw, to the inevitable. His decision making abilities made him the youngest multi-billionaire CEO in America. Usually ruthless, he didn't turn back from a goal and the death of Millicent had become a goal.

Feeling the Christmas Spirit, Millicent volunteered to work with John Harris on the Hospital Fund raiser, an annual effort for the cancer patients in the children's section. Doctor Harris usually coordinated the hospital staff with the volunteers, but this year, due to a newly discovered abscess in his own pericardium, his wife had stepped in to fill her husband's shoes. The reason for his declining was never given the hospital, or the publicity people. So this year Doctor John Harris let Johnnie Harris, his wife, coordinate the Fund raiser.

Matt Laurie loved the outdoor life, Millicent barely functioned in the backyard, or at a lawn party. He never talked about his love of the outdoors, too many people now a days frowned upon killing and eating wild things. Matt could survive, without a gun or prepared foods, or camping gear for two to three weeks. To sustain his hidden pleasure, he'd advice the company he had urgent but hush-hush business. Only for an extreme emergency would he come back and only if Millicent contacted him. The company accepted his demands and never once questioned his absence.

On Friday, April 11, 2003, Matt and Millicent headed out in their boat for a spur of the moment visit to her mother in Martha's Vineyard. Matt planned it, Millicent thought it a wonderful surprise. Millicent lolled back to enjoy the brisk sea breezes flaying the small whitecaps. The drugged drink Matt had warmed for her took effect at once. He headed out to sea.

"Millicent, my sweet, you betrayed me. You betrayed our love. For this betrayal you are to die." Matt's voice held no bitterness as he spoke. His eyes constantly flitted up and down the drugged body sprawled in the chair. "You thought I didn't know, didn't you?" The query was answered when Millicent's head bobbed to the bouncing of the boat.

Matt's voice raised a few notes to this response. "You knew, I knew? No, you didn't know. I came home while you spoke to John on the phone. I heard you say how wonderful it was at his house while I had been in Detroit." Matt's voice broke. "You said that love making was a pleasure. A pleasure. You always said our love making was a pleasure." Matt's tears mixed with the sea spray.

Matt emptied the water bottle and chucked it into the garbage container. Don't litter the environment. Millicent stirred, Matt sat back and watched her, dreaming no doubt about her lover. Damn, he should have gone after Doctor Harris first. Later would do. His thoughts fixated on the loss of Millicent. He wished he knew what had really come between them.

Had he really paid attention, even for a moment. Just to hear the words he thought he heard. Millicent talking on the phone to Johnnie. Woman talk. Talk of the latest romance novels and their intrigues. They discussed the Hospital Fund raiser. The woman volunteers had met at Doctor Harris' home. Afterward the two woman spent time together with woman talk. Oh Matt, you screwed this up. You'll never know.

When the last drop of gasoline vaporized the boat sputtered and Matt commenced his terrible deed. Millicent sunk below the waves, a series of small swirls and various size bubbles broke the surface. Her hand seemed to reach up. Matt recoiled from the gunnel. He had only to wait. Wait for his rescue. He could survive for several days without food. They had brought none. Why bring anything for so short a trip. No water supply, other than the bottle he had emptied. He could drink his urine and survive. This would make his story very creditable to his rescuers.

Matt was found adrift on the 14th of April, dying. For three days he recycled his urine. Each time the fluid became more toxic to his body. True, your urea will perhaps quench your thirst, but there's only so much to recycle. Finally it becomes pure poison.

RUNNER

The prisoner ran his fingers over the name scratched into the wall. RUNNER

"Gee, I knew him way back." he said to his cell mate. "Way back. As a kid even."

"I never heard of him."

"Oh, he was an old timer. I'd say he did this in the late 40's, early 50's."

. Ralph "Runner" Greene ran wherever and whenever he went anywhere. As a child his fat legs and rapid waddle brought smiles to the faces in the neighborhood. As a teen they brought cries, when Runner snatched purses and packages from unsuspecting people walking the streets. Running behind trucks he'd pilfer their cargoes, then his broken field style of running made escaping easy and any pursuers cursing in the distance.

He graduated to running errands for the big guys. He ran around for the bookies and the floating crap games. When he knocked up Rosario's sister, he married her, "Or else." But he ran out on her when her brother died in a shootout   Runner ran up a few gambling debts, but got into some snook's business and bankrupted it to clear his debts. When "Dippy" Dan Druce ran for office, it was Runner that got his campaign stuff out.

"He mustta got caught with those other crooked politicians."

"No. He must have carve this in the wall before he got into politics."

Runner should have stayed off his feet. "Fleece" DeFellicio talked him into a sure thing heist of a currency exchange, hitting a truck delivering cash at Cottage Grove and 79th Street. No one expected a Grand Crossing squad car to blunder into the heist and block the get away car Runner was driving. That put him on his feet.

He ran east, to the I.C. railroad tracks, where the cops spotted him ducking under the suburban train platform and flushed him out. Darting for a passing freight train, he ran along side grabbing a ladder and pulling himself aboard. So did a cop. At 87th Street, he slipped between cars and dropped off. As the freight train passed, he bolted.

The express engineer never saw Runner. The pursuing police found his legs a short distance from the body. Officer Ostrowski knew Runner and identified him.

Runner's time had run out.

COMPLETE KILLER

Arnold was a klutz before birth, he turned as he dropped in the birth canal and became a breech birth. Most things after that didn't turn out well for Arnold. Chosen last for school teams, forgot assignments, made blunders in experiments and usually failed at anything he attempted. Many tasks he was sent to do by friends, actually cruel acquaintances, made him the butt of their sick humor. Only Frankie, the leader of the small gang of hoodlums, gave him true sympathy, even prevented some of their pranks against Arnold. Frankie always said, "Arnold may screw it up, but he tries."

Arnold and Frankie became close, very close. Over the years Arnold would listen to Frankie, never offering advice, just listen. He listened to dreams, hopes, desires and fears. Frankie had them all. Shrewd and willing to take chances, Frankie moved among the hierarchy of the underground. In the passing decades he became The Don. Arnold's tormentors came and went, Arnold stayed.

The night Frankie's heart failed him, Arnold called 911. Arnold went to the hospital. Arnold sat through the night at Frankie's bedside. Arnold kept all visitors out of Frankie's room, except the priest. These things he did because he and Frankie had talked about it many times over many years.

Doctor Malone folded his stethoscope and placed it in the smock pocket. A determined set of jaw caught Frankie's eye. "So Doc, you're not pleased."

"Not at all. I told you, once it begins to break up, the end will follow shortly. There is no way a new heart can help you."

"Tell me, exactly what's going to happen?" Frankie's calmness belied a deep fear, not of death. Incapacitation. Frankie feared being bedridden.

Doctor Malign fussed with his ring. "For how long, I can't say. One, two months. A year."

"Awe Christ Doc. I'm going to be bedridden, ain't I?"

"Simple truth. Yes.'

Arnold sat in his chair taking in every word. As usual he listened, but didn't offer advice. Tears welled up and cascaded down his thin cheeks. Frankie observed his behavior and wondered how Arnold would do without him.

"Hey. What's with the tears?" The assumed gruffness in his voice startled Arnold.

"Gosh Frankie, you know. I ain't so good with bad news."

"Shit Arnold, we all die. Again the gruffness as he spoke.

"I'll stop." He whipped his handkerchief across his entire face. "See? Gone."

"See you later, Doc. We got things to discuss."

Their conversation covered conversations of years gone by. But Frankie spoke of one unsettling fear. Being paralyzed, bedridden, unable to control his own body, Frankie feared more than meeting God. Arnold listened.

Late that night, as the tubes and monitors cradled Frankie in a peaceful sleep, Arnold left the room. He had developed a plan, Frankie would not agree to his plan, he knew that, so it went unmentioned. The mob bosses would not go along with his plan. He would explain it all later.

Arnold broke into the drug cabinet and removed some cyanide and took a box of Band-Aids. In the washroom he emptied a capsule of cyanide onto the Band-aid and returned to Frankie's bedside. No one would notice an extra bandage on the taped up body. Frankie smiled as he felt Arnold squeeze the Band-aid unto his forearm. Arnold smiled back, as he settled back into his chair.

The alarms went off in Frankie's room. Code blue was flashed to the attendants. Their efforts were in vain. They found Arnold bedside, in his chair, dead too. Frankie had nothing to fear. Arnold, ever the klutz, had handled cyanide and it had seeped through his skin. He had poisoned himself. The entire story would reveal that he had killed himself and his best friend.

BUCKLE UP

"Morris, if you go out anywhere you make sure you buckle that baby up."

"Yeah, yeah. Christ woman, you think I don't know what to do."

"You buckle your belt too." Ida hollered back as she went out the closing door.

Morris stood before the open refrigerator door scanning the contents. "No beer. A warm day, the Bears playing the Pack and no beer. And me stuck watching the baby." The baby didn't understand a word this man was saying to himself, but gurgled in response. "Maybe next door... Nah, ain't nobody home." Checking under the sink, he continued his one man conversation. "Shit! Should've checked before that woman left. Shit!"

Morris picked the baby up, waving its bottom near his nose. "Ain't dirty. Come on little guy, we're going shopping." His big arms blanketing the tiny figure, he headed for the door, stopping to put a small caliber pistol in his pocket. Sweat dripping from his forehead, Morris dutifully attempted to strap the infant into the safety seat in the car's back seat, cussing, in sweet baby talk, at the straps and buckles resisting his efforts.

Morris knew of a little shop in a near-by neighborhood and drove to it. Without money, he didn't want anyone recognizing him for holding-up the place. Some cigarettes, cold beer and what cash the register held wasn't worth another year in the can. Morris, adjusting the gun and baby in his arms, entered the store.

A dark skinned, foreign looking guy behind the counter eye-balled Morris as he walked in. A kid, loading the cooler, looked up as Morris removed two six packs. The rest of the store was empty. Everyone's watching the game he guessed.

Staring at the gun pointing from beneath the baby diaper, the counterman put the beer, cigarettes and cash into a bag, as Morris demanded. Morris headed toward the car as the clerk, ducking down, grabbed the phone dialing 911.

A near-by squad car pulled in immediately. The clerk ran out hollering and pointing at Morris. "He gotta gun! Under the baby, he gotta gun!"

It was a warm day. Morris would have no beer or Bears game. The police arrested him as he was cussing and fighting with the baby seat straps and buckles.

JUST BE NATURAL

"Lester."

Mike "Lion" DeLeo, motioned for Lester with a ham most of us consider a hand. The movement caught Lester's attention since he hadn't expected meeting anyone in the small eatery. Recognition by the leader of local hoodlum hierarchy made Lester beam, wave and with a gulp and a little fear, head for the Lion's table.

The peasant stopped a step from the king's table. Awed, he waited for permission to approach or speak. Eyes lowered, alert and taking in the other three men that watched his every move, Lester knew his place.

"Pull a chair from the table behind you and sit with us." said the Lion.

Bewildered but obedient, Lester sat. "Thank you."

"Want something to eat Lester? Or coffee?" purred the Lion.

Lester noted the empty dishes and half-filled cups. "Coffee, OK?"

A snap of Lion's fingers and the waitress jumped with two coffee pots and a cup. Lester tapped the decafe coffee pot, she poured and left. He never thought such service would happen to him. All eyes stared at him, even the other customers stared. He was being checked out.

"Lester, I seen you around and hear you do some small jobs now and again. I also hear that sometimes things have been difficult for you." Lion swept that ham across the table, "A couple of these guys think you might like to help us. A small job, maybe not too big for you?"

"Me? Not if you think I can help do it Li... Mr. DeLeo."

"Yes. Can you do a small job for the Lion Friday afternoon?"

"Tomorrow." said a voice at the table.

The Lion glared at the speaker. Silence, not a breath could be heard.

"Wantta work for me, tooomooorrooww?"

"Yeah. Sure. Tomorrow."

All the men left together crossing the street to sit on the park bench and garden wall. Fingers were pointed, men stood and moved as the chess master bade them. A charade played out for the benefit of the participants, a comedy for passerbys.

"Now when you walk in to Kleist's Jewelery store, walk in casual. Just be very natural. Ask to look at some ah... some watches. When it's clear, place your hand behind your head. We'll come in and clean the place out."

"I'll act natural Mr. DeLeo. No problem. Natural."

Lester walked into the store at 4:30p.m. He checked his Timex as he stepped into the coolness of Kleist's Fine Jewelry. The shop was empty, except for the man on the phone.

"Go ahead and finish. I'm in no hurry. I'll just look around."

The man waved his hand and continued to talk. He watched Lester at the watch display. Lester lay his watch on the counter and seemed to compare it with those in the case. Lester then moved toward the front window, saw the man still on the phone and waved to him.

When the phone conversation ended and the man came toward Lester, his hand quickly touched the back of his head. Lester pointed to the watches and began to discuss which he could afford. A sale might be in the making.

Three masked men entered the front door. They pushed

the man and Lester together, tied them and sat them behind the display counter. They smashed the glass and scooped up the various gems, jewels and watches into ready bags. In less than a minute the robbers were prepared to leave the store.

As they stepped from the store, the police grabbed them. The police were waiting. They knew the place was being robbed.

Police District 9 roared with laughter every time a newcomer heard the story. The newspeople fell all over themselves as they told their viewers the story of the bumbling escapades of the robbery.

When Lester walked in, the proprietor was talking to the mayor's assistant PR man. Lester's natural behavior didn't fit Lester. His glances out the window and at the watches were not the glances of a shopper. The owner mentioned this to the PR man and finished his conversation. The PR man called the police. The police solved this one on the spot. By the way, Lester looks perfectly natural in his latest mugshot.

LADIES CHOICE

Haree Bridgeman and his half brother Johnee Lopes needed money. They needed lots of money right now. They had bluffed their way into the Big Guy's poker game and lost. The Big Guy blew his cork when they didn't cough up on the spot. His games didn't function as charity affairs. They had until midnight to pay up or get whacked. Four and a half hours to live. Where the hell could they get a grand in that time?

Neither of them would measure half way up to normal on an standard IQ test. They were not yet in their forties, and both had spent 12 years in the local state prison. They had a tendency to botch minor robberies or burglaries. It wasn't that they didn't plan their jobs well, they just didn't look ahead and they'd get caught.

"Them sisters. You know them old lady sisters. They got money." said Haree.

"Don't know. Never see them spending anything." Johnee grumbled. "We get whacked dead if we don't pay the Big Guy."

"Whatta you wanna do? Huh? We can't run away."

"Look Haree, maybe we can get some from mom and pay a little..."

"Mom. Shit, she'd throw her beer bottle at us and laugh when it hit or missed us."

"Yeah. OK. We try the old ladies. We don't take no crap from 'um either. We kick their asses 'til they give us their stash."

Haree knocked softly on the front door. He looked through the glass window and could see the old biddy, with a cane, move down the hallway. The porch light went on and the door opened a crack. Both men pushed violently on the door, which sent the old woman to the floor. Haree pounced on her, covered her mouth with his hand and whispered into her ear.

Johnee, with one swift move shut the door and flipped the porch light off.

"Old lady," Haree whispered, "where's that sister of yours?"

As if cued, a voice called from the back end of the hallway.

"Who knocked Rosie?"

Rose didn't answer. She couldn't with the filthy hand, smelling of tobacco, covering her mouth. A violent jerk pulled her to her feet and a shearing stab of pain twisted her back. The three of them advanced on the voice in the back room.

A small woman, a floral apron over her dress, spoon and pot in her hand, stood at the supper table. Her mouth opened but shut at once when the man holding her sister spoke.

"Don't say nothing. Nothing. Understand?'

The small gray head nodded.

"Put the pot down over on the stove."

Johnee followed her. His eyes opened wide at the table setting and the smell of the prepared food.

"What ja cook old lady?"

"Hey! No crap. Who cares what she cooked." said Haree.

"Shucks, Haree, I know, but it smells good and I really am awfully hungry."

"No crap."

"It's Louisiana gumbo." the little woman said in a frightened voice.

"Jeez, Haree, gumbo. Haven't had that in a long time."

"If you're hungry, I can serve you some." the little old woman said.

"Shut up old lady, or this Rose sister of yours gets her neck broke."

"Shit, Haree, she's only doing what old ladies are suppose to do. They learned that way. Like in the movies."

"Johnee, shut your face. We come to get the money. Remember? The money? The Big Guy?"

"I know. Come on man we got time now. We're in here and the old ladies will get us the money. Just a bowl full? OK? One bowl full?"

Haree pushed Rose into a chair, the force made her wince. "Shut your face."

Rose nodded. May, her sister, approached the table with two more bowls.

"There's hot buns in the oven. If you want them, help yourselves."

"No, Johnee, we watch them. They do everything so we can see them."

"OK, Haree." came a muffled response from a mouth filled with hot gumbo.

"You bring the buns. And get some butter too. You got real butter?"

"Real butter." said May. "Wine too?"

"Christ, wine too." said Johnee. "Hot damn. A party. Who wouldda guessed."

"Wine? Sure. And don't try no funny stuff." Haree ignored the offered wine glass and put the bottle to his mouth. "I had better." He wiped his mouth with his cuff.

"Haree, if you drink from that bottle, I want a bottle too."

"There more. There, on the shelf behind you. Want me to fetch it?"

The two men ate and drank. They drank more than they should have, with results they should have expected. Earlier May had a chill and pushed the thermostat up a few degrees. The spicy meal, the warm wine and the warm air soon played havoc with their equilibrium. Haree, a ladies' man began to paw both women. They protested in a quiet way, then offered him cognac. A treat

Haree had never tried. Johnee moved to an easy chair and turned on the TV and dozed off.

"Wherish the munney?" Haree's voice spoke in a slurred angry tone.

"We keep it under the mattress of our bed." said a very timid voice.

"Liss get it." said the listing Haree, as he rose from his chair. "Mon Johnee."

The huddled body snorted and remained asleep.

"Come along with me." Rose lead the man through the door. "This way."

Haree leaned over the bed, tugged at the mattress and fell face forward.

"You're pathetic." said the policeman, as the cuffs clicked behind Haree's back.

Through the foggy numbness of a befuddled mind, Haree saw the old ladies through the door. They were talking to other officers. Johnee, slid to the floor, his hands cuffed behind him and continued to snore. The brothers had screwed up, again.

OPEN SESAME

A typical Chicago April wind blew Lester around the corner of the building and down the alley, numb fingers pulling the frayed, stained coat closer to his hungry body. Heading for the soup kitchen, hoping for some warmth, but mostly wanting some hot food, he pushed into the wind. He had had food squirreled away in his room; however, he forgot to lock the door yesterday and some thoughtless thief cleaned him out.

The loud clatter of garbage cans startled him, actually scared him would be more accurate. Flattening against the wall, Lester looked back toward the noise making cans. No one there, but the cylinder of a pistol was rolling along the pavement. Lester continued looking about, up and down the alley and up and down the buildings. Nothing and no one to give him a clue as to where the cylinder came from. Looking behind the garbage cans, he found the rest of the gun.

Pushing his body into the shallow doorway and examining his find, he whistled a low note An old broken pistol without bullets. The barrel was plugged, no, not plugged never there. A starter's pistol. Looked real, felt real and might scare anyone looking into it. Lester dropped it into his coat pocket. Later, in the warmth of the soup kitchen's toilet, he'd checked it out more closely.

Now Lester always had trouble adding facts to facts and getting conclusions. His walk to the soup kitchen allowing him to daydream about that broken weapon. He envisioned some easy and ready cash using the pistol as a persuader. Just walk into that little bank office, that one across the street, point the gun at a teller, take the cash and run. Run like Hell. By God, he'd do it, right now.

He pushed his way into the small lobby, walked right up to the closest teller and pointed the gun in her face. "Just gimme the paper money. The big stuff."

She didn't scream, her eyes grew huge and her dark skin grayed, as she pushed several packets of paper money toward the gun. "Yes Sir. Here Sir." Then she stood there, a hatching chrysalis, mouth trembling, bug-eyed and body twitching.

Lester turned and with three or four quick steps, slammed into the door he had just entered. It didn't budge. He took a step back and threw his body at the door and bounced back into the lobby. Desperately he looked about, no one coming toward him, the teller seemed to be grinning. He rushed the door again, his head banged off the door this time and whirling him back into the lobby again.

"OK. OK. Someone, locked the door. Open the God Damn door! Open the door or I'll shoot someone!" Lester waved his gun high above his head. "You", he looked at the teller. "Open that door! Now! Open it!"

She was laughing, "It's not locked Sir. Honest." The giggles pouring forth, "Honest it's not locked."

"You." He looked at the teller. "Here's your money back. I ain't stealing nothing. No robbery. OK?" Waving the gun, now coming apart and falling in pieces on the floor, literally sobbing, "It ain't a loaded gun. It's broken even." Advancing toward the door, "Just open the door and let me out." Lester bawled.

Outside, a small child came charging toward the door. A woman with another child in her arms, reached toward the running child. The child hit the door, shoving it open. All the way.

Only as Lester fled from his demons did he read LLUP on his side of the glass door

The child continued to HSUP against the door, keeping

it open for mommy. Lester ran into another demon, Officer Ostrowski on his way into the bank.

OLD TIMERS

"Mitchell? Poole?" Max Pearl stood and poured his not so dulcet voice over the cubical walls of the District VII, Metropolitan Police office. "Which smart ass put these two files on my desk?"

Half a head poked through the space two cubicles to the right of Max. "I did Sarg. Your name is on the cover of each one."

"It should be. I busted those two my first week on the job. September, '72."

Paul O'Connor stuck his face into Pearl's, the gray fabric cubical surface separated them by inches, and gave him a know-it-all smile. "They've come back to haunt you."

"Bullshit."

"Nope." The eerie child's voice from Poltergeist, rasped, "They're here."

"My god. You're kidding. Something for my retirement party, right?"

"Nope." Again O"Connor spoke in the child's voice, "They're here."

Paul came around the cubical and faced Max. "Your first huh? In '72?"

"Shit, Paul, they're dead." He waved the files. "Or still in the can at Joliet."

"Sorry Max, but these two are alive, out of Joliet and downstairs. I'll take you down." Paul swept one arm in a grand theatrical gesture, "Come into my parlor."

After looking over a pair of chunky, balding, unshaved for several days, dressed like bums prisoners, Max admitted they were Tommy "Sparks" Mitchell a.k.a. "Fireball" and Larry "Leadfoot" Poole, a.k.a. "Speedy Gonzales". "Sparks" set himself afire hot-wiring a car and "Speedy Gonzales" tried to talk himself out of a ticket, speaking Spanish to Officer Ortiz. Without a word to either of the two under lock and key, the two detectives returned to the upstairs offices. Max popped for two cokes, from the hallway cooler, while Paul shook the candy dispenser to drop the coins through and deliver some chocolate.

Max sat in his chair behind the desk. Paul settled in the old leather relic, the one the wheel fell off if it moved. It came off, so Paul sprawled forward onto the desk.

"I'm waiting." Max grinned as the words faded in the small space. "Gonna tell me?"

"Christ Max, You ain't gonna believe me. No way. You'll think it's a set-up. Like you said, for your retirement."

"OK. It ain't a set-up. Tell me what those two are doing downstairs."

"Waiting for a hearing." Paul swallowed some coke, some dribbled from his mouth.

"That Cuban girl, came from the Academy last week, and Arnie, grabbed them in the mall parking lot yesterday. You'll bust your ass laughing at this one." Paul leaned back and the chair lurched.

"I'd bust it laughing at you."

"OK. OK." Paul readjusted the chair, then slowly leaned back, touching the soft rug wall. "Here's the skinny on these two."

The phone rang. "Pearl." A short pause and a head nod. "Call you back in fifteen, twenty minutes."

Paul began, "The two downstairs, from what we have been able to piece together, stole a truck for a robbery. They stole a City Highway Department truck, with all the cones and signs. Poole drove it over to the mall, Mitchell drove over ahead of him with a getaway car. They were going to rob the bank in the food store, had it cased and everything. They knew the armor company left extra cash on the fifteenth of the month."

Max just sat, didn't even bother to munch the chocolate or swig his coke.

"They were clever with this job. Planned every detail, to the minute." Paul dribbled more coke on his shirt. "They set out cones and signs, on the highway, near Entrance D. They even got a traffic cop to direct traffic around the set-up."

"No shit. The Chief will come down on that cop."

"Did. Inside for a couple a weeks." Paul rolled his eyes. "To continue, they even started to paint over the crosswalk. Then they quit painting and walked over to the store. They stopped the money delivery just inside the door. With the money and a guard in pursuit, they raced to their car and, zzzzzip, they were out of there. Except, they can't get out of there. Their cones and signs had directed traffic into a hugh snarl. Nothing moved, couldn't. The guard from the store walks over and holds them 'til Arnie and his partner arrest them. Arnie and the girl were in the mall lot passing out parking tickets. Just like that. Fini."

"Fini." said Max.

RANTING AND RAVING

CARD SHARP

Gasping lungs pumped vapor clouds into the Chicago night air. Watery eyes watching the red lights on the back of the train grow smaller. Walking into the two-toned gray waiting room, Mel saw the door on the far end of the station open. Someone else had missed the 1:17.

Mel's companion was a tall, well dressed black man. Walking close to the coal burning stove, he pulled his foggy horn-rimmed glasses down a wide, flat nose. Extending two hands with long thin fingers ringed with gold toward the heat, he began rubbing them together.

"An hour wait?" a voice, distinctly southern, asked.

"Yeap. One hour."

Flashing a wide smile, he continued rubbing his hands. "Nearly froze them. Don't need gloves where I come from."

His jeweled fingers slide down the front of a soft gray overcoat, revealing a paisley lining, "Might as well be comfortable." Sitting on the bench he plucked a deck of playing cards from an inner pocket of his blue pin-striped double-breasted suit. "Can't practice enough."

Mel was staring in awe, as the man separated the deck with one hand and began flipping the cards over and over. He's a magician Mel thought. The nimble fingers exposing the top card, a deuce of hearts, then dealing out four hands of five cards, with the red deuce never moving.

"You're good. Magician?"

The corners of his eyes wrinkled, his large smile flashed a

gold incisor. His laugh was melodious. He was charming Mel and he didn't realize it.

"Thank you. I'm not a magician I'm a gambler."

"Really?"

"Really. Watch. Catch me moving this top card."

Turning over the top card, a ten of clubs, he shuffled. The top card never moving, but staying on top with each riffle. Dealing to four imaginary players five cards, the ten remaining in plain view at all times.

Grinning, as they say, from ear to ear. "I'm dealing seconds, not off the top."

"I didn't see the top card move."

"Better not. You see I'm cheating. If I were caught I could get killed. Don't ever cheat at cards. If you're playing for money with friends and you cheat, you'll lose your friends. Cheat other people they'll beat the tar out of you or kill you. Don't ever cheat."

"I hear you. But you cheat, don't you?" Mel implied with his question.

"Don't have any friends. And I've got caught. Look here." He tilted his head upward revealing acne scars and an uglier, lumpy track along his neck, up behind the ear and into his gray hairline. "And here". Pulling the frayed sleeve of his suit coat back, he pointed to a large bump sticking up from his forearm. "Both bones broke."

"Getting caught? Cheating? Can't you just be a magician?"

"Looking for the easy life I'd say. But I'm a black man, an older black man. I'll never really get to the easy life."

"If you played honest, maybe?"

"Let's put it this way. The white guys can go back and forth on the ocean boats. I can't even get on one, much less play cards with white, rich men. I ride the cross country trains. Some times the not-so-rich men lets me play. Correction, 'let' me play."

"Do you cheat them?"

"Often. But, I'm guessing you ain't going to tell."

"Good guess."

"I respect your word. Shake. I'm David."

"Mel."

His grip was velvet, firm and warm. Our closeness hinted of stale sweat and a hint of alcohol on his breath. The mints he was popping into his mouth might mask these odors. Mel quietly declining his offer of several.

"How do you practice if no one's watching you? Like I'm watching?"

"I sit in front of a mirror trying to catch myself. I really try."

"I see. Can you cheat other ways? Did you ever catch someone else cheating?"

Mel, warming to David's openness, felt free to ask questions.

"Yes and yes. I just drop out of the game." A bit of froth glistening in the corner of his full lower lip. Checking a large gold and jeweled pocket watch, "Forty minutes yet." Then looking at a watch on his wrist, also large and gold, "Won this one," David said, tapping the crystal. "Sometimes you can stay in a game without cash. Worth a hundred. If you're still interested, see if you can catch this."

Once again the agile fingers were shuffling the cards and dealing them out. A jack was on top now. Each imaginary player had two pair, his pair, aces over jacks. He dealt several times and knew every card. He never lost.

"I'm shuffling through. It takes a lot of practice. Time for one more before our train gets here. Cut the deck, look at the top card and put it back on top. What is it?"

"Four of clubs."

Flipping the top card over with his pinkie, revealing an eight of hearts. "Nope."

David's eyes were twinkling, revealing his pleasure of showing Mel his dexterity and skills and mystifying Mel.. Engrossed in showing Mel a few more tricks, even how to palm cards, they almost didn't hear the approaching train.

Sitting together in the smoking car, they rode to 79th Street where they parted. After the door closed, and the train began moving, Mel saw David leaning against the window, mouthing, "Don't ever cheat."

LOVE, MATCH

Every aging muscle ached. A droplet of perspiration rolled into the slight furrow above her eyebrow, connecting to another to run down the nose, there to form a hanging drop. Her eyes were burning from concentration and the bright pitiless sun. For over two hours she's tried, watched, waited for this moment. Her throat desert dry, breaths coming in faster, measured quantities. She licks the parched lips, pressing her teeth together. Her arm falls, then comes up straight, swiftly steel blue lasers pick-up their arching target. The other arm coils over her shoulder, the aching body, responds. Every fiber, every muscle, every bone throbs in pain as she bends into her effort. Watching the ball's progress, she automatically begins the next movement of the often repeated ritual. In intense pain she pushed herself.

She plants her burning, knotted feet half way to the back of the service line. Straining to keep her balance, she watches her opponent's feet shuffle, the racquet coming back. Anticipation! Watch! Watch! Are her shoulders turned or straight back? Watch her feet! Are they close together? Watch her! Watch! Analyze the ball bounce. Watch the angle. Your serve is going wide. She's late. She missed.

An ace! An ace!

Game!

Set!

Match!

The crowd's roar rings in her ears, as she rushes to the net for an acknowledgement of her win. Elated feelings flood her screaming body. Tears of joy and pain blind and distort the scene as they bathe her cheeks. The players shake hands at the net and walk to the sidelines. It's not her first win, but her last. Even champions age and retire.

YOU CAN'T GO BACK

"Dad" came the voice from behind the magazine. "Did Mom spell her name, VINOWEISKY?"

"Huh, huh. Vinoweisky. Why?"

"There's an article in this magazine about Grace Vino-weisky, a clothing designer that may be in trouble with the I.R.S."

"Could be your mom. Is there a picture?"

"Nope. Just the name. Who really cares anyway?"

"Guess we don't, right Dom?"

Leaning back into the privacy of his recliner, Henry Mull-erman shut his eyes and drifted back to New Year's Eve, Chicago, 1975. It was smoky and dark in Fuzzy's back booth. The chill of the night didn't reach back to this quiet corner. Even the exuber-ance of the celebrating, liquored up crowd didn't reach into the quiet booth.

The clock tolled the old year out and Henry looked into Grace's eyes, slipping a small diamond ring onto her finger. No words between them, the cheers of Auld Lang Syne deafened the neon Hamm's bear. Her kiss said yes. They cuddled for hours, too happy to drink or share time with the other patrons. Fuzzy brought the iced bottle of domestic champaign Henry had bought earlier, winked and let them be. They had a City Hall wedding on Valentine's Day.

As a switchman on the EJ&E Railroad Henry put in over-time and banked every cent. Gracie waited tables at the Blackhawk using her paycheck and tips for living expenses and the luxury of a movie now and then or a pair of bleacher seats at Wrigley Field.

Both bought little items on birthdays or the holidays, these usually benefited both of them. It took six months to pay off Polk Brothers for a table model color TV.

"Dad, you wanna see this article?'

"Naw" The break in Henry's reveries didn't sidetrack him, they continued.

Grace's Christmas wish for 1977, a house. "Let's buy a house." He had never thought of the two of them in a house, their own house. Their rented flat continued as home 'til they looked at a place in Oak Lawn. It had four rooms, a garage, a small linked fence surrounding an area of grass and flowers in the back and grass in the front too. The amenities of suburban living made the location, "Everything we'll ever need." Grace cooed. "Everything."

For her birthday, April 24th, Grace wanted a kitten. Henry detested cats. However, he succumbed to her desire. She came home with two. The house smelled of cat, cat urine, cat food, cat hairballs and cat reproductive fluids. Their furniture aged to scratches and tears, their food had extra protein in it, known as cat hair and the little yard became the stage for nightly arias sung by TomTom and other Toms.

The hopelessness of a childless marriage crystallized when the doctor told them, Grace's body, her reproductive organs, had been scared in her childhood. They had discussed adoption sometime ago. Holding each other that night, they decided to file papers as soon as possible. What God denied them, He let others give. They adopted Dom.

We knew nothing about his background, his parents, his genetic or psychiatric history. How do we care for him. Henry worried about what they had done and honestly wished they hadn't. Looking over to Dom, he knew he'd surely miss him if he lost him. He loved having him for a son.

"Want something Dad?"

"No son, just looking about. Do you have homework tonight?"

"Dad, it's summer vacation, remember? No homework."

"Oh. Yeah. Forgot." Henry said, slipping back into the past.

Cleaning up after Dom, while Grace pouring over a catalog delivered that day, was a familiar scene. She sat on many nights with her face buried in a "dream-book", while Henry assumed more and more of the household chores and the care of Dom. Henry's seniority allowed him a steady run each night from Acme Steel to the Harvey yards, while Grace waitressed days at Le Brothers, just off 87th and Central. They were a typical suburban blue collar family. Until that night.

"Henry, I want to go back to school." Grace said. "I want to have a better life for us. For Dom. Whatta ya think?" her eyes seeming to dare Henry to think otherwise.

"This is pretty sudden isn't it?" said a pale, wide eyed, open mouth Henry.

"Well yes and no. I thought about it and I found some classes I could take at Moraine Valley Community College. You can take care of Dom before you leave for work. It's only ten minutes from here and a bus goes out there. Think about it Honey, will ya? Classes start soon."

Henry almost stepped into a switchlight that night. He blind-sided himself thinking about Grace going to school. He mentioned it to Hoover, the engineer, as they moved out of the Harvey yards. Hoover thought it was a good idea and wished his wife would go too. Moe, the yardmaster spoke highly of continuing adult education. So Henry agreed and Grace became a college student.

It became a matter of pride for Henry, telling everyone his wife went to college. He worked hard the next couple of years. Grace struggled at first but kept going. She seemed very happy, bubbling with excitement with her projects, modeling them for Henry's approval. One night she called and said the group decided to stay after class and work on their designs. The next week she went out with her class, getting home in the wee hours. This happened off and on all Spring term.

One night, the first week in June, Henry asked why the class stayed out late so often. Tears oozing out of those soft brown eyes, Grace's chest began to heave, words blubbering from a dry throat as she confessed an infidelity. It just happened. It wouldn't happen again. He thought their marriage too important to break up. He forgave her. Dom needed both of them. Things settled down and she tried selling some of her designs.

In July, with a heavy heart Henry opened Dom's bedroom door and peeked in. Young Dom turned and continued the soft snoring of calm childish sleep. The note in Henry's hand didn't seem threatening now.

Grace's note read, "I got a job in California. You can get a divorce and keep Dominick, I don't want him. I don't have any reasons for doing this to you. I just want a life."

She never wrote, sent a card at Christmas or even a Birthday card. She left with no worry they'd cope with such a life change. Pushing out of the chair, Henry began his bedtime routine, turning off the lights, setting the alarm and plopping into the bed he had once shared with Grace. Pulling the blanket to his chin, he reckoned Dom and he have had a pretty good life without her. She won't become a part of it now.

"Night Dad. Love ya." Dom said, walking down the hall to his room.

EMPTY

Richard casually slid the automatic's chamber open, discharging the bullet, released it, and removed the clip. He remembered, never assume a gun is empty 'til you check it.

Twisting and turning the automatic in his hand, he looked down the muzzle and pulled the trigger.

Now the gun was empty.

WALKING

My baby is dead. I know he is. But I can't put him down and leave him to the scavengers. Not my baby. He hasn't moved during the night nor had a body function since the previous sunset. No whimper of hunger or thirst. No nuzz to my breast to suck.

One hand pushed down on the walking stick while her back strained against the mud wall. Finally she stood, gaunt and bowed by the weight she shifted at her chest. Stepping into the already dusty road she mingled with the other early risers. The sun pushed the horizon down and promised another hot day.

When have I eaten last or had a drop of liquid? I am walking with the hopes of those who walk with me. Yet, there are others walking toward me. Where are they going? Where am I going? Look at them skinny, dirty, eyes rolling, shuffling their feet. I must never sink that low.

I hear people. Up ahead there's a crowd. Maybe there's food or water. I would like a little. Just a little bit.

A man is hollering. What did he say? Did he say there is food and water in my home village? Did I hear my village name?

No one answered her questions.

Hadn't she asked them? Can't you hear me? Don't push me. Don't turn me back.

Slowly everyone seems bent on walking back. Back to the place they left in the morning. Was it this morning or yesterday, or the yesterdays before? Back.

The high sun cast no shadows a monochromatic ocher dusts everything, living or dead. Tramping feet moving people in one direction, other people in the opposite direction, creating a moving ever shifting cloud of ocher, without guidance or purpose.

Is that the wall I leaned on last night? I've gone nowhere, done nothing. I'm so tired... thirsty... hungry... Where are these people going? I just came from there, there is nothing there. They say there is drink and food in my village. Go that way. I must rest. I'll show you the way after I rest. Just rest for a spell. Cradle my baby. Maybe he'll wake soon? Let me rest. For a while.

BETTER NOT
TO SPEAK AT ALL

Mike shrunk back into the music filled elevator, watching the two well dressed men stitching the air with their flashing fingers. Smiles, nodding and slight body movements accompanied their dancing hands during the slow descent of the hospital elevator. Both men exited on the Neo-natal floor, proceeding down the hallway, arms waving as loosely as a marionette's.

"Dummies." A near audible whisper came from the back corner.

The white coated gentleman in the front of the elevator turned, his stethoscope dangling from his neck. He stared at Mike, as Mike stared at the badge snapped with a silver clip to the jacket pocket. Matthew Huddleson, M.D. Mike's jaw tightened, his face contorting to a familiar feature among humans. Without speaking Mike's face said, "What?"

"Dummies?" said Dr. Huddleson. "You would reconsider your word if you knew those two men. You just saw two brain surgeons telling each other the success they had in using the latest methods, developed by them, for removing brain tumors from children."

The door opened, the doctor stood aside and Mike stepped out. He heard, "Dummy, " as the elevator door closed.

POINT OF VIEW

Junron looked around her parents' bedroom, everything seemed the same, but things would be different now. Standing in the doorway, she asked the same question she had asked her father the day her mother died.

"Why Daddy? Why? Why did Mommy have to die?"

She just couldn't understand why God wanted her mommy. Mommy had been sick and in pain for two years. She took medicine the doctor said would stop some of her pain, but that it would hurt Marel, a six year old sister, or her if they took it. Mommy's medicine was for sick people. Junron had been told by her mother, if she felt a little better later, they would bake a cake for daddy's birthday. Marel would help too. Grandma and mommy's sister, Aunt Ronnie, would bring ice cream and presents. Now Mommy was dead. Why?

Her childish concepts of God and death were confusing. She had trouble understanding that God loved her mother and wanted her to live with Him. Didn't God love her too. Why didn't He take her too? That first night Marel cried in her bed and Junron held her and sang her to sleep, like Mommy did. She heard Daddy crying too.

The day after the funeral Aunt Ronnie brought a casserole for supper. Daddy wasn't home so she ate dinner with us. During dinner she explained that people die to make room for new people to live on earth. Just like the baby Mrs. Davies was going to have next month. She said Mommy was probably looking down on us as we're eating and is happy being with God. For the umpteenth time she told us everything would be all right.

After Daddy came home he came in to hear our prayers. He hid his face because he had been crying. To stop Marel's crying he again told us Mommy was happy to be with God and both He and Mommy were watching over us. He held us in his arms as we fell asleep, but I felt a tear drop on my head.

After the funeral Junron couldn't concentrate on her schoolwork. Her mind skipped from person to person, from comment to comment. Sorting them occupied all her time. Ironically she remembered who said what about God, heaven, happiness, etc.

Pastor Phil said, at the funeral services, "God is in all our hearts and we should rejoice in God's love for us. We should remember that death returns us to His bosom, to our home. Our tears are for us not the deceased loved one. If we continue to think about death, we can sicken ourselves. Instead we must recognize the love of God and thank Him for the time we had with Mommy. We should also do good works during our lifetime, so we may join Him and be reunited with Mommy."

Grandma said, "It's difficult to understand dying now, but you will some day. That only the good die young. Heaven is a beautiful place. It is everything you want it to be. Worrying about what's going to happen, will make you sick." At the casserole supper, Aunt Ronnie said, "Everybody dies, even us, some day."

Sitting in the classroom, Junron remembered the comments as she began to write. She had learned to write last year. Her teacher, Mrs. Quig, said her handwriting was very nest. How she was extra careful, her letters and words were neat and legible. She would slip the note under Grandma's apartment door when she went home after school. That way Grandma would see it right after she got home from work.

Thursday Grandma worked late, she arrived home at nine forty. After reading the note, she called 911 and left for her son's house. The police arrived as she did. She explained that she was worried when the phone wasn't answered. When she unlocked the door, a policewoman took her by the arm, the one holding Junron's note. The house was an ice chest, the silence screaming for attention. Grandma guided the officers through each room, toward the family room in the back. The sight was too much, the note fell from her hand as she sank to the floor.

It was now the officers understood the babbled voice that called 911. What they saw was clarified in the note.

Grandma,

I am making a surprise. I would ask you to come but you are not young now and you know about only the young dying. I am fixing a birthday cake for Daddy and Marel with Mommy's medicine. We will be happy with her tonight.

Love, Junron

EQUAL DOESN'T MEAN EQUAL

Dink pushed his tawny, bony body through the open door. Dangling from a lop-sided grimace hung the latest victim of his feline prowness, a young chipmunk. He padded onto the linoleum covered kitchen to settle under the table and play with his future meal.

"Dink! Drop it this instant!"

The exasperated tone of her voice indicated this was not the first time Dink had decided to eat in the kitchen. Mrs. Hermes wasn't about to tolerate another creature to meet its maker in her kitchen. Dropping to her knees she grabbed the hunter's scruffy neck and yanked him up to her eye level. The protesting meow allowed the tiny prey to thud to the floor, making no effort to escape its fate, it labored for breath.

Dink was unceremoniously hustled out the back screen door, to slide across the weather worn painted surface. Urgent piteous cries protesting this separation of hunter and meal. Dink tried to reenter but the closed screen door allowed only a view not entry. The bottom half of the Dutch door soon blocked that too.

"Poor thing." said its gray headed savior. "What has that nasty Dink done to you." Held in the warm cupped hand and caressed, the dazed bit of fluff emptied its bowels and shivered.

"Well now, not exactly what I expected, but you're still with us."

Mrs. Hermes set the animal in a small glass bowl and rinsed her hands. It didn't move. She reached in and ran a finger along a black stripe, then a white one. Scratching the head between the small ears caused no movement. The chest hairs moved slightly, showing there was life in the battered body.

"You may make it little one. Keep trying." She hollered at the noise maker on the back porch. "You'll not get this one, Dink. Not this one."

Aside from what the old lady ascertained as a comatose condition, she saw no battle scars on the supine body in the bowl. A good sign she thought. Yet she felt a desire to consult with someone with more animal knowledge than a one time mid-wife to a litter of pups born beneath the shelving in her garage. She knew she could care for animals but some times help is appreciated.

Cradling the old black phone on her shoulder, she continued stroking the unresponsive chipmunk "Doctor Goodman, Mrs. Hermes. Oh no, Dink is fine. Not sick, not in need of a shot or anything. I have a different Dink problem. Do you have time to answer some questions?" Her head nodded into the telephone as she continued to quiz the veterinarian.

"And you feel you should see this animal before letting me keep it? I shouldn't keep a wild animal. I know. But it can't fend for itself and I feel I owe it. You know, with my cat catching it in the first place. When it's better out the door, but away from here. Honest."

Opening the screendoor and checking for Dink, Mrs. Hermes stepped off the porch and into the garden area of her backyard. She clutched a shoebox and towel under her arm. Selecting a sun warmed rock she wrapped it in the kitchen towel and placed the bundle in the shoebox now containing the chipmunk. There were a few raisins and a dab of applebutter along with a water dampened sponge lined beside the patient. Backing her car out of the driveway, she thought if she had a siren and flashing lights she'd be at the doctor's in no time.

Doc Goodman twisted the tiny body, pinched the cheeks and blew the hair this way and that. Pointing to several pink pin pricks of color on the chipmunk's body, he muttered, "We could have internal bleeding in here." The good doctor explained how punctures beneath the skin may have ruptured and caused internal bleeding. "However, no broken bones that I can see. He's just shook up, nothing more."

"Think I can care for the poor thing? A day or two? Or three? A week at most?"

"Sure Mrs. Hermes. I"ll call the DNR and get Merlin, the officer in charge of our area and get him to OK your caring for the animal."

That evening while sitting before the TV, the phone rang. Someone had informed the local TV station of her rescue and wished an interview. Wouldn't you know it, she wanted privacy about this business: however, she would do an interview. The local newspaper picked up on the interview and did a story. Mrs. Hermes was getting her fifteen minutes of fame.

"Women Loves All God's Creatures" headlined the story. It gave Mrs. Hermes' views about the importance of treating animals with love and care. That the world would be better if everyone took the time to care for the other things in our world. The local DNR representative praised Mrs. Hermes and said he would allow even more time if Mrs. Hermes thought "Chippy" needed additional recover time. She reveled in the simple notoriety.

Six days later the TV people returned to watch Chippy go free. Mrs. Hermes reached into the box to retrieve the animal. He bit her thumb and the box fell to the ground. Chippy flicked his tail and disappeared before the camera could catch him darting under a near-by stump. The camera did catch Mrs. Hermes hurt expression and the expletives weren't deleted for the evening showing.

Three weeks later Mrs. Hermes made the news again. National news this time. She didn't want the publicity this time. No way.

According to the assistant county sheriff's report, Mrs.

Hermes shot a man near her residence. Upon investigating the shooting, called in by Mrs. Hermes, the police found a dying man just outside the garden fence, next to the stump Chippy had gone under. An ambulance had also responded to the shooting report, but the man was dead before they loaded him into the vehicle. It was mentioned that this was the first shooting death in the county in 61 years. The sheriff immediately took over but charges would not be filed until tomorrow.

Mr. Smyth's dying statement accused Mrs. Hermes of shooting him because he wouldn't get off her property. When the rain started, quite heavily, he sought shelter under a plastic sheet partially attached to the garden fence. Mr. Smith reached through the fence and purloined several tomatoes to satiate his hunger. As the rain abated Mrs. Hermes went out, with shotgun and ordered the stranger from under the plastic sheet and away from her fence. At this point opinions differ as to what happened.

Mr. Smyth's statement says he lost his footing. became trapped in the plastic material and fell. Mrs. Hermes says the man attacked her and attempted to take her shotgun. Mrs. Hermes, with the advice of her lawyer, will say nothing further. The Grand Jury will meet next week. The truth of both statements will be decided then.

The local newspaper editorial condemns Mrs. Hermes for treating a chipmunk with TLC and killing a human being. Some similarities exist between the two incidents and in this case humans fair lower on her scale of brotherly love.

HEAVENLY SEX

A letter in a local newspaper caught my attention, as a nude would, walking down a church aisle. The letter said, her minister told her there is no sex in heaven. Where did this person get that information?

Here on Earth, most healthy creatures have some sexual urges, whether as procreation, recreational, or for mutual or self gratification. The Creator specifically made two distinct sexes, which we humans, it seems, recreated for our own amusement. There is, if one examines the possibilities, no end to our fascination with sex. It is used to sell cars and coffins. We write about it, read about it or talk about it more than the weather.

God surely has a bizarre sense of humor. Aside from making humans, lawyers and politicians, the Almighty created sex. Not two different beings, but the act of sex, so consuming of human actions and time. We must appreciate God's sense of humor when we consider the various applications and method achieving sex we humans use.

Accept that we are made in the image of God. Is God male or female? Well? Or accept that God is three persons in one, you know the idea Saint Patrick was supposed to have proved with a shamrock. Does that mean God is gay? Think about it. Think about this too. What is the most important part of a human being? Heart? Mind? Soul? Sex? You pick one, I'll pick one, perhaps we picked the same one or a different one all together. Which might God pick?

Could it be sex? I don't know where the soul is (By the

way, does the soul have a sex?), or if the heart is such a critical factor in human behavior. The mind is in the head and our body functions without it, often. If you need proof that a body can perform without a mind look at Congress. God put sexual parts in humans up center and up front, even fixed it so one sex part fits into the other sex part. God's plan, not just an evolutionary development.

Is there sex in heaven? Heaven is eternal with absolute happiness. What will make you happy in heaven?

HOLIDAYS ARE HERE

"So Harry, got plans for the holiday? Thanksgiving Day is tomorrow."

Harry looked up at Max Shult, proprietor of the restaurant they were in. "Sure I got plans. Kid's are getting together, like the old days. I told you that yesterday. Forget?"

"No, I didn't forget. But I remember last year you said you were going with your kids. Then I found out you holed up in your room all afternoon and you didn't even watch the Detroit game or even eat dinner."

"Jeez Max, I told you I fell asleep and forgot to go. I must'a been feeling a little sick and my body dictated sleep, so I slept."

Max shrugged his huge shoulders and wiped at Harry's table with a damp cloth. "Harry, when the WW two Veterans got together, you mentioned to Swede and me, Shine and Paulie too, that your kids forgot you couldn't drive to their house for Christmas."

"Christmas? Oh, yeah. Well they did, Junior called and apologized for forgetting. He told me that both Trish and Shawn thought the other one was picking me up." Harry lowered his eyes, "You know, things like that happen."

"Yeah."

"Well they do. Tomorrow is all planned, we're having dinner at Junior's house. He'll pick me up about noon and we'll drive to his house. Everyone will be there." Harry smiled, drained the last drop of cold coffee from his cup and stood to leave. He wrapped his arm over Max Shult's shoulder and grinned, "Everything's planned. See you for breakfast on Friday."

"See ya." Max turned the door key in the direction that Harry had gone. "Liar."

Late Thursday morning Harry slouched in his chair before the TV, a bowl of cold cereal in his lap. His best suit jacket and black pants draped over the folding chair near his closet waited for Harry. He had shaved and bathed and at a quarter to noon he began to dress. He'd be ready for his ride, to spend some time with the kids and grandchildren. After Ramona had died, three years ago, the kids didn't visit as often. The phone rang, disturbing the light sleep Harry had fallen into. The TV football game had a disputed replay. His clock showed 2:38. Harry's mind was a bit befuddled.

It was Junior's voice apologizing for not being there, something about a screw up and he had gone to the shop first. He told Shawn to get dad, but Shawn came early and the football game had started. Harry heard the grandkids shouting in the background, that it was snowing. He could hear laughter and greetings as Trish arrived and someone swearing at something happening on the television. He heard, without listening to his son's pitiful excuse for not picking him up.

"Sure. Yes it's OK you can't get me. Shawn sure likes his ball games. I know everyone's sorry I'm not there. OK. OK. Trish will detour on her way home with some leftovers. Tell her not to, with the snow and all, she'd have to rush because of the kids in the car. Why don't you stop in the morning?" Harry heard, "Happy Thanksgiving." as he set the phone down.

Friday morning Officer Bennet blew on his coffee and said, "Say Max, wasn't that guy, the retired bus driver, one of your steady customers?"

"Harry? Sure. Most very day he comes in, since his wife died. He sits right there, where you're sitting." Max set hot coffee before the police officer. "Why?"

"You ain't heard yet, huh? They picked him up, D.O.A. this

morning. Found him sitting in his chair, all dressed up, with a bowl of cereal in his lap. The guys that picked him up found seven or eight different kinds of pills mixed in with the cereal."

Max banged his fist on the table, the coffee cup rose and fell, the hot contents rushed to fill the officer's lap. "Shit. They didn't come and get him. He was so lonesome he copped out. Son of a bitch." Max turned as his tears flushed the bitterness from his eyes. "I should have realized how lonesome he had gotten. I really shoulda. Ya know, maybe I coulda done something? Something? Maybe?" The words were hardly audible, as the shaking body turned and moved behind the counter as the damp cloth came to his face and wiped away a fallen tear.

EVENING PRAYER

May Beonitti, Maybee, to those who knew her, sunned her small nude frame on white beach sand, against the low stone wall that separated her from her noisy weekend neighbors. An environmental activist, Maybee fought her neighbors when they planned a "weekend cottage" a sprawling nine room cottage, a walled enclave of noise and late night parties. The visiting birds and small animals to her feeder would disappear, as would her peace and quiet, especially on week ends.

"We're going to bid on the cottage next door and keep bidding 'til we get it." came the voice from next door. "For Christ sake, who wants a bunch of Jews for neighbors. It's bad enough we got this old Nature Nut next door."

Maybee recognized the voice and the clinking of ice cubes in a glass. They belonged to Donaldson, her neighbor. She thought of him as a pest and now knew him as a bigot. She felt like rising up and challenging him, then and there. But held back, as he continued his anti-semantic and anti social mutterings.

"Don't want people around that make me uncomfortable with their different ways." He sighed, after a sip of the drink. "Particularly Jews. Got that fussbudget broad next door that's different enough. Always out feeding those damned dirty birds and rats that come out of the bushes there. I'd clear all that stuff out and get a landscaper in."

Maybee cringed. She heard Donaldson suggest going in to cool off in the air conditioned bar. She wrapped a towel around herself, her green eyes pierced the boundary between the two houses. Flying insects avoided the electrical current around her body. Something brewed inside her sharp devious mind. So he didn't like people that were different. She'd show him different. Yes, she would.

Maybee, a one sixteenth Huron Indian, collected western art and memorabilia. Her cottage walls were a tiny museum decorated with skins, pottery and other artifacts. Hanging in a display-case, was a white doeskin Indian dress, decorated elaborate with beads and shells and a handsome pair of soft moccasin's. A small knotted quirt rested in a case on her hearth, below a framed document declaring that the quirt belonged to her great-great grandfather, who's grandfather had fought in the Blackhawk Wars, against Abraham Lincoln.

The following day, June 21st., Donaldson's party began a little after five. The crowd, the woman in elegant evening gowns and jewelery, the man sweating in tuxedos, became louder as the band's music became louder. The woods became silent with night's approach. Etiquette went out the dooor as shoeless guests strolled about the sandy area, they pointed, laughed, wildly danced about and fawned over their hosts. Often their words of praise for Donaldson's plans, weaved their way through the air, to stop in Maybee's ear.

There are people who honor the ending of the longest day of the year in a more somber fashion.

A shrill whistle broke through the musical noise of the Donaldson's party. Heads turned and talking stopped. Maybee, in a white doeskin dress, her small fist thumped a drum to the wood-wind music played on a tape. She began a slow descent to a flat sand area. She uttered a strange gutteral chant, her body swayed and bowed, her silver ornamented arms flayed the still air with lavish, provocative gestures. Donaldson's visitors stopped in their tracks, moved toward the wall and gawked. Donaldson choked on his drink.

Maybee pulled a tied package from beneath the shrubs. A

bearskin rug became her altar and a beautiful pot the vessel of burned offerings. An awful stench from burning herbal smoke wrapped around her twirling body and sweat beaded and sparkled on it's surface. Maybee's chants grew louder. They soon became recognizable English words and the words reached the invited people at the Donaldson's.

"Hear my pleas God of the Universe. Bring shame and dishonor upon those that will not share Your world with others of different ethnic backgrounds. Deny them the power to control the destines of your children. Let their friends know their evil intentions and cause them to walk away from them. As this day ends, find it in Your wisdom to guide their steps. Great Spirit, keep Your eyes upon us, upon the flowers and the animals and the Earth we share."

Maybee rose, poured water into the smoking pot, rolled the bearskin rug, reentered her home, shut off the music and dosed the lights. A subtle fighter, a very clever woman, she stood in the dark and watched as some guests of the Donaldson party departed. In her heart, beat the music of her people, she hummed, "This land is my land..."

I AM WITH YOU

I am your friend, your devoted servant. Your confidant and succor. I will be with you always.

I remember our first meeting. Let's see fifty, no fifty-one years ago. The desire in your eyes as we first touched. There was fear in your eyes also. Was it the fear of being caught, or the fear of disapproval? How I seized upon your inexperience. Your body reacted to my powers. Your throat constricted as I touched your lips. Your eyes filled with tears as I danced before them, even your hands shook. Was it tenderness?

Over the years we have become the closest of companions. Night or day you have called upon me. I answered, never turning from your call. When you sought attention, there I was. I let you use me to break the ice at formal or informal encounters. I helped you through school, the long night of studying, as well as the hours between classes. I was with you just before your first job interview, as well as immediately after. I accompanied you to the hospital when the babies arrived. I even stayed away from you, when you wanted me so desperately to share with you, that night you sat and watched your mother die. I was her friend too.

Now, as you face death, I am with you. And now you realize what has been the truth all along. I was not the friend you thought. Perhaps I was unwelcomed, but as an old friend, you kept me around. A crutch? Maybe you would still need my services? You're dying. Light up. Go ahead. One last time. My slave.

XAVIER

"Xavier," said the man from town, "we need a road to the next town."

The farmer asked "Why? No one goes there."

"We could go there. We could sell our things there."

Xavier thought for a moment. "I can sell my things in our town."

"Think, Xavier. You could buy things in the next town."

"But I buy things in our town now."

Becoming angry, "The town people want a road to the next town. The best and easiest route is through your place. Give us the land or we will take it."

Eventually the town bought Xavier's land. For a very, very cheap price. They built a very cheap road. The people from each town went back and forth, seldom to buy, or sell for more than they got before. Why travel back and forth, people soon bought farms along the road, to make shorter trips. The road fell apart.

"Xavier," said the man from town. "We need some money to fix the road."

"I have little money. Certainly none to fix a road I didn't want or use."

"The people along the road and the people in town want it fixed. If you have no money you must work ten days each year to repair the road."

After several years the road continued to need repairs. Many more people lived along the road and further demands soon were asked of Xavier.

"Xavier," said the man from town. "We need water for the people. The best and easiest route is from the mountains through your land."

"And if I don't give you this land you will take it?" asked Xavier.

"Most certainly my friend. Or, we may buy it. Cheaply."

The water flowed to everyone. But, each year the weeds would grow in the channel and block the flow of water.

"Xavier," said the man from town. "We need money to clear the weeds from the channel. Without money you must work seven days each wet season to clear the weeds."

"I didn't want the water channel on my property. Why must I work for others to have it?"

The man said, "It is for everyone."

So, the people had a road and water. Soon they had money and goods and wanted to protect it from thieves and from fire.

"Xavier," said the man from town, "We need to protect our goods. Everyone must pay for a sheriff and a watchman. One to keep thieves away the other to watch for fire."

"You know I have little money," said Xavier.

"And you know we will have these workers, paid for with money or with time. You will work seven days and seven nights each year as a watchman."

Xavier had enough of these demands for time and money. Always he lost the arguments and his property or time. He went to town to see the mayor. The books were opened and checked for accuracy and fairness. Xavier noted that behind each entry for his name was "TAX"

"What does this mean?" he asked.

"That", said the mayor, "Is the short way of saying, Take it Away from Xavier. We call it a tax."

I'LL FIX THEM

"Wake up girl. Come on, wake up."

She stirred to the soft muffled urgings, softer still were the pastel colors surrounding her, silent and blurred and comforting, they kept interrupting a calm she had never known. She turned her face from the soft voice, her body retreating into a fetal coil.

"I will call 'til you acknowledge me. Come on Micki. Wake up."

"Whaaa? Leave me alone. Leave me be."

"Ahhh. Good." The voice continued. "I am Veluss your escort. Your celestial escort."

"Huh? What escort?" Micki's voice raspy and weak was also befuddled.

"I need your attention. Come on, help me. I must determine why you're here."

"Here? Where here?" Micki swung her head and stared, but nothing came to mind. "Where am I?"

Veluus perused the pages of a small book, her lips were pursed, her eyes digging out the words on the page. "I have these facts written here. You are Micki. Your parents hoped for a child for twelve years before you were born. You were a healthy normal girl. You dreamed of becoming a writer. You had few friends and thought one boy may have liked you. At eighteen you attempted suicide."

Veluus closed the book and looked into Micki's eyes. Veluus sighed and taking Micki's hands, pulled her into a sitting position.

"I am not allowed to judge you; however, if you wish I am allowed to listen and determine if you belong here."

"Where am I?"

"You are in the Portals."

"That doesn't tell where I am. Really, where am I?"

"The Portals. Waiting. Waiting for eternity"

A frown crossed Micki's face while her eyes attempted to pierce the blurred colors. To comprehend what she didn't understand.

"I jumped."

Veluus sat and waited for her to continue. The wait was long. "I know."

"I jumped to show them. To make them sorry they hurt me. To...to..to teach them a lesson."

Again Veluus waited. If only questions didn't influence people's reasoning, a determination could be made sooner. Oh, well. Eternity is a long time.

Veluus didn't ask and Micki didn't know what to say. Wrinkles creased her forehead. The strain of determining who had hurt her or how wasn't very clear. Her reasons were clear when she wrote the note to her folks. They were clear when she stood at the fifth floor railing in the mall. She visualized their shame and regrets when she was no longer there. They'd be sorry, very sorry. The reasons were clear then.

Veluus head dropped down.

"I just wanted them to feel bad. Just enough to know how hurt I was."

Waiting for Micki to relate her story finally pressured Veluus to speak. "You'd hurt yourself to hurt them?"

"Yes."

"Great pain?"

"You know? You understand? Yes. I was in deep pain"

Micki's eyes glazed, looking into the nothingness wrapped around her. In her mind she saw her parents crying, holding each other, whispering regrets for their selfish treatment of a beloved daughter. They had denied her simple pleas for understanding of just how a young lady feels, how she needs to fly, free, into..into.

She saw her class, that special boy, how he had laughed at the mistake she made by misunderstanding the teacher's directions. She knew it seemed funny but to be laughed at. Oh, no, no. And the pimples that seemed to pop up every time something particular happened, always, always big, ugly, painful pimples. And why wasn't she a women yet, eighteen and hadn't started her periods. Was she a freak?

Veluus interrupted. "I can see your thoughts.

"Huh? My thoughts? Really?"

"True. Your parets were sorry, but only in your thoughts."

"They didn't regret what they did?"

"People do not understand why loved ones try suicide. They regret the loss and their pain is real, but they never understand why. They feel shame even more than their pain."

"They should. They made me do it."

"Do it?" asked Veluus. "Do it?"

"Yes, they made me kill myself."

Veluus waggled a finger, no.

Micki's eyes centered on the finger. "What?"

"You weren't listening. I said you attempted suicide and I was sent to determine why you are here. Now I know."

"What? Know what?"

"You did not die. Now, as in Dicken's Christmas Carol, I will show you your life. What is ahead for you. However, unlike Scrooge, you will not be able to influence the future. Your future is already decided."

Micki sees two figures sitting next to a bed. Her mother's voice is broken by weak sobs as she strokes the hand of the figure in bed. It is Micki's hand. The other person is completing a form for care at the Crother's Rehabilitation Center.

"Yes, Micki did fall from the fifth level of the mall. Some

people say she jumped, but I know she didn't. She fell. The fall broke her neck, which left her a quadriplegic, unable to perform any body function. Can't even speak." She wrung the handkerchief tighter around her fingers and sobbed. "The family thinks she's deaf and blind too since she responds to nothing. Well, sometimes, when you jab her with a needle, the muscle twitches. Sometimes."

"You know, as Micki's caseworker, I must ask these questions. I'm sorry they must be asked and answered again."

"I understand." came a mumbled reply.

"I'll make it as easy as I can for you. I'll tape everything you say and type it up later, back in my office. OK?"

"OK."

The recording machine clicked and hummed, papers shuffled.

"Oh." said the councilor. "If I feel something is unclear, I'll interrupt. OK?"

"OK."

Micki and Veluus listened as her mother told the story. "I came home from work and found Micki's note. Before I could call my husband or do anything, the police knocked on the door. My daughter was in the hospital, injured in a fall at the mall. At this point I did not tell the police about Micki's note. When I met my husband in the hospital, I told him.

"The family doctor, with several concurring opinions, told us Micki was a vegetable. He urged us to seek institutional help for Micki. We were stubborn, wanted her at home, where loving care might bring her back to us. My health deteriorated and my husband gave up after a year and blew his brains out. Because he committed suicide the insurance company refused payment. I quit my job, started working at home.

"I've been doing that for three years now. I don't make enough money to pay all our bills and the extra for Micki's care. I'm sick now and I'm still trying. I try and I know I can't. It's too much."

Micki heard and saw it all. She looked at Veluus then ran to her mother. She thrust her arms out in an attempt to hug her. Micki's arms passed right through her mother. There was no reaction, it wasn't noticed. Micki shouted and got no reaction.

"You can not interfere. You can do nothing. Come, sit beside me while we see what else will happen in the future." Veluus pointed back, the room had changed.

She saw herself in bed in a small white room, hanging on the wall a print of Jesus in the Garden of Gethsemane. There were various medical machines near-by, all keeping her, a vegetable, alive. The door opens and a young man in a scrub suit enters. Coming to the side of the bed, he pulls down the blanket, opens her gown and begins to fondle her.

"It's Thursday Sweety. Our date night. You gonna give me a little tonight?"

Micki shrieked as she witnessed his attentions on her helpless body. She didn't influence this situation either. He mounted and raped her.

"When did this happen? Can't I stop it?"

"It will happen." said Veluus in quiet monotone. "This too will happen, later."

Within the same room, still lying in the same bed, the voices from the group near-by discussed her condition. No words of Micki's told them the problem, her bloated belly told them of her pregnancy. Now they were going to abort her baby. They didn't know the father, guessing an employee, but to prevent a reoccurrence the uterus would be removed. This would also eleminate some female problems for now and perhaps later. After all, she was a young woman and they couldn't predict how long she'd live.

She watched the prostrate figure in the bed, she watched herself shrivel a little, growing older and wrinkling. Day by slow day sped passed, night by dark night, more awful visitors. Time inexorably passed. No friendly visitors, mom had died within two years of Micki's entering the Center. Interveinous meals dripped into her but sometimes these too were forgotten. A machine forced oxygen through her body and drains removed wastes. No radio or TV, not even a change of seasons in her windowless box.

She turned to Veluus only to find the Portals and Veluus gone.

Now she heard voices, real voices. "She jumped." "Poor kid." "Is she dead?" "She's breathing." 'Not dead." Micki recognized none of the voices, but felt a icy chill in the last voice. "She may wish she was."

DEATH PENALTY

Governor Ivers turning from his office window poked the lighted button on his private phone. The digital clock flipped to 10:54 p.m. as the arthritic pain flashed from finger to brain. He forgot, again, a jolted joint inflicts pain.

He heard the phone lifted on the other end. "Jamie, don't bother getting Mather ready. I'm calling the execution off."

"Sure, Mike. Sure. You really OK with this?"

"Sure," exhaling deeply. "You know I've given it a hell've a lot of thought." Again a deep breath passing his lips. "Considering the newspeople with their arguments for and against, it's been rough."

"Geez, Mike, we both know things get tough when the courts order an execution. This one... Well the decision on this one turned nasty the day the kid's body turned up." Jamie's voice sounding concerned, but in his heart, glad the decision wasn't his. "I'll inform Mather. Want me to tell the media, or do want to go on the speaker?"

"You do it Jamie. I feel like shit. And I don't want to answer their idiotic questions. Tell them, I had trouble with the confession and some doubts about Mather's mental capacity. You know, some of the details didn't jibe?"

"OK Mike."

"Thanks Jamie. See you at the State office party next week. And I owe you one."

Corky Mather lifted his head as the lock opened, expecting one scene and seeing another. A smile. Anticipating the worst, his body, tensing as the door creaked, now saw a smile. Something was happening, changing the mood in the cell, filling it with light and warmth. A smile, he hadn't seen a smile in quite a while.

The smile spoke, "Corky, the Governor has stopped your execution." Mather heard only, "stopped your execution." The Warden's mouth contoured but nothing came out, a silent film of Chaplin's crossed Corky's his mind. He'd live. He'd see tomorrow, next week, next year. He'd not die today. "Stopped your execution."

Depending on their point of view the news media blessed or damned Ivers decision. Foes of the death penalty now demanded a pardon for Mather. His confession, under duress, made him a victim and he should go free. Arguments against Ivers stated that Mather's confession contained facts only the killer knew.

Mather sentenced to life without parole soon dropped from public view, yesterday's news. He could live like that, after all where there's life there's hope. Mather, along with every jailed mind hoped to be free. Free, not from guilt, he had killed the child and others, but free from his prison.

Corky Mather loved beautiful children. Since his teen years he would reach out and caress the face or brush the hair of children. He would smile at the parent, rarely if the father were present, and pat the child, boy or girl. He offered to babysit little ones, being very careful to fondle them and masturbate. In the early years he didn't violate their small bodies. He almost hurt the Harlow baby, his desires were so intense, but grandmother Harlow stopped in unannounced.

The kidnapping of the Brown baby from the front vestibule of the Casson Street Library made the front pages and TV news for nearly two weeks. Simon Brown, sleeping in the stroller, had been left in the hallway while his mother returned a few books. "Just a few minutes," she told the police. As Mather entered the library, he noted the sleeping child and no adult about. He snatched the infant, shoved the small bundle into his partial zipped coat and went straight to his car, parked near the library entrance.

Mather had molested and killed the child and dumped the body before the first newscast about the abduction. Mather worried for a couple of days, but stopped as the news items became smaller as clues failed to materialize. He felt power in the success of the abduction and evading the police, a feeling of pride. Now he began looking for opportunities and schemed to steal another infant.

Robin Rolwell wandered between the store aisles, doing the forbidden. She touched stuffed animals, stroking and patting them. Momma Rolwell stood arguing with the store clerk, glancing, infrequently, at the bobbing head among the toys. An old hunter's axiom says for every pair of eyes you see, a hundred more see you. Corky's eyes were on a prize, Robin.

"Would you like to see a real puppy?" asked the hunter.

Bright eyes and a child's shy smile accompanied an affirmative nod from Robin.

"In my car." The child and abductor stepped into the elevator.

Mrs. Rolwell didn't see the small head moving so she shifted away from the clerk to look. "Robin. Robin. You're in trouble young lady." The voice, a little more urgent and shriller, moved faster through the area. Then a scream of realization. Something had happened, Robin had vanished in the twinkle of the eye.

Mather had moved quickly out the store door, picking up and holding the child tightly to his shoulder, closing off her breathing, rendering his victim unconscious. Now appearing more a parent carrying a sleeping child. Slipping into his car, he left the parking area. A normal scene in most cities. He drove a short way, parked and then gagged and tied the child, throwing a blanket over the small body on the floor of the back seat.

The emboldened Mather kept the child for two days, before dismembering the abused body. He drove around the county highways flicking small parts onto the roadside for small animals to find and devour. No clues. No body. No closure.

That was in the past, now it was different. If only the garage door had closed properly? If only the bitch across the street had taken her mail out a minute or two either way? If only the kid hadn't gotten out of the car? If only? If only? Yes all of these ifs caught a killer.

Yesterday, or the day before, the garage door had slipped down on his car roof. Using a piece of wood, Corky had temporarily held it in place. It came down again as he drove in with the Natachi child. Dazed and hands tied, the child stepped from the car as Corky inserted his wooden door stop. The neighbor across the street came out of her house as Corky frantically grabbed the child. The closing garage door hid the scene before she could make more of what took place. Oh, well.

After watching the six o'clock news, Mrs. Racker, the neighbor, called the police. She thought she saw a small child, maybe a boy, in a purple shirt, at a neighbor's house and he doesn't have children. The police eventually arrived at Mather's place to ask a few questions and then went to the Racker house. Their questions and his answers didn't fit together. Officer Mullen sat in the car and radioed for information. Officer Bunge returned to Mather's for more questions. Mather didn't answer the door.

Knowing Mather had not left his house, they received radio permission to break in, suspecting the resident had an accident. Looking for him, they found instead the child's body on the bed. Further searching found Corky hiding in a false backed utility cabinet in the garage. The neighborhood couldn't believe a killer was living among them. They told the TV interviewers they couldn't believe it too.

Questioned about many child abductions and disappearances, Mather coolly denied any knowledge. Nothing stuck to him except the Natachi murder. He would say nothing to his lawyer or the investigative team of doctors. He did get the press to investigate his claims of police brutality during his questioning. He even exhibited signs of mental slowness, further hinting his confession of guilt questionable. The jury didn't buy his act, found him guilty of murder and approved the death penalty.

Ivers bought it.

Three years, two months, and four days later, Mike Ivers, voted out of office by the reform party, sat in his office, part of the law firm of Brooks, Cupton, Lee and Ivers, talking to his wife and young daughter before they went shopping. Tilly, his secretary, came in and mentioned the escape of Corky Mather. He killed a guard and intern in the hospital when they took him in for a complaint of chest pains.

"My God. That's right next door," Mike said. "When?"

"Not too long ago."

"Mike, what should I do?" asked Mrs. Ivers.

"Go shop. The two of you go shopping. Right now, nothing is changed. Go."

Recognized by the officer as Mrs. Ivers approached the parking lot gate, he pushed the gate open and waved the vehicle through. This happened nearly very time she came to the gate. If the guard had looked into the car, on the back floor, he would have seen the Ivers girl. Corky Mather sat with her under the brown picnic blanket, a pistol stuck in her ear. Mather peeked at the guard and driver, sweat dotting his forehead, determination curling his lip, stroking the child's leg. A smile.

A phone ringing in the woods is uncommon, but Russell Byes, walking from the lake with his small catch, heard a phone ringing. He peered into the weedy underbrush, but saw no one. The ringing continued.

"Somebody lost their phone," he said to himself. One step into the overgrown area and he fell into the leaf covered gully containing a leaf covered partially clothed body. The ringing phone begged to be answered.

He pushed the button, "I don't know you or who're calling, but you call the police right now. Tell them a body is in the Boone

Lake parking lot just off the north end. Hurry." Russell Byes left his fish and the broken pole, climbed up the slope and waited, with a prayer, for the police.

"Yes Tilly." Mike Ivers said , as the woman walked in un-announced.

"Mr. Ivers, the police, Detective Handy, wants to talk to you." she gulped.

With a questioning look, he waved his hand, an approval for his entrance.

"Detective Handy, if you don't mind, I'd like my secretary to stay while we talk?'

"It's very personal. But if you wish OK."

"She stays." Ivers looked for a reaction and clicked on a hidden recorder.

"Shoot."

Ivers collapsed to the plush rug as the detective said, "The county police have found a woman's body at Boone Lake. A re-ceipt in her coat pocket identifies her as Mrs. Patricia Ivers. One officer thought he recognized her as the former governor's wife and called our office. Do you know where your wife is at the mo-ment?"

In a trembling voice, bearly audible, Ivers said that when she left his office about two hours ago, she and his daughter were going to shop 'til about one thirty, call him and have lunch wher-ever they wanted. Ivers trembling voice continued, "She went to the car, downstairs, to get something to return. She's shopping, I know. That receipt must belong to someone else. It must."

"Mr. Ivers, can you come with me? Identify the body, may-be. If you want, I'll get you over and back. If it's not your wife, well, that'll be a relief." Detective Handy reached into his pocket and withdrew a clear plastic bag. "Were you calling your wife's cell phone about an hour ago?"

"No."

"Would you call it now, please?"

The bagged phone began ringing.

"Oh God. Dear God. No."

Mike Ivers sat in his dark office, the television news droned on with drivel. It broke in with a helicopter chase in progress. The escapee, Corky Mather, driving the Ivers car is being pursued on the interstate. Several cars were hit by the reckless driving escapee. He is trapped in a construction site and shooting at police. They shot him. An unidentified child was found dead in the back of the car.

Hours later, lying on his hospital bed, Mather told his guard, "I'm sorry for the governor, He's a nice guy. I saw this lady and kid and wanted their car after I broke out. I didn't know who they were. I ain't saying what happened. But I don't think Mr. Ivers, or this Governor, will let me off this time."

WHITE ON WHITE

Lie back. Eyes closed. You see nothing. Nothing at all. Slowly, very slowly the space is brightening. Soft white light fills the space. It comes from nowhere, yet it fills the area. There are no shadows, just light. White light.

You began to float in the light. No fear. It's quiet. Step, yes step, there is nothing below your feet but white light. You can walk on it. Turn, and walk where you will. Walk slowly. No place to walk to, no direction to move toward.

Within the light a something develops. It too is white. It has form, yet no shape. A free form. A floating white free form. You can touch it, but it can not be felt. What do you want it to be? It can be anything, anything you wish. It will remain white, but you will create it. It is yours.

Hold it. Bring it with you. Go where you wish, but bring it with you. Imagine a white wall. Now a room with walls. No doors, no windows. There are stairs, there off to your right. There are stairs going down into a white room below. Go there. Take your creation with you. Grab the banister on your left. Go slowly, no rush.

Are you comfortable? Can you let loose your creation? Yes it will be all right. Look about you, the walls are soft white and soft. Lean into them, touch them. The floor is white and soft. Touch it. Lie down on it and relax. Feel the softness surround you. Your eyes are still closed. Keep them closed. Feel the softness of the darkness. Relax. Relax. Slowly, feel yourself relax. You're floating. Soft darkness. Relax.

SLEEP. Sleep. sleep........zzzzzzzzzz

CHUCK McCANN

I am the first born son of a sixteen year old high school drop out. For most of my first seven years relatives took care of me, the next eight years Catholic Charities sheltered, feed, clothed and guided me. I dropped out of school and started working one month after I turned sixteen.

Married at twenty-one, with a child on the way, I decided to return to school, but there was a hitch. I worked as a clerk on the railroad during the evening hours, so night school was out. Instead I attended school during the day as a regular student. It took from 1951 until 1964 to get a Master's Degree. Incidentally I've taken a class in something every year since 1951.

I became a teacher, then a naturalist and back to teaching junior high science until I retired. I retired early due to Parkinson's Disease, which effected my ability to read and write notes on student's paper. I have taught at every level from Pre-school to college. After retiring I tried professional bowling. I found more success as an artist. A story of my early childhood is in the Willow Review, 2005.

Printed in the United States
39461LVS00004B/94-150